Dear Reader,

I am a survivor of sexual assault. I didn't report what happened to me, because at the time I believed I'd somehow sent the message that I had wanted this person—someone I knew and trusted—to do what he did. I buried the shame I felt into the darkest corner of my soul, but still, the memory of him—of his hand on the back of my head, pushing—has stayed with me for years, following me like a second shadow.

I'm not alone. It's estimated that a sexual assault occurs once every two minutes in the United States. More than 80 percent of these attacks are never reported, and four out of five victims know their assailant, which means the majority of men who commit sexual assault fly under the radar. They are our fathers, husbands, and sons; our neighbors, our coworkers, and our best friends. They are practically impossible to detect.

This terrifying fact pushed my writer's mind into a game of "what if"—what if a young man, a generally good person, raped his best friend? What about his upbringing, his internal wiring, his environment, would contribute to the pinnacle moment when she told him to stop and he didn't listen? What if the young woman didn't go to the police, but instead took matters into her own hands? How would each of them be forever changed?

I wrote *It Happens All the Time* because we need to talk about why we still blame the victim for what she said or did or wore or how much she drank—and then, in the next breath, look at her attacker and say, "But he's such a nice guy . . . he'd never do something like that." We need to talk about why we educate our girls on how to protect themselves from getting raped, but don't do enough to teach our boys how to ask for and identify consent.

By including both the victim's and the perpetrator's points of view, I wasn't trying to create false empathy for rapists; rather,

I wanted to help readers recognize rape culture as not just a woman's problem but as a societal problem, and one that we each have a hand (and a stake) in solving. I don't want to start a controversy—but I do want to start a conversation.

Thank you in advance for reading. I hope the story means as much to you as it did to me in writing it.

All my best,
Amy Hatvany

ALSO BY AMY HATVANY

Best Kept Secret

Outside the Lines

The Language of Sisters

Heart Like Mine

Safe with Me

Somewhere Out There

it happens all the time

A NOVEL

AMY HATVANY

ATRIA BOOKS

New York London Toronto Sydney New Delhi

ATRIA BOOKS
An Imprint of Simon & Schuster, Inc.
1230 Avenue of the Americas
New York, NY 10020

This book is a work of fiction. Any references to historical events, real people, or real places are used fictitiously. Other names, characters, places, and events are products of the author's imagination, and any resemblance to actual events or places or persons, living or dead, is entirely coincidental.

Copyright © 2017 by Amy Hatvany

All rights reserved, including the right to reproduce this book or portions thereof in any form whatsoever. For information, address Atria Books Subsidiary Rights Department, 1230 Avenue of the Americas, New York, NY 10020

First Atria Books hardcover edition March 2017

ATRIA BOOKS and colophon are trademarks of Simon & Schuster, Inc.

For information about special discounts for bulk purchases, please contact Simon & Schuster Special Sales at 1-866-506-1949 or business@simonandschuster.com.

The Simon & Schuster Speakers Bureau can bring authors to your live event. For more information, or to book an event, contact the Simon & Schuster Speakers Bureau at 1-866-248-3049 or visit our website at www.simonspeakers.com.

Interior design by [[tk]]

Manufactured in the United States of America

10 9 8 7 6 5 4 3 2 1

Library of Congress Cataloging-in-Publication Data

Names: Hatvany, Amy, 1972– author.
Title: It happens all the time : a novel / Amy Hatvany.
Description: First Atria Books hardcover edition. | New York : Atria Books, 2017.
Identifiers: LCCN 2016015251 (print) | LCCN 2016021600 (ebook) | ISBN 9781476704456 (hardcover) | ISBN 9781501153907 (softcover) | ISBN 9781476704463 (ebook) | ISBN 9781476704463 (Ebook)
Classification: LCC PS3608.A8658 I8 2017 (print) | LCC PS3608.A8658 (ebook) | DDC 813/.6—dc23
LC record available at https://lccn.loc.gov/2016015251

ISBN 978-1-4767-0445-6
ISBN 978-1-4767-0446-3 (ebook)

For my daughters and my son,
who made it essential to consider both sides of this story.

Violators cannot live with the truth: survivors cannot live without it.

—*Chrystine Oksana*

it happens
all the time

Tyler

I don't see the gun until it's pointed right at me.

"Drive," she says, shifting her upper body toward me. We are in the cab of my truck, me behind the wheel, Amber in the passenger seat. Her arm trembles, from uncertainty or the weight of the weapon, it's impossible to tell.

I look at her, blinking fast. "Amber, wait—"

"Shut up." Her voice is stone. Unyielding. She cocks the hammer with her thumb and I jerk to the left, toward the driver's side window. My shoulders hunch up around my ears and then—I can't help it—I say her name again.

"I said, shut up!" Amber repeats, this time with a shrill, unstable edge. She tilts her head toward the parking lot's exit. "Go." Her index finger rests against the side of the trigger. One twitch, one small movement, and it could all be over.

I straighten and try to steady my breath. *Just do what she says.* I put the key in the ignition, turn it, and the engine springs to life. The radio blasts and Amber and I both startle; she hurries to snap it off. A bead of sweat slides down my forehead, despite the bone-chilling bite in the air. It's early November, and it strikes me that it has been almost a year since she came home for Christmas and found me waiting for her at her parents' house. So much has happened since then. Everything has changed.

I pull out onto the street, telling myself that one of my coworkers inside the red-brick station house must have noticed the two of us together, that something in Amber's stance or facial expression hinted at what she was about to do. Someone will follow us or, at the very least, call the police. But even as I think these things, I know they won't happen. My partner, Mason, had already left for home, for his wife and daughter. The paramedic team who took over for us was behind the closed doors of the garage, double-checking inventory in the rig. The firefighters were upstairs in the bunk room, sleeping if they needed it, or in the gym, shooting the shit and lifting weights to pass the time. As first responders, we are accustomed to crises, our bodies conditioned to react. We race toward disaster instead of from it, but we don't stand by the window, scanning our surroundings, expecting to see it as it strikes.

When I first stepped outside and saw Amber waiting for me in the dimly lit parking lot, I was foolish enough to feel a spark of hope. "We need to talk," she said, and I nodded, noting that she was thinner than I'd seen her in years. Her face was gaunt, sharp cheekbones and enormous hazel eyes in darkened sockets. Her thin brown hair fell in messy waves to her jawline, and she wore a puffy black ski jacket that only emphasized her stick-slim legs. She couldn't have weighed much more than a hundred pounds. Nine years ago, when she was fifteen, in the hospital at her worst, she had weighed eighty-two.

"Get on the freeway," Amber says now, releasing the hammer and dropping the gun to her lap, where she cradles it, staring straight ahead. Her face is shrouded in shadow, making it impossible for me to guess what she is thinking. "Go south."

"You don't need to do this," I say, hoping I might be able to reason with her. "You said we need to talk, so please . . . let's talk."

"Just drive where I tell you to drive." She lifts the gun and points it at me again, this time holding it with two hands, one cupped under the other, her finger still lying next to the trigger.

"Okay, okay! Sorry." A familiar, tightly wound panic coils in my chest; I worry what might happen if it springs loose. "You don't need the gun."

Her eyes narrow into slits. "Don't tell me what I need." She jabs the nose of the weapon into my ribs and cocks the hammer once more.

I gasp, and then pump the brakes, slowing to a stop at a red light. My eyes flit to our surroundings, searching for someone on the street, anyone I can signal for help, but it's three in the morning in our sleepy college town. There are no other cars around.

The tips of my nerves burn beneath my skin, and then I hear my dad's deep voice in my head: "Don't just sit there, Son. *Do* something."

The light turns green, and Amber pushes the gun deeper into my side, urging me forward. I ease my foot down on the gas pedal, contemplating the ways my father might take control of a situation like this. I see him shooting out his right arm and grabbing Amber by the back of the neck, slamming her head against the dashboard. I imagine his thick fingers curling into a fist and punching her in the face.

But I don't want to hurt Amber, not more than I already have. What I want is for everything to go back the way it was when we first met—before my parents' divorce and her illness, before we grew apart and then came back together, closer than ever, last June, after she came home from school with an engagement ring on her finger. I want to rewind the clock, take back the night when the world shattered. I want to erase everything that went wrong.

"I hate you," she says. Her voice sounds diseased, infected with disgust. "I hate you so fucking much."

I wince, suspecting that I deserve every bit of that venom, the pain of the gun jammed against my ribs. I might even deserve the bullets inside it. I turn onto the freeway onramp, accelerate, and then, unsure what Amber's plan might be, I look at her. "I know," I say. "I hate me, too."

Amber

It was just after midnight when I turned the corner onto my parents' street, three hours later than I'd told them I'd be home for Christmas break. As I coasted down the gravel driveway that ran alongside the house, I switched off my headlights, just as I had in high school when I showed up past curfew, hoping that the cover of darkness would allow me to sneak inside without getting caught. I might be able to get away with this now, having been away at college for almost four years, but back then, there was no doubt my parents would be waiting up for me, sitting at the kitchen table, my mother sipping at a cup of hot peppermint tea and my father nursing a two-finger pour of Scotch, concern etched into deep lines on both of their foreheads.

"Where have you been?" my father would demand when I finally walked through the back door. "Your mother and I have been worried sick!"

"Sorry," I'd mumble, shoving my fists into the pockets of my coat and dropping my gaze to the floor. I knew it was pointless to make excuses; it was better to appear penitent and promise to never let it happen again. I understood that their concern was simply a side effect of my being an only child—a child who almost didn't survive. I came into the world nine weeks early via an emergency C-section, and the neonatal team in the delivery room had to whisk me away after I was lifted, unmoving, from my mother's womb. I hadn't cried the way a newborn should. I couldn't, because I wasn't breathing. As the doctors called out codes and pumped air into my deflated lungs, my mother lay on the operating table and sobbed, terrified of losing me, while my father squeezed her hand, telling her over and over again that everything would be okay.

"You almost died," my mom said, the first time she told me this story. Her eyes, the same green-gold color as mine, welled with tears as she produced a picture of me inside what she said was an incubator, where I stayed for the first two months of my life. I couldn't believe how small I was—just three and a half pounds —how the map of my veins glowed like tiny blue rivers beneath translucent, epidermal parchment. "They literally had to jump-start your heart," she said. "It was a miracle that you lived. You're a *miracle,* sweetie. Don't ever forget that."

I was only seven at the time, and so I nodded, wanting her to think that her words had made me feel treasured and special, but hearing that my mother thought my birth was miraculous sent an uncomfortable shiver up my spine. I imagined that I'd better do something exceptional, *be* someone exceptional, to live up to that birth story. They chose not to have any more children because of my perilous arrival; instead, they focused their energies, and all their hopes and dreams, on me.

I sighed as I turned off the engine of my car, landing on the only other time I'd been in a hospital, in an uncomfortable bed, hooked up to monitors, wires, and tubes—it was my own fault. Choices I'd made that put both my parents' hearts and my life at risk. I squeezed my eyes tightly shut, as if that might stop me from seeing the painful reel of memories playing inside my head. *I'm better now,* I told myself. *I'm not that person anymore.*

I lifted my backpack and cell phone from the passenger seat, and peered up at the cozy, two-story Victorian-style house where I'd spent the first eighteen years of my life. Black December clouds obscured the moon, but the glow from the streetlamp was enough to illuminate the hundred-year-old structure that my parents had painstakingly updated as time and money allowed. They replaced the plumbing, the knob-and-tube wiring, and finally, after all the rooms had been fully remodeled and everything brought up to code, they sanded and lacquered the original blond maple floors. The outside was painted robin egg's blue, and the wraparound porch and steep eaves were edged in white gingerbread trim, both of which were currently covered in hundreds of festive, twinkling lights. Even if the last few years I lived there hadn't exactly been a fairy tale, it still *looked* like a storybook house, and it would always be a place I could call home.

Hiking my bag over my left shoulder, I opened the trunk of my car and hefted my black suitcase up and out, setting it on the ground. I was anxious to get inside, climb the stairs, and slip into my childhood bed. The entire time I'd been living in Pullman for school, my mom left the room I grew up in untouched—hopeful, I was sure, that I might return to Bellingham and move back in with them once I graduated, in six months. But the truth was, if I had had a choice in the matter, I wouldn't even have come home for Christmas. After suffering through a brutal finals week, all I wanted was to snuggle up with Daniel and talk about our plans for moving to Seattle together next fall, where he'd be attending the University of Washington medical school and I would start studying for my official certification by the American College of Sports Medicine. Just sitting for the test required a four-year degree in nutrition and physiological science, and afterward I'd be able to start working toward my ultimate goal of working as a trainer for professional athletes, specifically, for the Seahawks, the team I'd grown up rooting for with my dad. But instead of Daniel and me spending the holidays with each other, he flew home to Denver to see his family and I packed my bags to drive home and see mine. He and I had only been dating since July, when we met at the gym, but things were already feeling serious between us. Serious enough that when my parents had driven over the pass to spend Thanksgiving break with me, I introduced them to him, something I'd never done with someone I was dating before. All of my other relationships had been short-lived—lasting a few weeks, a month at the most. But Daniel and I had slept together practically every night for the last four months, either at his place or at mine, and the idea of being away from him for winter break felt like torture.

I snuck through the side door, locked it behind me, and then sent Daniel a text. "Made it," I said. "Missing you like crazy." I set my backpack on a kitchen chair, glancing around the dark space, listening for the telltale footsteps from the creaky floor upstairs that would mean one or both of my parents were still awake. My phone dinged, but before I could unlock the screen, a deep voice sounded from the couch in the family room, a space adjacent to the kitchen.

"Hey, Amber," it said, and I dropped my phone. It clattered on the hardwood floor as I splayed a flat hand over my chest, feeling like my heart might pound right through it.

"Jesus!" I said. My gaze flew to the couch, where I saw the shadow of a familiar blond head. I reached over to the wall near the door and flipped on the overhead light so I could see his face. "Tyler!" I exclaimed. "You scared the shit out of me!"

"Sorry," he said. He stood up and walked around the couch, and I was struck, as I always was since I'd moved away, by how much he had changed since the day we met eleven years ago, when his family moved into our neighborhood. Back then, he was gangly-limbed, all knobby joints and too-big feet and hands. Now twenty-five, he was six-foot-two and had filled out substantially, with broad shoulders and well-muscled arms and legs, a younger, better-looking version of his father. He had full lips, a strong jaw, and pronounced cheekbones that drew direct attention to his eyes. I had a hard time reconciling these two versions of Tyler; whenever I thought of him, my mind flashed to an image of the shy, awkward boy I'd grown up with, not the strong, attractive man he had become.

"What are you doing here?" I asked. It wasn't unusual for Tyler to treat our house like his own—he was an only child, too, and after his parents divorced, and his mom, Liz, had to start working full-time, Tyler spent many of the evenings she had to stay late at the hospital pharmacy with us. He and I would do our homework together, and then he'd join us for dinner, sometimes even spending the night on our couch if Liz was stuck with the swing shift. During football season, he would spend every Sunday afternoon watching a game with me and my dad, yelling at the TV and high-fiving when our team scored a touchdown or sacked the opposing team's quarterback. Tyler was here so often, in fact, that my mother began referring to him as her surrogate son. But the last time I'd been home, we hadn't parted on the best of terms, so I couldn't help but feel a little uncomfortable having him here now.

"Your parents had Mom and me over for dinner," he said. "I told them I'd stay up and make sure you got in okay so they could go to bed." He pulled me into a hug. "It's good to see you."

"You, too." I turned my head so my cheek pressed into his chest. His body was hard and warm; his shirt held a whisper of a sweet, but earthy-scented cologne. I didn't remember him wear-ing it before, which immediately made me wonder if he had a girlfriend who might have bought it for him. Or perhaps he bought it because of her. It would make everything so much easier if he was dating someone, too.

I stepped back and picked up my phone from the floor, checking to see if the notification chime I'd heard moments before had been a return text from Daniel. "Miss you, too, babe," he said. "Can't sleep without you next to me. Love you."

My cheeks flushed as I read his words, and I felt Tyler's eyes on me, intent. Back in September, when at my parents' insistence I came home for Labor Day weekend, Tyler and I had hit Cafe Akroteri for dinner on Saturday night, and then hung out at his apartment, half-watching a preseason NFL game he'd recorded while we talked. At some point, I'd told him about Daniel, and his reaction had been less than enthusiastic.

"Is it serious?" he asked.

"I don't know," I said. "It's getting there, I guess. I like him."

"But who is the guy?" he demanded. "How long have you known him? Have you talked to any of the other girls he's dated, or his friends? Did you Google him, at least?" He peppered me with questions like these until I finally snapped.

"You know what, Ty? It's none of your business," I said. "I get enough of this kind of shit from my parents."

He scowled. "I'm just worried about you."

"No. You're just jealous," I shot back, and then, seeing how his shoulders curled forward and his face crumpled, I knew that my words had poked at a wound in his heart that had yet to fully heal.

He dropped his gaze to the floor and sat back hard in his seat.

"Ty, wait. I didn't mean—"

"I think you should go," he said, cutting me off. He looked at me, his eyes the same light, clear color as sea glass. Without another word, he stood up, went into his bedroom, and closed the door. A second later, there was a loud thump, followed by another, and then one more. I wasn't sure what he was doing—hitting the wall?—but it seemed clear that going after him would only make things worse.

I returned to my parents' house that night, then drove the six hours back to school the next day. Since then, I'd basically avoided any complicated interaction with Tyler, wanting to keep things light between us, knowing all too well how sensitive he was, and certainly not wanting to hurt him again.

Standing in the kitchen with him now, I hoped that his offer to wait for my arrival was his way of saying that all was well. "So," I said. "How are you?"

"You'd know if you ever answered my texts with more than emojis," he said, playfully, but I still heard a tinge of reproach.

"I know, I know," I said, holding my hands up in surrender. "I'm a sucky friend. My schedule has been brutal. Emojis are pretty much all I can manage." This was mostly true. On top of the fifteen- to seventeen-credit class load I took each semester, I worked as a personal trainer at a gym near my tiny apartment. Most of my clients were mothers trying to get their prepregnancy bodies back, or older women attempting to halt the inevitable ravages of time, neither of which fit in with my long-term career goals. But I tried to look at the job as a stepping-stone, and it paid fairly well. For the most part, I could set my own hours, and to tell the truth, I enjoyed seeing the progress these women made—a pound lost here, a heavier weight added to the leg press there. It reminded me that even the smallest of changes can reap meaningful rewards.

Tyler stayed silent, shuffling his feet and avoiding eye contact, as though he, too, was unsure exactly how to behave after the fight we'd both swept under the rug.

I yawned, and then slapped a hand over my mouth. "Sorry," I said through my fingers. "Long day." I knew we needed to talk things out, but I was too tired to do it now.

"I should let you get some sleep. We've got the tree farm field trip in the morning."

"Oh god," I groaned. "What time?" Each year, both our families went to pick out our Christmas trees together, sipping tongue-scalding hot cocoa and eating slightly stale spritz cookies. It was something my parents had done with me since I was born, and we invited Liz and Tyler to join us after her ex-husband, Jason, left them and moved across town to a condo in Fairhaven. Only a lost limb or the threat of deathly illness could excuse me from participating, and even then it was possible my mother would rent a wheelchair and pop a morphine drip in my arm so I wouldn't miss out. Traditions were kind of her thing.

"We're meeting here at ten." Tyler smiled. "I'm glad you're home." He grabbed his jacket off the back of the couch and then, as suddenly as his head had popped up from the couch, he was gone.

My mother had roused me from sleep the same way for as long as I could remember. I'd be curled up beneath the weight of my blankets and she would sneak into my bed, tucking herself around me. "Good morning, sunshine," she'd whisper, her mouth resting near my ear. "Time to wake up, sweet girl." She would rest her hand on my hip, which she'd pat a few times, then shake gently if I didn't respond, then more vigorously if I ignored her.

When I was little, I adored feeling her body against mine, the smell of the vanilla bean lotion she applied religiously after she got out of the shower. The mornings I woke on my own, I would feign sleep until she arrived, craving her warmth—the absolute sense of security I felt in her arms. It wasn't until middle school that I began setting an alarm so I would be sure to already be out of bed before she came to get me. I wanted to be responsible for myself, to take control of the choices I made, even something as insignificant as when and how I started my day.

So now, at twenty-four, a small part of me squirmed in rebellion when I felt her climb into my bed the morning after I'd come home. "Good morning, sunshine," she murmured. "Time to wake up, sweet girl."

"Mom . . . it's too *early*," I moaned, pulling my comforter up tight beneath my chin. Despite how tired I'd been the night before, I was also wired from the surprise of finding Tyler waiting for me, so it had taken me longer than I thought it would to fall asleep. The last thing I felt like doing this morning was get out of bed in order to trek through the woods.

"It's almost ten, honey," my mom said. She threw her right leg over mine and pinned me to her. "I let you sleep in a little when Tyler told us how late you got home. He and Liz are already downstairs having coffee." She paused. "I made cinnamon rolls."

I stifled a sigh, unable to ignore what her deliberate mention of the baked goods meant. There was no doubt I'd have to eat my mother's cooking while I was here, or else risk her hovering over me, policing every bite I did or didn't put in my mouth. Normally, I precooked all of my meals for the week on Sunday nights—four-ounce portions of baked chicken breast or salmon, brown rice, and two-cup containers of kale salad, snack bags of toasted almonds and one-inch cubes of low-fat cheese—but I couldn't do that here. I'd simply have to eat controlled amounts of whatever she prepared, and get in as much exercise as I could to counteract the onslaught of excess calories.

I rolled over onto my back and peered at my mother, blinking to bring her into focus. She was already dressed in black boots, jeans, and a thick, blue wool sweater. Her auburn hair was pulled into a messy bun atop her head and I noticed a few streaks of silver running through it that hadn't been there when I last was home. "Don't we usually go in the afternoon?"

"We've always gone in the morning, but nice try. You still have to get up." She threw her arms around me and squeezed, hard.

I grunted, but also hugged her back with just as much strength, letting myself give in to the old sense of safety I felt in her embrace. Whatever my problems with my parents over the years, how much we loved each other had never been an issue. She kissed my forehead and stood up, then yanked back my comforter, exposing my body.

"Gah!" I exclaimed. Still resting on my side, I brought my knees to my chest and wrapped my arms around them in order to protect my skin from the cool air in the room. I only had on a tank top and underwear, and part of me couldn't help but wonder if she'd pulled back the covers just so she could check to see—as she used to almost every day after I was released from the hospital—if the xylophone of my rib cage showed through my skin or if the valley between my jutting hip bones had deepened.

She must have been satisfied with what she saw, because she didn't say a word about my appearance. "No more stalling. We want to be out of the house by eleven, at the latest. Tyler has to be at work by four, so we have to be back before then."

It was pointless to argue with her, I knew, so after she left, I got up and staggered to the bathroom across the hall. "Be sure to dress warmly!" my mom called out as she made her way down the stairs. "It's only supposed to get up to thirty-four today!"

Great, I thought as I closed the bathroom door. I jogged in place and did two quick sets of jumping jacks and squats, hoping the exertion would perk me up. If I was lucky, I could fit in a run later this afternoon, and maybe a trip to the gym.

It only took me ten minutes to dress and head downstairs—having such a tight schedule between my classes and work had trained me to whittle my routine down to the barest of necessities: dark hair brushed and put into a ponytail, a swipe of mascara and lip gloss to help brighten my face. I heard voices as I walked through the living room into the kitchen, and before I'd even had a chance to say hello, my dad, who stood at the end of the counter, turned around and swooped me into his arms.

"Hey, Pops," I said, and the threat of tears stung my eyes. I never realized how much I missed my parents until I came home.

"Hey, yourself." He pulled back and held me at arm's length, gripping my shoulders with thick fingers. He searched my face with his dark blue eyes, while I surreptitiously took in the fact that his beer belly had expanded several inches over the last few months. My father wasn't a tall man—at five-foot-ten, he was only four inches taller than me—but he was burly and strong, and his presence made me feel like all was right with the world. With his black hair and wide smile he was still handsome, but part of me worried about the dangers of this extra weight settling near his heart. Maybe I could get him to head to the gym with me later, and skip the spritz cookies. I often had to hold myself back from scolding my mother for the kinds of meals she typically cooked— things like meat loaf and buttery mashed potatoes, chicken pot pies, and always some kind of rich dessert—but I reminded myself that just as I hated when she lectured me about what I did or didn't eat, she didn't need me to lecture her.

"Beautiful as ever, I see," my dad said.

"She sure is," Liz said from across the room, where she sat at the kitchen table with a mug of coffee in hand. "So grown up!" She smiled, revealing ultrawhite teeth that set off what I knew had to be a spray tan. Her stick-straight, highly processed blond hair grazed her shoulders, and her blue eyes were expertly lined in wing-tipped black. Since divorcing Jason, Liz had gone through a succession of boyfriends, most of whom ended up having just as many issues as her ex. My mom tried setting her up a few times with men who would likely have been good to her, but Liz seemed to only be attracted to big personalities and short fuses.

I chuckled internally at her statement about my being "grown up," since technically, I was an adult, but I also knew that, in Liz's mind, a part of me would always be the chubby eighth grader she was introduced to, just as Tyler would be the younger version of himself to me.

"How are you, honey?" Liz asked.

"She's anxious to graduate," my mom said, answering for me as she pushed a plate with a giant glazed cinnamon roll upon it toward me on the counter. We made brief eye contact, and I grabbed a fork from the silverware drawer and used it to break off a good-size hunk. She watched as I put it in my mouth and chewed, trying not to cringe from the cloying cream cheese frosting that attacked my taste buds. When I swallowed and the bite hit the back of my throat, I almost gagged. Outside of fruit, I rarely ate any kind of sugar, and when I did, it was usually just a few squares of dark chocolate, and then only for the antioxidants.

Satisfied, my mom turned toward Tyler. "You sure you don't want another one, honey?"

"Oh no," he said, patting his stomach. "It was awesome, but I'm stuffed." He glanced sidelong at me, and I took another bite of the roll, washing down the sticky dough with a swig of black coffee, then stepped over to the refrigerator and pulled a few slices of roasted turkey from the deli drawer, hoping a quick influx of protein would keep my blood sugar from spiking and making me feel sick.

"I thought Liz could ride with us and you and Tyler could take his truck," my mom said as she lifted her coat off the hook next to the back door. "I'm sure you kids want to catch up." She raised her eyebrows, giving me a look laced with meaning, and I instantly regretted having told her about the fight I'd had with Tyler. I often vacillated between telling my mother everything and telling her nothing—if I shared everything, she automatically felt entitled to give me her opinion on what she thought I should do, and if I shared nothing, she poked and prodded for details about what was going on my life—a kind of verbal Chinese water torture—until I was tempted to make things up in order to get her to stop. Regarding the way I'd left things with Tyler in August, she'd said, "You can't change the fact that he had deeper feelings for you than you had for him, but you two are so important to each other. You worked it out before—you can do it again, as long as you keep the lines of communication open. Don't shut him out just because it's easier than having the hard conversations." She was right, I knew, so I resolved to bring up the argument on our way to the tree farm. I didn't want the remainder of my two weeks at home to be strained beneath the weight of unspoken words.

"Sounds good," Tyler said now, and a few minutes later, we were outside, greeting the clear morning. The sky was the bright kind of blue that forced me to squint when I looked up—there wasn't a cloud in sight. Still, it was cold enough that the lawn was stiff with frost, and each breath we exhaled instantly turned into a puffy white mist. Fortunately, the heat was blasting inside Tyler's truck. As the engine rumbled, I held my gloved hands up to the vent, my fingers already aching from just a few minutes exposed to the winter air.

"How's work?" I asked as he backed out of our driveway, thinking this was as good a segue as any into a more meaningful conversation. After graduating high school two years before me, Tyler had decided to forgo attending a four-year university, instead opting to get his associate's degree as an EMT, then entered the paramedic training program with the Bellingham fire department. He'd been working as an official paramedic for the last year, a career choice—considering his acrimonious relationship with his firefighting father—that I was still surprised he had made.

"It's good," he said, keeping his eyes on the road. "Stressful, at times, but I'm learning a lot. My partner is great."

"Mark, right?" I asked, trying to remember what he'd told me about the man he was working with.

"Mason," he corrected. "He's a cool dude. Supersmart. Been on the job for eight years, so he manages to teach me without making me feel like an idiot. His wife, Gia, just had a baby. You should meet them while you're here."

"Sure," I said. "If I have time. You know my mom already has my entire visit planned down to the nanosecond." I made my voice go high-pitched, in an exaggerated imitation of my mother. "'Cookie dough prep, nine thirty. Stringing popcorn and cranberries, ten forty-five. Watching *Love Actually* for the twenty-sixth time, twelve thirty-three. Bathroom break, one thirty.'"

"If you're lucky," Tyler said, laughing.

"No joke. I swear she preps for the holidays the same way a football player gets ready for a new season, only her training camp consists of testing out recipes and browsing for decorating ideas on Pinterest."

He kept laughing, so I decided to take advantage of this moment of levity between us. "So, are we good?" I said. "After . . . August?"

"Yeah," he said. His voice was soft, but reassuring. He kept his eyes on the road, his large hands gripping the steering wheel. "Of course. I've missed you."

"Me, too."

"I was an asshole about you dating that guy," he said as he drove past the Sunset Square Shopping Center, toward the Mount Baker Highway. "I'm sorry."

"It's okay," I said. Even though he referred to Daniel as "that guy" instead of by name, I finally relaxed for the first time since seeing him last night. This was the Tyler I knew—my sweet, kind best friend. The texts he'd sent me over the last few months had been vaguely apologetic—"You know I just want what's best for you, right?"—to which I'd send him a smiley face emoji in return. He'd never addressed that night in his apartment directly, but then again, neither had I. "I wasn't exactly nice to you, either," I said.

"I kind of deserved it. I just worry, you know? I want you to be happy. And safe."

"Like any good big brother should." I lightly punched his shoulder. "Don't worry. I'm fine."

"You're sure? You're doing okay?" He glanced over to me again, letting his eyes travel the length of my body with a fleeting, but clearly assessing gaze. "You look good."

"Thanks," I said, through gritted teeth, knowing that "good" actually translated as "not too skinny." My weight had been a topic of discussion for so many years, I dreaded every time a conversation even hinted at it. I'd worked hard to stay in the low end of a reasonable range, one that all the medical charts and my doctor said was healthy for someone my height, so the fact that my loved ones still seemed like they were still holding their breath, waiting for me to waste away again, was infuriating. The way they held on to the past, judging who I was now against the girl I used to be, made it all that much harder for me to leave her behind.

"You look good, too," I told Ty, then paused, deciding to go ahead and risk asking about his dating life. "Are you seeing anyone?"

"Nope." The edges of his tone were sharp enough that I knew not to push the subject. "You're still with Daniel?" he asked, in an entirely different, lighter voice, and I took it as a good sign that he'd actually used my boyfriend's name.

"Yeah."

"It's going well?"

"Yep," I said, knowing that even though things felt better between us, it still wasn't a smart idea to go into details of how amazing the relationship was. I certainly wasn't going to tell Tyler that Daniel and I planned to move to Seattle together next fall. At least, not yet.

"That's awesome," Tyler said. "I hope things work out for you guys. Seriously." He smiled, nodding his head as though lending emphasis to the sincerity of his words.

"Thanks," I said again, giving him my best smile in return. But even as I did, I couldn't help but wonder if Tyler truly meant what he said, or if, for the sake of our friendship, he was only telling me what he knew I needed to hear.

Tyler

I met Amber Bryant on a Saturday, the Labor Day weekend before I would start my sophomore year at a new high school in a new city. My parents had moved us from Seattle to Bellingham in late August, after a series of state budget cuts had forced my dad to leave the fire station where he had worked for over a decade.

"Fucking bureaucrats," my father had muttered when he got the notice of his pending layoff and optional transfer. "I lose *my* job because bleeding heart liberals decide to use all our tax dollars to support these stupid girls who keep spitting out babies because they don't know how to close their slutty legs." He'd looked at me as we sat across from each other at our kitchen table, eating the lasagna my mom had made for us before she left for her shift at the pharmacy, and pointed a thick finger in my direction. "Be careful who you stick it to, Ty. No matter what they say about being on the Pill, don't forget—no erection without protection."

I was fourteen at the time, and I'd nodded, uncomfortable with my father's graphic and casual reference to sex, but also unable to clear the images that suddenly filled my mind at hearing his words: images of slutty girls—girls like the ones in the Victoria's Secret catalogs I kept hidden under my bed, who wore nothing but spiked high heels, push-up bras, and black lace thongs. Without meaning to, I pictured them spreading their legs, then ended up flushed and squirming in my seat, trying to find a way to change the subject.

Three months after that conversation, my parents and I packed up our house and drove northward, eventually pulling up in front of the yellow, two-bedroom house we'd bought, which turned out to be only four doors down from the Bryants' place. The movers hadn't even taken the first box off of the truck when Amber's mom, Helen, showed up in our front yard holding a plate full of chocolate chip cookies and an invitation to the neighborhood's yearly end-of-summer party.

"It's at our place this weekend," Helen said. "Hopefully the weather will hold out so we can still use the pool!" She smiled at me, and I could immediately tell she was someone I would like. She was shorter and heavier than my mom, but there was something inviting about Helen's round, soft edges, and the kind light in her eyes. She had long, dark red hair and freckles, reminding me of a teacher I'd had in second grade who told me that someday, with my dedicated interest in dinosaurs and bugs at the time, I might make a good scientist. Helen seemed like the kind of mom who would sit you down after school, feed you a snack, and ask to hear about your day—unlike my mother, who more often sat me down, poured herself a glass of chardonnay, and proceeded to tell me all about hers.

"Do you like to swim, Tyler?" Helen asked.

"Nope," my dad said, crossing his big arms across his chest. "He's afraid of water."

My cheeks flamed as I lowered my eyes to the grass.

"Jason, please," my mom said.

"Please, what?" my dad replied.

My mom ignored him in favor of giving Helen an apologetic look, then offered explanation in a low voice. "Tyler had a scare a couple of years ago. He went over the side of a canoe at summer camp and got tangled up in some lily pads. It took a while for the counselor to cut him loose, and he hasn't really been crazy about swimming since." She put her arm around my waist, which I knew was meant to be comforting, but I yanked away from her touch. My dad had already made me feel like a baby—I didn't need her to make it worse by coddling me, too.

"Well," Helen said, "there are lots of other things to do at the party besides swim. Lawn darts and badminton. And so much good food! We like to eat in this neighborhood! My daughter, Amber, is about to start eighth grade. What about you, Tyler?"

"He'll be a sophomore at Sehome," my mom answered for me. "He just turned fifteen last week."

"Oh, that's a great school. Amber will go there next year, too." She smiled again. "I should leave you all to unpack. Just wanted to welcome you, and say I hope we see you Saturday!" She waved as she turned and walked down the street toward her house.

After she was out of earshot, my mom turned to my dad, her blue eyes flashing. "You think it's funny, embarrassing your son like that?"

I held my breath, waiting for my father's response, worried that they might get into a screaming argument on the lawn. My parents had fought with each other for as long as I could remember, bickering over things as silly as taking out the garbage and more serious issues, like his long shifts at the station or my mom's tendency to charge too much on their credit cards. Over the past couple of years, though, things had gotten worse. Their fights had become louder and more frequent; they'd started calling each other names. I would lie on my bed with my pillow over my head, trying not to hear the ugly words they said to each other. My heart shook inside my chest—I was terrified that my dad might come into my room and direct his anger at me, if only for another place to put it. Part of me hoped that moving to a new place would somehow press a reset button for them. Maybe it would help our family make a fresh start.

"A little embarrassment might do him some good," my dad said, talking about me like I wasn't standing right there. "Maybe he'll man up and get over it."

His last words were the ones that floated through my head when we arrived at the party a few days later. "Man up, Son," might as well have been tattooed on the backs of my eyelids, my father said it to me so often. It was a hot afternoon, already eighty-five degrees at one o'clock, so my dad insisted I wear my swim trunks, and I knew better than to argue. He wore his trunks, too, but my mom put on a denim sundress, saying that if she got too hot, she'd just stick her feet in the water.

The Bryants' backyard was full of people when we made our way through the gate, most of them engaged in animated conversations, laughing and talking like they'd known each other for years, which they likely had. There were mostly adults, a few teenagers, and lots of younger kids; many of the littler ones were already in the pool. I told myself that I was going to get into the deep end on my own, even if it killed me, just to prove to my dad that I wasn't the scared little boy he kept making me out to be. Everyone told me how much I looked like him, only a skinnier version. I was five-foot-nine, and he was six-two; I ate like my entire body was hollow and needed to be constantly refilled, yet I remained scrawny, while my dad spent enough time fighting fires and lifting weights at the station house that he maintained an impressive physique.

As my parents shut the gate behind us, I scanned the crowd and saw Helen standing over by the tables of food, which were in the shade, beneath a covered part of the patio. As she moved things around to accommodate what everyone had brought, she looked up, saw us, and headed over. On the way, she grabbed the hand of a dark-haired girl who had been standing alone near the back door.

"You made it!" Helen said as she and the girl stood in front of us. They had the same hazel eyes and heart-shaped faces, so I assumed that this had to be Helen's daughter. Helen's cheeks were bright pink, and she waved her hand in front of her face as though it were a fan. "Whew! It's a scorcher, isn't it? Can I get you something to drink? A bucket of ice to pour over your head?" She laughed, speaking so quickly, she didn't pause between sentences long enough to give us a chance to reply. She smiled and put her arm around the girl's shoulders. "This is Amber. My husband, Tom, is hiding somewhere around here, too. Probably inside, in front of a fan."

"Hi," Amber said, holding a single hand up in greeting. Like her mother, she had round, soft edges, and they both wore summery dresses. I struggled to maintain eye contact with Amber, which was a particular challenge because her outfit was doing a pretty awesome job of showing off her cleavage.

"This is Liz and Jason Hicks, honey," Helen said. "And their son, Tyler. Our new neighbors. I told you he's starting at Sehome as a sophomore, right?"

"Yep," Amber said as she gave me a slight roll of her eyes, which I interpreted as meaning "Parents are so annoying."

"Hey," I said, managing a smile.

"You're such a pretty thing," my mom said to Amber, and then turned to my dad. "Isn't she pretty, Jason?"

"Very pretty," my dad said, his eyes roving over Amber, and I saw a strange look flash across her mom's face.

"Want something to drink?" Amber asked me, apparently

oblivious to, or perhaps blatantly ignoring, what was being said by the adults. I nodded, following her to the big green Coleman ice chest that sat on the patio closer to the house. "There's soda, iced tea, or water," she said, grabbing a bottle of water for herself, and I grabbed a Coke.

We stood together in silence for a moment, watching the younger kids splashing in the pool, until Amber finally spoke. "Where'd you move from?"

"Seattle," I said after I took a long swallow of soda. "My dad got transferred to a fire station up here."

"He's a fireman? That's so cool. My dad just sells insurance." She paused. "Well, actually, he owns the insurance company, but still. That's nothing like saving people's lives."

"Yeah, I guess. He's gone a lot. Like, twenty-four hours at a time. Sometimes more."

"That sucks," Amber said, screwing up her face. "What about your mom?"

"She's a pharmacist, but she only works part-time, since my dad is gone so much. She doesn't like to leave me alone. Which is stupid, because it's not like I'm going to burn the house down or anything."

Amber bobbed her head. "I know, right? My mom's so protective. When I started kindergarten, she decided to get a job at the elementary school so she could have all the same vacations as me. She's like a stalker, but a nice one who bakes me cookies and does my laundry." She made another funny face, and I laughed. It usually took me a while to get comfortable talking with someone, especially a girl, but something about Amber made me feel like we'd known each other for years.

"Does she still work there?" I asked.

"Yep. She's the secretary. She offered to try and get a job at my middle school, but I told her I'd kill her if she did. Of course, she still joined the freaking PTA."

We went silent again for a minute, until this time, I found my voice. "Want to get something to eat?" I asked. Just looking at the tables overflowing with food made my stomach growl, even though I'd eaten a sandwich at home only an hour before.

Amber's eyes followed mine, and then she quickly looked away, almost as though she'd been caught doing something wrong. "No, thanks," she said, her voice at a higher pitch than it had been when she was talking about her mom. "You can, but I'm not really hungry." She chugged from her water bottle until the entire contents were gone, then grabbed a red Solo cup from a stack of them on a table and filled it with ice from the green chest. "I like to chew on it like it's popcorn," she explained, holding up the cup, rattling its contents.

"Oh," I said. "Okay." It felt like kind of a random thing to tell me, but I didn't comment on it because I wanted to keep talking with her.

"Hey, Tyler!" my dad yelled from across the yard, interrupting my train of thought. He stood next to the pool with a beer bottle in hand. "Time to bite the bullet!" His voice was full of mischief.

"What bullet?" Amber asked, tucking her long, dark hair behind one ear. "What's he talking about?"

"Nothing," I mumbled, setting my soda down on a table. I looked up and saw that my dad had put down his drink as well, and was now charging toward us with a determined look on his face. My stomach clenched, and the Coke I'd just sipped burned in the back of my throat. I glanced around and realized that everyone else was busy, even my mom, who was already sitting at a table with Helen, each holding a glass of white wine, heads together, looking like they were deep in conversation. I willed her to sense my eyes on her and then do something to intervene.

"Are you okay?" Amber asked, but before I could answer, my dad stood in front of me, his body only inches from my own, his hands on his hips. Amber took a step to the side, away from us, but didn't leave, and before I knew what was happening, without a word, my dad scooped me up, cradling me like a baby.

"Dad, stop!" I screeched, my voice cracking on the words. I kicked my legs, trying to break free as he turned around and carried me toward the pool. "Please, don't!" I begged, continuing to kick, but his arms were thick with ropy muscles; it was useless for me to protest. He held me over the water for a couple of seconds, locking his green eyes on mine. "This is for your own good, Son," he said, and then he dropped me, fully dressed, in front of the entire party, into the deep end.

The world went silent as I plunged into the pool. Chlorinated water assaulted my eyes, then filled my mouth and ears, making them sting. Bubbles rose up as I coughed and choked, flailing and panicking the same way I had when the lily pad tendrils had wrapped themselves around my legs. When I bobbed to the surface, I opened my eyes, blinking fast, treading water as best I could, feeling like I might be sick. The muscles in my chin twitched, involuntarily pulling down the corners of my mouth. *Don't fucking cry. Keep your shit together.*

My dad stood by the edge of the pool, watching me with a satisfied look on his face. "There you go," he said. "That wasn't so bad, was it?"

I didn't answer; instead, I fought my way to the shallow end, where my mom had rushed. "Are you okay, sweetie?" she asked, putting a hand on my back as I stumbled up the steps to the patio. I had to throw out a hand and grab on to the railing so I wouldn't fall. All of the other people at the party had stopped their conversations and were staring at the pool. At my dad and me.

"I'm fine!" I jerked away from her touch, keeping my head down as I grabbed the towel she held and wrapped it around my body. Despite the heat, I shuddered, and rivulets of water raced down my legs. My flip-flops had come off in the water, but I didn't even care. I just wanted to leave.

"C'mon, Ty," my dad said from the other side of the pool. "Don't be a spoilsport!"

"Please, Jason!" my mom snapped. "Enough!"

"I'll decide what's enough, *Liz,*" he replied, leaning hard on her name. His brows furrowed as he made his way over to join us.

Out of the corner of my eye, I saw Amber look at her mom, like *what should we do?* But Helen simply pressed her lips together and gave a small shake of her head. I couldn't believe my parents were fighting in front of everyone, that this was the first impression they wanted to make. So much for our family getting a new start.

"We were just horsing around," Dad said, in a much more controlled, lighthearted voice, glancing around at the other people at the party, as though only now realizing he was being watched. "That's what fathers and sons do. Right, Ty?" He gave a hearty, friendly-sounding laugh, one so convincing that if people didn't know him, they would think it was genuine.

I stood still and didn't answer, refusing to look at him.

Just then, there was a commotion of activity as the gate opened and more people arrived. With the distraction of the new company, the strain in the air dissipated. While the younger kids began to play in the pool again, the adults grabbed drinks and food, sitting in the shade or lounging in the sun, chatting with each other and keeping an eye on their children. Someone turned on some music, and a stocky man with black hair and a friendly smile greeted my father. If I had to guess by the way he clapped my dad on the back and maneuvered him away from me and over to the food table, I would have said that this was Helen's husband, Tom, trying to assure that the situation remained diffused. My mom sat down with Helen again at a table by themselves, and they put their heads close together again, talking. In between sips of wine, my mother kept biting her bottom lip and shaking her head, looking like she was trying not to cry.

Seeing this, I left the patio and strode across the lawn, knowing that witnessing her tears might bring on my own, which was the absolute last thing I needed—I'd had enough humiliation for one day. I sat alone near the back fence, staring at the thick grass, kicking at one spot with my big toe until a small chunk of the lawn lifted. I thought about leaving. About running away from this stupid small college town and going back to Seattle, even if there was nothing for me there. For the most part, I kept to myself. I didn't really have any friends, certainly not the kind that would invite me to live with them. I was too quiet, too hesitant to engage in the sort of rough-and-tumble activities other boys my age seemed to love. My grandparents on my father's side lived in Southern California, where he'd grown up, and after some sort of squabble they'd had with my dad years ago, we didn't talk with them. My mom's parents had had her later in life, when they were in their early forties, and now they lived in an assisted-living community in Bellevue that didn't allow residents under the age of fifty-five, so I couldn't stay there. I had nowhere to go, no one in my life to save me. As I looked up at the cloudless blue sky, a shadow fell over me, and Amber dropped my flip-flops on the ground next to my feet.

"Thought you might want those," she said, plunking into the empty chair next to me.

"Thanks." I was too embarrassed to look at her, so I pulled the towel from my shoulders and wadded it up into a ball in my lap. It was hot enough that my hair and T-shirt were already almost dry.

"It must suck to move somewhere new, huh?" Amber said. "I've lived here all my life. Same house, same people, same everything. Talk about boring." She pretended to snore, and I couldn't help but laugh—a short, dry sound that emanated from my chest.

"It does suck. I don't know anyone."

"Well . . . you know me," she said, with a lilt in her voice. "And I'm pretty great. Just ask me." She grinned, revealing straight white teeth and a single dimple in her full, round cheek.

I laughed again, this time from my belly, and the tension in my body slowly began to melt away. I fiddled with the thick hem on my towel, then gave her a grim look. "Sorry about my dad."

"What are *you* sorry for?"

I shrugged.

She waited a moment before speaking again. "Why'd he do it?"

The words "Because he's an asshole," almost came out of my mouth, but instead, I said what my mother always told me when he acted like a jerk. "He just wants me to be more like him."

"Oh." Amber cleared her throat, and then looked at me. "Are you?"

"Am I what?"

"Like him."

I glanced over at my dad, who by this time had left Tom's company to sit near the pool and a woman in a bathing suit that showed off her big boobs. She laughed at something my dad said, and in response, he briefly brushed the backs of his dangling fingers against her bare leg. "No," I told Amber. My voice was flat. "I'm not."

"Maybe that's a good thing."

"Yeah," I said, wondering how it was possible that after barely a ten-minute conversation, this girl might already understand me.

"C'mon," she said. "You wanted to eat, right? So let's eat. I can tell you what's good."

"Sure," I said. "Thanks." I gave her another shy smile then, grateful for the way she made me feel. It didn't matter that she was two years younger than me or that we were going to different schools. In that moment, one thing felt clear. Amber and I were going to be friends.

"What about that one?" Amber asked me as we stomped our way through the plot of forest that the tree farm opened to the public during the holidays. Her parents and my mother had gone off in a different direction to pick out the Bryants' tree, while Amber and I were put in charge of finding a smaller one for my mom's house.

"You two know what I like," she told me as they waved us away. The truth was that Helen was much more particular about these kinds of things than my mother was. If Helen, who was my mom's closest friend, wouldn't have given her a bad time about it, my mom most likely wouldn't have bothered putting up a tree. But when my parents divorced only six months after moving to Bellingham, the Bryants basically adopted my mom and me into their family, and my mother's gratitude for their kindness ran deep. So did mine.

I stopped and stared at the tree Amber pointed at, a lush noble fir that was about the same height as her. "I don't think my mom has enough ornaments to decorate one that big," I said.

"She can borrow from the ten million extra ones my mom has in the attic," Amber said, laughing. Her cheeks were pink from the cold, highlighting the scattering of tiny brown freckles that peppered her nose, and her eyes were bright with amusement. I was happy we'd managed to resolve the tension between us on the drive to the farm, even if it had required me to lie to her about my hoping her relationship with Daniel would work out. I loved her so much, it made my stomach hurt, and that made me willing to do anything—say anything—to make sure I didn't lose her.

"Remember the time we poured some of her boxed wine into coffee mugs and snuck it up there to drink?" I asked.

"Oh my god!" Amber exclaimed. "I totally forgot about that. How old were we?"

"You were a freshman and I was a junior. It was during spring break and we were bored out of our minds so we decided to see what it would be like to get drunk."

"That's right." She shoved her hands into the pockets of her puffy black ski jacket and jogged in place a minute, presumably to warm up, which made me have to fight the urge to offer her my body's heat. "You chugged the whole mug in, like, thirty seconds," she said. "You were so dizzy when you stood up, you knocked over a box of ornaments."

I cringed and shook my head, remembering the thud of the box as it hit the floor, the sound of shattering glass. "I was seriously terrified your mom was going to kill me."

"But then *I* insisted that you keep your trap shut and she'd just assume it fell over on its own. Which she did." Amber gave me a triumphant look, and I laughed.

"You corrupted me. I never lied to anyone until I met you."

"Pfft, whatever!" she said, and then shot out her right arm, grabbing the noble fir near its tip, wiggling it. "Come on, your mom will love this one. Chop the sucker down so we can go get some damn cocoa and stop freezing our asses off!"

"Okay, okay!" I said. "Bossy, much?" I lifted the hatchet I carried, and then took a few steps over to crouch down next to the tree. I whacked at the base of the trunk a few times, while Amber stood by with her arms crossed over her chest, watching.

"You need me to do that for you, big man?" she asked. "I wouldn't want you to hurt yourself."

"You're so not funny," I said, smiling. This was what I loved most about Amber. She forced me not to take myself so seriously. She made me feel like the absolute best version of myself.

"Oh, I'm hilarious. Just ask me." This was one of our private jokes, after she had used the "just ask me" phrase at the party where we first met, and I later confessed that was one of the funniest things anyone had ever said to me, the moment I knew we would be friends. Her use of it now confirmed the fact that she had fully forgiven me for what had happened in August.

"Smart-ass." I shook my head and put my focus back on chopping down the tree.

"Better than a dumb-ass." She jumped up and down a few times, her arms still crossed and her fingers shoved under her biceps. "How's your dad?" she asked. "You going to see him for the holiday?"

"Probably." I hit the trunk with the hatchet with as much force as I could muster, and it finally began to lean to one side. "And he's fine, I guess. We don't talk that much."

"You don't see him at work?"

"Not really," I said, glancing up at her. "We're assigned to different station houses, so the only time we see each other on the job is if there's an emergency that requires more than one team of responders and we happen to be working the same shift."

"Ah, got it," Amber said. "Is he still living with that one chick . . . what's her name? The one with the smelly gray cat?"

"Diana. And no, he broke up with her. As usual." Like my mother, my dad had never remarried; instead, he plowed through relationships with mostly younger women—some of them the same age as me—leaving a trail of broken hearts in his wake.

"I need to sow my oats," he once told me, not long before I graduated high school. "Your mom trapped me into getting married too young, and I'm never gonna fall for that again. I spent too many years giving her everything she wanted. It's about getting *my* needs met now." He winked at me, like we were in on some kind of secret together, and I didn't know what to say. I couldn't deny my dad's ability to charm women. I'd watched over the years when we went out for dinner on the weekends I had to spend at his house, how he had a way of talking and touching women—plying them compliments, making them laugh, and discreetly brushing his knuckles somewhere against their bare skin. It almost always got him what he wanted—them, at his house, in his bed.

"Sorry," Amber said, and I knew her well enough to understand that she wasn't just referring to the fact that my dad had broken up with yet another woman. She was sorry that he and I didn't have the kind of relationship that she had with her parents. She was sorry that I used to come home from a weekend at his condo and lock myself in my bedroom, wishing I never had to go back there again, that I never had to wake up to find some half-naked, strange girl in his kitchen—to make stupid, awkward conversation with her until my dad told her she needed to leave.

"It's fine," I said, giving the tree trunk one last strike. It fell over, hit the ground, and I thought about the other lie I'd told Amber in the truck—the one where I said that I wasn't dating anyone. *It's just a white lie,* I told myself as I picked the trunk up and Amber held on to the tip, slowly making our way back to the barn where, I hoped, our parents would be, too. I wasn't dating Whitney, my twenty-year-old, college-student neighbor, I was sleeping with her. I'd met her back in September—not long after my argument with Amber—in our building's parking lot, where she was lifting a backpack out of her car.

"Here," I said, striding over to her. "Let me get that for you." I smiled, taking in her petite frame, her straight, long black hair, and equally dark, almond-shaped eyes. She wore a red, form-fitting dress that was short enough to make it clear what would show if she bent over.

"That's okay," she said. "I've got it."

"I can see that," I said, "but I'm trying to impress you with my gentlemanly skills, so please, let me." I reached out, took the bag from her, and she finally smiled, too.

"I'm Tyler."

"Whitney Cho." Her gaze swept over me, and I was happy that I was in uniform. I still was getting used to how much attention women gave me when I wore it.

"Well, Whitney Cho, are you busy right now? I just got off work, and I'm thinking about watching a movie. Want to join me?"

"I don't know . . . I kind of need to study." She looked upward, where I assumed her apartment was.

"Okay," I said. "I'll just go home and try not to think about how lonely I am." I fake-sniffled and wiped beneath my eyes with the back of my hand.

Her posture relaxed and she laughed. Five minutes later we were in my apartment, the television on while we sat together on the couch. We chatted a little, and I learned that she was a business major, and that she had grown up in Bellevue. Currently, she lived with three other roommates in a two-bedroom apartment upstairs, and she only got along with one of them.

"Do you have a boyfriend?" I asked, thinking about Amber sitting in the exact spot where Whitney was now, telling me about Daniel—the harsh edge in my friend's voice when she said, "You're just jealous." My skin began to itch and my heart, to pound. I set my hand on the top of Whitney's leg.

"No," she said. "I kind of like older guys." Her cheeks flushed, and taking this revelation as permission, I kissed her. I rolled to my side, pressing my erection against her hip, and she didn't pull away. When I gently lifted her hand and put it on me, she hesitated, but didn't protest. She kept her eyes closed.

It was over quickly, and afterward, when she had gone home, I lay in bed, telling myself that I deserved something like this—

something fun, something casual—something that was nothing more than no strings attached. Because the truth was, while Whitney was many things—she was young, she was hot, she was available—she would never be enough.

She would never be Amber.

Amber

It was snowing in Eastern Washington on New Year's Day, making my drive back to Pullman more treacherous than usual. The roads over Snoqualmie Pass were icy, and chains were required, so I was happy my father had insisted I learn how to put them on my tires without anyone's help. After a tense, seven-hour trip—an hour longer than it normally would take—I opened the door to my apartment to find Daniel stretched out on my bed, waiting for me, just as he'd told me he'd be.

"Hey, you," he said, standing up to his full six-foot height.

"Hey," I said, with a big smile. I dropped my bags to the floor and jumped up, locking my arms around his neck and my legs around his waist. He held me like that, neither of us speaking, his face pressed into the crook of my neck and mine in his, breathing each other in. I thought about the first time I'd seen him, back in July, when he started working out during the same hours I was on shift as a trainer at the gym. We'd smile and nod at each other, and sometimes I'd catch him watching me with a client as I issued instructions on how to use the medicine ball or free weights, until, finally, I approached him at the juice bar, putting one hand on my hip. "Are you trying to decide if you want to hire me?" I asked.

"Not exactly," he said, and his mouth curled into an amused smile. He had short, thick, black hair and heavily lashed brown eyes. His skin was naturally tan, and I guessed that he was of some kind of Hispanic descent. He was muscular, but not overtly so, and he wore loose gray nylon shorts and a blue tank top.

"Then why, exactly, have you been staring at me?" I said, standing up a bit straighter. I was not a high-maintenance girl—I came to the gym to work, not to be the hottest chick in the room, so I was bare-faced, sweaty, and my hair was in a topknot bun. I found myself checking out his biceps, wondering if I could bench-press as much as he could.

"I'm Daniel," he said, holding out his hand, which I stared at for a moment before shaking it and giving him my name. "So, Amber," he continued. "Would you like to go rock climbing with me this weekend?"

It took me a moment to respond, realizing that I'd been expecting him to ask me out, but to a frat party or a bar, like most guys my age would do, which was a huge reason that I'd never had a serious boyfriend. The ones I'd dated all seemed like little boys trapped in men's bodies, and I wasn't interested in having a long-term relationship with an adolescent. The fact that Daniel wanted to do something adventurous and physically challenging immediately made him stand out.

I accepted his invitation, and after we spent a long, sweaty Saturday afternoon together climbing rocks at Minnehaha just outside of Spokane, we went for sushi, which it turned out we both loved. I learned that his last name was Garcia, and that he was the youngest sibling in his immediate family. All three of his older sisters were makeup artists who'd started a business together in Los Angeles, leaving their parents in Denver with the rest of his numerous extended relatives. "Fun fact," he said. "I have thirty-two first cousins."

"Shut up," I said, holding my empty chopsticks, midair, above my plate. "You do not."

He laughed and nodded. "No joke."

"How do you remember all their names?" My eyes went wide, trying to imagine how it would feel to be part of such a huge family. I had exactly three cousins, all of whom lived in Oregon, and who I saw only at our infrequent reunions.

"A lot of the guys are named Jesus," Daniel said. "So that helps."

We both laughed, and he went on to tell me that he'd chosen Washington State University for its exceptional premed, physiological bachelor's of science program. "I'm going to be a sports medicine doctor," he said. "Maybe work for the NFL someday."

"No way," I said. "It's, like, my dream job to be a trainer for the Seahawks."

"You like football?"

"Love it. Grew up watching with my dad."

"Awesome," Daniel said. "We should hit a few Cougar games this season then."

"I'd love to," I said, unable to eat anything more due to the giddy, skipping feeling inside my belly. Even though it was still the middle of summer and we were only on our first date, he was already talking about the two of us being together in the fall. I was attracted to Daniel's looks, but even more so to his easygoing nature, intelligence, and sense of humor. I loved that, like me, he was a goal setter, someone who knew what he wanted out of life and was willing to work hard to get it. The arousal I felt in his presence, the chemistry between us, was undeniable.

When he walked me to my door after dinner, Daniel cupped my face with both of his hands. "So, that was fun," he said, leaning in to kiss me, softly at first, then more insistent. I felt an ache between my legs that took me over, and then I did something I hadn't done before on a first date—I grabbed him by the hand and pulled him inside my apartment, then led him to my bed.

"You're sure?" he asked as we toppled over and I began to push down his shorts. He was above me, bracing himself with both arms so he wouldn't squish me.

"Yes," I hissed. I wanted to sleep with Daniel, and the fact that he paused to make sure of that made me want him even more.

"Do you have condoms? I didn't think—"

"In the nightstand," I said, pulling him back down to me and cutting him off with another kiss. I'd bought the condoms several months before, after a series of seemingly promising dates with a guy I'd met in my biomechanics class, who eventually revealed that he already had a girlfriend in Seattle.

Daniel opened the drawer, pulled out one square package from the still-sealed box, and then set it on the mattress. Turning his attention back to me, he began to work his mouth over my neck, pushing the length of his body against me. Frantically, we peeled each other's clothes away, his hands moving over each newly exposed piece of my skin. I ran my hands down his arms to his well-defined waist, dipping my fingers lower, stroking.

He groaned with his lips on my breasts while his fingers brushed over the heat between my legs. He kissed my stomach, then shifted his body downward, his mouth following suit, tasting and touching me. I began to tense, feeling the pressure in my pelvis build and build. My nerves tingled, standing at attention, begging for release. Daniel went still, only for a moment. "Look at me," he said, his voice ragged with lust, and so I did. I opened my eyes, locked them on his, and then, his fingers took over where his mouth had been.

A moment later I was falling, wild spasms pulsing through my entire body; a meteor shower of brilliant lights flashed behind my eyelids. He rolled on a condom and was inside me then, moving slowly until he, too, was trembling.

When he finally collapsed next to me, his legs still entwined with mine, both our bodies were slick with sweat. Breathing hard, Daniel kept one of his long arms around my waist and kissed the closest part of my flesh he could find—my elbow. "Wow," he said, and I rolled over onto my side, resting my head on an outstretched arm.

"No kidding," I said, smiling shyly. I hesitated to speak what came to my mind next, but felt compelled to share it. "That was the first time I've ever . . ."

"You've never had an orgasm?" Daniel asked, with evident disbelief.

"No, no," I hurried to say. "I have, of course. But not . . . well . . . no one has ever *given* me one." I paused. "Except me." It wasn't like I was a virgin, but I was particular about who I invited into my bed, and once they were there, I had a hard time relaxing enough to let go. Being with Daniel felt different. He made me feel safe.

"Ohh," Daniel said. "Well, that's tragic." He raised a single eyebrow and grinned. "Want to do it again?"

Seeing him now, after two weeks apart, I felt the same sensation as I had that first night. I clung to him for a few minutes, until he finally dropped me back to the floor. He kissed me, set his forehead against mine, and then asked, "How'd it go?" We'd texted each other pretty constantly throughout our separation, but it wasn't the same as talking face-to-face.

"I probably gained ten pounds, but otherwise, good," I said, stepping back from him and patting my belly. I'd forced myself not to get on the scale when I was home, too afraid of seeing a number that might spin me into a negative place.

"You look exactly the same," Daniel assured me. He knew

about the struggles in my past, and was a huge help in making sure I stayed on the right track. He understood that my choice of career was my way of maintaining balance, both physically and mentally—focusing on being healthy and strong instead of being thin. He didn't worry about it the way my parents did; they feared that my becoming a fitness and nutrition professional would keep me walking too fine a line between my illness and my recovery.

"You should check out your fridge," Daniel said.

"What? Why?"

"Just look."

"What did you do?" I asked, as I took a few steps over to the tiny kitchenette, which was on the other side of the studio. I opened the refrigerator door and saw that the shelves were filled with a week's worth of my typical meals—baked chicken and brown rice, kale salad, baggies of chopped vegetables, and individual half-cup containers of plain Greek yogurt. "Babe," I said, looking back at him. "You didn't have to do this."

"I know. I wanted to. I figured you'd be too tired to cook tonight, so when I made mine, I just made enough for you, too." Daniel wasn't quite as rigid with his diet as I was with mine, but he did like to eat clean, so it made it easier for both of us to stick to it. Unlike me, he gave himself one cheat day a week, when he enjoyed a cheeseburger or an entire pepperoni pizza, but he exercised enough that his body didn't show it. Not that how his body looked was the most important thing to me. He could have weighed three hundred pounds and I was certain I'd love him just as much.

"You're so sweet to me," I said. "I swear to god my mom purposely slathered everything I ate in extra butter while I was home."

"I doubt that," Daniel said. "And remember, everything in moderation, right?"

I nodded, though a part of me knew that while Daniel understood the mechanics and medical details of my eating disorder, he hadn't lived through it with me like Tyler had, so there were some things he would never fully comprehend. He never saw me looking like a skeleton, my skin stretched over my bones, my joints red with sores simply from rubbing against my clothes. He didn't see just how close to dying I'd ended up. And now, no matter how far I'd come in recovery, I knew that anorexia was as much a part of me as my hair color or height; I needed to stay vigilant, or else run the risk of letting it devour me again.

I'd been dating Daniel a little over a month when I shared the basics of how my disorder began. I told him how my issues with food started early, that because I'd been only three and a half pounds when I was born, I was bottle-fed on a special formula that was engineered to help me gain weight. Later, as a toddler, I drank calorie-boosted nutritional shakes instead of regular milk. My mother added butter to my rice, heavy cream and extra cheese to my macaroni, and every night, if I wanted to, I could have ice cream for dessert.

Still, I remained a diminutive creature, delicate and sprite-like in the midst of other children, so when I was five and I should have begun kindergarten, my parents decided to give me another year to grow. When I finally did start school, their decision to hold me back resulted in the odd contradiction of me being the oldest, yet also the smallest, person in my class.

"Be careful of Amber!" Mrs. Benson, my elementary school gym teacher would call out whenever I was part of a game. At my parents' request, she wouldn't let me participate in the more vigorous activities, like flag football or dodgeball; instead, I was allowed to sit at her desk and read or color until class was over.

Other kids, mostly other girls, were often jealous of the preferential treatment I received. "I wish *I* was tiny like you" was a line I heard over and over again, and their envy eventually transformed into a warm light burning inside my chest, making me feel like maybe I was a little more important than everyone else because of my size.

It was in the middle of sixth grade that everything changed. I remained the shortest girl in my class, but over the course of several months, I also became the one of the heaviest. It was as though someone had flipped a switch, and all the additional calories I'd been fed over the years erupted into rapidly multiplying, juicy fat cells beneath my skin. With each passing week, my body seemed to swell, rounding out my sharp edges, causing me to burst out of my clothes.

"Don't worry," my mother said when she had to take me shopping for a new, bigger wardrobe full of elastic waists and shapeless, stomach-hiding tops. "You'll get taller and eventually, it will all even out."

"But I don't *want* to be fat," I said, thinking about all the times I had heard her bemoan her weight. She always seemed to be on some kind of new diet—low-carb, high-protein, seafood only—Weight Watchers, Jenny Craig, and Nutrisystem—but none of them seemed to have a permanent effect. She lost and regained the same twenty pounds over and over, cursing her slow metabolism and sighing every time she had to put on what she called her "fat jeans" again. And then she'd bake a big pan of brownies—"for your dad"—to make herself feel better.

"Oh, honey, you're not fat!" she insisted. "You're just having a growing spurt."

I nodded at the time, but the weight I'd gained made me feel panicky, like there was a huge balloon expanding inside my body, pushing at my seams, threatening to destroy what made me feel special. If I was the same size as or bigger than everyone else—if I was *fat*—I'd be ordinary, the one thing I never thought I'd be.

More than a year after that conversation with my mom, a couple of days before I met Tyler in our backyard, I stood in front of the full-length mirror that hung on the back of my bedroom door, squeezing the dimpled pudge of my belly between tight fingers, wishing I could take the scissors from my desk drawer and cut it off.

"Disgusting," I muttered. I dug my nails into my skin, enduring the pain for as long as I could before I finally let go. I thought about what had happened earlier that week, at a park that edged the northwest shore of Lake Whatcom. Kids would line up at the bridge crossing over it so they could jump the ten feet or so into the deep water below, and that's where my friend Heather and I were when Brittany Tripp—who, with her long black hair, blue eyes, and lithe body, was the most popular girl in our class—cut in front of me with two of her equally popular friends. They all wore tiny bikinis, showing off their tan skin and budding breasts. Thanks to my mother's Irish heritage, my skin had two colors only: snow white and lobster red, and I wore a sensible black one-piece to cover as much of it as I could, especially my breasts, which, since the beginning of seventh grade, had doubled in size. Heather was blond, with blue eyes. She was also a ballerina, slender, and already a head taller than most of the boys we knew.

"Hey," Heather said. "We were next."

"Like I could miss you guys," Brittany said. "Amber's ass takes up half the line." She looked at her friends with a single, perfectly arched, dark eyebrow raised. "Why doesn't she just go *lose* a hundred pounds?"

My eyes filled with tears and my throat seized up, preventing me from speaking. I didn't know how to handle Brittany's brutal words. For most of my life, when people had commented about my size, it was complimentary. "Oh, look at you! So petite! So cute!" So I did the only thing I could think of—I whipped around and ran toward the spot on the grass where Heather and I had left our towels. Even there, I could hear Brittany and her friends laughing.

"Don't listen to her," Heather said when she caught up with me. "She's a bitch." Heather and I had met back in first grade, when her family moved here for her father's professorship at the university. She, her younger sister, and her parents were going camping over Labor Day weekend, so they would miss the party.

"She's right," I said. "I'm so fat."

"Stop it. You are not."

I rolled my eyes, pointed to my chubby middle, and Heather shook her head. But she had no idea what it felt like to want to crawl away from her own body; to wish, as I had countless times since I began to gain weight, to be struck with some kind of horrible, nonfatal disease that would magically melt all my fat away.

When I got home from the lake, I immediately got online and put the phrase "how to lose weight fast" in a search engine. I clicked on one link after another, skipping the names of diets I'd seen my mother go on, ignoring the articles written by doctors who recommended that a slow and steady weight loss of a pound or two a week was best. I wanted to be thin, and I wanted it now.

I redesigned my search by typing in "how to be the skinniest girl," and then landed on a site called "Thin Intentions," hoping to find a way to get more immediate results. There was a list of "thinspo," which was a shortened version of "thinspiration," and it was filled with suggestions of how to combat food cravings. I could chew sugar-free gum or crunch on ice cubes; I could drink tons of ice water or hot green tea. When I did have to eat, I could cut my meal into a hundred tiny pieces and chew each tiny bite at least thirty times. There were pictures of perfectly thin women, glorifying the substantial gaps between their thighs. There were quotes that said things like "Hungry to bed, hungry to rise, makes a girl a smaller size," and "Keep calm and the hunger will pass."

I didn't put another bite of food in my mouth that night, chanting those phrases over and over again. I lay in bed, my stomach empty and growling, feeling oddly powerful about my decision to do whatever it took to force my body back into shape. I would lose weight and everything would be okay again. I'd go back to being the smallest girl in my class—to being special—and everyone would want to be like me. Brittany and her friends would give me envious looks, and I'd know that they were wishing their bodies looked like mine. They might even ask me for diet tips, which I'd refuse to give them, of course, so they'd know what it was like to feel powerless, to feel disgusted by their own shapes. *My* body, how thin I became, would become the standard by which they measured their worth.

I started skipping breakfast, then throwing away the lunch my mother had packed for me to take to school. At dinner with my parents, I did as the websites suggested—I cut my food into tiny pieces, chewing a few of them slowly, hiding the rest beneath piles of mashed potatoes or rice, shaping and forming my food into piles that made it look like I'd eaten more than I had. It only took a couple of weeks for me to lose ten pounds, and one more week to lose another eight. My face slimmed down, and by Thanksgiving of my eighth-grade year, I started to be able to fit back into the clothes I used to wear. But by Christmas, those were hanging off of me, too. I weighed myself up to ten times a day, training myself to do jumping jacks or sit-ups in my room if the scale tipped even a few ounces in the wrong direction. I took up jogging, since my thinspo websites insisted that running was the absolute most efficient way to burn off any calories I ate.

As the number on the scale dipped lower, the number of compliments I received went up, and that warm light in my chest returned. When I started my freshman year, even the popular upper-class girls would ask me to share my secrets for staying thin. "I just exercise a lot," I told them. "And I'm supercareful about what I eat." What I didn't tell them was how I used my allowance and birthday money to buy phentermine, the one still-legal prescription medication of the fen-phen weight loss pill phenomenon, off one of the girls in Heather's ballet class. I'd learned about the drug on one of my favorite websites, which touted how taking it made you forget about food and eating altogether. It also gave me a crazy, jittery amount of energy, amping me up enough that I could get by on just a few hours of sleep a night. I hid the pills inside a pair of black boots that I kept in the back of my closet, spending the hours I should have been asleep in front of the mirror, examining my body, pinching at skin I was convinced was still thick with fat, sucking in my gut, counting my ribs, and relishing the empty space that remained between my thighs, no matter how hard I tried to push them together.

"Do you think Brittany Tripp is fatter than me?" I asked Tyler one autumn afternoon during my freshman and his junior year. It was a Tuesday, and we were sitting in the family room off our kitchen, doing our homework together. His mom was working at the hospital pharmacy until six, and then she had a date with an orthopedic surgeon, so Tyler was going to spend the evening with my family for "taco night." I had already decided that for appearances' sake, I would force myself to eat two one-inch cubes of chicken, four grape tomatoes, and one quarter cup of shredded lettuce. That way, if my mom or dad said I hadn't eaten, I could point out that yes, in fact, I had. Both of my parents had expressed their concern over how little I was eating—my mother had gone so far as to take me to the doctor, to whom I lied about how many calories a day I was taking in, and who believed I was heavier than I actually was because I'd used a trick I learned about on one of my thinspo websites—I wore two extra layers of clothes, thick-bottomed hiking boots, and put a handful of lead weights in my coat and jeans pockets when the nurse made me step on the office scale. Since then, the only place I put any food in my mouth was at the dinner table, in order to help keep my parents off my back.

"You're not fat, period," Tyler said, looking up at me. His pencil was poised over the notebook that rested in his lap. "If anything, you could stand to gain some weight."

"No way," I said. "I want to lose at least ten more pounds." Dropping that amount would put me just under a hundred on the scale, and according to my websites, double digits were the only acceptable place to be.

"That's crazy." He shook his head and made his longish blond hair fall over his eyes. "If you lose any more, you'll disappear. Like your boobs."

"Hey!" I said, shooting out my leg to kick his. "Be nice!" I crossed my arms over my chest and curled my shoulders forward, even though I knew what he'd said was true. My boobs had gone from a D to barely an A cup since Tyler and I first met, something that secretly pleased me, since it had stopped all the weird stares I'd been getting from boys.

"I didn't mean it like that," he said, quickly backtracking. "You're still pretty and everything, but you have lost a lot of weight."

"I know," I said. "But it's only because I needed to. Ten more pounds and I'll look perfect."

"I think you're perfect no matter what you look like," Tyler said, ducking his head down so I couldn't see his face.

"Thanks," I said, feeling a twist of pleasure inside my stomach. He always seemed to know exactly the right thing to say.

Of course, when I told Daniel the story about Tyler pointing out how my boobs had shrunk, I made a joke out of it, leaving out the part where Tyler also told me I was perfect. Daniel knew that my best friend was a guy, that Heather had moved to San Francisco with her family right after we finished our freshman year, leaving Tyler as the person with whom I spent the most time.

"You two never hooked up?" Daniel had asked me when I told him about my friendship with Tyler.

"Nope," I'd said, though that wasn't one hundred percent true. I'd certainly never slept with Tyler, and I reasoned that that was what Daniel had meant. "He's like my brother."

"That's cool," Daniel had said, and then never mentioned it again. I didn't tell him about the fight Tyler and I had had back in August, and now that it was resolved, I didn't see the point in bringing it up.

I closed the refrigerator door and walked back over to Daniel, slipping my arms around his waist. "You know what's *not* good in moderation?"

"Hmm," he said, with a slow smile. He reached his long arms down and cupped my ass in his hands. "I'm not sure that I do."

I kissed him, then, letting the tip of my tongue brush over his lips. "Let me show you," I said, and a moment later, our clothes were off, and we were welcoming each other back home.

Tyler

"Hicks!" Mason's loud voice boomed in the station's bathroom, echoing off the walls as I stood in front of the sink, washing my hands, mentally replaying the last few hours I'd spent with Amber and our respective families the night before, on New Year's Eve, watching college semifinals football, playing poker, and toasting with champagne at the end of the night. I could still see her freckled face, the twinkle in her eyes when she laughed as she tried to get her father to believe her bluff. If I tried hard enough, I could almost feel her body against mine as we hugged goodbye.

"Yeah?" I said, grabbing a few paper towels in order to dry my hands.

"We got a call. House fire over on Jefferson."

"How many vics?" I asked as I tossed the crumpled towels into the garbage. I turned to see Mason standing in the doorway, holding the door open with one beefy arm. My partner was a thirty-two-year-old man of Colombian descent with broad shoulders and chiseled flesh built up by regular doses of protein and two workouts a day. When I stood next to him, I felt pretty much invisible to any woman in the immediate vicinity. Those women would be sorely disappointed, however, if they thought they stood a chance of getting anywhere with Mason. He was happily married to Gia, a short and curvy firecracker of a woman who had, as I told Amber, recently given birth to their daughter. I was pretty certain if another woman tried to make a move on her husband, Gia, despite her size, would slam said woman to the ground.

"Not sure yet," Mason said, smiling and smacking the wall with an open palm. "Git your butt in gear, boy! We got *lives* to save!" He lifted his chin and began to croon the chorus of the Fray's "How to Save a Life" in a high-pitched falsetto.

I chuckled and shook my head, trying to erase the thoughts of Amber from my mind so I could focus on doing my job. Focus was key, my first instructor had told me when I entered the EMT program at Bellingham Tech. If you weren't focused, people died. It was that simple.

"So. Did you have fun last night?" Mason asked, once we were in the front seats of the rig and the engine had roared to life. My partner knew that I'd requested the holiday off for the specific purpose of being able to spend it with Amber, since she would head back to WSU the next day. It was rare for me to confess my feelings about her to anyone, but over the last year, spending hours of downtime with Mason, waiting for a call to come in, I'd started talking about my friendship with her—how we met, how close we were back in high school—and my partner simply guessed—correctly—that I had a thing for her.

"How'd it go?" Mason turned a corner sharply enough that I had to throw out an arm to brace myself against the dash.

"Okay, I guess," I said, not wanting to tell him how my heart had squeezed with longing the instant I saw Amber standing in the kitchen last night. How just the smell of her made my muscles feel weak, and how, whenever she touched me, my breath stopped, wondering if her feelings for me might have finally—

miraculously—developed into something deeper. For my partner's sake—and my own—I needed to pretend that being Amber's friend was enough.

"She still with that other dude?"

"Yep." My voice clipped the edges of the word as it left my mouth.

"Sorry, man," Mason said. The tires on the rig screeched as he blew through a stoplight and took a left onto Jefferson Avenue.

I stayed quiet, keeping my gaze locked on the red trucks with their bright lights spinning already at the scene, bracing myself to be around the flames, grateful that I wasn't the one who had to fight them. I had originally thought I might follow in my father's footsteps and become a fireman, but only because when I was young, he made it seem that I had no other choice.

"You have to grab this world by the balls, Son!" my dad used to say, wrapping a thick forearm around my neck in a fake headlock. "Teach it who's boss! We'll teach it together! Team Hicks, to the rescue!"

Before we moved to Bellingham and my parents divorced, I would nod enthusiastically when my father would make these kinds of proclamations, but even as I did, my stomach churned, fearing I could never live up to my dad's expectations. I was the boy who carried dying bees out of our house into a shady place in the yard so the insects could spend their final moments peacefully, in their own habitat. The boy who had to force back tears when I saw a skinny, collarless dog wandering across a busy street. The boy who'd give my favorite turkey and cheddar sandwich to the homeless man sitting alone on a bench in the park. The boy whose father, seeing how anxious I always seemed to be, was constantly telling him to toughen up.

I flinched as I recalled the day that I decided there was no way I could do the same job as my dad. I was thirteen, and he took me to go see my "uncle" Curtis in the hospital. Curtis was my dad's best friend, and they were both fighting a warehouse fire in the Georgetown district of Seattle when one of the walls of the building caved in. My dad wasn't too badly hurt, but Curtis suffered third-degree burns on over eighty percent of his body. I still remembered the antiseptic stench of the burn unit as my dad and I stepped off the elevator. I remembered the other firefighters in the waiting room, the sobs of Kristin, Curtis's wife, as they gathered around her. She was huddled in a chair, her face in her hands, but looked up when my dad and I entered.

"Hi, honey," she said to me, reaching out with both arms. I took a few hesitant steps over to her and let her hug me. I had spent many afternoons at her house with Tracy, Curtis and Kristin's daughter, when my parents both had to work. I liked hanging out with Tracy, especially when she went into the closet with me and let me lift her shirt so I could touch her barely budding breasts. She was the first girl I ever kissed.

Now, Tracy sat next to her mother with tear-streaked cheeks. She stared at the floor, black hair pulled into a messy ponytail, her tiny shoulders shaking. I wished I knew what to say.

"Can I take Ty in to see him?" my dad asked Kristin, who told him he could.

I gave her another hug, feeling awkward when she dug her fingers into my back. She clung to me; it felt like she was desperate for a comfort I didn't know how to give.

"Come on, Son," my dad said, and I reluctantly followed him down the hall and into a glass-windowed room.

Curtis—or what remained of him—lay in a bed, unmoving. His hair and eyebrows were gone; the only skin left on his body was in red, ragged patches. The rest of his flesh was blackened and peeling, shiny and slick with some kind of ointment, other spots covered with gauze. His eyes were closed; various tubes pumped medication into his veins and oxygen into his lungs. He looked like a monster.

"Hey, buddy," my dad said, stepping over to stand next to his best friend. He swallowed hard. "It's me and Ty. He wanted to come say hello."

I hung back by the door, shaking my head when my father gestured for me to come closer.

"Get over here," my dad said, through clenched jaws. He glared at me, and I was scared to defy my father so blatantly, but the air reeked of scorched meat, and without warning, my stomach heaved and I raced to the garbage can, where I vomited until there was nothing left inside me.

When I was done, I looked up to my dad. "Sorry," I muttered. My eyes watered and the back of my throat burned. I didn't look at Curtis, worried I'd start puking again.

My father strode over to me, gripping the back of my neck with tight, thick fingers. "Damn it," he hissed under his breath as he led me out of the room. In the car on the way home, my dad preached to me about the responsibilities of brotherhood. "Be a man, Son," he said. "That's all I want for you." Even today, I could hear the disdain in my father's voice; I could feel the shame that settled inside my chest.

"You ready?" Mason asked now, interrupting my thoughts. He parked as close as he could get to the address on the GPS screen. I nodded, looking down the street at the target house, which was already completely engulfed in flames. Seeing this, I wondered if the structure would be a total loss. I wondered if the people inside had found a way out, or if the firefighters at the scene had rescued them. I hoped their smoke alarm had warned them. I hoped the only thing turned to ash was their home. Over the years, I'd realized that my reaction to seeing Curtis in that terrible state wasn't about being unable to handle its gory extremes but, rather, my fear that if I did his job, I'd end up just like him, burnt to a crisp in a hospital bed, dying three days later. It turned out that *helping* people like him, the victims of disaster, was something I was better suited to do.

After letting dispatch know we had arrived, Mason and I raced around the back of the ambulance and opened the doors, pulling out the gurney and grabbing the rest of the gear we'd need. Jogging down the street with my partner, I called out to one of the nearby fighters. "How many?"

"Just the one," the fighter answered, pointing with a gloved finger toward the front yard of the neighboring house. Eight other crew members stood around the burning house, four of them on two hoses, trying to extinguish the blaze from the top down as the flames reached into the night sky with long, jagged arms. Another fighter kneeled over what looked to be a petite young woman lying on the neighbor's grass on top of a yellow backboard.

"What we got?" Mason asked as we approached.

"Smoke inhalation. Female, unconscious, early twenties. Airway is clear, but breathing is rough. Neighbors say her name is Mollie. No one else on the premises." The fighter moved out of the way for me to take over, and I slipped into work mode, checking for her pulse: strong and steady. A good sign. Then I took the oxygen mask Mason offered me and put it over the woman's nose and mouth.

"She's got slight burn demarcations around her nostrils," I said. I checked the rest of her body for burns and saw several around her feet and ankles, a few big ones on her shins. They were red and blistering—likely second degree. I performed the rest of my ABC checks–airway, breathing, and circulation. "Skin color looks good."

Mason slipped the blood pressure cuff around Mollie's arm, and suddenly she began coughing, reaching up with a frantic hand to claw at the mask on her face. Her eyelids flipped open and she twisted her head back and forth hard, trying to gauge where she was.

"It's okay," I told her, touching her arm with the tips of my fingers to settle her. I needed to keep her calm. "You're all right. You were in a fire, but you're safe now. Try and lie still." She thrashed a bit more, but seemed to have heard me, because she stopped moving everything but her eyes. I put my hand on her shoulder while Mason expertly slipped a needle into the crook of her right elbow. "We're going to get some IV fluids and pain meds going for you." I knew the membranes in her lungs and esophagus were inflamed; my first concern was making sure the levels of carbon monoxide and possibly cyanide, depending on the kinds of materials inside the house, in her system weren't lethal. The fact that she was alert was a positive sign, but we needed to get her hydrated and straight to the ER so the doctors could run all the appropriate tests.

"You suffered a few burns on your feet and shins. Don't worry, the burns look pretty superficial. We're going to take care of you," I told her. She nodded again, keeping her eyes on my face. I gave her what I hoped was a reassuring smile. "I'm just checking for broken bones," I explained as I moved my hands down her arms, ribs, hips, and legs. Everything felt intact. I looked to Mason, who had finished putting in the IV. "Good to go?"

"Yep," Mason confirmed, and jumped up to pull the gurney closer to us, then lowered it. "Hold on, sweetheart," he said. "We're just gonna lift you onto your magic carriage. You never know . . . Tyler here might be your Prince Charming." He winked at Mollie, who was too disoriented to register the joke. Mason was determined to set me up with every cute, single victim we came across in the field, which occasionally got under my skin, but I knew my partner just wanted me to have as much happiness as he had with Gia. I wanted that, too, but it seemed like no matter what kinds of women I met, my heart compared them to what I felt when I was with Amber, and they all came up short.

I knew I wanted to become a paramedic the night nine years ago when Amber's parents were out of town and I'd found her unconscious in her room, facedown on the fluffy blue rug next to her bed. I remembered crying as I told the 911 operator that she wasn't breathing. I remembered riding in the ambulance while the paramedics shouted her stats into their radio, telling the ER what to expect. I watched, hand over my mouth, as they performed CPR and managed to restart her heart. I remembered thinking that this—saving people—was what I wanted to do with my life.

Tears stung the backs of my eyes as I recalled the terror I'd felt that night. Losing Amber was one of my greatest fears—a fate I'd only avoided by pushing down my feelings for her so deeply that I hoped she couldn't tell they were still there. When she'd told me about Daniel back in August, they'd risen up before I could stop them, and her words—"you're just jealous"—were not only painful, they were true. They also made me realize that I wasn't as good an actor as I had thought. The only way I managed to hold myself together in that moment—to prevent myself from dropping to my knees and begging her to love me the same way I loved her—was to tell her to leave while I locked myself in my bedroom and punched the side of my hard oak dresser until my knuckles were bruised.

I was happy that she and I had managed to smooth things out, because the truth was I couldn't imagine a life without her. Something had forever changed in me that first day we met, and I hoped that someday, maybe, that same exact something might change in Amber, too.

At six a.m., four hours after Mason and I safely delivered Mollie to St. Joseph's ER, it was finally the end of our shift. Tired and silent, we headed back to the station to clean and restock our rig. When we were done, Mason checked his phone as we walked to our cars. "Want to come over? Gia says she's making waffles."

"Really?" I asked, knowing full well that Gia's culinary talents were mostly limited to boxes of macaroni and cheese and Bagel Bites.

Mason grinned. "Yeah, probably toaster waffles, but it's the thought that counts. She might even manage to not burn them."

I laughed, thinking it was a good thing that in order to maintain his beefed-up physique, my partner basically subsisted on protein shakes and the cooked chicken breasts he bought in bulk from a local butcher. "Sorry, man, but I'm wiped. Think I'm just going to head home and crash."

"All right," Mason said. "See you later."

"You know it," I said. I climbed into my truck, and pointed it toward home.

As I accelerated onto the freeway, I wondered if, despite my fatigue, I'd be able to fall asleep. I often felt wired after work, an electric panic buzzing through me, and there were few things that sanded down that anxious, jagged edge. My training had taught me that the fits of anxiety I'd struggled with since I was a kid were functions of brain chemistry, linked to emotion via the limbic system. My response to stress was, for lack of a better phrase, simply the way I was wired. But as I'd gotten older, especially after I started dealing with the often nerve-racking circumstances of my job, the symptoms I experienced had become acutely physical—shortness of breath, aching muscles, hot, angry pinpricks traveling in raging currents over my skin. I'd never told anyone—not Mason, not my mom, not even Amber—how bad it sometimes got. I simply pushed it down as best I could, doing whatever I had to in order to keep it from controlling me.

Now, I gripped the steering wheel, the muscles in my legs tensing as unthinking, I pushed my right foot down harder on the gas pedal. Without signaling, I changed lanes at the last moment before I might have rear-ended a white sedan, then put even more pressure on the gas. My shoulders hunched and I thought about whether or not I could beat my record of getting from the station to my apartment in under ten minutes. I'd have to hit 100 miles an hour in order to do it, and a glance at the speedometer told me that I was already at 80.

I felt the tension in my body rise even further as I hit 90 miles an hour, then whipped in front of a red Jetta and crossed over another lane in order to keep from missing the Lakeway exit. Horns honked and I heard tires screeching as I jammed on the brakes, my heartbeat beginning to slow down as my vehicle did, too. That hard and fast rush, followed by a sudden drop of adrenaline, was the only thing that relieved the internal pressure I sometimes felt, that helped me relax.

My apartment was just a few blocks off the freeway, a one-bedroom place on the first floor of a converted house at the bottom of High Street. There was barely enough space in the living room for a small, slightly ratty couch that I'd picked up for fifty bucks on Craigslist. But I had a flat screen hanging there and one in my bedroom, where my bed consisted of a box spring and mattress on the floor, and that, coupled with a functioning bathroom and the tiny galley kitchen, was all I really needed.

At twenty-five, I sometimes felt like I should move into something more adult—whatever that might mean—but the apartment was cheap and my neighbors were mostly college students, which worked well for my weird schedule. They tended to be on campus when I was home during the day and needed to sleep. My shifts were typically overnight, which were the peak partying hours for the young people in my building. They all knew I was a paramedic, though, and a few times I'd awakened to pounding on my front door when one of the students had passed out from having too much to drink, and their friend wanted me to make sure no one was going to die.

After parking in the small lot behind the building, I opened my front door and stepped inside, heading immediately for the kitchen to search out something to eat. I found only a lone pizza in the freezer and stuck it in the microwave to cook while I headed into my bedroom to change my clothes.

After wolfing down my freezer-burned meal standing next to the sink, I drank a big glass of water and took the few steps back to my bedroom, where I collapsed onto my bed, propping myself up with a few pillows. I clicked on the TV, more for the background noise than anything else, and when the news showed a clip of a house fire somewhere down in Tacoma, I wondered how Mollie was doing. That was often the hardest part of my job: not knowing the end of the story for the people I treated. I liked to believe she was fine. I had to tell myself that so I could continue doing my job.

I wondered what Amber was doing right then, if she was with Daniel or if she was already at the gym for work. I grabbed my phone, thinking I would send her a text, but then remembered that I'd promised myself to wait at least a few days before contacting her after she'd gone back to school. I didn't want her to assume that I was just sitting around, thinking about her. Which I was, but she didn't need to know that.

Instead, my mind wandered back to her almost three-month-long stay in the hospital during her sophomore year, where doctors had immediately hooked her up to a feeding tube so she wouldn't die from malnutrition. I remember overhearing a nurse say that Amber was one of the worst cases of anorexia he'd ever seen. That some cancer patients weighed more than Amber did, even after they'd been through several rounds of chemo.

"What's the last thing you remember?" I'd asked her, when she was finally conscious long enough to have a conversation. I was there every day after school, sitting next to her bed, whether she was awake or not. I watched her sleep—her eyes twitching beneath closed lids, her emaciated limbs sticking out of her hospital gown, unmoving.

But that day, she was awake, and only a week into her hospital stay. She rolled her head to one side in order to look at me and pulled the oxygen mask from her face. "Walking up the stairs to my room, feeling dizzy," she said. "And then . . . waking up here." She glanced down at the PIC line in her chest that was delivering the nutrition she so badly needed. "I can't wait to get this thing out of me. I can totally feel it making me fat."

"Are you kidding me?" I demanded. I stood up from my chair and gripped the rail on the side of her bed. "Not eating is what landed you here, Amber. You can't fuck around with this shit anymore, okay? It's going to kill you. It almost did."

"Getting fat will kill me," she whispered, and then I couldn't help it, I started to cry. Not the quiet, silently weeping kind of crying, either. I sobbed. My shoulders shook and tears dripped down my cheeks and landed on her arm.

"You can't die," I said, my voice broken. "Okay? You're the only person who gets me. You have to get better."

She closed her eyes then, and rolled her head away so she didn't have to look at me anymore. "You should go," she said, but I didn't listen. I just sat back down and tried to get a handle on my emotions.

"I'm not going anywhere," I said, still sniffling, but with defiance. "You can't make me."

At this, she finally laughed, a dry, cackling sound. "What are you, six? Don't be such a baby. I'll be fine, okay? I'll get better."

"You promise?"

She turned to look at me again. "Yes. No. I think so." She sighed. "I don't know. I'm too fucking tired to decide right now."

"I'll make you a deal," I said, suddenly struck with an idea.

"What kind of deal?" she asked, her voice full of suspicion.

"If you do what your doctors tell you to—the whole group therapy thing, talking with the psychologist, trying to eat—everything, I'll take you to prom. I'll wear a tux, rent a limo, the whole thing."

"Well, now. This just got interesting," she said, raising her right eyebrow. Her breathing was labored as she spoke; the doctor had told her parents that Amber's heart was still in distress after the heart attack she'd had the night I found her on the floor. With her extreme weight loss, the muscles of her heart, just like the rest of her body, had weakened and wasted away. She'd missed so much school since the beginning of the year due to her health— her parents had taken her to multiple doctors and a few different counselors, desperate for help, to find a way to get her to *eat*—that it looked like she would need to repeat her entire sophomore year, which would mean she wouldn't graduate until she was nineteen and, because of her late September birthday, wouldn't start college until she turned twenty. "You haven't ever been to a dance. You said they're only for idiot jocks and cheerleaders."

"I know. Which should tell you just how serious I am about you doing whatever it takes to get well." She was right; I tended to think that school dances were just for the more popular kids, not guys like me who would much rather spend a Friday night watching a documentary on the Learning Channel than in some dark, sweaty gym, pretending to have a good time. Amber, on the other hand, loved to dance. And if I had to go to my senior prom, there was no other girl I'd rather be with. I held out my hand. "Do we have a deal?"

She stared at my hand for a minute, a small flicker of light having returned to her eyes, then gave a short bob of her head. She reached her bony hand out to shake mine. "Deal. But you actually have to dance when we're there. No standing by the wall bullshit, watching everyone else."

I agreed, and when she began to get better physically, her mood started to follow suit. She'd entered the hospital in early January, and wasn't released until late March, because at one point early in her treatment, despite the bargain we'd struck, she'd pulled out her feeding tube, and more than once, she was caught throwing up the nurse-supervised meal she'd just eaten. It was far from an easy process, and she only put back on twelve pounds while she was there, but when she got home, she continued to see a therapist and attend a support group for people who suffered from eating disorders. By the time prom came around, she was still thin, but she almost looked like herself again, like the Amber I knew and loved.

As I lay in my bed now, my thoughts returned to prom night itself—what Amber had said to me—and suddenly, that jittering, electric feeling I'd had in my truck on the drive home from the station took me over again. I forced myself to think instead about Whitney, who was likely upstairs in her apartment. I remembered what it felt like to be inside her, to have her young, firm flesh pressed against mine. And though my entire body burned with exhaustion, I turned off the TV, grabbed my cell phone, and tapped out a quick text, inviting her to join me. "I can't stop thinking about you," I wrote. "Come over." Not a request, a demand, knowing that, however I worded it, she would comply.

"I'm not even out of bed yet," she answered just a few seconds later.

"Perfect," I replied. "Neither am I." I added a winking smiling face, and then waited a moment. When she didn't text back right away, I typed more. "Come on. You know you want to."

I couldn't ignore the barbed, erratic pounding in my head—the tightness in my chest, making it difficult to breathe.

I needed to do something. I needed relief.

"OK," came Whitney's reply, and my body instantly began to relax, knowing that sex would do for the moment, quieting the torturous discomfort that I suspected would only be cured by one thing.

Amber

We are driving south on I-5 for a full twenty minutes before Tyler speaks again. "Amber, please," he says. "Don't do this."

"Don't do what?" I squeeze the butt of the gun tighter, the weight of it uncomfortable and unfamiliar in my lap. My dad taught me to shoot when I was sixteen, strictly for self-defense, but I'd never had cause to pick up a weapon before. Not until tonight. Not until it seemed like my only option.

"Whatever you're thinking about doing," Tyler says, throwing me a quick sidelong glance, his green eyes dropping to the weapon I'm holding.

"Just drive," I say, staring out at the long, straight stretch of the freeway in front of us. I was alone in the house the night I snuck the key for my father's safe from his desk. I stood in his office, feeling the cold steel of the gun in my hands, telling myself that when I used it to confront Tyler, it would help me stay strong—it would remind me that, unlike the night when he raped me, *I* was the one in control. I wanted to scare him. To make his body shudder in terror, the same way he'd terrified me back in July. I wanted him to freeze up, feel sick, and hope that, whatever I might do to him, it would be over quickly. It was a stupid idea, really, because there was no way he could feel what I had that night. There was no way for me to strip from him what he had taken from me.

I feel light-headed, a sensation that I used to love and now just feels too familiar. I can't turn off the skipping-record memories of that night. The crowded party. The smell of booze and sweat in the air. The way I danced. The number of tequila shots I took. The way Tyler led me upstairs. Even during the rare moments when I manage to quiet my mind, my body remembers everything. It remembers, and then it's happening all over again.

I try to focus on what comes next. I'm going to make Tyler drive us to my family's cabin on the Skykomish River. Our families had vacationed together there more than once. We'd go for spring break, Memorial Day weekend, and at least a week in the summer, taking hikes through the forest during the day and toasting marshmallows and telling ghost stories around the campfire at night. It was a place without electricity or running water, an A-frame, two-story log home with a wood-burning stove and an outhouse. It was an hour away from civilization, secluded enough that no one would hear a gun go off.

"I'm so, so sorry," Tyler whispers. "If you'd just—"

"If I'd just what, Tyler?" I said, my voice rising. "Forgive you? Move on? Fuck that. And fuck you." Even as I speak, I can barely believe that it's him I'm talking to like this. That Tyler, the boy who sat next to me in my hospital bed every day after school for three months straight, making me laugh and encouraging me to do everything I possibly could to *live,* is now the person who managed to make me feel like I want to die.

My mind flashes to the way he asked me to go to his prom. That even in the midst of the dark place I was in—stuck in a locked eating disorder treatment ward—how excited I'd been to think that I'd be one of the very few sophomores at the dance. It was something I looked forward to as I trudged my way through my individual and group sessions at the hospital with Greta, the therapist whose job it was to help me get well.

"What about eating scares you so much?" she asked me the first time I met with her alone. She was a blond, sturdily built German woman, whose sharp accent chopped off the ends of her words.

"I don't know. Getting fat, I guess."

"And what would be so terrible about that?"

I shrugged. "No one wants to be fat." *Fat is easy,* I thought. *Being thin takes work. It takes vigilance and commitment—it takes a kind of inner strength that other people don't have.*

"I doubt most people want to be so thin that their heart stops," Greta said, giving me a pointed look. "No one wants to end up in the hospital with damaged kidneys, pressure sores, and a feeding tube, either." She paused, letting her words sink in. "Do you like being here? Missing school? Not seeing your friends?"

Again, I shrugged, because the truth was that other than Tyler, I didn't really have any friends. Heather had moved away, and I didn't hang out with any other girls in my class. Most of them didn't like me—I never sat at anyone's table in the cafeteria because I spent my lunch period in the gym doing sit-ups, jumping jacks, and burpees. I didn't accept the few invitations I got to go to the mall or the movies because I had a strict exercise schedule I needed to stick to during the hours I wasn't at school: a ninety-minute run as soon as I got home, then another hour or two of calisthenics in my room before having to endure the torture of dinner with my parents. Gradually, the invitations to socialize stopped, and I assumed it was because the girls were jealous of how skinny I was. Their envy sustained me in a way that food never could.

"What does being thin mean to you?" Greta asked. "What do you get out of it?"

"It's just who I am," I said. I told her the story of my birth, of starting school late, and always being given more attention and preferential treatment because of my size. I told her how when I started to gain weight, I panicked.

"So being thin makes you feel special," she said. "And maybe better than everyone else who isn't?"

"I guess," I said, slowly, unsettled that she was able to so easily pinpoint what I thought were my very unique, privately held beliefs.

"Okay then," Greta said. "So can you consider, just for a moment, that maybe all of this isn't about food or even the size of your body? Maybe it's about your *identity* . . . how you've always seen yourself. You've been conditioned to feel set apart from everyone else, so the idea of being *like* them in any way is terrifying. Maybe when you think about gaining weight, what you're *really* scared of is not knowing who you are."

"Maybe . . ." I said. I kept my eyes on the floor.

"Your thoughts are more powerful than you know, Amber. You've learned to equate thinness with purity and superiority. Your self-worth and how you look are concepts that have become so entwined that your brain sees them as one. We have to try and disentangle them, and then recondition the way you think."

"Sounds fun," I said, feigning a lightheartedness I didn't feel.

"It's not," Greta said. "But it *is* a matter of life or death. Our focus won't just be on getting to a healthy weight, it will be about finding emotional and mental balance, and figuring out a very different way of defining what it means to be strong." Again, she paused. "Tell me something. Do you want to die? Or do you want to get well?"

I wasn't sure how to answer. I thought about my parents and Tyler, how frightened they'd looked when they first saw me in my hospital bed, how much I knew they loved me, and how devastated they'd be if my heart gave out for good. I thought about the self-loathing that never seemed to leave me, no matter how long I went without eating or how low the number on the scale dropped, and I felt a flash of desperation, a need to finally cry out for help.

"I don't want to die," I whispered, fighting back tears.

"Good," Greta said. "I don't want you to die, either."

And that's how it started, my recovery. Tyler's invitation to prom, and Greta's gentle but insistent counsel. I struggled a lot, at first, especially as I got to know the other girls on the ward and realized that I wasn't so special after all—that I was just another case for the doctors to deal with, another one of "those girls" who fell into the trap of wanting to be skinny. I had to turn everything I thought about myself upside down—that "smaller" didn't actually equal "better" when you were so thin that your hair fell out and your internal organs started disintegrating and shutting down. I constantly had to fight the urge to restrict what I put in my body because the more dizzied I was by hunger, the stronger I felt. I craved the rush of supremacy I felt when other girls looked at me in envy, and I worried that I'd never find another way to look in the mirror and be happy with who and what I saw.

After I left the hospital, striving to find balance was a constant battle, something I had to fight on a regular basis so I wouldn't get off track. When I returned to school in the fall to repeat my sophomore year, I turned seventeen at the end of September, two years older than my fellow classmates, which made it even more difficult to make friends. I felt different than everyone else—disconnected. I was the sick girl, the one who'd been stupid enough to get so skinny that she almost died, so I spent most of my time focusing on getting my GPA up and spending time with Tyler, who by then was attending Bellingham Tech so he could become a paramedic. We still watched football every Sunday with my dad, and went to home games of the WWU Vikings, cheering on our town's university team. In watching the players move the ball down the field, I thought about the kind of diet and exercise regimen they must stick to in order to maintain their muscular builds and abilities as athletes, and a proverbial lightbulb went off in my head about how that related to Greta wanting me to find a different way to define what it meant to be strong. The players inspired me, and when I went for a run or lifted weights, I did my best to stop thinking about how many calories I was burning and instead, focused on gaining strength and endurance.

Even so, it wasn't until I graduated, moved to Pullman, and took my first course in nutrition at WSU that something began to change for me on a fundamental level. In learning about the biological mechanics of how nutrition interacted with how well the body functioned, I was able to see mine more like a machine that needed fuel, and totally separate it from my value as a person. Gradually, my obsessive thinking patterns about food and exercise began to lessen their hold, and I was able to put them in their proper place. My goal shifted from being as thin as I possibly could to becoming healthy, nourished, and strong.

Of course, there were times when I still struggled—my pants might feel a little tight or I might see the number on the scale go up a few pounds—and in a reflexive panic, I'd stop eating and overexercise. But more often than not, I was able to catch myself before I went too far. I spent almost every weekend during the fall watching WSU Cougar football games, either at the campus stadium or on TV, and eventually sparked on the idea of someday using my degree to become a trainer for an NFL team. By the time I met Daniel, in my senior year, I felt proud about my decision to take the worst thing I'd ever gone through and transform it into a career that could help others focus on strength, balance, and health.

"Do you remember what I wore to prom?" I ask Tyler now.

"What?" he says, glancing over to me again.

"Keep your eyes on the road," I say, then clear my throat. "Your prom. Do you remember my dress?" He doesn't need to know why I'm asking the question, he just needs to answer it.

He nods, complying with my request to keep his eyes straight ahead.

"What color was it?" I can feel the hum of the truck's tires hitting the road vibrating through me, a sensation that would normally lull me but, tonight, seems only to amplify the adrenaline coursing through my blood.

"Green. Dark green."

"Do you remember what happened after the dance, in your car?"

"Amber—" he says, but I cut him off.

"Do you remember, Tyler? Tell me." The last two words slip through my gritted teeth.

He releases a long, slow breath. "Of course. We were talking and I just . . . kissed you."

"And what did I do?"

"You kissed me back."

"And then what?"

"You pushed me away."

"That's right." I think about that moment, when Tyler leaned in and put his lips against mine. It was the first time anyone had kissed me, ever. At first, I didn't know what to do other than let it happen. I closed my eyes and moved my lips against his, let his tongue touch mine, until a strange buzzing began to sound off in my head, a kind of internal alarm warning me that something didn't feel right.

"Don't!" I said, setting my palms on his chest.

"Amber, please," he replied, as though the words were a prayer.

"And then you told me you loved me," I say now. "That you were *in* love with me." I remember the look on his face when he spoke, the naked vulnerability in his eyes.

"And you said you didn't love me," he says. His voice is flat. "Not that way. Not ever."

"But I did love you. You were my best friend." Tears sting my eyes and I fight back what feels like a ball of barbed wire in my throat. "I told you that. I said how much you meant to me. And you still stopped talking to me. You didn't look at me when we were at school, you didn't come over to my house that entire summer. You totally shut down. It took months for things to go back to normal."

"I was hurt," he says.

My entire body tenses. I want to tell him that he doesn't know what it is to hurt. To ache so deeply that all you want is to scrub away your skin and peel back your muscles so you can get down to the black, malignant damage and gouge it out.

"Were you trying to punish me?" I say, instead. My voice rises again, finally getting to the point of why I'd brought up prom night now. "Is that why you did this? To make me pay for rejecting you? For falling in love with Daniel?"

"God, no," Tyler says, and I can hear the anguish underpinning his words. "I don't . . . I never . . . I have no idea why it happened, Amber."

"It didn't just 'happen,' Tyler," I say. Tears roll down my cheeks and I hate them. I hate them because they make me seem weak. I'm not weak—I'm seething, a bomb about to explode. "It wasn't some bullshit passive thing that you had no control over. You made a choice and you *did* it. You need to take some fucking responsibility for your actions. *Man up.*" I watch for his reaction to his father's phrase, the one I know he hates more than any other.

He doesn't look at me, but his long fingers grip the steering wheel tighter, causing his knuckles to go white. His chest moves up and down, slowly, deliberately, as though he is trying to control his breath. To pause and think about what he will say next. "If there was any way I could take it back," he finally says in a low, measured tone, "you have to know that I would. I'd do anything."

"It's too late." I turn my head and stare out the passenger side window into the dark, running my fingers down the cold steel barrel of the gun. I think about how there are some wounds unreachable by words, some sins immune to apology. I think about this, and then I think about Tyler. How there are some things you just can't forgive.

Tyler

I woke the morning of Amber's graduation party with what felt like an anvil resting on my chest. It was early June, and things had continued to be good between us—we'd been texting at least a few times a week since I last saw her at Christmas, keeping each other informed of any important, or unimportant, details of our lives, talking about her school and my work and the latest idiot my mother was dating. But the text she sent me yesterday turned my skin to shrink wrap.

"Daniel asked me to marry him," she said. "And I said yes." She wanted me to know before I saw them today, at her parents' house, for her celebration. "I just got off the phone with my mom and dad, and I wanted to make sure you heard it from me, first."

"Wow. I'm happy for you guys," I managed to respond, despite the wailing siren going off inside my head. "Congratulations." I knew that was all I could say. That anything else would be pointless.

"Thanks," she said, followed by a smiley face emoji.

"Can't wait to meet him," I said. Amber's boyfriend—fiancé, I corrected myself—would only be visiting Bellingham for a couple of days before he started summer session at the University of Washington in Seattle. "He's a total overachiever," Amber had told me a few weeks ago. "He enrolled in a couple of seminars that his adviser said would help jump-start his first year in med school." Amber planned to spend the summer at home, working to save money, and then join Daniel in the fall.

Now, almost twenty-four hours after she told me the news, I sat up and gripped the edge of my mattress. *Amber is getting married. To Daniel.* I took a deep breath, and the muscles in my chest pulled so tight I was afraid they might snap. I wondered if Whitney was home, and then remembered that spring quarter at WWU was over. She had already gone back to her parents' house for the summer.

I rolled out of bed, pacing back and forth between my small bedroom and living room, trying to return my pulse to normal. "Fuck it," I said aloud, to my empty apartment. If I couldn't get laid, I needed another way to force my spiking adrenaline into submission. I had taken the day off for Amber's party, which didn't start until three, so I pulled on a pair of jogging shorts, a T-shirt, and my sneakers, then grabbed my iPhone and keys, heading out the front door.

Only ten minutes into my run, my breathing was labored and my hamstrings were screaming at me to quit. But I dug my fingernails into my palms and pushed myself to keep going. It was a slightly overcast, cool, early June day, and still, beads of sweat gathered on my forehead and rolled into my eyes, causing them to sting. I wiped at them, stopping to jog in place on a busy street corner, waiting for the walk signal. I caught an attractive blond girl staring at me, and I immediately thought about how easy it would be to ask her to go out for coffee, then invite her to come to Amber's party. Maybe that would make meeting Daniel easier, having a date with me. A few flattering words, a few suggestive jokes—that was all it would take. As introverted as I had been as a teenager, as an adult, I never had a problem getting girls. Things changed significantly when my body filled out. And while I was still fairly quiet, most women tended to assume that my lack of wordy machismo meant I was the strong silent type, in search of a soul mate. But with how often I struggled with anxiety, I didn't *feel* very strong. And the truth was I didn't need to search—I already knew who my soul mate was.

Now, the blond girl smiled at me, and then ducked her head down. Flirting. But just as I was about to say hello, I realized how retaliatory and desperate bringing a stranger to Amber's party would make me seem—like "oh, look, you might be engaged, but here's a pretty girl I picked up on a street corner this morning!" I gave the girl quick, friendly nod, and then headed across the street, pumping my arms and lengthening my stride. I ran until I didn't think I could keep going. And then I ran some more.

When I finally returned to my apartment, my head was clear and my legs were shaking and weak, but the pressure in my chest was gone. I reveled in being able to take in deep, satisfying breaths. A few hours later, after a nap and a shower, I was on my way to Amber's house, the present I had wrapped for her resting on the passenger seat of my truck. I parked on the street, the buzz of music and conversation already overflowing from the backyard. Grabbing her gift, I slowly made my way down the driveway and opened the gate to find a small gathering of the Bryants' friends—people Helen worked with at the elementary school, Tom's coworkers from his office, and a few teachers from Sehome High School, none of whom seemed to notice me arrive.

My dad's voice was the first one I heard. "Ty, my boy!" he called out. "Come meet Layla!" I glanced toward where he sat, on the patio near the bar—of course—with a dark-haired woman who looked to be in her late thirties. She wore a too-tight, low-cut black dress. She sat in a lawn chair next to my dad, who had one arm around her shoulders, his thick fingers dangling over her ample cleavage. In his other hand, he held a beer.

"Hey, Dad," I said, holding up the gift I carried in greeting. "Let me put this inside first. Say hi to Amber and her parents." *And Daniel,* I thought, grinding my molars together until they squeaked. *Don't forget about Daniel.*

My dad nodded, and I walked from the gate to the French doors that led inside the kitchen, where I found my mom and Helen standing next to the counter, their backs to me.

"Can you believe he brought that woman?" my mom said. "She looks like a *hooker.*" My mom had had ten years to get used to the parade of women in and out of my dad's life, so it was likely that she was angrier with herself for not bringing a date than with my dad for bringing his.

Helen shook her head. "I'm sorry. I told you Tom ran into him at the hardware store the other day, and when Jason asked when Amber would be home from school, he felt like he had to invite him. You know I'd never—"

I cleared my throat, not wanting to hear more. They both turned, and my mother came over to hug me. "Hi, honey," she said, standing on her tiptoes in order to give me a kiss on the cheek. "How are you?"

"Good," I said. "Where should I put this?" I held up a small box, nothing expensive or flashy, but a gift that I hoped that Amber would like. I hoped it would mean something to her.

"Oh, aren't you sweet," Helen said. "The dining room table would be great. And I think Amber and Daniel are with Tom out in the living room." She paused. "Did you hear the news?"

"I did," I said, purposely keeping my tone light. "Amber texted me yesterday."

"He's just a doll," my mom said. "So smart. And handsome! Amber sure knows how to pick them."

"I have no doubt," I said, faking a smile. I'd never discussed my feelings for Amber with my mom, though from the sympathetic look on Helen's face, I suspected that Amber had discussed them with hers. Heat rose in my cheeks.

"I think you'll like him," Helen said.

"I'm sure I will," I said, hoping this would be true. Hoping that I could at least pretend for the duration of the party that I hadn't spent the last nine months, since learning of his existence, silently wishing that he would screw up somehow and the relationship would end. Amber had dated other guys over the years, but none as long as Daniel. And now they were engaged and I worried that I'd lost my chance to change her mind about me.

I headed into the dining room, where I set Amber's present on the table, then proceeded into the living room, where I saw Amber standing with her dad and a tall, tan guy with black hair. Amber's fingers were laced through his.

"Hey," I said, forcing another smile.

"Tyler!" Amber said, letting go of her fiancé's hand to come over and hug me. "I'm so glad you're here."

"Wouldn't miss it." I hugged her, and a familiar sensation of arousal and longing rushed over me. *Stop it,* I told myself. *Just knock it the fuck off.*

"Come here," she said, pulling back and grabbing me by the hand. She led me over to where her father and fiancé stood. "Daniel, this is Tyler. Tyler, Daniel."

"Nice to finally meet you, bro," Daniel said, holding out his hand for me to shake.

"You, too." I gripped his fingers maybe a little too tightly before I let them go, but he didn't seem to notice.

"How's it going, Ty?" Tom asked. He put his stocky arm

around his daughter's shoulders. "Can you believe our girl is all graduated?"

"It's pretty great," I said, nodding my head.

"Like you were expecting me not to?" Amber said in a teasing voice. She looked up at her dad, who kissed her on the forehead.

"I expect you to kick ass at whatever you decide to do," he said.

"Aw, thanks, Pops," Amber said, giving her dad an adoring look.

"So," I said. "I hear other congratulations are in order." I smiled at Daniel, who nodded.

"I'm a lucky guy," he said.

"The luckiest," Amber agreed, and we all laughed. She held out her left hand to show me the ring, a small, but sparkling round diamond on a silver band. "What do you think?" Her eyes were wide, a little worried, I suspected, that I might not be as happy for them as I seemed. After my behavior last August, I couldn't blame her, but I'd worked hard since Christmas to act nothing other than supportive of their relationship. "If you're happy," I'd told her, more than once, "so am I."

"Very nice," I said about the ring now.

"Amber tells me you're a paramedic," Daniel said. "One of my cousins in Denver does the same thing. I admire the hell out of you guys."

"Thanks," I said. "But you, heading off to become a doctor. That's something to admire." *I'm doing this for your sake,* I wanted to tell Amber. *I'm going to be nice to him. I'm going to be welcoming and friendly all because of you.* But even as I thought this, I couldn't help but concede that, so far, Daniel was a likable guy. However much I hated to admit it, I could see why Amber fell for him.

"Thanks, man," Daniel said.

"Well!" Tom exclaimed, drawing away from Amber. He rubbed

the palms of his thick hands together. "I'd better go fire up the grill if we're going to eat anytime tonight." He clapped me on the back and pulled me into a quick side hug. "Good to see you, Son. Don't be such a stranger. You know Amber doesn't have to be here for you to come see us."

"I know," I said. "Thanks." I watched as he headed through the arched doorway which led to the dining room and into the kitchen, then out the back door. Not for the first time, I wished that my dad was more like Tom—affable, laid-back, and easy to talk to—qualities my own father had never possessed.

"Did you see your dad?" Amber asked me as she scooted over next to Daniel again. "And his date?" She screwed up her face, raising a single, questioning eyebrow. There were a hundred meanings behind that one expression, years of conversations about the complicated nature of my relationship with my dad.

I suppressed a sigh. "Yep. On my way in. They seem very . . . content."

"No girlfriend for you, man?" Daniel asked.

I cringed a little at the continued use of "man" and "bro" at the ends of Daniel's sentences. I was nit-picking, I knew, but it was irritating. "Nope," I said. "I was seeing a girl in my building, but she went back to Bellevue to live with her parents for the summer."

"Wait, what?" Amber said. "Why didn't I know about this?"

I shrugged. "You didn't ask." I only mentioned Whitney because I knew the chance of Amber ever meeting her was basically zero. I just didn't want her or Daniel to think that, when I wasn't working, I spent all of my time alone—the poor, pathetic, miserable bachelor.

"I shouldn't have to!" Amber stepped forward and hit me on the arm.

"Ow! Sorry!" I said, rubbing my bicep and pretending that her punch hurt more than it did.

Daniel laughed. "Careful, dude," he said. "She's feisty."

I smiled, but inside I was screaming. *I'm not your dude, dude! And you think I don't know that she's feisty? I'm her best friend. I know more about her than you ever could. I love her more than you ever will.*

Instead, I said, "Don't I know it."

"All right," Amber said. "We should probably stop hiding and go socialize with all my parents' friends who were kind enough to write this feisty girl a graduation check." She grinned, and both Daniel and I followed her outside, where my mom and Helen had set up a table with appetizers, and Tom was standing in front of the grill, sipping a beer and chatting with a man I didn't recognize. I looked at the pool, remembering, and felt as though a rock had dropped from my chest into my gut. I wasn't afraid of the deep end anymore, but I had never been able to shake the humiliating memory of what my father did to me that day.

"Tyler!" my dad called out. He and Layla hadn't moved from their lawn chairs. "Come here, Son. I haven't seen you in ages."

You think that's an accident? I thought. Still, as Amber and Daniel walked over to talk with a group of her parents' friends closer to the pool, I made my way to my dad, shaking Layla's hand when I got there. "Nice to meet you."

"You, too, hon," she said, taking a sip of the beer she held. "Your dad's told me so much about you. That you're a fireman, just like him."

"I'm a paramedic, actually," I said, clenching my jaws at the idea that my father would lie about what I did for a living, as though my actual job were a shameful thing. Both jobs served important purposes. Both saved lives. I had been terrified to tell my father that I wasn't going to follow in his footsteps. But then, at the beginning of my senior year, on one of the two weekends a month I spent with him at his condo instead of home with my mom, I somehow worked up the courage. We had just finished breakfast in the small nook off the kitchen, and I asked him to join me in the living room.

"Should we sit?" I asked when we stood next to the couch, and then immediately regretted it. I'd just turned eighteen, and questions like that implied my father was still in charge of my decisions.

"I'm good," my dad said. He widened his stance and crossed his arms over his broad chest. "What's up?"

"I've made a decision." I forced myself to retain eye contact with him.

"About?"

Before I answered, I straightened my posture to my full six-foot-two height, which I'd reached over the summer, finally tall enough to look my dad in the eye. A small part of me believed that, if I stood my ground about what I wanted to do with my life, my father might actually respect me. Wasn't that what he always said he wanted from me—for me to "ball up" and "be a man"? I swallowed and went on. "I'm going to school to be a paramedic. I'm not going to be a firefighter."

I held my breath, waiting for my father's response. I hoped he might see that I was choosing a noble and important profession, even if it wasn't the one he wanted me to have. I didn't know how to articulate my need to differentiate from my father while at the same time wanting to make him proud.

My dad remained quiet for what felt like a long couple of minutes after I spoke, staring at me with void, blinking green eyes. "You gonna make fifteen dollars an hour for the rest of your life, Son?" he finally said. "Is that how you're going to take care of a family?"

Being a paramedic would allow me to make significantly more than that, but in that moment, my father's scorn had gutted me. It also made me even more determined to prove that I could be successful without being like him.

"Layla, honey," my dad said now. "Why don't you go get me another beer? And something to eat." He held up his empty bottle and gave it a little shake. She smiled, took the bottle, then stood up, and as she turned, my dad smacked her ass, loud enough that it made the people near us turn their heads.

"That woman is pure wildcat," my dad said under his breath, after she'd walked away. "Best blow jobs I've ever had."

"Jesus, Dad," I said. "Don't tell me shit like that."

"What?" he said, blustering. "Your little boy ears can't take it?"

I stared at him, but didn't say a word. It was safer not to.

"I hear Amber went and got herself engaged," he continued, as though that brief, tense exchange hadn't happened.

"Yep."

He lowered his voice again. "You ever ride that ride? You two spent enough time together."

"Shut up!" I said. The words came out as a hiss. "Right now, Dad. Do you understand me?" I glanced around to make sure that no one had heard him, grateful that it didn't seem like anyone was looking our way. Layla stood by the food table, using a toothpick to nibble on tiny blocks of cheese, then set a few different appetizers on a plate.

"Whoa!" he said, holding up both hands, his palms facing me. "Don't get your panties in a twist. I was joking."

"It wasn't funny," I said, even as I tried to steady my breath. My face was hot and my chest was instantly as tight as it had been that morning, before my run. *Don't lose it, now,* I thought. *Don't ruin this night for Amber.*

"Whatever you say," my dad said, staring me down. Daring me to push the argument further.

"I'm going to see if I can help Tom with anything," I said, standing up, towering over my father.

"You do that," he said, and I walked away, feeling sick, wishing, as I had the first time I stepped foot in Amber's backyard, that I could find a way to disappear.

I didn't hear from Amber for three days after her party, nor did I reach out to her. I suspected that she'd be spending all the time she could with Daniel before he left for Seattle, and the truth was that I didn't think I could handle witnessing more of what I already had of the two of them together—his long arm around her shoulders, his talented, going-to-be-a-doctor fingers resting on the small of her back. Whenever I looked at them during the party, he was constantly reaching out, holding her close, leaning in to kiss her. His touch was like a branding tool on her skin, a reminder that he possessed what I'd always wanted.

I left before she opened her gifts, citing my having to be up early the next morning for work. It wasn't until Tuesday that I woke to find a text from her on my phone. "Want to get coffee?" she asked. "Our usual place?"

"Sure. See you at eleven?" I knew she meant Espresso Avellino, a small, artisan coffee shop downtown on Railroad Avenue, where we sometimes used to hang out after school or on the weekends when we didn't have anything better to do. Her invite now confirmed that Daniel had left, and we could finally spend some time together.

Amber was already standing at the counter, placing an order, when I arrived a few minutes before eleven. The bell on the door chimed as I entered, and she turned and saw me, smiled, then signaled the barista to make two drinks. "Hey, you," she said, giving me a quick hug when I approached.

"Hey." I pulled a ten-dollar bill from my wallet and slid it across the counter. "Keep the change," I told the barista, and then Amber and I took a few steps over to the corner and sat down. I leaned back against my chair, resting my fingertips on the edge of the small, square table between us. "How are you? How's being home?"

"Weird." She screwed up her face in a classic Amber expression, a mixture of distaste and uncertainty. "I can't get used to the idea that I don't have to go back to school. I keep waking up in a panic, thinking I need to call my lab partner or finish a term paper."

I laughed, and the barista delivered our drinks. Amber lifted hers and took a small sip, closing her eyes as she did. "Do you have to work tonight?"

I nodded. "Yeah. My schedule lately is Friday through Tuesday. More incidents and accidents on the weekends." I thought of the last call of my shift the previous night, which had been to a house where an older man had fallen down the stairs. When Mason and I arrived, the man was bleeding profusely from a gash in his head, as well as from a fracture in his forearm that had broken through the skin. As we treated him, his feeble wife stood too close, hands wringing anxiously. "Is he going to die?" she kept asking as I tended to the man's wounds. Her thin, high-pitched voice wobbled. "They'll put me in a home if he dies." The house was a mess, both of them smelled like urine and sweat; it was clear they hadn't emptied the garbage or showered in weeks. Neither of them seemed very coherent, so, after getting them to the hospital, I had to report their living situation to Adult Protective Services. It was a part of the job I hated. Almost as much as when, despite my best efforts, someone I treated died on the scene.

"So you took a Saturday off to come to my party?" Amber asked.

"I figured you'd kick my ass if I didn't show."

"You figured right." She grinned, then set her mug on the table. "I just got around to opening my gifts last night."

"Well, that's good. I was a little worried when I didn't hear from you." I paused. "Did you like it?"

"Are you kidding?" She reached beneath the collar of her jacket and pulled out a thin chain, pressing the small circle of pounded silver between her fingers. Upon it, I'd had the jeweler etch the words "Just Ask Me" in a pretty, scrolled font. "It's perfect. I love it." She gave me a shy smile. "Thanks, Ty."

"You're welcome," I said, and my chest burned with pleasure, knowing that I'd made her happy, that she and I were the only ones who understood what the engraving meant. "So, I take it Daniel's in Seattle?"

"Yeah." A shadow passed over her face as she looked down at the ring on her finger. "He left this morning."

"Miss him already, huh?"

"I guess." She didn't make eye contact as she spoke.

"Is something wrong? Did you guys have a fight or something?" I kept my tone as casual as possible, considering the flash of optimism I felt.

"No." She sighed. "I guess I'm just overwhelmed with everything. Graduating, getting engaged, now having to be apart from him, moving again in September . . ." Her voice trailed off, then she looked at me with bright eyes. "Never mind. I'm being an idiot."

"Being overwhelmed doesn't make you an idiot," I said. *Keep cool,* I thought. *Don't let her know how much you want her to realize this engagement was a mistake.* "It makes you normal. It's a lot to have going on."

"Yeah," she said. "It is. I love him, Tyler. You know that. But I just feel so . . . awkward, somehow. He's really the first guy I've been really serious with."

"That's true," I said.

"And the only time we ever even *talked* about marriage was

when he told me that he would rather do it before he actually became a doctor, so he'd know the person he was with wasn't pretending to love him for his money. I thought he was just being theoretical, you know? Like we were just having a general conversation, not planning *our* future. We haven't even been together a year."

"So it feels like he made the decision without you? Like it's more about want *he* wants instead of what you *both* want?" *Careful,* I thought. *Don't criticize him too much.*

"Exactly!" she said. "I knew you'd get it." She sighed again. "But he's so great. I don't know what else I'd want from a guy that he's not already giving me."

I bit my tongue to keep myself from blurting out anything that might prevent her from telling me more about what she was feeling. The more I let her talk about it, the more I'd know how to fan the flames beneath her doubt and turn her attention toward the possibility of having a relationship with me. It wouldn't be the first time a girl finally realized that the guy who has been there all along, her reliable best friend, is really the one she loves. It could happen to us.

"You remember that I went home with him over spring break and met his parents, right?"

"Yep." *Tell me it was horrible,* I thought. *Tell me his family is a bunch of assholes.*

"They were awesome. His mom made me a special fleece blanket because Daniel had mentioned to her that I tended to get cold easier than most people. I mean, Jesus. How would it have looked if I had said no when he proposed?"

It was everything I could do not to ask, *You thought about saying no?* but I didn't think I could contain the glee in my voice if I did. "What do your parents think?" I asked, instead.

"They think it's a little fast, but as long as we don't get married right away, they're good with it. They like him. And you know they got married when they were both twenty-two, so it's not like they can tell me these kinds of relationships never work out."

"That's true," I said, disappointed that Helen and Tom hadn't shown their usual overprotectiveness of Amber in this particular situation. Either they really *did* approve of Daniel and the engagement, or they expected the relationship to run its course and end on its own without their interference.

"Whatever," she said, rolling her eyes, as though she was annoyed with herself. "Enough about that!" She reached over and smacked my forearm. "Tell me about this neighbor girl of yours."

I waited a moment, contemplating what details to share. "Her name is Whitney," I finally said, deciding to keep it simple. "She's a business marketing student, very smart and very cute." If Amber was going to believe I had been dating someone, she might as well know that the girl was intelligent and attractive.

"Oh, really?" Amber said, widening her eyes. "And how old is Whitney?"

"Twenty-one," I said, fudging the truth by a year. I worried that, somehow, seeing a girl who couldn't legally drink yet, would make me seem perverted.

"Hmm. Is it serious?"

I shook my head. I wanted Amber to be a little jealous or, at the very least, relieved that I wasn't pining for her, but I didn't want her to think that I was unavailable. "We have fun," I said. "But we're not in love or anything."

"Well, good. Because she needs the best friend seal of approval before you can say that."

"Ha! Like you waited for my approval with Daniel?"

"I know," she said. Her tone was soft, and a little regretful. "I'm sorry it took so long for you to meet him. And I appreciate how supportive you've been after a sort of a . . . rocky start."

"He seems like a good guy."

"He is," Amber said, but I couldn't help but latch on to the tinge of ambivalence in her voice, thinking that, with the proper amount of convincing, my dream of a life with Amber might actually have a chance at coming true.

Amber

Initially, when Daniel decided to spend the summer in Seattle while I stayed in Bellingham with my parents in order to save up money, we'd agreed that we wouldn't go more than two weeks without seeing each other. But after he left and as June progressed, it became clear that the seminars he had enrolled in were more intense and demanding of his time than he'd thought they would be. He was also working full-time at a twenty-four-hour gym, so by the Fourth of July weekend, it had been almost an entire month filled only with daily texts, FaceTiming, and, when our schedules aligned, a longer call on Skype.

"Love you, baby," Daniel said at the end of every one of our conversations. "Can't wait until you're here with me."

"I love you, too," I always replied, because it was true. I did love Daniel. I missed him. But that didn't erase the fact that since talking with Tyler about my feelings over coffee the day Daniel left, I hadn't been able to shake the nagging sensation that getting engaged might not have been the smartest choice. I didn't know if I was really ready to make that kind of commitment. Before Daniel asked me to marry him, I'd been excited to move to Seattle, to embark together on the adventure of figuring out what we would do with our lives and who we'd eventually become as individuals. There was no pressure, just the limitless, open-road future stretched out in front of us. But now, the ring on my finger seemed to signify something so weighty, so final and constricting, the excitement I had felt shifted into something less thrilling and more uncertain. Something that filled me with doubt.

I did my best not to think about it, telling myself that everything would be fine once I made the move to Seattle and Daniel and I were together again. I kept busy, spending time with my parents and Tyler, focusing on my own job at a locally owned gym. I started work at six a.m., five days a week, and was there until two in the afternoon. It was a smaller establishment that prided itself on a family-friendly atmosphere and personalized fitness plans for the customers. They scheduled me to see at least five clients a day, and I was happy for the chance to show them what I could do.

The Friday morning before the holiday weekend, I began my day with a dark-haired, attractive, but pudgy bank manager, who informed me that he wanted to try to find his abs again after ten years of feeding them nothing but fast food and beer. The next hour, I met with a client who seemed more interested in watching the *Today* show while she walked on the treadmill than in listening to what I had to suggest about letting go of the handles and bumping up the incline on the machine so she might actually break a sweat.

"I want to have a body like yours," she had said when I first introduced myself and inquired about her fitness goals. She was in her late forties, and was round on top with long, thin legs.

"Well," I said, in a measured tone. My first job as a trainer was to get a client to set reasonable and realistic goals. "I tend to focus more on getting you healthy and strong rather than trying to help you reach a specific body type. We *can* get your body in the absolute best shape for *you*."

"Huh." She gave me a sour look. "I bet you're one of those women who can eat and eat and never gain weight."

I suppressed a sigh, suspecting that if I told her about my struggle with body image and how close I'd come to dying—if I said that learning to make sure I ate *enough* food every day was as much of a challenge as her learning to eat *less*—she wouldn't believe me. I knew from my time in the hospital and the years of struggle to find balance that followed, that unless this woman changed her mind-set, her body would stay exactly as it was.

Still, I encouraged her through a workout, and she told me she would be back for another session on Tuesday, so it was still possible for her attitude to shift in the right direction. I reminded myself that I didn't get better overnight—it had been a process, a relearning of everything my calorie-deprived brain told me was true. That even ten years later, I still had to fight the voice inside my head telling me I was too fat, that I shouldn't eat this or that or, on some days, anything at all. After she left, I took an hour to get in my own workout—being able to do so while I was still on the clock was a perk of the job. Now, at a little before ten, I stood behind the front desk, watching it for the receptionist while he took his morning break.

"Can I help you?" I asked an older woman who entered the doors of the gym, clad in a red velour tracksuit, looking a bit uncertain once she was inside.

The woman directed her bright blue eyes at me. "Yes, please," she said. "I'm Doris Carter, and I have an appointment with Amber Bryant?" Her voice wavered a bit as she spoke, and I guessed from the crinkled state of her pale skin and slightly hunched shoulders that she was somewhere in her seventies.

"I'm Amber," I said with a welcoming smile. "Is this your first time meeting with a personal trainer?"

She nodded. "My doctor said walking my dog isn't enough. I need to lift weights to help support my bones." She looked me over from head to toe. "How old are you, dear, if you don't mind me asking?"

"I'm twenty-three."

"And you know what you're doing?"

"I do," I said, continuing to smile. "I have a degree in nutrition and physiology, as well as a personal training certification. I'd be happy to show you my credentials."

"Oh no," she said, waving the suggestion away. "If Harold hired you, then I'm sure you're wonderful."

"How do you know Harold?" I asked as I grabbed the intake sheet I would need Doris to fill out before we started our session. Harold Richards was my boss, the owner of the gym, and a client of my father's, which was how I'd secured the job.

"I was his high school English teacher," Doris said. "He was a terrible nuisance in class, but it seems as though he's finally made something of himself here." She took the piece of paper I held out to her and looked it over. " 'Is there any possibility you might be pregnant?' " she read out loud, and then winked at me. "I doubt it, but I sure wish I had someone to practice with again."

I laughed, immediately knowing I would like working with her. "You're not married?"

"I was. For fifty-two wonderful years. My Steven passed away four years ago."

"I'm so sorry," I said, wondering if my marriage to Daniel would last that long. If it would last at all.

"Thank you," Doris said, as she continued to fill out the form in front of her. She glanced at my left hand. "You're engaged?" I nodded, and my conflicting emotions must have shown on my face because Doris made a clucking sound and gave a little shake of her head. "Uh-oh. If there's even a drop of doubt in your heart, honey, you should listen to it. That voice inside you is the wisest part of your soul."

I nodded, pressing my lips together so my eyes wouldn't tear up. So much for my job distracting me from the indecision I felt. "Maybe we should barter our services," I said. "I help you to build up your strength and you can teach me about life."

Doris smiled, a lovely motion that lit up her entire face, giving me a glimpse of the young woman she used to be. "Oh no, dear," she said. "The only thing I'm qualified to teach is English. Everything we learn about life comes from the living of it, good and bad choices alike. And each of us needs to make our own. That's just the way of it." She signed the bottom of the form with a flourish, then set down her pen, looking at me expectantly.

Just then, Trevor, the receptionist, returned from his break. "All set?" I asked Doris, and she nodded, then followed me into the gym. I talked with her about the importance of stretching her muscles before any kind of exertion, and then led her through a series of gentle warm-ups, including a fifteen-minute walk on the treadmill.

"How did you and your young man meet?" she asked me as I stood next to her, monitoring her heart rate via the machine to make sure she wasn't overdoing it. I told her the story, and then she spoke again. "Did you know he was going to propose?"

"No," I said, recalling the afternoon in early June that Daniel and I went rock climbing in the same spot as we had on our first date.

"Can you grab my water for me, babe?" he asked when we reached the top of our first ascent. It was a beautiful, sunshine-filled day and we both were sweating. "My calf is totally cramping." He set the heel of his right foot on a small rock and pointed his toes toward the sky, grabbing on to them with the tips of his fingers, stretching the muscle out.

"Sure," I said. I leaned over, unzipped the backpack he'd just set on the ground, and pulled out the silver metal bottle he always carried with him when he worked out. But when I turned to hand it to him, he had stopped stretching and was down on one knee, holding a black velvet jewelry box in his hand.

"Oh my god," I said, slapping a hand over my mouth. "What are you doing?" Of course, I knew what he was doing, but the words were the only ones my shock-addled mind allowed me to speak.

"What I've wanted to for a long time now," he said. He opened the box, revealing a small but glittering round solitaire set upon a slender silver band. "I love you, Amber. I want to be with you, always. Will you marry me?"

A hundred thoughts raced through my mind as I stared at him. I loved him so much in that moment—the sweet simplicity of his proposal, the fact that he had chosen to ask me privately, just the two of us, out in nature doing something we both loved, as opposed to in a fancy restaurant in front of a bunch of strangers. He knew me well enough to understand I would have despised something like that. But along with the love I felt came a sharp spike of confusion. We'd been together less than a year. Was that enough time to really know each other, down to our cores? Oddly enough, I thought about Tyler, that even with the few bumps in the road we'd experienced, how our friendship had lasted longer than I'd been with Daniel. Was I being fair to myself, committing myself to only one person when I was still so young? My parents had done it, but they had dated for three years before they got engaged. I knew the longevity of their relationship was a rarity—that more than half of marriages that began in a couple's early twenties ended in divorce. There was no way to know if Daniel and I would withstand the odds.

"What do you say, babe?" he asked when I didn't answer

right away. "There's no one on earth I'd want to build a life with but you."

The sincerity of his words melted away my hesitation. I threw my arms around his neck, and, in the process, almost toppled us both over onto the dirt. "Yes," I whispered. "Yes, yes, yes."

He kissed me, and then slipped the ring on my finger. "It was my abuela's," he said. "I promise I'll buy you something bigger and better when I'm a doctor."

I shook my head. "No way," I said. "It's perfect. You're perfect. I love you so much."

"He sounds wonderful," Doris said now, as I finished telling her the story. Her blue eyes stayed intent on me. "But you're still not sure."

"Is it possible to be totally sure of anything? Or anyone?" I asked, more of myself than of her.

Before she could answer, I heard my name called out from across the gym floor, and then turned to see Tyler striding toward us. "Hey," he said, as he approached. He was in uniform; he must have just gotten off an overnight shift. We'd been spending a lot of time together since Daniel left, grabbing dinner or a coffee a few nights a week, after I got off work at the gym and before he had to be at the station. We watched movies at his place or with my parents at mine, laughing and talking like we had back in high school, before he'd taken me to prom. Being around him again made me feel comfortable. It made me feel like I was one hundred percent, totally myself.

"Hey, you," I said. "Everything okay?"

"Oh yeah. Sorry to bug you when you're working, but I was nearby."

"No worries," I said. "Doris, this is Tyler. Tyler, this is Doris." I glanced at the time remaining on her treadmill; I'd programmed it for fifteen minutes, and she still had three to go. I reached over and pushed the down arrow to slow her pace in order to return her heart rate to normal.

"Nice to meet you, ma'am," Tyler said, giving Doris a charming smile. Not for the first time since I'd been home, I found myself thinking how attractive Tyler was, how much more at ease in his skin he seemed to have become. I wondered if the younger girl he'd been seeing, Whitney, had had something to do with this, and was surprised to feel a barb of jealousy.

"You must be the fiancé," Doris said. "Aren't you a handsome devil?"

A shadow briefly clouded Tyler's face, even as he kept smiling. "Just a friend," he said.

"My *best* friend, actually," I said. "We've known each other since we were kids. And please don't tell him he's handsome. It'll go straight to his already giant head." I grinned, and Tyler laughed, reaching over to give my ponytail a light tug, a motion that sent a surprising, pleasurable shiver across my skin.

"I see," Doris said, her eyes darting back and forth between us. She looked at me. "Is it okay if I stop now, honey? I need to use the restroom."

"Of course," I said, hitting the red button that stopped the treadmill belt. Doris's cheeks were pink as she turned to take a step off of the machine, and as she grabbed on to one of the handlebars for support, Tyler stepped closer and offered her his hand.

"Thank you, sir," she said as she let him assist her onto the floor. She patted her short, silver hair and straightened her stance. "I'll be right back."

"I'll be waiting," I said, as she walked toward the ladies' locker room.

"She's a sweetheart," Tyler said. "Have you been working with her long?"

"Just started today," I said, crossing my arms over my chest. "So, what's up?"

"Well, you know Mason has been all over me about meeting you, which really means Gia has been all over him."

"Ha," I said. "Yep." I hadn't been introduced to Tyler's partner and his wife yet, because their daughter, Sofia, had been struggling with an ear infection that wouldn't clear up, despite two rounds of antibiotics. Neither parent was getting much sleep, so socializing was pretty much their last priority. "Is the baby any better?"

Tyler nodded. "She is. Enough that they're going to get a sitter for her on Sunday night, for the Fourth. I guess one of their friends is having a party at his parents' place out in the county. I thought maybe, if you want to go, you could meet them there." He paused. "Unless Daniel is coming up and you'd spending the holiday with him."

"Nope," I said. "He has to work. So it's a date."

"A date, huh?" Tyler said, raising his eyebrows. His green eyes twinkled and we held each other's gaze for a moment longer than we normally would. I had a sudden giddy feeling in my gut. *What the heck is that about?* I wondered. *Am I flirting with him? Is he flirting with me?*

Doris reemerged from the locker room and made her way toward us. "I'll pick you up Sunday at six?" Tyler said, before she arrived.

So I did the only thing I could manage—I nodded, let him hug me, and then watched him walk away.

Tyler

"She called it a date, huh?" Mason asked as he pulled out of the station parking lot onto the street, flipping on the lights and siren of our rig. "Sounds like you might actually have a chance with the girl."

"Maybe," I said, trying not to get my hopes up too high. Spending time with Amber since she'd come home from school was everything I'd wanted it to be. Even though we worked opposite hours—my swing shifts to her early mornings into the afternoons—we still found a few evenings a week to go on runs together and then grab sushi for dinner, or just hang out at her parents' house or mine. We talked and laughed like we had when we were in high school, before the night my confession of being in love with her threw up a wall between us that had never quite gone away.

There was no sign of that wall yesterday, when I went to see her at the gym. She was bubbly toward me—flirtatious, even—and when her eyes locked on mine, I couldn't deny the arousal I felt, or the heated flush I saw rise in her cheeks. *Maybe being away from Daniel was exactly what she needed to figure out how she really feels,* I thought as I left her on the gym floor with her client. *Maybe spending so much time with me is showing her that marrying him would be a mistake—that she would be happiest if she chose me.*

Now, it was just past eight on Saturday night, and dispatch had called for all units at the station house to get to a multicar accident on I-5 near the Fairhaven exit. Several other firefighting and medic teams were already on the scene—my dad's likely included—but there were so many injured, they needed more. A tanker truck had jackknifed when the driver in front of it slammed on his brakes; the domino effect of crunching metal and broken windshields quickly took over all of the southbound lanes. Multiple car fires and possible fatalities had been reported—not a great way to begin a shift, even on the best of days. And today certainly didn't fall into that category. Despite how well things were going with Amber, I'd still woken up that morning with what felt like a giant stone settled on top of my sternum. My entire body was shaky; my hands trembled, and I had no idea why. There was no rhyme or reason to when anxiety would hit me—no inciting event or emotional precursor. It just showed up, dug in its claws, and threatened to take over.

Mason turned a tight corner, carefully edging his way around the inattentive drivers who didn't pull to the side of the road to get out of the ambulance's way, finally managing to get on the onramp heading south. The freeway was a parking lot; we'd have to drive along the shoulder. My partner flipped the siren on and off a few times to encourage the cars in front of us to pull to the side so we could change lanes and get where we needed to be. "Out of the way, dumbass!" he yelled. Every minute we weren't on the scene, another life could be lost.

The thick ache in my chest pulsed as I looked down the road and saw the enormous plume of black smoke rising up from where we were headed. "Damn," I said. "Looks bad." The words stuck in my throat and came out sounding strangled.

Mason gave me a quick, worried look out of the corner of his eye. "You okay?"

"Yeah," I said, drumming my fingers on the tops of my legs.

"You sure? You seem kinda jumpy."

"I'm sure. Ready to get to work," I said. *Calm down,* I told myself, curling my hands into fists, digging my nails into my palms. *Just do your fucking job.*

As we inched down the side of the road, we listened to the scanner for more information from dispatch, but none came through. "Unit forty-nine, approaching the scene on I-5 south," I said into the radio.

"Heard, unit forty-nine," the operator said. "Firefighters extracting multiple vics right now. Do not approach the vehicles. I repeat. Do not approach the vehicles. Fighters will bring vics to you."

"Copy that, dispatch," I said. "Unit forty-nine, out." I glanced at Mason, who had gotten us as close to where we needed to be as we were likely going to get, about a hundred feet from the tanker, which was now lying on its side. Behind that, I saw the source of the black smoke: at least five cars in flames, countless yellow-jacketed fighters spraying water and chemical fire retardant everywhere, in an effort to prevent gas tank explosions. I knew one of those fighters was my father, but it was impossible to tell which he might be. My heartbeat thudded in a wild rhythm with the added pressure of possibly running into him, having to perform my work under his scrutiny. *He'll be too busy doing his job to care about yours,* I thought. *Get over yourself. Get your head in the game.*

"Let's hit it," Mason said, jumping out of the driver's side door and running toward the back of the ambulance. After a deep breath, I followed him. We grabbed the gurney and our supply bags, weaving through the cars trapped by the blocked lanes. The thick gray clouds that filled the sky began to spit raindrops; I hoped it would pour and help extinguish the flames.

"Over here!" one of the firefighters yelled, spotting the two of us coming their way. He pointed and, as we approached, I saw a young man lying on the cement, half of his face burned away. His skin was red-blistered and scorched all the way down his right side, ending just below his knee.

Oh, Christ. My stomach lurched, and my mind immediately flashed on the memory of being in the burn unit with Curtis. The smell of roasting flesh. The way his nose and both ears had turned to ash. I'd been around other burn victims since then, but something about this one—paired with the anxiety-spiked adrenaline already raging through my blood—made me feel dizzy and weak.

"You got him?" the fighter yelled as Mason dropped to his knees next to the young man and began taking his vitals.

I gave the fighter a thumbs-up sign but didn't speak. *Damn it. Get your shit together, Hicks!* I swallowed and tried to steady my breathing.

The fighter ran back toward the smoldering cars, and I saw several other paramedic units on the other side of the disaster. They must have come from the south.

"Ty!" Mason yelled. "You need to get a line in, now!"

I realized I was still standing there, staring at the burning cars, leaving my partner to fend for himself. I dropped to the ground, kneeling on the other side of the young man Mason was treating. I heard my father's voice, echoing inside my head: *Man up, Son!* The victim's eyes were closed, but he was moaning, rolling his head back and forth. The rest of his body didn't move or respond to stimulation.

"We need to get him on a board," Mason said. "Could be a spinal."

On a three count, I rolled the man carefully onto one side so Mason could slip the yellow backboard beneath him. The man shrieked when we eased him down, startling me so badly, I almost dropped him.

"You sure you're okay?" Mason asked again, his dark brows furrowed.

Hands shaking, I bobbed my head once. "Sorry." I grabbed what I'd need for running an IV from my black bag while Mason checked the man's pupils. The victim screeched again, a howling, animalistic sound. Thunder cracked, the sky opened up, and the rain began to pour.

"He needs pain meds and fluids," Mason said. "Hurry up. We need to get him stable."

I nodded again, but the smell of the man's cooking flesh rose up and I was thirteen again, standing in Curtis's hospital room in my father's angry presence, feeling like a disgrace. The anxiety that had been coiling tightly within me, stockpiling inside my chest all day long, began to unwind, gaining speed until it spun out of control.

Before I knew it, I had dropped the tubing and the needle onto the wet cement. "I can't do it," I whispered, shaking my head. "I can't." My heart jackhammered and the contents of my stomach twisted. I felt certain I was going to vomit. Again, my father's voice: *Only newbies and pussies puke.*

"What the fuck?" Mason said. He grabbed the necessary tubing and needles from his own bag and came around to the man's undamaged side, pushing me out of the way.

I watched my partner work, my own skin feeling as though it was peeling away from my body, as the victim's had, all his nerves exposed. I felt too disoriented to stand, but I forced myself upward, groping and grabbing on to the back of my partner's shirt for support, which almost toppled both of us over.

"Get off me!" Mason said, pushing me away. "Jesus, Ty! What's wrong with you?"

I couldn't speak. I could only feel the terror pushing through my blood like a toxin, poisoning every cell.

Mason stood up, grabbed me by my biceps, and squeezed them, hard. "Tyler!" he shouted. "Look at me."

I blinked heavily, then lifted my gaze to my partner's. My body trembled and my chest heaved; I could barely catch my breath.

"I don't know what's going on," Mason said, giving me a quick, violent shake. "But it needs to stop. Right. Now." He let go of one of my arms and grasped my chin instead. "Do you hear me? I need you to help me get this man to the ER."

I shook my head, unsure if I could do what needed to be done. My partner's voice sounded distant, muffled and cloudy inside my head.

"Goddamn it, Hicks!" Mason smacked my cheek with his thick fingers. The sting of that impact was finally enough to jar me out of my foggy state, enough to get me to stumble over to the injured man's feet and lift him, with Mason's help, onto the gurney. Though I was still trembling, I met Mason's steely gaze with my own. *I can do this. Just try not to breathe in too deeply. Ignore the smell. Save this man's life.* My heart still pounded.

"All right then," Mason said, guiding the gurney back through the maze of cars to our rig. Once we got the gurney secured in the back of the ambulance, Mason radioed ahead to notify St. Joseph's that we were on our way with an accident victim. Then he held the keys out to me. "You drive. Okay?"

I looked at Mason, then allowed my eyes to dart back toward the injured man. *There's no way I can treat him,* I realized. *Not when I'm feeling like this. I'd probably make a fatal mistake. I could kill him.* I snatched the keys from Mason's hand and jogged around the vehicle to the driver's side, steeling myself against any thought but the need to deliver this man safely to the hospital.

I started the engine, glancing behind me to make sure Mason was inside and ready to go. "Punch it," my partner said as he wrapped a blood pressure cuff around the man's uninjured arm. Fortunately, the pain meds Mason had administered had kicked in, and the man was finally—mercifully—silent.

I put the vehicle in reverse, and the cars around the ambulance shifted out of the way so we could turn around and drive north in the southbound lanes. With the tanker truck still blocking the road, it was the only way off the freeway. I gripped the steering wheel as tightly as I could, taking in deep breaths through my nose and blowing them out through my mouth to try to steady my erratic pulse.

My right foot longed to press down hard on the gas pedal, to push the ambulance's speed up and up and up; to feel that sense of relief when the adrenaline in my bloodstream finally dropped, then leveled off. But with all the cars around us, there was no way to go faster than five miles per hour. There was no way for me to get relief.

"You doing okay up there?" Mason yelled over the sound of the siren.

"Yeah!" I managed to reply. I hunched over the steering wheel, maneuvering around the last few cars that were preventing us from reaching the exit. I drove the wrong way up the ramp, staying perilously close to the edge of the shoulder, honking the horn and swearing at the few drivers who still would not get out of my way. "Move, goddamn it!"

"We're almost there," Mason said, sensing that I needed some reassurance. "You got this, brother. Everything's cool."

Buoyed by my friend's support, I felt a surge of confidence. My jerky pulse slowed, and my breathing began to regulate. Less than five minutes later, I pulled into the ER ambulance bay, jumped out of the rig, and helped Mason deliver the burn victim to the doctors and nurses awaiting us there.

Walking back to our vehicle a few minutes later, Mason clapped a hand on my shoulder, then let it go. "You had me worried back there, man," he said with a frown. "What's going on?"

I shrugged, unsure how to articulate a proper response. What would my partner think of me if I told him the truth? That I was riddled with anxiety, and had some sort of PTSD flashback when I saw our burn victim?

"I'm fucked up," I finally said, thinking that was as honest as any other statement I could make.

"All right," Mason said as he climbed into the driver's seat of our vehicle and I settled into the passenger's. "So what're we going to do about that?"

I managed a small smile at my partner's use of the word "we." "I'll figure it out," I said.

Mason gave me a wary look. "I won't tell the captain that you lost it," he finally said. "As long as you promise to find a way to deal with whatever caused it." He paused. "You got me?"

I nodded.

"Seriously, bro. If I see even a hint of that kind of shit again, I'm reporting it."

"Right. Absolutely." While my partner had my back, I knew there was no way Mason would risk putting another victim we were treating in even further danger.

"I'll get a handle on it," I said, having every intention of doing just that. I'd go for more runs—I'd make them longer and more intense, every night before work, draining my body of the same excess adrenaline that, for whatever reason, had sent me over the edge today. If I was going to have the kind of life I wanted, I needed to wipe out the weakest parts of me. I needed to become the kind of man a woman like Amber deserved.

I woke up the next morning to the sound of pounding on my front door. My eyes creaked open, my lashes sticking together as I peered at the clock on the nightstand. It was just past noon, and I'd only been asleep for five hours. My shift—the rest of which to my relief was much less eventful than the rollover accident—had ended at three a.m. And while I'd been exhausted when I got home, I still had a hard time winding down, the residual stress hormones in my body serving up the worst kind of emotional hangover there is—my head pounded and my limbs trembled, my heart thumped a disturbing, discordant rhythm inside my chest. When I finally did drift off, it was into a restless slumber, filled with vivid images of bodies on fire—of flesh melting away from bone.

The person outside my apartment pounded again. "Coming!" I shouted as I pulled on a pair of shorts and a T-shirt, and then stumbled into the living room. I yanked open the door, surprised to see my father standing in front of me, his right arm raised, hand in a fist. "Dad," I said, keeping my hand on the doorknob, blinking fast in order to bring my eyes into better focus.

"We need to talk," he said, barreling past me, not waiting for an invitation.

"Come on in," I said, unable to keep the sarcasm from my voice as I shut the door behind him. The last time he had been to my apartment was when I first moved in, two years before, and I needed to borrow his truck, before I had bought my own. I hadn't seen him since the brief, tense conversation we'd had at Amber's graduation party three weeks ago. Now, I watched as he dropped onto my couch and crossed his arms over his broad chest.

"You got any coffee?" he barked. "None of that prissy latte-mochaccino shit, either. The real thing."

"Yeah," I said. "Hold on." I headed into my small kitchen, grabbed a mug from the cupboard, and popped a French roast pod into my Keurig machine, gripping the edge of the counter while I waited for it to brew, wondering what the hell was so important that my dad needed to come over and wake me up on a Sunday morning. Despite my best intentions to remain calm, my heartbeat sped up, and I felt my face get hot. Once the first mug of coffee was done, I made another for myself and carried them both back into my living room, handing one to my father. He took a short sip and then set the mug on the small table in front of him. "I heard you worked the tanker accident last night."

"I did." I sat in the chair opposite him, and my first swallow of coffee burned the roof of my mouth, all the way down my throat to my belly. I coughed, sputtering a bit when I continued. "I think most units in the area were called, weren't they? I figured you were helping put out the car fires."

"You figured right." He stared at me intently. "What you didn't figure is that one of my boys delivered that burn victim to you and your partner. Or that he watched you stumble all over the goddamn place instead of doing your fucking job."

I froze, my mug in midair, and forced myself to hold his gaze. "It wasn't that bad," I said, instantly set on the defensive, thinking this was the absolute last thing I needed right now—my father tearing me down. *You're not thirteen anymore,* I told myself. *You don't have to put up with his shit.*

He narrowed his eyes. "Not that bad, huh? You got the line in right away? You didn't sit there doing nothing, leaving the victim to lay there writhing in pain? How do you think I felt, being told my son looked like a pussy?"

I dropped the mug I held to the table, not caring when the hot liquid sloshed over the side. "What the hell does it have to do with you?" I demanded.

"It has to do with me because what you do, however you fuck up, reflects right back on me."

"Oh, I see," I said, curling my hands into fists, trying to control the rising tide of my anger. I couldn't believe he had the audacity to criticize me like this. Or maybe I could. It was what he'd always done. The stormy rage I'd felt toward him for years rose up and I wanted to call him out on every bullshit thing he had ever done or said. I wanted to make him pay. "It's always about you! About you and what *you* want! Never me or Mom. No wonder she divorced you!"

"I don't know what you've been smoking, Son, but that's not what went down. *I'm* the one who divorced *her*. And now she can't stand the fact that I don't have to put up with her crap to get laid." He gave me a look so full of pride, it took everything in me to not punch his smug face.

"You're disgusting," I said in a low voice. "You think it's something I aspire to, sleeping with the skanky women you date? You think that makes me jealous?"

"I think you'd do just about anything to get into your sweet little Amber's panties."

I glared at him, my jaws clenched. "Don't talk about her like that."

He leaned forward, resting his elbows on his knees, fingers laced together, and smirked. "I see the way you look at her. The way you've always looked at her. You'd give your left nut to get a piece of that ass." He shook his head. "It's never going to happen. Not with a girl like her. You're too fucking scared to step up and be anything but a whiny little lapdog, following behind her. Yap, yap, yap."

"Shut up," I said with as much venom as I could muster. I stood, knocking into the table with my shins. My entire body quaked as I pointed to the door. "Get out."

He didn't move. Instead, he calmly reached for his coffee and took another sip, then looked up at me after he set the mug back down. "What do you think your captain will do when he hears how you fucked up? That partner of yours might keep his mouth shut, but he's not the only one who saw what happened." He paused, and then stood up, too, his gaze locked on mine. "My guess is you'd be ordered to talk to the department shrink. Maybe get put on leave. Even lose your job, if they find out you don't have the balls to do it."

"You need to go," I growled. Hatred coursed through me. I couldn't believe that this man, the one person I should be able to look up to and go to for support, was threatening to destroy my career for the sake of his own ego. Because he thought *my* failure might make *him* look bad.

He took the few steps to the door and put his meaty hand on the knob, pausing before turning it. "You know what, Son?" he said, looking over his shoulder. "I'm glad you didn't decide to become a firefighter. Because no matter how hard I tried to toughen you up, you never had it in you. You just don't have what it takes."

Before I could respond, he slammed the door behind him. I didn't move, his words banging their way through my entire body. I listened to the ragged edges of my own breath and the rumble of his truck's engine as he drove away. Would he go straight to my captain and tell him how I'd screwed up, or was he just playing a power game with me, putting on a show? My work was everything to me—I loved helping people in need, being there for them in the midst of the worst moments in their lives. I loved having an experienced partner like Mason to show me the ropes. I'd worked hard to get where I was, and I worried that just when things with

Amber seemed to be going well, a suspension—or even the loss of my job—might send her right back into Daniel's arms.

I worried about these things, but mostly, as I stood in the silence, my heartbeat throbbing like an open wound inside my chest, I worried that my father might know me better than I knew myself. That all the horrible things he'd said about me, the painful jabs he'd thrown, might just end up being true.

Amber

"Come on, Pops!" I said, jogging in place at the end of our block, looking back at him about twenty feet behind me. "You can do it!" It was a little after three o'clock on the Fourth of July, which had turned out to be a warm, sunny Sunday after a stormy night of hard-driving rain. I had convinced my dad to take a walk with me, and now was encouraging him to jog part of the way home, which would help shift his metabolism into fat-burning mode and keep it there for the rest of the day.

"I'm glad one of us thinks so!" he gasped as he pumped his arms a little harder in order to catch up. His round face was red, his black hair damp, and his forehead beaded with sweat. But while his breathing was labored, he could still talk without too much effort, so I knew his body wasn't being pushed past an unreasonable limit.

"There you go!" I said, when he came up next to me. "You did it! And now we walk to cool down." I patted him on the back and smiled. "I'm proud of you."

He leaned forward and set his hands on his knees, arms bent and elbows out, breathing hard. "Isn't that supposed to be my job . . . being proud of you?"

"I'm an adult now," I said in my normal voice. At this level of exertion, I hadn't even broken a sweat. "It's a two-way street."

"An adult? No way. You're still my baby girl," he said, straightening back up. He wiped the moisture from his brow with his forearm. "And a taskmaster, it seems."

"I'll take that as a compliment," I said, as we began to amble down the sidewalk.

"You should."

I grinned. "I love what I do. I can't wait to take it to the next level."

"That's what that certification will do, right? After you take the test?" my dad asked. "Give you bigger and better job opportunities?"

"I hope so," I said. "That, and moving to Seattle should really help. I can spend a few years building a strong clientele working at a gym, and then use that experience to eventually apply for a job at the Seahawks training facility. I figure if I start at the bottom, maybe as an assistant to a coach or trainer, they'll have to at least *consider* me if a senior position working directly with the players becomes available. It might not happen right away, but it *will* happen."

"That's my girl," he said, smiling wide. "No goal too high."

"Thanks, Pops." I smiled in return, even as the muscles in my throat tingled with the threat of impending tears, knowing how hard I'd worked to get where I was, and how close I'd come to losing it all back when I'd been sick. It had been a bit of a struggle to stay on my regular food plan since I'd been home, but it helped that, after some subtle prompts, my dad had agreed to try to start eating healthier, too, so I'd managed to reach a compromise with my mom: I would eat whatever she made for dinner each night that I wasn't out with Tyler, and she and my dad would eat the low-fat, protein-packed breakfasts and lunches I prepared for us all. It was working well so far, and my dad had already lost six pounds.

"Hey, Mom," I said, once we were back inside the house. She stood at the kitchen counter, using a cookie cutter on a rolled-out round of pastry. The air smelled of apples and cinnamon stewing on the stove, and I assumed she would be covering the top of the pie with the stars made out of dough, just like the image she'd shown me on her Pinterest account the night before.

"Hello, my loves," she said, looking up from her work. "How was your walk?"

"Brutal," my dad said as he dropped into a chair at the table. He winked me. "Our girl's a gladiator. You should have come with."

"Maybe next time," my mom said. "I had to get this done for tonight." She looked at me. "You're sure you and Tyler don't want to join us at the Millers'? Liz is coming, too."

The Fourth of July was the one summer holiday that my parents didn't throw a party at our house. Instead, we always spent it with their friends Sara and Jeremy Miller, who lived in a big place out on Eldridge Drive. Their back deck overlooked Bellingham Bay, lending an amazing view of the city's fireworks show.

I shook my head as I opened the fridge and grabbed two bottles of water. "Tyler's partner and his wife are going to be at this party we're going to," I said. "We've been trying to get together with them for weeks."

My mother drew her brows together over the bridge of her nose. "Okay," she said, which I suspected was a two-syllable code for "You're ruining a family tradition."

"Daniel's not driving up?" my dad asked as I handed him one of the bottles.

"Nope. He volunteered to work," I said. "The gym pays him double time on the holiday."

"I'm surprised Tyler's free tonight," my mom said. "Don't they usually need more paramedics and firemen on the Fourth?"

"He and Mason lucked out and didn't get scheduled." My phone, which I'd left on the counter, buzzed, vibrating against the granite. I picked it up and saw a text from Daniel. "Hey baby," it said. "Time for a quick call?"

"Yes!" I responded, and then turned to my parents, bottle of water and phone still in hand. "I'm going to take a shower," I said, leaving them alone as I headed down the hall and upstairs to my room.

Once the door was closed and I was lying on my bed, I quickly pressed the call button next to Daniel's picture on the screen, and a single ring later, his voice was in my ear. "Hi, gorgeous," he said. "How are you?"

"I'm good," I said. I told him about the walk-slash-jog with my dad, and my mom's giving me an unspoken hard time about not going with them to the Millers' party.

"What are you doing instead?" he asked.

I stared up at the small spiderweb crack in one corner of my ceiling. When I was little, I used to pretend that Charlotte, from *Charlotte's Web,* lived there. "Tyler invited me to a party with some of his friends. It should be fun."

Daniel was silent, so I waited a moment, and then went on. "Everything okay, babe?" I asked, wondering if, in our being separated from each other, Daniel was having any of the same doubts regarding our engagement that seemed to be haunting me. *What if he ended it?* I thought. *How upset would I really be?*

"You seem to be spending an awful lot of time with him," he finally said, in a quiet, controlled voice.

I felt a pang of guilt in my chest, despite having done nothing with Tyler that could have caused it. Nothing tangible, at least. Appreciating how handsome he had become wasn't cheating. I thought about something I'd once overheard my mom tell Liz when she was still married to Tyler's dad and found herself attracted to a single doctor at the hospital: "You can look at the menu all you want, as long as you eat at home."

"Well, yeah," I said to Daniel now. "He's my best friend. You know that."

"I guess," Daniel said, and then cleared his throat. "But if it was me spending all my time with some other girl, someone I was really close to, how would it make you feel?"

"I'm not spending *all* my time with him," I snapped, immediately set on the defensive. "I'm at home with my parents a lot. And working full-time, too."

"You didn't answer the question," Daniel said, his voice beginning to rise. "I think it's reasonable to be a little worried about this dude."

"No, it's not," I said. "We've known each other forever, and he's really my only friend here. With all the shit I went through in high school, he was the only one who stuck by me. I'm not going to stop hanging out with him just because you're feeling insecure." As soon as the words left my mouth, I regretted them.

"Really," Daniel said. The word was a statement, not a question.

"I didn't mean it like that." I sighed. "Look, I'm sorry. But I need you to trust me. Especially if we're going to get married."

"If?"

Shit. "You know what I meant," I said, wincing at his tone. This conversation was not going well at all.

"Okay, sure," he said.

When he didn't say more, I spoke again. "So, we're good?"

"Sure," he repeated, but I didn't believe him.

"I love you," I said, trying to lighten the moment. "I miss you so much."

"Have a good night," he said. And then, without warning, he hung up the phone. For the first time since we'd been apart, he didn't say that he loved me, too.

When Tyler turned onto the gravel driveway near the intersection of Hannegan and Kelly Roads, he looked at me and smiled. "You look great," he said. "Did I already tell you that you look great?"

"You did," I said, glancing down at the outfit I'd decided to wear, a V-necked, spaghetti-strapped, red sundress. It had a white and blue bandanna print around the hem, which hit me midthigh, and was sexier than what I normally wore, its style too revealing to allow me to wear a bra, but it flattered my figure and made me feel confident and strong, so I threw on a pair of wedge-heeled, white sandals to complete the patriotic-slash-sexy look.

"Well, it's true. Your hair looks pretty like that," Tyler said as he directed his truck toward the large gray house at the end of the drive.

"Thanks," I said, feeling my cheeks flush as I reached up to smooth the beachy waves I'd managed to achieve with a curling iron. The style was a definite departure from the typical ponytail or messy high bun I tended toward most days. As I was getting ready, I had decided the best way to forget about the tense conversation with Daniel was to go to this party with Tyler and have an amazing time. I was going to look good, have a few drinks, dance my ass off. Being so focused on health and fitness throughout college, I'd never had much of a social life, but tonight, I needed to blow off some steam. I looked over at Tyler, knowing I could trust him to take care of me, even if he'd seemed a little tense when he first picked me up. He was distracted, somehow, his fingers drumming against his legs and a weird sort of stiffness stretched across his face.

"You okay?" I'd asked him at my parents' house, as he opened the passenger side door of his truck.

"Yeah," he said, not looking directly at me.

"I don't believe you." I poked him in the ribs, and he jumped, giving me a startled look, which almost immediately transformed into a smile.

"Can't hide anything from you, can I?" he said.

"Nope," I said. "Spill."

He sighed. "My dad showed up at my apartment a few hours ago. We had a fight."

"What about?" Tyler's father had more of an emotional hold over him than my best friend would like to admit. He talked a good game about not caring what his dad said or thought, but his behavior whenever Jason did something to hurt Tyler told an entirely different story. There were injuries between them that if prodded, still bled—their relationship was basically a minefield composed of deeply buried, potentially explosive pain.

"Just his usual bullshit." Tyler held out his hand and helped me climb into the truck.

"Daniel and I sort of had a fight, too," I said, as I plopped into the passenger seat. "He thinks I've been spending too much time with you."

Tyler had been about to close my door, but then hesitated. "Do *you* think you've been spending too much time with me?"

"No," I said. "I do not."

I'd left the explanation at that, and now, as Tyler found a place to park amid the row of other vehicles on the grass, his body was more relaxed and his energy seemed to have shifted into a better place. "Ready?" he asked, and I nodded. He jumped out of the truck and came around to get the door for me, offering his arm in support as I climbed down and stood next to him. The air smelled of roasting meat and gunpowder—fireworks were illegal within Bellingham city limits, but out in the county, with so much more open space, the police were less likely to bother trying to regulate their use, a fact that the party's host seemed to be taking clear advantage of.

Tyler locked the truck and we walked toward the house together, through the front door and then directly into the backyard, where it seemed everyone else was already gathered. Loud music blasted through outside speakers, and several small groups of men and women sat around the patio, talking and laughing, drinks in hand.

"There they are," Tyler said, nodding his head toward a dark-haired, muscular man and a petite woman in the corner of the patio. Tyler took my hand and led me to join them. Both stood up from their seats when they saw us coming. Gia's long black hair was pulled up into a slicked-back ponytail, exposing her narrow neck and the large silver hoops in her ears. She was a full foot shorter than her husband, but her stance was the shoulders-back, steel-rod-spine variety, giving off the impression that you wouldn't want to mess with her.

"Ty, my man!" Mason said, reaching over to give Tyler a shoulders-only hug. "You're late!"

"Sorry," Tyler said when he pulled back. "My fault."

"You feeling better?" Mason asked.

"I'm good," Tyler said, but the muscles along his jawline tightened, making me wonder if something else was going on with him, other than the argument with his dad.

"Were you sick?" I asked, looking back and forth between the two men.

"No," Tyler said. "Just kind of a rough night at work. The tanker accident." He stared at Mason with unblinking eyes, and his partner gave an almost imperceptible nod.

"Oh!" I said. "I read about that on Facebook this morning. You guys were there?"

"Yeah," Mason said, grimly. "It was pretty awful."

"Okay, that's enough!" Gia said, stepping in front of her husband. "No more shoptalk tonight!" She looked at Tyler, pointing a perfectly manicured red fingernail in his direction. "And you. Are you going to introduce us to your lady friend or not?"

"I'm Amber," I said, smiling as I leaned forward and gave Gia a quick hug. "It's so great to finally meet you both. I've heard a lot about you."

"It's great to meet you, too," she said, giving me a quick kiss on the cheek, and then pulled back.

"Hey, Amber," Mason said, giving me a hug as well.

"According to Mason, Tyler hasn't shut up about you," Gia said. "I figured I'd better let him know if you're a keeper."

I widened my eyes, feeling a little dismayed by Gia's bold pronouncement, wondering what kind of relationship, exactly, Tyler had told them he and I had.

Tyler stepped in to rescue me. "She's joking," he said, giving Gia a stern look. "Right, Gia?"

"Of course, *mijo,*" she said. She turned to her husband. "Baby, why don't you get us something to drink?"

"Anyone up for shots?" I suggested, and Mason did a double take as he looked at me, raising a single eyebrow.

"I like you already," he said with a grin. "Tequila?"

"Why not?" I said, glancing at Tyler, who nodded.

"All right, then," Mason said, then headed over to the table that was covered in various bottles of booze and mixers. He looked around to see if anyone was watching, then returned with a full bottle of Patrón in hand. "We're among friends, right?" he asked, before popping out the cork and putting the bottle to his lips, taking only a tiny sip of the clear liquid inside. "That's it for me," he said, handing the bottle to his wife. "Go for it, babe. I'm driving."

"Here's to a night of freedom!" she said, lifting the bottle into the air before taking a bigger swig than her husband had. "And pumping and dumping!"

"Um, what?" Tyler said, screwing up his face.

Gia laughed, pointing at her chest with the bottle. "I'm breast-feeding," she said. "I can drink, but I'll have to pump and dump the milk so I don't pass my debauchery on to the baby." She handed the Patrón to me, and after I took a long shot, feeling the warm burn of alcohol slide down my esophagus into my belly, so did Tyler.

"Happy birthday, 'Murica!" Gia yelled when Tyler handed her the bottle again, causing several people to turn and to gawk at us. "What're you lookin' at?" she said. "Don't you love your country? Aren't you *patriots*?"

I laughed, as did the crowd around us, and then startled when a loud firework shot off, sending out a proliferation of brilliant white sparkles against the rapidly darkening sky. I took another pull from the bottle, a bigger one this time, shaking my head as the alcohol pulsed its way through my blood, making my joints feel liquid and loose. No wonder people liked to drink—all of the tension I'd felt after my phone call with Daniel had vanished, like it had never been there at all.

"I need the bathroom," Gia said, then looked at me. "You?"

"Sure," I said. Even though I didn't have to go, I suspected she just wanted to get me alone so we could talk without the guys there. Gia grabbed me by the hand and led me toward the house, leaving Tyler and Mason on the patio. We stumbled our way through the kitchen and down the hall to a small powder room, where she pulled me in with her, closing the door behind us.

I leaned against the wall, averting my eyes while Gia lifted her black skirt and dropped onto the toilet. I was a lightweight—the two shots I'd taken were already making me dizzy. I also hadn't eaten since lunch, and since I knew booze was high in calories, I decided then and there to not eat anything at the party.

After Gia finished and stood up at the sink to wash her hands, I looked over her petite physique and spoke again, my tongue already feeling thick inside my mouth. "You'd never guess you just had a baby. You look amazing."

Gia laughed as she dried her hands on a green towel. "Thanks. Breast feeding definitely helps, but even after eight months, my stomach still looks like a pile of cottage cheese when I'm naked. It's totally worth it, though. She's the best thing I've ever done." She paused, turning around to rest her butt against the counter. "Do you want kids?"

"Maybe someday," I said, thinking about the conversation Daniel and I had had after our trip to see his parents and extended family over spring break. On the flight home, we'd talked about children, and he'd confessed that he wanted to have at least three, something I wasn't sure I wanted, too. I hadn't spent much time around babies, and when I had, I'd felt more awkward than maternal. I had a hard enough time keeping a handle on my own issues; I didn't think I was properly equipped to guide them through theirs, too. "I'll have them as long as you're the one to stay home," I'd said, only partially joking. Daniel had surprised me by nodding. "You got it," he'd said, and while I wasn't sure if he had really meant it, the conversation had ended and we hadn't discussed the subject since.

"You know our boy Tyler's in love with you," Gia said and, once again, I was taken aback by her blunt approach.

"Well, he was . . ." I sputtered, dropping my gaze to the ring on my left finger, spinning it around and around again using my thumb. I still hadn't gotten used to wearing it. "But that was back in high school. We're just good friends now." Even as I spoke, I thought about the shiver that had crossed my skin at the gym the other day, when Tyler had gently yanked my ponytail. I thought about the pull of attraction I'd felt over the last couple of weeks whenever we spent time together, which only seemed to fuel the hesitance I felt about my sudden engagement to Daniel. *If I really loved him, if he really was the person I should marry, would I be having these feelings about Tyler?*

"Uh-huh," Gia said, nodding, but not looking like she believed me. "You two need to get your stories straight."

"I don't know about Tyler," I said, waving a hand in the general direction of the backyard, "but what *I* need is another drink. *Many* 'nother drinks!" I gave her what felt like a sloppy grin, and she laughed.

"Let's do it!" she said, and we headed back outside, where the night sky had darkened even more, and the speakers were blasting "Sweet Home Alabama." Everyone had clumped together on the large patio, where they were dancing, arms in the air, bodies moving to the music, many sipping from red Solo cups. I searched the crowd for Tyler's familiar blond head, and then felt him sidle up next to me.

"Hey," he said, leaning down in order to whisper in my ear. I felt his lips against my skin, smelled his sweet cologne and the booze on his breath, and I wondered how much more he had had to drink while I was inside. And maybe it was my own growing intoxication, or the party atmosphere itself, but as I turned to face him, I slowly turned my head so that my lips trailed against his cheek in what could be interpreted as a light and teasing, drawn-out kiss, taking pleasure from the fact that my touch made him quiver.

"Hey, yourself," I said, taking the bottle he held from him and knocking back another long pull of tequila, swallowing twice, then a third time, keeping my eyes on his the whole time. "Wanna dance?" I asked in a raspy voice, the muscles in my throat both fiery and numb from the rapid influx of alcohol.

He nodded, his lips pressed together, his normally light green eyes dark with desire. It was so different from how Daniel looked at me, which was always so adoring, so sweet and kind and accepting. But Tyler's eyes hooked into my soul. He saw right through me. He knew every detail of my life, the good along with the bad. I could always talk with him because I didn't have to explain myself, to waste time trying to make sense of why I was the way I was. He already knew my story. He already knew *me*.

I tucked the bottle up against my chest and led Tyler into the middle of the throng of people moving to the music. The song changed to Def Leppard's "Pour Some Sugar on Me," and Tyler snatched the bottle from me and took another drink, then held it back to me, challenging me to do the same.

"You're on," I said, putting the bottle to my mouth one last time, swallowing as much of the sharp liquid as I could without gagging. As we danced, my body began to feel like molten steel, viscous and hot, and my mind went blank. I was only the music, the beats of the bass line, the movements of my limbs. Someone took the bottle from my hand, but I barely noticed. Tyler pressed himself up close against me, his hips grinding against mine. I could feel his arousal, and my own rose to meet it. We locked gazes, his long leg tucked between mine, his pelvis circling, and his hand on my lower back. It was intimate enough to feel as though we were the only two people at the party. My edges seemed to melt away, and a thousand words were spoken in the looks we gave each other.

The song stopped, and in the brief moment before another started, I stood on my tiptoes and pressed my lips against his, opening my mouth to use my tongue. He answered by running his hands up and down my back, pressing his hips even harder against me. I didn't care that we were surrounded by so many other people. I didn't care that there was a ring on my finger or that I was cheating on my fiancé. All I knew was to try to hold onto this sensation of falling, to feel instead of think, to let the warm, loose sensation in my body take me over.

When we finally stopped kissing, we were breathing hard, but neither of us said a word. Tyler grabbed my hand and pulled me through the small crowd back into the house. "Where are we going?" I asked.

"Somewhere private," he said. The two words slurred together in a muddy mix, and he spoke again, more deliberately. "I want to be alone with you." He led me down the hallway, past the bathroom where Gia and I had talked, then found the stairs. We stumbled our way up to the top of them, holding on to each other for support, stopping every few steps to kiss again. Tyler opened the first door we came across, and then surprised me by scooping me up in his arms, the same way his father had done to him, holding him over the pool the day we met.

I giggled, wrapping my arms around his neck, kissing him as he kicked the door shut behind us, then carried me over to the bed, dropping me onto it. My head swam and I had to shut my eyes to keep the room from spinning. Tyler lay down next to me and began to run his large hands over my body, pushing up the hem of my skirt, using his fingers to drift along the skin of my inner thigh. The heat between my legs twitched in response.

"You're so beautiful," he said, nuzzling my neck. "It's always been you, Amber. No one else but you."

I kept my eyes closed, feeling his body pressed against mine, the stiffness of his erection straining inside his jeans. And then, out of nowhere, as suddenly as on the night we'd gone to prom, a bolt of revulsion pulsed through me. This was Tyler, my best friend. And I was engaged. This was wrong. So, so wrong. I couldn't do this to Daniel. I couldn't cheat on him. I needed it to stop.

"Don't," I said, finally opening my eyes. He answered by rolling over on top of me. "Tyler, wait!" I felt a spark of panic ignite inside my chest. I put my hands on his shoulders and tried to push him off of me, but my arms were weakened by how much I'd had to drink. He kissed me again, forcefully this time, slipping his tongue inside my mouth and rolling it around like a fat slug, the weight of him crushing me, making me feel like I couldn't breathe.

"I've wanted you for so long," he said, his own words coming out in a drunk jumble.

"Stop, Tyler! Please!" I struggled against him, but couldn't get him off of me. With one hand, he reached down and unbuttoned his jeans.

"I don't want to do this!" I said, turning my head to one side as tears began to roll down my cheeks. I wanted to scream, but my mind and voice couldn't seem to make the proper connection. My stomach churned, and alcohol-soaked acid rose up and burned the back of my throat. I gagged as I swallowed it back down.

Intent on pulling his jeans off, Tyler didn't seem to hear me. The heft of his well-muscled frame was enough to keep me held down while he pushed my skirt higher and yanked my panties down to my knees. "I love you so much," he murmured, running his hands roughly up the curves of my hips to my waist, and then to my breasts, where with one hand he gripped me and tried to hold me still. "You feel so good."

I froze then, biting my bottom lip as I realized that fighting was useless. I couldn't move; my head felt like it was stuffed full of cotton. He outweighed me by more than a hundred pounds. His eyes were closed, and as he shifted his body against mine, I could feel the wiry hairs on his legs rubbing like sharp steel wool against my skin. He tilted and shifted his pelvis, trying to slip inside me without the aid of his hands. When he finally managed it, it was one fast, violent jab, with what felt like a hot, hard sword shoved into the core of me, slicing and scorching my tender flesh. He plunged into me again and again while I wept, my fingernails pressed deeply enough into my palms that they began to bleed. I tried to concentrate on that pain instead of the one between my legs. I tried to pretend it wasn't happening at all. I lay motionless, my eyes squeezed shut, waiting for it to be over. For him to be done. He grunted and moaned as he stabbed himself inside me, not sounding like himself. This was some other man, some animal, not the boy I'd known and loved. He was a stranger violating my body, a monster taking what he wanted and not caring about the carnage left in his wake.

This was me, having led him on to the point where he thought that it was okay to keep going, even after I told him to stop.

This was me, opening my eyes and staring at the ceiling, my soul floating up above my body, trying to deny that I was being raped by my best friend.

Tyler

I know where Amber is taking me as soon as she instructs me to take the Highway 2 exit off of I-5 south in Everett. The highway runs through the smaller towns of Monroe, Sultan, and Gold Bar, past the famous Zeke's Drive-in, where back when we were in high school, our families would sometimes stop for burgers and thick, homemade ice cream shakes on the way to the Bryants' cabin. Before her stay in the hospital, when she was still restricting what she ate, Amber refused to touch the meal her parents would order for her, but after her release, she would at least pick apart the burger she'd ordered, removing the bun, eating the lettuce and tomato, along with most of the cheese-covered, charbroiled meat itself. The first time she reached over, grabbed my chocolate and peanut butter shake from me, and took a long pull on the straw, I remember thinking that therapy was finally working for her. That she might actually end up staying well.

Looking at her gaunt body now, in the cab of my truck as we drive along the highway in the dark, I know whatever progress she had made with her health over the last nine years had been erased by what happened on the Fourth of July. I had made her sick again. There was no one else to blame.

"So . . . we're going to the cabin," I say, as I reduce my speed to thirty, per the sign on the side of the road, even though I'm tempted to slam my foot down on the gas pedal and maybe draw the attention of a cop and get pulled over. But I don't, because I'm afraid of what Amber might do. Her small hands still cradle the gun, its muzzle aimed at me.

"You guessed it," she says, still staring straight ahead, out the windshield. "Congratulations. Your prize is to keep driving and shut the fuck up."

"Amber . . ." I say, desperately searching for the right words to get through to her. To make her stop whatever crazy plan she might have concocted.

"Do me a favor," she says. "Stop saying my name. Every time you do, I want to vomit. I want to shove this gun down your throat and pull the trigger." Her chest heaves. "Which might just give you some tiny idea of how it felt. What you did to me."

"I thought you wanted it, too," I said, quietly, and she laughed.

"I wanted it, huh?" she says, scornfully. "Did you think that when I told you to wait? To fucking *stop*? When I said I didn't want to do it?"

I'm quiet for a moment, soaking in her questions, trying to remember everything she said to me that night and when she said it. But what I remember most is the way her lips brushed against my cheek when I came up next to her on the patio. The way we were dancing, the way she kissed me and then took my hand and led me into the house, up into a bedroom, saying she wanted to be alone with me. I remember her pushing me onto the bed. I remember feeling the heat between her legs, the sweet taste of her mouth. I remember the wanting, the way her body moved against mine, everything between us feeling so good and powerful and *right*. I remember thinking about my father's words earlier that afternoon in my apartment, thinking that once Amber and I were together, he would finally know how wrong he was about me.

But that was before I woke up early the next morning, head pounding and alone in that same room, remembering how I'd pushed up Amber's skirt and yanked down her panties—I remembered being inside her—then struggled to recall exactly what had happened next. My stomach roiled and panic fluttered in my chest, as I realized that how much I'd had to drink had caused me to pass out. I had no idea where Amber had gone or when she had left. My jeans were down around my ankles, my boxers were twisted at my knees. My mouth felt as though it had been lined in thick, wet fur.

"I was so drunk," I say now, knowing it's the worst kind of excuse, but it's the only one I can offer.

"We both were," she says. "But I still told you to stop. And you raped me anyway."

I recoil at her use of the term, unable to comprehend that what had happened between us could be construed that way. For almost five months, I'd told myself that it happens all the time— these drunk hookups between men and women, both of them remembering different versions of the truth, the woman later regretting the decision and crying rape to make herself feel better. But I couldn't imagine Amber being vindictive like that. Even if my memories of that night were foggy, I couldn't imagine she'd make something like that up. I couldn't believe she'd lie. Still, I can't help trying to explain away what led us to that moment, to justify it, somehow, to prove that the sex had been something we both wanted. I keep going back to how we danced, how we kissed, and how, no matter what she says now, I never heard her use the word "no."

We drive along in the pitch black for another half an hour, until we reach the logging road that will lead us where Amber wants to go. Much of the paved road between the town of Index and the Bryants' property had been washed away by flooding on the Skykomish more than a decade ago, and since it wasn't exactly a priority for the state to repair, the only way to access the cabin is to go up and over the mountain, adding an extra hour or more to the route. "You sure this is safe to do at night?" I ask, knowing the terrain is uneven and the road often cuts close to the edge of a steep, treacherous drop.

"I don't care," she says. "Put on your high beams and drive."

I do as she asks, keeping my speed low, staying jutted against the left side of the road as best I can.

"Does Daniel know where you are?" I say as we bump along. I'm trying to get her to talk to me, to make her realize that what she's doing is crazy.

"Daniel and I broke up in July."

"Oh, wow. Sorry," I say, shocked to hear this, but then realize that if they were still together, Daniel would have more than likely shown up at my front door to kick my ass.

"No, you're not," she snaps. "Just shut up. I don't want you talking about him."

I comply, and a silent hour later, we reach the main gate of the property. Amber jumps out of the truck to unlock the gate, and as she pushes it out of our way, I am briefly tempted to throw the truck into reverse and leave her there, alone, in the woods and the dark. But even now, I don't want to put her in danger. Part of me feels responsible for her pain. At the very least, I am responsible for the annihilation of an important and meaningful friendship.

Amber climbs back into the cab, and I drive us over the narrow bridge that leads to the cabin. The ground is covered in a few inches of early November, slushy snow, but my truck's four-wheel drive easily gets us through it, and a few minutes later, I pull up into the one parking spot at the top of a small incline, at the bottom of which is the cabin. I turn off the engine, and almost immediately, the chill from outside begins to seep through the windows and eats up the remaining heat in the cab.

"What now?" I ask Amber, who hasn't said a word since she told me to shut up about Daniel.

She shifts her head and looks at me, her hazel eyes dark, the bruised spots beneath them making it appear as though she has been beaten. "You're going to admit what really happened," she says. Her voice sounds detached, far away from her body, and I worry that she might be having some kind of serious mental break. Even though I could overpower her if I wanted to, I can't help imagining the kind of white-hot agony she must be in to have taken things this far. However much has broken between us, I still love her. I probably always will.

"I didn't mean to hurt you," I say, feeling helpless.

She finally looks at me, the dim light from the moon catching the shine of tears in her eyes, turning them into impossibly deep, swirling pools of green and gold. "What you meant doesn't matter," she says. "You still need to pay for what you *did*."

Amber

The moment Tyler was finished, he rolled off me and passed out with one of his long arms thrown across my body. I couldn't look at him. All I could feel was the burning between my legs, the knots in my stomach, and the tears running down my cheeks. I felt paralyzed, as though the entire weight of him was still pinning me to the bed, pressing all the air from my lungs.

Loud music blasted out on the patio, punctuated by the occasional firework. I heard laughter and happy, shouting conversation—the world had gone on, continuing to spin on its axis, even as mine had slammed to a jarring, neck-snapping halt.

I didn't know what to do. I was still drunk. Tyler had driven me to the party. How could I get home without him? That was all I could think to do. Get home. Climb in the shower. Scrub away the stain and smell of him from my skin. Never see him again.

I could feel his hot breath on my bare arm as he slept. Light snores escaped him as I forced myself to get out from under his touch, shifting oh so slowly, terrified of waking him. My head ached, my insides felt as though they'd been stirred with a hot poker. My body moved like it was full of heavy, wet sand.

When I finally managed to sit upright on the side of the bed, more tears filled my eyes and a sob seized my throat. I slapped a hand over my mouth to keep from making a sound. *Get away . . . don't wake him* were the only thoughts in my head. My chest heaved a few times as I swallowed back my revulsion and grief, and as soon as I could, I leaned over and grabbed my underwear, pulling it up as I stood. A warm, sticky liquid oozed between my thighs, and in response, I gagged.

I need to get to a bathroom. I grabbed my sandals from the floor and tiptoed as quietly as I could out of the room, closing the door behind me. I stumbled down the stairs, grasping the railing so I wouldn't fall. The small powder room I'd been in with Gia was empty, so I locked myself inside it, turned on the light, and forced myself to clean up as best I could. I let loose a few hiccuping sobs as I finished, pulling up my panties again, flushing the toilet, and then stood in front of the mirror, not recognizing who I saw. My hair was a tangled mess and my eyes were smudged with mascara; black streaks ran down my cheeks. My bottom lip was swollen and had a cut, either from Tyler's forceful kisses or from my teeth biting into it. The girl I'd been just an hour ago was gone; she'd been obliterated. I had no idea who I was now.

Oh my god, what am I going to tell Daniel? I thought. *What will he think of me? What will he do? Will he believe that Tyler forced me to have sex, or will he think that I'm lying to assuage my guilt?*

Shaking, I snatched several tissues from the box on the counter and cleaned my face up as best I could, then dampened and smoothed my hair, trying to put my fiancé out of my mind and focus on what to do next. I hadn't brought my phone or a purse, since I didn't want to worry about having to keep track of them at the party. I was trapped. I couldn't call my parents and ask them to come get me. They'd ask too many questions. They'd want to talk to Tyler. There was no way I could tell them what he had done. I just needed to get home and climb into bed. I needed to sleep, to figure out a way to move forward as if this night never happened.

Find Mason and Gia, I thought. *They can give you a ride.* But then, just as I was about to open the door, a wave of nausea hit me with such intensity that I barely made it to the toilet, where I heaved until my throat burned and there was nothing left to come up. I slumped on the floor, resting my head against the wall, disgusted by the rancid stench of stomach acid and tequila. I tried to catch my breath, feeling just the tiniest bit less drunk.

A couple of minutes later, I managed to get up, rinse out my mouth with water, and head back out to the patio, where I saw Mason and Gia slow-dancing. The look of adoration on his face as he gazed at his wife stopped me in my tracks. *That's how Daniel looks at me,* I thought, and a wave of sorrow rushed over me as I wondered if he would ever see me like that again. I hesitated, debating whether I could bear talking to them. But I had to. I didn't have a choice. I walked over and touched Mason's arm.

"Hey!" he said, smiling. "Where'd you two disappear to?"

"Tyler's passed out upstairs," I said, my chin trembling as I spoke. I ground my teeth together in order to get it to stop. "And I'm sick."

"Oh no, *mija,*" Gia said. "You poor thing." She sounded as drunk as I felt.

"I hate to ask, but is there any way you guys could take me home? I could call an Uber, but with the holiday and being out in the county, it might take forever . . ." *Please, please, please.. Don't make me stay here any longer than I already have. Don't make me call my parents.*

"No worries. I'll drive you," Mason said. He looked down at his wife. "Do you want to stay, and I can come back?"

Gia shook her head. "Nah." She swayed a bit, and her husband reached out to steady her. "I may have overestimated my ability to party like I used to." She grinned. "I've had my fun. Let's go home."

"Thank you so much," I said, crossing my arms over my chest and rubbing my triceps to combat the chill in the air.

"Of course," Mason said, but then he hesitated and looked upward, to the second story of the house. "Maybe we should take Ty home, too."

"No!" I said, sharply. Both Mason and Gia gave me a strange look, so I quickly backtracked. "I mean, he's really out of it. I tried to wake him up, but couldn't. It's probably better to just let him sleep it off and he can drive himself home in the morning." *How am I doing this?* I wondered. *How am I standing here, talking with them like my life wasn't just destroyed?*

"She's right," Gia said. "Tyler's a big boy. He can take care of himself."

Mason nodded, and the three of us made our way to the front of the house, where we climbed into their car. I sat next to the empty infant car seat in the back, curling my shoulders forward, trying to make myself as small as I possibly could. I couldn't stop shivering.

"You okay back there?" Mason asked as he pulled out of the driveway and onto the main road.

"I'm fine," I said, but my voice cracked, so I cleared my throat. "Don't worry. I already threw up back at the house."

Gia laughed, turning around to look at me. "Guess neither of us are party animals."

"I guess not," I said, trying to ignore the pain between my legs. *Just get me home. Please. I just want to go home.*

Mason glanced in the rearview mirror, making eye contact with me. "Are you sure you're all right?"

"I'm sure," I said, fighting back a swell of tears. "Just not feeling well." I couldn't imagine telling them the truth. And what would

I say, anyway? I was certain that they had seen the way Tyler and I were dancing, the way I'd kissed him and let him grind his hips on mine. They wouldn't believe that what happened up in that bedroom was against my will. They'd chalk it up to a drunk girl regretting her decision to have sex. They'd call me a liar. A cheater. A slut. Maybe they'd be right.

"What's your address?" Gia asked, and I recited it, watching as she punched it into the car's GPS. I sat back, closing my eyes, trying not to think, focusing as much as I could on the vibration of the tires as they hit the road, a low buzz humming through me.

For the rest of the ride, Mason and Gia talked with each other up front, but I couldn't pay attention to what they were saying. All I could think about was getting home. When the car stopped in front of my parents' house, I practically leaped out of the backseat.

"G'night, *mija*!" Gia said, turning around again. "The four of us should do dinner together, soon!" She giggled, then burped. "Oh, wow. Sorry. That was gross."

"That's okay," I said, forcing a smile as I opened my door to climb out. "Good night."

Mason exited the car, too, and stood next to me, offering his arm for support, but I didn't want him to touch me. I couldn't imagine wanting anyone to touch me ever again.

"Thanks," I said, taking a quick, jerky step back from his reach. "I'm fine."

"You don't seem fine," he said, with a calm, assessing gaze. I could suddenly see him in work mode, treating injured victims in their houses or on the side of the road. "Let me walk you to the door, at least." His low tone soothed me, and so I nodded, allowing him accompany me to the side of the house, to the door that led into the kitchen, where Tyler had surprised me back in December. Mason stood at least a couple of feet to my side, giving me the space I so desperately needed. Feeling his eyes still on me,

I leaned down and lifted the realistic-looking but fake rock next to the stairs that held a spare key, taking it out and slipping it into the lock on the door. "Thanks," I repeated. "I appreciate the ride."

"Amber, wait," Mason said.

I stopped what I was doing, freezing at the top of the steps, my heart thumping like a jackrabbit's leg inside my chest. I didn't look at him. I didn't speak. I was too afraid of what might come out of my mouth. I was afraid I might start screaming and never stop.

"Take care of yourself, okay?" Mason said. "Take a few ibuprofen and drink lots of water before you go to sleep. It'll help."

I almost laughed, thinking how neither of those things would come close to fixing what was wrong with me now. Still, I bobbed my head and then rushed inside, shutting and locking the door behind me, relieved to finally be alone. I glanced at the clock on the microwave and saw it was only ten thirty—my parents wouldn't be home for at least a couple of hours. I wove my way down the hall and up the stairs, stripping off my dress and panties in the bathroom, turning the water in the shower on to run as hot as it could get. I grabbed a pair of scissors from the vanity drawer and took them to my clothes, cutting and snipping until there was only a handful of red and white fabric-confetti left. I wrapped all of it in toilet paper and shoved it to the bottom of the garbage can, then yanked back the shower curtain and climbed inside the tub, letting the scalding water hit my body for as long as I could stand it, watching my skin turn bright red. I turned the handle so the water would cool to a slightly more tolerable temperature, then grabbed the neon green mesh scrub from the hook on the tile wall and soaked it in foaming body wash, running it back and forth across my body as roughly as I could, trying to scour away every skin cell that Tyler had touched. Trying to erase what he had done.

It was only when I finished scrubbing that more tears finally came, body-racking cries that made me shake so violently I couldn't continue to stand. I leaned my shoulder against the wall and slid downward, howling as I pulled my legs to my chest and wrapped my arms around them, setting my forehead on my bent knees. I rocked in place, sobbing, letting the hot water wash over me, trying to make it not be true, to find a way to make myself believe it didn't happen. I tried not to feel the weight of him still on me, tried to expunge the memory of the violent, insistent jabbing of his hips. He'd used enough force to make me bleed. I hadn't noticed it back in the bathroom at the house, but now, a narrow, red stream flowed from my body down the drain.

I stayed like this for as long as I could, keening and rocking until the water ran cold and I began to shiver, my teeth clacking. I felt numb, I felt empty. I was a shell, an abandoned chrysalis, a tomb lying in wait for the dead.

Once I was out of the tub and wrapped in a thick blue towel, I opened the door to let the steam out of the bathroom, then used my hand to wipe the condensation from the mirror. A stranger stared back at me.

I heard Tyler's voice in my head: *Your hair looks pretty like that,* and another wave of nausea rolled through me. I looked down, and my eyes caught the gleam of the silver scissors I'd left on the edge of the counter. Before I knew what I was doing, I grabbed them with one hand and a strip of my hair with the other. I held it away from my head and began to cut, one chunk after another, leaving haggard ends and uneven lengths in a bob that stopped near the bottoms of my ears.

When I finished, I stared at myself in the mirror, hoping that I would feel better, somehow, no longer looking like the girl who had flirted with her best friend when she was engaged to someone else; the girl who had been the one to kiss Tyler first, to let him grind his crotch against her and lead her upstairs to a room.

I knew what was going to happen. I couldn't deny that. I'd encouraged him, purposely turned him on. I'd let myself get drunk; I'd wanted to lose control. And this was the result: a girl standing in the bathroom, staring in the mirror with a trickle of blood running down the inside of her leg. A girl who had changed her mind when it was already too late, and now, no matter what she did, would never be the same again.

That night, I didn't sleep so much as surf along the edge of consciousness, startling awake with every distant firework boom, sitting up in my bed and turning on the light to make sure that I was still alone. What if Tyler woke up and decided to drive to my house? What if he came in my room and took what he wanted from me again? It was doubtful, I knew, but the fear cloaking my thoughts was relentless, driving roots deep into my brain, choking out any sense of security I had hoped being home would provide.

I heard my parents get home a little after midnight, but I stayed quiet when my mom opened the door and peeked in my room. I was too afraid to open my mouth. Too terrified of what she might make me do. She might make me say what Tyler did to me out loud. She might make me go to the hospital and call the police. Or worse, she might not believe me. She might blame me, like I did myself, for sending the wrong kind of message and leading him on. I couldn't fathom doing any of those things. I just wanted to pretend it never happened. I just wanted to escape into the thick, black bliss of sleep.

But sleep wouldn't come. I lay in bed for hours, curled up as tightly as I could beneath my covers, pillows surrounding me. Through my window, I watched the moon drop lower and lower in the cloudless night sky, and the pale, lavender whisper of dawn begin to lighten it. I was scheduled to be at the gym at seven o'clock, but I knew there was no way I could get up, no possible way I could work, so around four, I grabbed my cell phone and left Harold a message, saying I was sick and wouldn't be in. I couldn't face my clients. I couldn't face anyone. I turned my phone off and dropped it on the floor.

The throbbing between my thighs wouldn't stop. Every time I rolled over or moved at all, a piercing spiral of pain shot through my pelvis. Somewhere around five a.m., the reality of the fact that Tyler hadn't used a condom hit me, and while I was on the Pill, that wouldn't protect me from whatever diseases he might carry. Before last night, I would never have fathomed thinking something so horrible about him. But everything I thought I knew about my friend no longer held true. There was something sinister and violent and dark inside him I'd never experienced before. In one instant, he had become a stranger to me, someone I never wanted to see again.

It's all my fault, I thought. *I called it a date. I wore that dress and no bra. I drank too much, I kissed him. I used his body like he was the pole and I was the stripper out on the patio. I let him take me upstairs to that bed. Maybe he was too drunk to hear me when I told him to stop. Maybe I didn't say it loudly enough. Maybe I didn't say it enough times.*

Finally, around six, I drifted off into a restless sleep. But an hour later, my pounding head and empty, burning stomach woke me again. My mouth was so dry I could barely swallow, and I wished that I had taken Mason's advice. The last thing I wanted to do was get up, but I needed to hydrate or my headache would only intensify.

Slowly, I rolled out of bed and tried to stand, feeling like I had the worst sort of all-over body flu. My rib cage felt bruised, my joints creaked, and my muscles barely cooperated as I left my room and stepped into the hall, where my mom stood at the top of the stairs, about ten feet away from me, still dressed in her loose black pajama bottoms and one of my dad's blue and green Seahawks jerseys.

"Amber!" she exclaimed, the sharpness in her voice assaulting my senses. "What happened to your hair?"

I didn't move. I didn't look at her. "I cut it." *Keep it together. Don't say a word. Just act like everything is fine.*

"I can see that," she said, walking toward me. "But when? And why? You've always loved it long."

I shrugged. "Last night, when I got home. I just . . . did it." I stood still as she hugged me, keeping my eyes on the floor.

"Whew!" she said when she pulled back. "Had a little to drink, did you? It's coming out your pores."

I nodded, finally meeting her eyes. "I'm not going to work. I feel awful."

"I bet," she said. She paused, then reached up to push my hair back from my face, staring at me with an assessing look. "I like it," she declared. "We need to clean up the ends, but it actually suits you. Probably easier to take care of, too."

I nodded again. It was all I could manage.

She pursed her lips and tilted her head to one side. "Are you all right, honey? Did something happen? I didn't think you'd get home earlier than us last night."

"I just drank too much. I've never done that before."

She kept looking at me, like she was trying to decide whether or not to believe what I said. "Okay," she finally replied. "I'll go make you some ginger tea and dry toast. It'll help."

My gut twisted at the thought of trying to put any kind of food in my mouth, but I nodded, if only to make her leave me alone. When she turned to walk away, part of me wanted to call out, to start crying and tell her everything. To ask her to wrap herself around me in my bed the way she used to when I was a little girl, back when the monsters in my imagination weren't real. When they weren't actually someone I loved, someone I thought I could trust.

And then, I couldn't help myself. "Mom?"

"Yes?" she said, stopping her descent down the stairs to look back at me.

Tell her. Say it out loud. I opened my mouth, ready to convey the entire sordid story, but then, only two words came out. "Thank you," I said, and she smiled.

"Of course, sweetie. I love you."

"Love you, too." I entered the bathroom, where I forced myself to drink handful after handful of water, ignoring the mirror, staring at the contents of the wastebasket next to the sink. Before I'd gone to bed, I'd shoved all the strands of my cut-off hair on top of the toilet-paper-wrapped, chopped-up dress and panties, and now it lay there looking like a messy, dark brown nest. The girl I used to be, sitting in the trash.

I washed my face over the sink, then decided to take another hot shower, hoping it might actually make me feel clean. But when I took off the long T-shirt I wore and looked down at my body, I gasped. The evidence was everywhere—fingerprint bruises around my breasts and waist, fat smudges of purple on my rib cage and inner thighs, blood-crusted, half-moon indentations on the palms of my hands. I couldn't risk my mother walking in on me and seeing any of it. Hurriedly, I pulled the T-shirt back on and raced into my bedroom, where I changed into an oversize, gray WSU sweatshirt and black leggings. Once I was back in bed, a few tears snuck out of the corners of my eyes and rolled down the side of my face into my hair. About five minutes later, my mom brought in a tray with the hot tea and toast she had promised, and again, as I had last night, I pretended to be asleep. She stroked my hair again, setting the back of her hand against my forehead, like she was checking to see if I had a temperature, and the tenderness of her touch brought more tears to my eyes.

"Just rest, my sweet girl," she whispered before she left the room, and I realized that she knew I was awake.

I thought I might cry more. I thought I might lie there, thoughts spinning as they had last night, but the sheer weight of my fatigue won out and I finally slept, soundly enough that I had no dreams. I woke several hours later to a knock on my bedroom door, to my name being spoken as it opened.

"Amber?" Tyler said, and my entire body seized up. My muscles froze, and a sharp rock in my throat blocked me from taking a breath. *What is he doing here? Who let him in?* My parents, of course. They didn't know better. I hadn't told them what he'd done.

"Are you okay?" he asked, coming in and closing the door behind him. "I was worried when I woke up and you weren't there."

I sat up, pressing my back against the padded headboard of my bed. *Did he expect me to stay there and cuddle with him?* The skin beneath his eyes was dark, and it appeared as though he hadn't changed or showered. He was frowning, like he was sad. For a flash, I felt myself soften, accustomed to comforting him. But then, a new kind of muscle memory set in: his weight on me, the way he had gored himself inside me, and I instantly felt like a cornered animal, wild and willing to do anything to find escape.

"Get out," I whispered.

"Amber . . ." he said, taking a couple of steps toward me.

I couldn't move. I couldn't breathe. He sat down on the edge of my bed, and that's when I managed to find my voice. "Get out!" I screamed, with enough intensity that my entire body vibrated and the muscles in my throat felt singed. I kicked at him with both legs, as hard as I could, hard enough to push him onto the floor, fighting the way I should have fought last night. Instead, I'd let him hurt me. I'd let him win. "Get the fuck out!"

"Jesus, Amber," he said as he struggled to right himself.

"Get out!" I screamed again, and I kept on screaming it. "Get out! Get out! Get out!" Just those two words, the only ones I could think to say.

He stood up, his green eyes wide. Then, both my parents appeared in my doorway, their breathing labored after they'd clearly dashed up the stairs.

"What the hell is going on here?" my father demanded.

"Make him leave!" I said, barely able to speak. "Make him go!"

"What?" my mother said, her eyes darting back and forth between Tyler and me, confusion shrouding her face. "Tyler . . . ?"

Tyler didn't speak; instead, he simply turned around, pushed past both my parents, and strode out of the room.

My parents stood still for a minute, shocked, I supposed, by what had just occurred. "Honey, what happened?" my mom asked, coming over to sit down with me. She wrapped her arms around me and squeezed tightly, making me cry all over again.

"Did you two have a fight?" my dad asked.

I sobbed harder, unable to speak. I felt the mattress sag as my father sat down on the other side of me, putting his strong arms around me, too. "It's okay, baby," he said, and I could hear the tears in his own voice. "We've got you. Everything's going to be fine."

They held me like that for I don't know how long, until my eyes were swollen shut and my body felt like it had been drained of all my blood. I was so spent, I could barely move; I could barely draw a breath.

"Tell us," my mother said, her voice trembling. "Please."

And then, finally, I lifted my head and looked at my parents, and somehow found the strength to speak the truth.

Tyler

What the hell just happened? I thought as I let the Bryants' front door slam behind me, making my way to the street, where I'd parked my truck. I jumped inside, gripping the steering wheel and gunning the engine, picturing the wide-eyed, undeniable look of fear that had taken over Amber's face when I walked into her room. *She was scared of me. Totally terrified.* The tires squealed as I pulled out of my parking spot and pointed my truck toward home, running through three almost-red lights and scaring the hell out of a pedestrian on the way to the freeway.

"Watch it, jerkwad!" the man yelled at me as he jumped back on the curb to avoid getting plowed into by my truck. I flipped him off, then zipped past three cars, cutting them all off so I could merge onto the freeway before them.

Something was seriously wrong. When I'd woken up in the bed without Amber there, I'd called her, but her phone must have been off because it went straight to voice mail. I decided I'd better head over to her house to make sure she had gotten home okay and, also, to find out why she had left. With all the tequila I'd had, I still wasn't thinking clearly, and the entire night was a sort of fuzzy, amorphous blob in my mind. I remembered the way she and I had danced, how she'd been the one to kiss me. How she'd led me upstairs to the bedroom, how she tore off my clothes, writhing against me and pulling me down on the bed. I remembered how amazing it felt to be inside her. After that, everything sort of went dark, the specifics of the sex we'd had flashing in and out of my head in fractured, disjointed pieces. *Why was she afraid of me? Why would she scream at me like that? Had I gotten too rough with her? Had I done something to her in my sleep?*

The thought that I'd possibly hurt Amber caused me to reflexively press my foot down on the gas pedal, accelerating to sixty, sixty-five, seventy, then eighty. My blood pressure pounded in my eardrums, the rush of adrenaline filling my veins made my limbs feel heavy, aching with the need for release. *What is* wrong *with me? Just calm the fuck down!* Out of sheer frustration, I pounded the heel of my right palm hard enough against the top of the steering wheel that the front of my truck jerked into the next lane. The brakes on the car beside mine screeched, and the driver slammed on his horn.

"Shit!" I said, rushing to right my vehicle. But it was too late. Red and blue lights flashed behind me and the *whoop-whoop* of the siren sounded. My pulse jittered through my body as I slowed down, using my indicator to signal as I moved over to the side of the road. I turned off the engine and turned on the hazard lights, reaching for my license in my wallet and the truck's registration from the glove box.

When the officer approached, I didn't even bother to speak; I just held the documents out the window, wanting to get home, desperate to figure out why Amber had freaked when she saw me.

"Do you know why I pulled you over, sir?" The officer's blond hair was tucked up into a bun at the base of her neck, and her lips were so thin and pale, it almost looked as though she didn't have a mouth at all.

"I was speeding," I said, flatly. *Please don't have me do a Breathalyzer,* I thought. I might still be hovering near the limit of legally drunk.

"And you almost drove that Lexus off the road," the officer said. "Were you on your cell?" She looked to the passenger seat, where my cell phone lay along with my jacket.

"No, I was not." I reached over and offered the phone to her. "Feel free to check the text or call history for a time stamp of when I last used it."

She waved it away, then made a note on the clipboard she carried. "You in a hurry to get somewhere this morning?"

I held the tops of my thighs in a tight grip. "No, ma'am. Just wasn't paying attention. I apologize."

"You seem agitated. Everything all right?"

I had to restrain myself from unleashing the truth. That everything was far from all right. And just then, as I stared at the officer standing next to my truck, the sound of Amber's voice pleading with me last night went off like loud bell inside my head—*Tyler, wait!* she'd said as I was lying on top of her, and a sinking sense of horror crept through me. *Did she think that I forced her to have sex? Did she think I raped her? Oh god. Oh fuck. I have to talk to her. She has to let me. I have to make her understand she has it all wrong. I would never do something like that!*

I clenched my jaws, feeling the muscles working beneath my skin, before I answered. "Can you just give me the fucking ticket so I can get on my way?"

The officer paused, looking at me with cool brown eyes. "There's no need for that kind of language, sir."

I took a deep breath, then let it out slowly. "I'm sorry. Really." Getting arrested was all I needed right now; I needed to tone it down. "The thing is, I'm a paramedic and I guess I'm used to being able to push the limit, you know? Sometimes it happens off-shift without me even realizing." I didn't mention that Mason drove our rig the majority of the time.

"What district are you with?"

"City of Bellingham, under Captain Duncan." I held my breath, hoping that this thin alliance between my job and hers might encourage her to let me off with a warning.

The officer looked as though she were contemplating a decision to do just that, and then she spoke. "You might want to avoid driving when you're this upset," the officer said as she finished writing out the ticket and handed it to me. "I'm dinging you for the speeding, not reckless endangerment, but I'd better not catch you out here pulling that crap again."

"You won't," I said, taking the ticket, setting it on top of my jacket. "Thank you." After the officer had returned to her vehicle, I slowly drove away, trying to figure out where I should go next. Heading home wouldn't do me any good. I needed to sort out the events from last night, and I could only think of one person who could help me do just that.

Ten minutes later, I pulled up in front of Mason and Gia's house, a small two-bedroom, sky blue Craftsman in a neighborhood a few blocks off Cornwall Avenue, similar in size and design to the one I'd lived in with my parents across town. Before I left my truck, I shot my partner a text, not wanting to just knock on the door and wake him and Gia or the baby. It was a little after eleven, but I wasn't sure what time they had gotten in. All I knew was that Mason hadn't been drinking last night and could maybe help me figure out what had happened with Amber. Maybe he had seen something I couldn't remember.

Instead of answering my text, Mason opened the front door and motioned for me to come up the front steps and inside. I noted that his dark hair was pushed flat on one side, as though he'd recently gotten out of bed. A moment later I was sitting on the brown leather couch in their living room, a big glass of water that he said it looked like I needed in my hand.

"We'll have to keep our voices down," Mason said as he settled into the rocking chair on the other side of the square table in the center of the room. "Gia and the baby are still sleeping."

"Okay, sure," I said, the glass trembling in my hands.

Mason saw this and cocked his head. "You okay, bro? Have you talked with Amber?"

"Not really," I said, in answer to both of his questions. I drank down almost the entire contents of the glass, knowing it was the best thing for me, and then put the glass onto the table. "Do you know how she got home?"

"We drove her," Mason said, frowning. "She said you were passed out and she felt sick, so she asked for a ride."

"Oh." My mind reeled, relieved that regardless of what Amber might think had happened, she hadn't voiced it to Mason and Gia.

"What's going on, Ty? You two looked mighty happy with each other out on the dance floor, before you took her into the house—"

"Before *I* took *her*?" I said, cutting him off.

"Yeah," Mason said, giving me a strange look. "You don't remember that?"

I sat back against the couch, hard, and closed my eyes. "I thought she took me inside. I could have sworn . . ." My words trailed off as I tried to organize the jumbled mess of images flickering inside my head. *What else did I get wrong? What else had I forgotten? What did I do that made Amber scream at me and kick me off the bed?*

"You were both hammered," Mason said. "Have you blacked out like this before?"

"I didn't black out!" I insisted, opening my eyes again.

"Dude! Keep it down, please."

"Sorry," I said, lowering my voice. "I just don't know what's going on. I went over to her house this morning to check on her and she freaked out. She didn't want me anywhere near her."

"Freaked out how?" Mason asked in what I recognized as the same deliberately calm, information-gathering tone he used with victims in the field.

"She screamed at me to leave. Like, crazy screaming. And when I sat down on her bed to try to talk with her, she went nuts and kicked me off it. Then her parents came in and I just . . . bolted. I didn't know what the hell was going on."

Mason was quiet a moment before speaking again. "Did you have sex with her?"

I nodded, fighting the harshly edged ache that had risen in my throat, recalling the look of terror on my best friend's face when I walked into her bedroom. I'd seen her through many dark moments in her life, but I'd never seen her look anything like that. It finally registered that part of why she seemed so different was her hair. Since last night, she'd chopped it off, up to the line of her jaw.

"And she was into it, right?"

"Yeah," I said, but my voice faltered, and I shook my head. "I thought it was all her idea. I mean, I wanted it, too. You know that. But you saw the way she was dancing with me. Did you see her kissing me?"

"I did." Mason didn't say more, he just stared at me, expectantly.

"I thought it was finally happening, you know? That she realized she'd made a mistake being with Daniel and it was me she wanted. She's been having second thoughts about getting engaged. She's been flirting with me since she got home . . . we've been flirting with each other. I know we have. And we were kissing all the way up the stairs until we got to the bedroom. It felt like we couldn't get there fast enough. I didn't imagine that. I *know* it happened." My head ached as I tried to remember exactly what came next. My hand on her leg, pushing up her skirt. Feeling how hot she was for me, how ready. I remembered rolling on top of her. And then again, those two words, her voice, exploding inside my head: *Tyler, wait!*

"You made sure she wanted to do it, though, right?" Mason asked, quietly.

I didn't answer, but inside, I was thinking that of course Amber wanted to do it. She wouldn't have danced with me the way she did if she didn't want to have sex. She wouldn't have let me press my erection against her; she wouldn't have kissed me or let me take her up to the bedroom. She gave off every sign of wanting it as much as I did. I thought about Whitney, how I'd never had to stop and ask her if she really wanted to sleep with me—her willingness to come inside my apartment that first day, the way she let me touch her was permission enough.

But Amber told you to wait, I thought, and the realization that I hadn't listened, that I didn't hear her over the loud roar of my desire, made me feel as though I might be sick. *What if I did hear her,* I wondered, *and I went ahead with it anyway?*

"Tyler," Mason said, loudly enough to snap me out of my thoughts. "Please tell me you asked if she was okay with what was happening. Tell me she didn't say no."

"She never used that word," I said, my voice breaking. I cleared my throat. "But I think she told me to wait. She might have told me to stop." I breathed in, feeling the air hitch and get stuck inside my lungs.

"Jesus, man," Mason said. His shook his head in disbelief, and his thick fingers gripped the arms of his chair. "Are you *kidding* me? I thought there was something wrong with her. She seemed jumpy and kind of out of it, like she was in shock or something.

But I chalked it up to the booze . . . I told myself I didn't know her well enough to actually be right about that."

"We were drunk," I said. "Both of us, right? So maybe she's just having second thoughts. Maybe she's feeling guilty about cheating on her boyfriend and that's why she was acting weird."

"Her fiancé, you mean," Mason said, giving me a pointed look.

I stood up from the couch and began to pace behind it, desperate to think of any explanation other than the one that made me a monster. "Maybe she's just confused, like me. Maybe her mind is all fucked up because we were drinking. Maybe she's just trying to figure out exactly what happened, too."

"Maybe . . ." Mason said, but he didn't look convinced.

"I wouldn't hurt her!" I said, coming to a sudden stop. I gave my partner an imploring look. "You *know* me. I've loved her my whole life. All I want . . . all I've *ever* wanted . . . is to be with her. To make her happy."

"I get that," Mason said, "but you know as well as I do that people do some crazy shit when they've been drinking. How many drunk drivers have we taken to the hospital after they've killed someone with their car? Most of them don't remember the accident. All of them say they didn't mean to do anything wrong, but the fact that they were fucked up doesn't absolve them of responsibility for what they did."

"Are you saying that you think I *raped* her? That I could do something like that?" The pressure that had been building in my body since the moment I left Amber's house, increasing since the officer pulled me over and gave me a ticket, amped up and felt like it might burst open the valves of my heart.

"I think under the right set of circumstances," Mason said, carefully, his eyes not leaving mine, "pretty much anyone is capable of horrific behavior."

I was silent, unmoving, bracing myself with my fingertips

pressed against the spine of the couch, staring at him. I let what he'd said sink in as best I could, still trying to fight off the worst-case scenario as possibly being true. This had to be a misunder-standing. Maybe Amber and I both just needed to recover from our nasty hangovers, and then try to talk again. Even during the most difficult times in our lives, we'd always been able to sort out our differences. I told myself that that would happen again. Amber and I would talk and the truth would find its way to the surface, and everything—and everyone—would be just fine. I had to tell myself these things, because the alternative, a world with-out Amber in it, a world where I'd committed an unthinkable sin, was one I didn't want to be a part of.

Amber

"I'm going to *kill* him," my dad said, after I finished telling my parents what happened with Tyler at the party. "I'm going to *tear him apart*." He stood up and paced in my room, his hands clenched into tight fists at his sides. I'd never heard his voice sound like that before, flooded with enough contempt and disgust that I believed he meant to follow through on his threats.

"Daddy, no," I said, sniffling and wiping my eyes with the edge of my sleeve. I hadn't called him "daddy" since I was eight.

He stopped pacing, staring at me with tears in his blue eyes. "Baby girl," he said. His voice cracked, and he didn't go on, looking like he was struggling to hold himself together.

"I can't believe it," my mom said, tears running down her cheeks. "I just can't. How could he *do* something like this?"

"It wasn't just him," I said, leaning back against my headboard. My eyes were practically swollen shut from all the crying I'd done in the last fourteen hours. I'd never felt so tired or drained in my life. All I wanted to do was go back to sleep. All I needed was oblivion. "I was drunk, too. I shouldn't have danced with him the way I did. I shouldn't have—"

"Stop that!" my mom said, cutting me off. "None of this is your fault. Do you hear me, Amber? None of it. I don't care if you were drinking or not." Her voice rose as she spoke, becoming more tense and shrill as she went on. "You told him to stop. You told him you didn't want to do it. Right?" I nodded, numbly, and she bobbed her head, too. "Then what he did to you he did without your permission. He *raped* you, honey. That's what it was, pure and simple." Her shoulders began to shake and she pressed a curled fist against her mouth. "I can't believe it," she said again. "How *could* he?"

"I'm going to find him," my dad said, turning toward the door, but my mother leapt up and grabbed him by the arm.

"Tom, don't," she said. "We have to take Amber to the hospital. We have to call the police. They'll handle it."

"No!" I said, shaking my head. "I just want to stay here! Please, don't make me go." My bottom lip trembled as I pictured having to lie back on a hospital bed, my legs spread, enduring a doctor's poking and prodding between my legs. I couldn't bear it. There was no way. "I already took a shower. They wouldn't find anything." *Except the bruises,* I thought. *Except the way that he used his body like a knife inside me and made me bleed.*

"But you have to report what happened," my mom said. "He needs to be held accountable for what he did!"

"And how would I prove it?" I said. "Everyone at the party saw the way I was dancing with him. I made out with him, too. No one's going to believe me . . . that I told him to stop. It'll be my word against his."

"The police can get him to confess," my dad said. "That's their job. You just have to tell them what happened, like you told us, and they'll take it from there."

"I don't want to talk to the police!" I said, spittle flying from my mouth. "I won't! Please, leave it alone. I just want to be left alone!" I started crying again, and I wondered how it was possible for my body to produce this many tears, if I'd ever be able to stop. I kept seeing the look on Tyler's face when he'd walked into my room, the confusion and concern, and it didn't make sense. Did he not remember what happened? Did he black out? Would he blame his actions last night on alcohol? Would he proclaim his innocence because of an inability to recall what he did?

My parents were silent for a moment, frozen where they stood, looking at each other, then back to me. "I just need to sleep," I said, trying to calm down. "Let me sleep and we can talk about it later. Right now I can't think about anything. I can't make any decisions. My head's a fucking mess." I never swore in front of my mother—crass language was one of her pet peeves—but my energy levels were so depleted, I couldn't stop myself. I didn't care what she thought.

"Okay," my dad said, but I could tell it pained him to agree with my request. He took a couple of steps over and cupped my head with his hand, leaning down to kiss me on the forehead. "I'm so sorry this happened to you, sweetheart. Your mom and I are here for you, okay? We'll support you, no matter what."

I nodded, and my mom opened and then closed her mouth, like she changed her mind about what she was going to say. "We'll be right downstairs," she finally said. "We're not going anywhere."

They left, and I sunk down beneath my covers again, lying on my side and tucking the blanket tightly up under my chin, the same way I had when I was a child and woke from a bad dream, telling myself if I just closed my eyes and rocked back and forth, I would eventually lull myself back to sleep. Escape was all I could think about, and the only escape route I had was the ability to fall into unconsciousness. But just like last night, after my shower, my mind spun with too many thoughts to let me drift off. I tossed and turned, my body aching, until I remembered a trick that I'd used to use when the phentermine I took at the height of my eating disorder made it impossible for me to sleep.

As quietly as I could, not wanting my parents to hear me and come back upstairs, I slipped out of bed and opened my door, sneaking across the hallway to the bathroom, where I rummaged around in the medicine cabinet until I found the clear bottle full of tiny pink pills I needed. A standard dose of antihistamines always made me drowsy; a double dose would give me the relief I so desperately needed now. I took two pills, swallowing them down with a few handfuls of water from the sink, again making sure to avoid looking in the mirror. I stared at the bottle a bit longer, wondering what might happen if I took three, then four, or even the entire contents. That would give me a way out of having to deal with any of this. It would make this entire nightmare go away.

No, I thought, screwing the cap back on and returning the bottle to the cabinet. *I can't do that to my parents. No matter how much it hurts, no matter how unbearable my feelings might be, I can't just give up like that. I won't.*

Within minutes after returning to bed, I felt the comfortable buzz of impending sleep roaming around in my head. The allergy meds had numbed out my thoughts, quieting them down enough that my eyes stayed closed, and my heart stopped racing.

It was almost dark outside when I woke up, with my mouth so dry, my tongue stuck to the roof of my mouth. I blinked, trying to get my eyes to focus on the digital clock next to my bed. It was a few minutes past eight—I'd slept almost ten hours—and I saw that my mom had removed the tray of untouched tea and toast from earlier and replaced it with a bowl of cut-up fruit and two bottles of water. I knew I couldn't eat, but I did drink down both bottles in just a few minutes, knowing that the antihistamine I'd taken had dehydrated me even more than the tequila from the night before.

I forced myself to swing my legs over the side of the bed; I still felt woozy and bruised, so I took several deep breaths in through my nose, blowing them out of my mouth, trying to restore a proper level of oxygen to my brain. It was a trick I shared with my clients who struggled catching their breath after a particularly intense workout. "Press one nostril closed, and then take in three quick, hard sniffs of air through the other, like you're snorting some kind of drug. Then slowly blow the air out your mouth, as controlled as you can manage." This instruction always garnered me strange looks, but when they complied, my clients always felt better. "Your brain functions best when it gets lots of oxygen," I'd tell them. "That's why exercise strengthens your mind, as well as your body. Oxygen rinses it clean."

I almost laughed as I thought about this now, guessing there was nothing in the world that would ever make me feel clean again. I stood up, planning to go back across the hall and take another hot shower, but as soon as I opened the door, I found my mom waiting for me.

"Hey, sweetie," she said, reaching out to brush my messy hair out of my face. "How are you feeling? I came in to check on you a few hours ago and you were totally passed out."

I nodded, knowing I couldn't tell her about the pills I'd taken. "I need to take a shower," I said. "I feel disgusting."

She winced, upset, I was sure, picturing what Tyler had done to me to make me feel that way. I took another step, but she rested a hand on my shoulder, stopping me. "Honey, wait," she said. "Daniel is here."

"What?" I said, practically hissing the word. "Jesus, Mom. Did you *call* him? Did you tell him what happened?" My heartbeat, which had been calm just seconds ago, ramped up again, banging around behind my rib cage. I'd forced myself not to think about Daniel since I'd come home from the party; I'd been too overwhelmed by everything else. I didn't know how to fit him into the messy, imbalanced equation of it all.

"No, of course not," she said hurriedly. "I wouldn't do that. He just showed up about an hour ago. He said you two had argued, and he felt horrible about it. He just wants to talk."

"I can't see him," I said, the tears already returning to my eyes. "Not like this. Mom, please. Make him leave."

"Oh, honey," she said, pulling me into her arms, where I stood stiff as a board, afraid of what might happen if I let myself succumb to the comfort in her touch, worried I might lose control and never get it back. "Daniel loves you. He needs to know what Tyler did."

A thought struck me, and I yanked back, glaring at her. "Have you told anyone else? Did you tell *Liz*?"

A dark, fractured look passed over my mother's face. "No," she said. Her voice was strangled. "I haven't. But I want to. She needs to know. So does Jason. They need to know what their son did."

"What have you and Dad been doing all day?" I crossed my arms over my chest, preparing myself to hear the worst: that they'd gone against my wishes and called the police.

"Nothing," she said, and her chin trembled. "We've just been sitting together, waiting for you to wake up. Your dad is going out of his mind. He's so angry. I don't know what he'll do if Tyler shows up here again."

"He can't do anything," I said. "He knows that, right? He'll just make it worse." Part of me felt better knowing my dad wanted to hurt Tyler for hurting me, but I also couldn't stand the idea of the man who'd raised me answering one violent act with another. I hated what Tyler had done, but beating him up wasn't going to solve a thing.

"Yes, he knows," my mom said. She was about to say more, but then we both turned our heads, hearing my name spoken from the bottom of the stairs.

"Amber?" Daniel called out.

"Mom, please," I said, and she grabbed my hand, squeezing it tightly.

"You need to tell him," she said. "He deserves to hear the truth."

My already racing pulse sped up more. How would I tell Daniel anything? How would I tell him that I'd flirted with Tyler for weeks, how I'd dressed slutty for him last night, then danced with him like a stripper, kissed him, and let him lead me upstairs. The rest of what happened last night rolled through my body in waves that threatened to drown me.

"Hey, baby," Daniel said when he reached the top of the stairs, looking as though he hadn't slept much either. He walked toward me, and my mother let go of my hand, but not before giving it one more squeeze. She gave me a reassuring look, then headed back to where Daniel had just come from.

"Hey," I said, my voice dull, watching my mother's retreat, wondering how in the hell I was going to handle a conversation with my fiancé right now.

Daniel hugged me, and again, I stayed stiff. "You're still mad at me?" he asked when he pulled back.

I shrugged and walked into my bedroom again, retreating to the furthest corner of the bed, against the wall, pulling as many pillows and blankets around myself as I could. Daniel followed behind me, shut the door, then leaned up against it.

"I feel shitty about our fight," he said, and I almost laughed, thinking how ridiculous and small our argument was compared to the one I imagined we were about to have, once I told him that his suspicions about my best friend hadn't been unwarranted.

"It doesn't matter," I said, spinning my engagement ring over and over again with my left thumb. It felt heavy and wrong on my finger. I didn't deserve it. I didn't deserve Daniel. "But it did make me think," I continued. "A lot, actually."

"About what?" Daniel asked, the weight of him sitting on the edge of the bed sinking the mattress down.

I huddled closer to the wall. "About us. About getting engaged."

"Amber—" he said, but I interrupted him.

"Wait," I said. "Let me finish." I didn't want to cry more. "I care about you, Daniel, but I just don't think I'm ready to get married. You should be with someone who is."

"Are you being serious right now?" he asked, his brows stitched together, creating a small v in his otherwise smooth forehead.

"Yes," I said, feeling my heart sink down inside my chest. I couldn't tell him what had happened. It would hurt him too much. My silence would save him the devastation of knowing what I'd done, how I'd blocked him out of my mind, rationalized my behavior, and betrayed his trust. I was a broken person now—a pile of damaged goods. He needed to be with someone better than me. I was sure he would find someone else. "I'm sorry, Daniel," I said, pulling the ring off of my finger. "But it's over. We're over."

I held my hand out, palm up, offering him the ring. He dropped his gaze to it, then raised it back to me. "No," he said. "I'm not going to let you do this, Amber. It was one stupid fight. We'll work it out. We'll find a way to spend more time together. I took two days off to come up here, and I want to spend them with you. We just need to talk—"

"Don't you get it?" I said, raising my voice, even as a few tears slipped down my cheeks. I held on to the ring. "I don't want to talk. I don't want to try and make this work. You moved too fast. You pushed me into getting engaged when I wasn't ready. All you were thinking about was your own time line . . . your stupid master plan to get married before you started making a bunch of money. You weren't thinking about me and what *I* want. You didn't even *ask*. And you know what, Daniel? I don't want that life. I don't want kids. I don't want a life with *you*."

He stared at me, his brown eyes clouded with confusion and hurt. "Is this about Tyler?" he asked, slowly. "Was I right? Is something happening with you two?"

"No!" I said, maybe a little too sharply, because Daniel just shook his head.

"I knew it," he fumed. "I fucking *knew* it." He stood up and glared at me. "Did you sleep with him last night? Is that why you're doing this now? I pissed you off so you decided to fuck him. Jesus, Amber! What the hell is wrong with you?"

My throat flooded with so many tears, I couldn't speak. I just stared at him through glassy eyes, wishing I had it in me to tell him what had happened. Wishing I could say that he was wrong. I heard my mother's voice inside my head, *He* raped *you, honey,* and I thought about showing Daniel my bruises as proof that while I may have been guilty of leading Tyler on, he was guilty of something far worse. All the things I'd heard at orientation my freshman year at college started to run through my head: *Be careful if you're drinking at a party. Don't go into a room with a guy alone. If someone tries to force you to do something you don't want to do, fight back with everything you have. Gouge him in the eyes with your thumbs. Knee him in the balls. Hurt him before he can hurt you.*

I'd done none of those things, because I'd been with someone I trusted. Someone I never thought might hurt me. And here I was, hurting Daniel, trying to save him from a more excruciating kind of pain.

"I'm sorry," I whispered, and once again, I held out my hand, offering him the ring.

"Yeah," he said. "I bet you are. I hope you're happy with that asshole." Daniel snatched the ring from my palm and shoved it into his front pocket. "I never should have given that to you. You're a fucking cheater."

The disgust in his voice sliced through me. But he was right. I *had* cheated on him the past few weeks, a hundred times over in my head. I'd pictured how it would feel to kiss Tyler, to let him touch me the way I knew he'd always wanted. I'd thought about what it would be like to sleep with him—visualizing our bodies together, imagining how gentle he'd be as his fingers tenderly trailed across my skin. I'd wondered if *he* was the one I should actually be with, the one who already knew and loved me, even after everything we'd both gone through. And now, after last night, I couldn't be with either of them, with anyone. I couldn't imagine feeling safe with anyone else, ever again.

"Do me a favor," Daniel said. "Pretend we never met."

I nodded, knowing there was nothing I could say to make up for what I'd just done. He spun around and charged out of my room, leaving the door open. I sat in the silence staring at the wall, feeling the ghost of the ring on my skin, as though it was still on my finger. I felt like I should break down, but my eyes stayed dry. I wondered if I'd finally reached the limit of my tears—if there was only so much one person could cry in one day.

My parents appeared in my doorway, and then walked through it. "What happened?" my mom asked. "Daniel just ran past us and didn't say a word."

"Did you tell him? Is he going after Tyler?" my dad asked, looking as though if that were true, he might just follow my fiancé. *Ex-fiancé,* I reminded myself, and then I shook my head.

"I didn't tell him. I broke it off. I gave him back the ring."

"Honey, no!" my mom said, coming to sit next to me on the bed. She rested a hand on my leg, and I pulled away from her touch. She sighed. "You didn't even give him a chance? I think he would have understood. He would have supported you."

"It's not that big of a deal." Strangely enough, I meant those words. I didn't feel anything about breaking up with Daniel. All I felt was the giant, aching bruise my body had become. I felt the sudden absence of emotion, the all-encompassing lethargy that, even after so many hours of sleep, wouldn't let me go.

"Sweetie . . ." my mom began, but I held up my hand to stop her.

"Please," I said. "No lectures. That's the last thing I need."

"What *do* you need?" my dad asked, gently.

"She needs to eat something," my mom answered, glancing at the untouched, slightly wilted bowl of fruit on my nightstand.

"Not now, Mom!" I said. "Please." I sunk back down beneath my covers, not answering my father's question. I wasn't sure what, exactly, I needed. I needed for them to leave me alone. I needed more sleep. But mostly, I needed to turn back time, take back my bad decisions, and find a way to pretend I didn't feel like I wanted to die.

Tyler

After I left Mason's house, I took a long shower, hoping the hot water would help release some the tension in my body. But all I could think about was the look on Amber's face when I walked into her bedroom. All I could hear was her screaming for me to get out.

I'm not a rapist, I told myself over and over as I dried off and got dressed. *This is just a misunderstanding.* My head throbbed, so I grabbed some ibuprofen from the cupboard above the stove in my kitchen, and poured myself an enormous tumbler of water and drank it down, knowing that hydration was the only road back from a hangover. Dropping onto the couch, I picked up my phone from the coffee table, where I'd set it when I first got home. I unlocked the screen and clicked on Amber's contact info, assuming that, if I called, she wouldn't pick up, but if I texted, she might at least read what I had to say.

"Amber, please. Talk to me," I wrote. "Whatever happened last night that made you freak out when you saw me, I didn't mean to do. I love you. I would never hurt you. You have to know that. We can work this out." I pressed send, wondering if her parents had pushed her into telling them why she'd screamed at me. Would they believe her if she said what happened was rape? Would they make her report me to the police?

With this thought, at the idea of being arrested and taken to jail, I stood up and began pacing in my small living room, just as I had at Mason's. The anxious energy coursing through my body was a giant, revving engine. I couldn't sit still.

"Fuck it," I muttered, then headed into my bedroom, where I picked up a pair of socks from the dresser and my running shoes from the floor. I put them both on, snatched my keys from the table, and headed out, not caring that going for a run was the absolute last thing I felt up to doing. The only thing I cared about was quieting the fear twisting my mind into knots—trying to escape the mistake I might have made.

As I ran, I went over the last couple of days in my head, thinking about my panic attack the night of the tanker truck accident, the fight with my father, and the way Amber had looked at me on the dance floor. It was the same look Whitney used to give me when she'd come over to my apartment and let me lay her down on my bed—a look that said we both wanted the same thing.

But then I remembered the last time we were together, a couple of days before she went home for the summer. "Damn," she said, once we were done. "You were on a mission. I'm gonna have bruises." She rolled onto her side in order to curl up with me, not seeming to notice my body flinching in response to her touch.

"Sorry," I said. She didn't understand that my physical intensity wasn't a result of how much she, specifically, turned me on or how desperately I wanted her. It was the swell of my anxiety, adrenaline seeking release—the only thing I was desperate for was relief.

"That's okay. I kind of liked it."

The hopeful tone of her voice only amplified my discomfort.

She thought I had something to offer her. I turned so I could sit sideways on the edge of the bed, half-facing her. "I hate to do this," I said, "but I'm pretty wiped. Do you mind . . . ?" I trailed off.

She stared at me with hurt in her dark brown eyes, which she quickly attempted to mask by looking away. "You can't sleep with me here?"

"Sorry," I said again. "I'm sort of used to sleeping alone."

She sat up then, too, yanking the sheet up over her breasts. "Oh," she said. "Okay."

"I'll text you later." I pulled on a pair of boxers, waiting for her to take the hint.

"Want to maybe catch a movie sometime this week?" she asked

instead.

"I wish I could, but with work and it being my mom's birthday and everything . . ." It wasn't my mom's birthday. I was simply willing to say anything, tell any lie, to get her to leave.

"Oh," Whitney said, laying a small, cool hand on my bare back. "Do you ever talk with her about me?"

"No, I don't." My insides itched. I stood up to get away from her hand on my body. "Listen. I like hanging out with you. It's fun. But I can't do a relationship right now, okay? I'm just not there." *Not with you, anyway.*

"But I like you. I mean, like, *really* like you." She dropped her gaze to the floor and then lifted it back to mine. In that moment, she looked so much younger than her twenty years. So vulnerable and insecure. "I just want to know . . . is there any chance . . . ?" She trailed off, waiting for me to fill in the empty spaces of her questions.

"No," I said. "I'm sorry."

"Oh," she said again. Her voice was small. She scooted down to the bottom of the bed to avoid having to climb over me, then quickly got dressed. I did the same.

"So this is done?" she asked as she slipped on her shoes. "Is that what you're saying?"

"Yeah," I said. "It is."

Now, I remembered feeling relieved when I'd finally locked the door behind her, despite the fact that sex with her was the best remedy I'd ever found for the anxiety that coursed through my blood. And then it hit me—I *had* used her. I'd taken advantage of her age and compliant nature and said all the right things, whatever it took to get her to sleep with me. I'd done exactly what I'd watched my father do with women for years. Realizing this made me stop running. I stood in the middle of the sidewalk, breathing hard, terrified to think I was capable of that kind of behavior— that, despite my best efforts, I might still be like the man I sometimes hated. If I'd basically manipulated Whitney into having sex, did that mean I was capable of forcing myself on Amber, too? *No, I thought. No way. I love her too much. I would never do that. We were both drunk, and we both wanted it. I am not my father. Having sex was her decision as much as mine.*

On my way back home, I made those last two sentences my mantra. I repeated them as I showered again and then forced myself to eat a peanut butter sandwich, along with two more big glasses of water. I checked my phone for a message from Amber, but there was only a short text from Mason. "You hear from Amber yet?" it said, but I couldn't bring myself to tell him the truth. If I said that she still wouldn't talk with me, he might take it to mean that she really did have a reason to be scared. That maybe I actually did force myself upon her.

Having sex was her decision as much as mine. This was the only thought I could allow myself to have. Anything else was too horrifying to comprehend.

I watched a little television, trying to get lost in the convoluted plotline of a stupid movie, and finally, around six o'clock, I felt drowsy enough to pull down my room-darkening shades and collapse into bed, still fighting the lingering aftereffects of my hangover. Mason and I weren't back on shift until the next evening, so I planned to get all the sleep I possibly could to make up for the alcohol I'd had to drink. Sleep would let me escape. It would erase, at least temporarily, the look of terror that had taken over Amber's face when I stepped inside her room. It would silence the sound of her screaming, and I could pretend, at least while I slept, that my life wasn't about to fall apart.

I didn't wake up until seven the next morning, when the sound of my phone ringing served as an annoying alarm. *Amber* was the first thought in my head, so I scrambled to answer the call, disappointed when I saw my mom's face on the screen.

"Good morning," I said. My voice was more graveled than usual, so I coughed to clear it.

"Honey," she said, not bothering to greet me. "Did something happen between you and Amber? I went over there last night and Helen wouldn't even let me inside." She paused. "She was *so* upset, Ty. I've never seen her like that. She could barely look at me. When I asked her why, she said I should talk to you."

I froze, not knowing how to tell her everything that happened. I couldn't bring myself to say the words "She thinks I raped her" to my own mother. I couldn't imagine saying them to anyone.

"Tyler," she prompted. "For god's sake, tell me what's going on!"

"I'm not really sure," I said, thinking that this was actually true. Amber hadn't accused me of anything. Not yet. I still didn't know what she was thinking. "We got drunk at the party we went to, and Mason and Gia ended up driving her home."

"What? Why?"

"I overdid it," I said, trying to be as honest as I possibly could. "I passed out."

"Oh, Tyler," my mom said. "What were you thinking?"

"She was drunk, too," I said, realizing that I sounded like a child again, trying to defend myself by saying, "She hit me first!"

"That doesn't matter," my mom said. "You were her ride, and it sounds like you basically deserted her." She sighed. "But why would Helen be so angry? Amber got home okay, right?"

"Yeah," I said. I didn't want to think about any of this. I just wanted to go back to sleep. *Having sex was her decision as much as mine.*

"Did anything else happen? Did you and Amber have a fight?"

"Not exactly," I said, realizing that there was no way I could avoid telling my mom what really happened. If I didn't, I knew Helen eventually would. At least if the story came from me, I had a chance to explain my side.

"Then, what?" she asked, exasperated. "Helen's my best friend, Tyler. If she's angry enough to barely speak to me . . . to not let me inside her house . . . then she must think something awful happened." She waited for me to fill in the blanks.

"I'm not sure," I said, again, another honest statement. "Amber's been flirting with me since she got home from school, Mom. We've been flirting with each other. And at the party . . . well, we got pretty close. When we were dancing, she kissed me."

"She *what?*" my mom exclaimed. "Amber wouldn't do that. She's engaged!"

"I know that. But it's what happened." *That's right,* I told myself. *Amber started this. I only followed through on what she made it clear she wanted.* I took a deep breath, and then spoke again. "We ended up having sex. And now I think Amber regrets it or something. I don't know, for sure."

"Why don't you know?" my mom asked, dragging out the words.

"Because I went straight over there when I left the party the next morning to make sure she was okay. I was worried when I woke up and she wasn't there. But when I tried to talk with her, she basically kicked me out. I have no idea what she told her parents." *There,* I thought. *I'm not lying. Every bit of what I just said is true.*

"Well, that's just ridiculous," my mom said. "You need to go back over there and straighten things out."

"I'm not sure that's the best idea."

"If it was just between you and her, I would agree with that, honey. But she obviously told her parents something that made Helen angry enough to turn me away. I can't possibly think what could be so bad . . ." She trailed off, and I waited for her to draw her own conclusions so I wouldn't have to say the words myself. "Oh no," she finally said. "Do you think she told them that she didn't *want* to have sex with you? That you *forced* her?"

And there was Amber's voice again, inside my head: *Tyler, wait!* I closed my eyes and suddenly flashed back to the moment when she put her hands on my chest and attempted to push me off of her. The way she started to cry. *Fuck.* I rolled onto my back, throwing my one free arm over my forehead. "It crossed my mind," I said to my mother. "But you know I would never—"

"Of *course* you wouldn't!" my mom said, cutting me off. "That's just insane. Helen has to know that. Tom, too. I mean, good lord. You're not a rapist. You're a paramedic. You *save* people's lives."

I nodded, not sure, exactly, what one thing had to do with the other, but still desperate to allow my mother's words to make me feel better. She was right. I wasn't a bad person. Yes, I'd treated Whitney poorly, but I wasn't the kind of man who stalked women, then hid in the bushes, waiting for the right opportunity to attack. I only did what millions of other guys my age are known to do—I got drunk with a girl at a party, and we ended up having sex. I didn't tie Amber up or hold a knife to her throat. Even if she regretted it, an accusation of force would be almost impossible to prove. Everyone saw how she was dressed, how we were drinking and kissing and dancing. They saw us go inside the house, holding hands.

"Have you talked with your dad?" my mom asked.

"No," I said. "Why?"

"Because it's possible he could give you some advice here," my mom said, with more than a touch of bitterness. "You know he beat a sexual harassment suit right after we got divorced."

"What?" I said, sitting up and resting against the wall. My room smelled stale, of sweat and sleep. The curtain was edged in a bright square of sunlight. Birds chirped noisily, right outside my window. "No, I didn't know that. What happened?"

My mom exhaled, loudly. "A woman who worked with him claimed that he promised that if she slept with him, he would use his friendship with their captain to get her off of night shifts so she could spend more time with her kids. There was an investigation, but because he wasn't her superior and it was shown that she willingly initiated meeting with him multiple times over a course of several months, he was cleared."

"Wow," I said, shaking my head. "I can't believe he never told me."

"I think it scared him," my mom explained. "And since then, you know he's slept with a disgusting number of women, but I'm pretty certain none of them have been from work."

I thought about how, over the last few years, since I started my job, my dad had warned me about doing just that. "Don't shit where you eat, Son," he'd say. "Don't dip your pen in the department ink." Now, the frequency with which he'd said it made sense.

"I don't want him to know about this," I said, trying not to sound like I was begging. "Okay, Mom? He'll just make it worse." I could already hear how my father would berate me for getting stuck in a situation like this. For finally have the courage to make a move on Amber, but then royally fucking it up. It would only add fuel to what he'd said about me. It would only prove his point.

"All right," she said, reluctantly. "But you need to work things out with Amber. And I'll try to talk with Helen again."

"No!" I said, feeling panicked at the idea of her hearing details from Helen that I couldn't control. "Let me handle this, please."

"I'm sorry, Tyler, but I can't stand the idea of my best friend thinking you would be capable of hurting her daughter. I don't work until five tonight, so I'm going back over there this morning. You can come with me or not. It's up to you."

I felt torn. Part of me was worried that if I showed up at her house again unannounced, Amber would freak out. But another part of me reasoned that maybe all she had needed, like me, was a good night's sleep to put the events of the party in proper perspective. Maybe she had come to terms with the fact that she was just as liable for what had happened.

It was this last thought that had me meet my mom at the Bryants' house a few hours later. I'd showered and eaten a good breakfast, grateful that my hangover was gone and, for the most part, my head felt clear. Both Helen's and Tom's cars were in their driveway; I knew Helen's job at the elementary school gave her the summer off, but Tom was typically so busy meeting with clients, he rarely worked from home. The fact that he was here made me uneasy. An uncomfortable lump formed in my gut.

"It'll be fine," my mom said, running her hand down the side of my arm. "We'll work it out." She wore jeans and a light blue top that I had given her for Mother's Day.

I gave her a weak smile, nodding my head once as we made

our way to the front steps, which felt a little odd—too formal. I was so accustomed to entering on the side of the house, like family, through the kitchen. I raised my hand and rapped on the door three times, lightly.

When it swung open, Tom stood in front of us, his hand still on the knob. He glared at me with a look so hateful, I dropped my eyes to the ground. "You have some balls showing back up here," he said, practically growling the words.

"Tom, please," my mom said, reaching out her hand to try to touch his arm, but he jerked out of her reach.

"Please what, Liz?" he said, forcefully. "Ask your son to come into my house for a sit-down? He *raped* my daughter. He *raped* her. And now he's standing on my fucking front porch, acting like nothing's wrong."

"That's not what happened," I said, glancing around to see if any of the neighbors were watching from their windows. "You have to believe me—"

"No, Tyler. I don't." Tom's face was red and his blue eyes were dark. I'd never seen him like this. "I believe my daughter. I believe you got her drunk and you forced yourself on her. And now she won't leave her bedroom. She won't eat. She's in more pain than I've ever seen before and it's *your* fault." He paused, breathing hard, looking like he wanted nothing more than to punch me. "So forgive me if I don't invite you inside. Just be glad I'm not holding a gun."

"Hold on, Tom!" my mom said. "This is crazy. You know Tyler. You know he'd never—"

"The only thing I know is what I saw," Tom said. "I saw how frightened Amber was of him when he was in her room yesterday. She was *terrified,* Liz. I've never seen anyone so scared in my entire life. I know he's your son and you'd do anything to protect him—"

"I don't need to protect him because he didn't do anything wrong!" my mom said, throwing her arms up in the air, then letting them drop back down to her sides. "Amber got drunk! She kissed him and led him to believe she wanted to have sex with him, even though she's engaged to someone else! So who, exactly, is in the wrong here?" My mom was breathing hard, too. Her previously calm demeanor had vanished. "Amber cheated on Daniel and now she's just looking for someone to blame!"

"Shut up, Liz!" Helen appeared out of nowhere next to her husband, as though she'd been hiding behind the door, listening. Her red hair was a tangled mess and her skin was pale beneath her freckles. She crossed her arms over her chest and shot a look full of daggers at both my mother and me. "Just shut the hell up! My daughter is upstairs, still shaking after what your son did to her. I always told you if you didn't get him into counseling he'd end up just like his father, and now he has! He *raped* my daughter! He took advantage of her trust and now she can't stop crying. She'll never be the same." Tears rolled down Helen's cheeks as she spoke, and she angrily brushed them away. She looked at me. "How could you do this, Tyler? Tell me, please. *How?*"

"I didn't mean to hurt her," I stammered, hating the thought that Helen believed I was anything like my father. That she had told my mother I might turn out just like him. "I just . . . I thought . . . we've been flirting so much since she's been home . . ."

"Honey, you don't need to say another word," my mom said, but she was too late. Tom flung the door open and it crashed against the wall with a loud thud. He curled his fingers into fists.

"Don't you dare blame Amber for what you did!" he said. His words dripped with disgust. "Don't you fucking *dare!*"

I stumbled backward, down the steps, holding on to the railing so I wouldn't fall. Amber had told her parents that I raped her, and they believed her. She could go to the police. I could be arrested, prosecuted, and put in jail. I gave Tom an imploring look. "Please, you don't understand. It was a mistake. She wanted it, too. She kissed me. She let me take her up to the bedroom . . ."

"She told you to stop!" Tom roared, and before I knew it was coming, he flew toward me, down the steps, his right arm pulled back. I thought about ducking, about turning around and running to my car. But then it was too late. His fist made hard and fast contact with my cheekbone, sending a shock wave of pain through the side of my face. The next thing I knew, I fell backward, hit the ground, and the world around me went black.

Amber

I stayed in bed for days after the party. I didn't go to work, I didn't eat. I didn't leave my room except to shower, thinking that if I sloughed off enough skin, I might be able to erase the damage my best friend had done.

I'm sick, I told myself. *I feel like I have a fever.* That's what it was. A sickness. Nothing else. My immune system attempting to incinerate the images flashing through my mind. If I just hid beneath the covers long enough, I might wake up in a day, a week, or a month, fully cured. I might be able to believe the night never happened.

I kept my eyes closed as much as possible, constantly trying to force myself to sleep. I took more Benadryl, relishing the black, dreamless oblivion the tiny pink pills brought about. But when I awoke, when I kicked my legs, rising to the surface of that fuzzy, self-induced sea of escape, all that waited for me was the weight of Tyler pressing down on my bones. All I felt was his strong hands, gripping, his knees forcing my thighs to open, the pain shooting through my pelvis like a flesh-tearing bullet, one that was now lodged inside my gut.

Why hadn't I screamed? Why didn't I hit and claw and scratch at him until he was forced to stop? Instead, I froze, I gave up and gave in, and let it happen. If I had fought the way I should have, if I had actually said *NO,* if I had shrieked it in his ear over and over again, he might have heard me. He might have stopped. The Tyler I knew *would* have stopped. I started to wonder if I had imagined saying anything to him at all. I'd been so drunk, maybe I only *thought* I'd asked him to wait? Maybe the only protestations I'd made were inside my head.

My parents hovered around me the same way they had when I was a teenager, trying to get me to talk, trying to force bits of food into my mouth. "I made you baked chicken and brown rice," my mother said a few days after Liz and Tyler had showed up. It was close to noon, and my dad was at work. "No butter, just a little salt and pepper, a drizzle of olive oil. The way you made it for us."

"I'm not hungry," I said. This was true. I knew my stomach was empty, that I needed the sustenance, but I couldn't fathom putting anything other than water in my body. I felt certain if I did, I'd throw it right back up.

"Honey, please," my mom said. I could hear the desperation in her voice.

"Maybe later," I replied, which was the same answer I used to give her whenever she tried to get me to eat in high school. I lay in my bed in a ball, my knees brought up as close as possible to my chest. If I closed my eyes tight enough, maybe the memories couldn't find me. If I made myself small enough, maybe I could just disappear.

"Your dad and I are worried," she said, as she set the plate she carried onto my nightstand. "You need to talk to someone."

"No."

"We understand you don't want to—"

"I'm not doing it, Mom," I said, cutting her off. "So you can stop right now." I didn't tell her I was too afraid to talk to the police. I couldn't stand the idea of being told that I was wrong, that my worst fears would only be confirmed—that this was my fault as much as his, and I was just a drunk, stupid girl who decided too late that she'd made a mistake.

My mom sat down on the edge of my bed, placing a gentle hand on my hip. "You can't pretend this didn't happen, Amber. Pushing it down is just going to make it worse. Tyler needs to be held accountable."

"What about me?" I straightened my legs and rolled over onto my back, looking at my mother's angst-ridden face. She looked as tired as I felt, and her eyes were swollen, too. "Aren't I accountable, too?" She opened her mouth, like she was about to rebut what I'd said, but I held up my hand to stop her. "No, Mom. I'm serious. I totally led him on. I gave him every sign that I wanted to sleep with him. It's not just his fault."

"I know you think that's true, honey, but you're wrong. Even if you said yes at first, what matters . . . what makes what he did to you so wrong . . . is that you also told him to stop."

I considered her words; the guilt I might feel about leading Tyler to believe that I wanted to have sex with him—hell, even believing, temporarily, in my drunken state, that I wanted it, too—didn't make what he did to me any less heinous. It didn't make it any less of a betrayal. I racked my brain, trying to remember the moment that the word "no" left my mouth, and couldn't come up with it.

When I didn't say anything, my mother tried another approach. "What about a counselor?" she asked. "Someone who knows how to help with issues like this? I can make some calls—"

"Mom! Stop it, please. I'll be fine. I just need to rest." I shifted so I was on my side again, facing away from her. I knew she was only trying to help, but there was nothing she could do. Nothing anyone could say to take away the lightning bolt of pain in my chest every time I took a breath.

"You can't stay in bed forever," she said, quietly.

"Watch me," I said, and a moment later, she stood up and left the room.

But hiding in my room fixed nothing. As the hours and days passed, I grew antsy, unable to sleep as much as I wanted, and the antihistamines I took began to jack me up instead of knock me out. I finally forced myself to go back to work ten days after the party. Most of my bruises had faded by then, and my body didn't ache as much as it had the first week. Still, I dressed in full-length black leggings and a long-sleeved, moisture-wicking shirt, not wanting to risk my boss or any of my clients seeing the ghostly yellow smudges of Tyler's fingers on my skin.

I got to the gym early, around five thirty, thinking that I might be able to get in a quick workout of my own before my first client came in. I still wasn't eating any solid food—the thought of chewing anything made me nauseous—but I'd managed to sip down half of a protein shake my dad made for me in the kitchen before I left, the same kind of shake he'd been bringing to my room for several days.

"You sure you feel up to this?" he asked, looking at me with an equal mix of fear and sorrow in his blue eyes. He was up earlier than usual, too, unable to sleep, he said—too many thoughts spinning in his head. He was still in his pajamas.

I bobbed my head and glanced at his right hand. His knuckles weren't swollen anymore, but his skin held hints of black and blue. "Do they hurt?" I asked.

He flexed his fingers, and then curled them back into a fist. "Nah," he said. "And it would be worth it, even if they did."

I managed a small smile, and then hugged him. "I love you, Pops."

"Love you, too, baby girl," he said, and I knew he was fighting back tears.

Now, as I exited the locker room and went out onto the gym floor, I took several deep breaths, in and out, trying to steady my pulse. I felt shaky and a little weak, like I was recovering from the flu. *That's all it was,* I told myself again. *An illness. And now you're going to get over it by focusing on what you do best.*

I stepped onto the elliptical machine and started it up, setting a sixty-minute program for interval mountain climbing. My heartbeat began to pulse inside my head, and little by little, some of the tension inside me relaxed, which just confirmed that coming back to work was the right thing for me to do. I needed to bathe my brain in slippery gushes of serotonin. I needed to pretend that nothing had changed. I was still Amber, the girl who would soon sit for the certification test that would be the liftoff point for her career. I'd been foolish to get involved with Daniel, stupid to get sucked in by the false security of romance. I needed to focus on me and what I wanted for my life. Nothing else mattered. Not even what Tyler had done.

A few hours later, I was just finishing up my session with Doris when the front desk announced over the loudspeaker that I had a visitor. I felt myself go pale as I considered who it might be. *Would Tyler really come here? After what happened at my house with my dad, would he take that risk?*

"You all right, honey?" Doris asked with concern. She was lying on her back on one of the gym mats, going through a series of cooldown stretches I'd taught her. "Are you feeling sick again?"

"A little," I said, thinking this would explain why I'd broken out in a cold sweat. I gently helped pull her to a sitting position.

"Maybe you came back too soon," she said, grabbing a white towel from the floor and patting her face with it.

"Maybe." I kept my eyes on the doorway that led to the reception area, posed to sprint into the ladies' locker room if Tyler appeared. *He wouldn't follow me in there, would he?* I wondered, and then remembered that I had no idea what Tyler was capable of. What sins he would be willing to commit.

I stood up and held out my left hand, encouraging Doris to do the same. "Where's your ring?" she asked as she gripped my fingers with her knobbed joints and creped, tissue-paper-like skin. I carefully assisted her up to her feet.

I didn't answer right away, because I hadn't thought about what to tell people about me and Daniel. I didn't have a lie ready. "We broke up," I said, deciding that I should keep to the simple truth. No one needed to know the details.

"Anything to do with that handsome best friend of yours?" Doris raised her white brows and gave me a knowing look.

"No," I said, practically choking on the word. Tears sprang to my eyes and I had to fight hard to keep them from falling.

"Oh, honey, I'm sorry. I didn't mean to upset you."

"It's fine," I said. But it wasn't. Nothing would ever be fine again.

Doris put her hand on my forearm and squeezed. "It'll take some time to heal, but I promise, you will get over it. You're a strong young woman. You have your whole life ahead of you."

"Thank you," I said, forcing a smile. I glanced at the clock, and saw that I wouldn't have another client until noon, so that left me no excuse but to head up front and see who was waiting for me. "I'll see you Friday?" I asked Doris, and she nodded, then headed across the floor.

Just then, another gym employee, Tucker, walked by me. "Hey, Tuck," I said. "Can you do me a favor?"

"Sure," he said. He was in his early thirties, and his wife worked at the gym as a trainer, too. They both competed as professional bodybuilders, and Tuck had recently reached a national level.

"Will you go look up front and tell me if a tall blond guy is standing there?" *Please God, don't let it be him.*

"Everything okay?" he asked.

"Oh yeah," I said. "Just someone I really don't want to see right now." *Or ever, actually.* I couldn't believe I was thinking these things about Tyler. I'd thought we'd be friends forever. I'd thought he'd be the one person outside of my parents who I could always trust. Now, I worried if I saw him, I'd start screaming the way I did when he walked into my bedroom.

"Gotcha," Tuck said, and then he made his way toward the entrance to the building. He was back less than a minute later. "No blond guy. Just a long-legged, pretty girl sitting on the bench, looking at her phone."

"Thanks," I said, and felt a shiver of relief.

"No problem. If that guy you don't want to see shows up, you just let me know, and I'll boot his ass out."

I managed a smile, and then wove my way through the equipment toward the reception area. The girl's head was down, intent on whatever she was looking at on her phone, and the sheet of her blond long hair covered her face. But when she looked up, I knew exactly who it was.

"Amber!" Heather exclaimed as she shoved her phone in her purse and leapt to her feet. She trotted over to me and we hugged.

"What are you doing here?" I asked, shocked to see my childhood friend standing in front of me. We had emailed a little after she moved to California, but as time went on, our communication lessened, until it ceased altogether.

"Seeing family," she said. "My grandparents moved back here in January, but this is the first time I've been able to visit." She pulled back and looked me over. I did the same to her, not surprised to see that she hadn't changed much. She was still several inches taller than me, ballerina thin, and the angles of her bone structure still made it impossible to look anywhere but her sky blue eyes. She wore a simple white sundress and tan, thin-strapped sandals. Her skin was golden, and her eyelashes were unnaturally long and black.

"Are those real?" I asked, before I could stop myself.

"My lashes or my tits?" she asked, and I laughed, something I hadn't done since the night of the party. I looked at her chest, and noticed that her breasts did seem larger than I remembered. For a dancer, a flat chest was the norm—even the goal.

"Well," I said, "now that you mention it . . ."

"Totally got my boobs done!" she said, laughing, too, seemingly oblivious to the stares of the receptionist and the few other gym goers in the immediate area. "And the lashes are extensions. I'm only, like, ninety-eight percent organic."

I laughed again, thrilled with the sense of normalcy it gave me. I'd done enough crying over the past ten days to last me a lifetime. "So you're visiting your grandparents," I said, "but how did you find me?"

"I stopped by your parents' place and your mom told me where you're working." Heather's eyes roamed to the handsome, well-muscled young receptionist at the desk, then came back to me. "Nice décor. I can see why you like it."

"Are you still in San Francisco? Are you still dancing?"

"Whoa!" Heather said. "Too many questions and not enough time. When are you off? Can we get a drink?"

My stomach rebelled at the idea of imbibing any alcohol, but I nodded. On top of working, spending some time with Heather while she was here would be an excellent distraction. A way to help me get back on track. "I'm off around three," I told her.

"Should we get dinner, too?" Heather asked.

"Sure," I said, knowing I still wouldn't be able to eat anything. I'd have to rely on the tricks I'd used as a teenager, cutting up and moving my food around the plate to make it look like some of it was gone.

"Yay!" Heather squealed and hugged me again. "It's so good to see you. I can't wait to catch up!"

"Me, too," I said, wondering how I would manage to make small talk without mentioning Tyler. I hoped Heather wouldn't ask about him; maybe if I didn't say his name, she wouldn't, either. I'd fill her head with stories about school and Daniel, about the engagement and our recent breakup, knowing she'd get sucked right into the drama of all that. I wouldn't say anything about the party on the Fourth of July. I wouldn't tell her that since that night, my insides had felt like a jumbled mass of broken glass.

"Where should we go?" Heather asked. "I want tapas and fancy cocktails!"

"Poppe's on Lakeway is good for that kind of thing," I said. "Or so I've heard." Tyler was the one, actually, who'd told me about that particular bar. He said I couldn't leave Bellingham without trying their steamed mussels or fish tacos.

"Perfect!" Heather said. "Pick you up at your house around eight?"

I nodded. "See you then!" I said, trying to imitate her upbeat, lighthearted tone. *Fake it till you make it,* I heard my own voice saying, the same cheesy line I'd feed my clients when they told me they couldn't finish their workouts. "Pretend that you can," I'd urge them. "Pretend it until it's actually true."

I waved to Heather as she headed out to the parking lot, thinking that maybe that was what my life would consist of from now on—playing pretend, a carefully orchestrated performance, a contrived but lovely outside shell covering up the nightmare of fear and dysfunction underneath. Maybe my mother was wrong and I *could* find a way to push down what had happened. If I asked my clients to fake it, to push past the limits of what they thought they had the capacity to do, then I should be able to do the same thing.

That was what I told myself later that night as I stood in the bathroom, getting ready to meet Heather. Since the ends of my hair were still uneven from how I'd chopped it off, I pinned it up, leaving a few pieces loose to frame my face. I put on more makeup than usual: foundation, blush, a dark slash of red lipstick, black cat-eye liner, and lots of mascara. Turning my head from side to side, pursing my lips as I stared at my reflection, I was relieved to not look like myself. The girl in the mirror was someone else entirely—a girl encased in armor thick enough to repel any memory, strong enough to protect her from further attack. She was the only one I could trust.

Before I went back to my room to get dressed, I hopped on the scale, unable to deny the rush of pleasure I felt in seeing that the number had gone down. Ten days without solid food had been long enough for me to start feeling a familiar and airy, elevated sense of strength—the ability to deny my body's primal, basic need for nourishment was a high better than any drug I could take. I told myself that my willpower had always been forged out of steel; the rest of me could be, too.

"Why don't you girls just hang out here?" my mom suggested when I walked into the kitchen, where she and my dad were sitting at the table, sipping glasses of white wine. Their dirty dinner plates were on the counter, and I had to look away before the sight of the gristly, gnawed-upon chicken bones made me sick.

"Heather wants to go out," I said, as I poured myself a glass of water from the Brita pitcher in the fridge. "I do, too." That was what I was telling myself, anyway.

"We're not sure it's a good idea," my dad said. He set his hands flat on the table, fingers widespread, as though he were bracing himself for an argument. "You've been through a lot, and you just started back to work."

"Which was good for me, by the way," I said. I chugged down

the entire contents of the glass, my stomach temporarily sated. "The sooner I get back to normal, the better."

My mom shook her head. "You're pushing yourself too hard, Amber. You need—"

I banged the now-empty glass I held on to the counter, cutting her off, giving them a defiant look. "You don't get to decide what I need." I wished I'd never told them what happened at the party. I should have kept my mouth shut. The more people who know a secret, the harder it is to keep.

"You're not thinking straight," my dad said, his voice firm. "We just want to help you do the right thing."

"You don't get to decide that, either." I heard a quick honk from outside, and I peeked out the kitchen window to see Heather waving at me from her white rental car, which she'd parked in the driveway. "See you later," I said, grabbing my purse from the counter. My mom started to say something else, but I cut her off by slamming the back door.

Ten minutes later, Heather and I were seated in a booth at the small hotel bar I'd told her about earlier. The place wasn't crowded yet, and the only music playing was some kind of jazz, low in the background, so we didn't need shout in order to be heard.

"Okay," she said, taking a sip of the lemon drop cocktail our server had just delivered. "Tell me everything. Work, school, men. In that order."

I smiled, and gave her the shorthand version of my history over the past nine years, since I'd seen her last, leaving out any mention of Tyler and the time I'd spent in the hospital. The only place I went into detail was my relationship with Daniel, telling her how we had dated, gotten engaged, and then, broke up.

"Oh my god," she said. "Why? He sounds so perfect." She paused, holding up her index finger. "Wait. Don't tell me. There has to be someone else. For you, or him?"

The smile on my face froze, and I shook my head. "Neither."

"Seriously? You just ended things with a hot, sweet guy who's going to be a doctor?"

"Yep," I said, reflexively taking a sip of the pomegranate martini I'd ordered when Heather had asked for her drink. I'd asked for it for appearances' sake, just to have something to do with my hands, but now, the alcohol warmed my belly and eased the tension in my muscles.

"That's nuts," Heather said. "I'd kill for a guy like that."

"He's living in Seattle," I said. "I'll give you his number. Go for it." I couldn't believe the words as they came out of my mouth; they were something I never would have said before.

"Girl, please," Heather said with a grin. "No way I'm settling for sloppy seconds. If you don't want him, he can't be all that great."

"He is, actually," I said, swallowing down a bit more of my drink. *I'll just have this one cocktail,* I thought. *I won't do any shots. Definitely no tequila.* "But I'm not ready to settle down yet. I'm too young. I want to focus on me."

"I get that," Heather said. She took a handful of the trail mix the server had set before us when we got there and popped it in her mouth. After she had chewed, she spoke again. "That's kind of what I told my parents when I said I wasn't going to college. My dad totally freaked. He had some weird idea in his head that I might follow in his footsteps and become an English professor, too. Which was crazy, because my grades begged to differ with *that* fantasy."

"Why didn't you want to go to college?" I asked, enjoying the there-but-not-there feeling the martini was giving me, especially on an empty stomach. I couldn't believe I was just sitting here like any other twenty-something girl, having drinks and conversation with a friend. I wondered what hidden, dark circumstances the lives of the people around us might hold. Maybe all of us were walking around, pretending to be normal, when inside, our worlds were falling apart.

"Mostly because I was focused on being a dancer for so long. I thought I'd go to New York and join some prestigious ballet company and make a name for myself. And then my knee gave out and that dream was over, so I started teaching at a private dance school in Berkeley. I love it. It's all I want to do, and even though I'm totally supporting myself, my parents are all over me to get a degree 'just in case.' "

"In case of what?" I asked. "If dance classes are outlawed or something?"

"Exactly!" Heather said. "See, *you* get it. The studio owner already is grooming me to take over for her when she retires, so I'm saving as much as I can, and working on a business plan to present to the bank so I can get a loan. I researched how to do it on the Internet. I don't need a degree."

"No," I said. "You don't." I paused, and allowed myself to eat three peanuts from the bowl of trail mix, just for appearances' sake, chewing each of them slowly, happy that I didn't have to fight the urge to throw them back up. Heather and I had been so busy talking, neither of us had mentioned ordering an actual meal, which was fine with me. It would be easier not to.

Just then, our server appeared again, as though my thoughts of food had summoned her. She held a tray with two more drinks in hand.

"We didn't order those," I said, looking at Heather and then raising a single eyebrow. "Did we?" I wasn't drunk, but I felt tipsy enough that I figured I should ask, just to be sure.

"No," the server said as she set the cocktails in front of us. "They're courtesy of the gentlemen sitting at the end of the bar." She nodded in that general direction, and the men sitting there lifted their pints of beer and smiled. They were older, in their mid-to late thirties, probably—suit-and-tie types who were likely married and looked like the sort to hit on younger women for sport.

"Awesome," Heather said, quickly finishing her first drink so the server could take the empty away. "Can I get the fish tacos, too, please?" The server made a note on the pad she carried and then asked me if I wanted something to eat, too.

"No, thanks," I said, and so she left, heading toward the kitchen. "I don't know if we should accept those," I went on, looking at Heather. It felt wrong, somehow, letting these strange men pay for our drinks, like we were giving them the right to the possibility of more than that.

"It's just drinks," Heather said, lifting the second cocktail up and smiling at the men, too. "It doesn't mean anything else."

I nodded, but I didn't know how to tell her how wrong she was. That it's possible for a man to interpret a woman's initial permission as license to steamroll over any boundary she might set after that. That once a woman says yes, it's possible a man might not give a shit when she changes her mind. He might tear off her clothes; he might bruise her body and send splinters of blistering fear into her soul. He might do this even if he's someone she knows, someone she loves and trusts. And then she might end up in a bar with a fake smile plastered on her face, trying to act like none of it mattered, trying to believe, despite the agony deep down inside her bones, that she's over what he did, desperate to pretend she's safe.

Tyler

If I'd had a choice in the matter, I wouldn't have gone to work after Tom punched me. The last thing I felt like doing was showing up for my shift, but sitting around in my apartment, staring at the walls while I replayed the events at the party over and over again in my head, wouldn't do me any good. I told myself that the distraction of work would help, that keeping busy was the best thing for me.

And so, after having rested on my mother's couch for a few hours with an ice pack on my face, I showed up at the station house with a burgeoning black and blue right eye. "Whoa," Captain Duncan said when I walked into the locker room. "I'd hate to see the other guy."

"Got into a brawl with a weight machine at the gym," I lied, forcing a smile. "It sprang loose and knocked me in the face."

My captain nodded, and looked as though he believed me. I couldn't imagine telling him what really happened. Mason, however, was a different story. I knew there was no way I could keep the truth from him—that after Tom had hit me, I'd lain on the grass for less than a minute, only briefly unconscious, dazed by my skull bouncing on the hard ground when I fell backward off the steps. I came to quickly, only to find my mother kneeling next to me, threatening to call the police.

"No, Mom. Don't," I said, feeling a bit dizzy as I sat up. My eye ached, and I touched it carefully, feeling around the socket to make sure I wasn't bleeding and that no bones had shattered. It hurt, but everything seemed intact. *Tom just* punched *me.* I couldn't believe it. Even my own father, with all his flaws, had never been physically violent with me.

"He just assaulted you!" my mom said, helping me get to my feet. She shot both Tom and Helen a furious look, which they met with their own.

"Mom," I said, grabbing her hand. "Stop. Let's just go." Having the police there would only have made the situation worse. They'd demand to know what incited Tom to hit me, and I couldn't handle the idea of being accused of rape, put in handcuffs, and driven off in the back of a squad car. I couldn't believe any of this was happening, at all.

"Don't come back here again," Tom said, cradling his right hand to his broad chest. "Either of you. You're not welcome." He was breathing hard, and winced when he tried to straighten his fingers. He might have broken them; from the redness of his skin, I could already see that his knuckles would bruise. My first instinct was to offer to take a look, but I knew he wouldn't let me.

I glanced up to the second story and saw the white, gauzy curtain in Amber's room shift. Her window was open, so I suspected she'd been listening in. She was probably happy her father had hit me. It took everything in me not to shove my way inside the house, run up the stairs, and beg her to talk to me.

"You should be ashamed of yourself," Helen said, tearfully. Her arms were crossed tightly over her chest, her hands running up and down her biceps. "What kind of monster *are* you?"

"It's Amber who should be ashamed," my mom said. "Do you know what a false accusation like this could do to my son?"

"Mom!" I said, yanking her arm as I took a step toward the street. "Enough. This was a bad idea." I could feel the blood pounding around my eye, the skin starting to stretch as it swelled. I knew I'd need to get ice on it as soon as I could. I'd gone there to find out what Amber's state of mind was—what she had told her parents—and now I knew. She was claiming that I'd raped her. At that point, no matter how much I wanted to prove her wrong—to fix things—there was nothing more I could do.

Now, after talking with my captain, I threw my bag into my locker, and then made my way into the garage, where I found Mason already double-checking the inventory on our rig. "Hey," I said, climbing into the back of the ambulance to join him.

He looked up, and his eyes went wide when he saw my face. But before he could say anything, I told him what had happened, keeping my voice low so no one else might hear. He listened, staying silent for what seemed a long moment after I was done.

"This is one fucked-up situation," he finally said.

"Yeah, it is." I didn't know what else to say. That single sentence pretty much summed things up.

"What're you gonna do?"

I shrugged. "I don't know if there's anything I *can* do. She won't talk to me."

"I don't think you should worry about that," he said. He sat back against the stainless-steel cabinets that lined the back of the rig and stared at me. "What should worry you is who she *is* going to talk to. Like the police."

I nodded, unable to speak, for fear I might lose my shit right then and there. An intense pressure expanded inside my chest—the kind of pressure I couldn't outrun. But I couldn't let what had happened the night of the tanker truck accident happen again. I couldn't let my partner see how messed up I really was.

"Maybe you should call a lawyer," Mason said, and even though we were friends, I felt like he was judging me, that it was possible he thought Amber's version of what happened was true.

"I'll think about it," I said, not wanting to discuss the issue further. I'd come to work in order to work, not sort out my personal life. "Thanks."

He bobbed his head, and we managed to make it through our shift without bringing the subject up again. We made it through the next few weeks, actually, during which time I didn't hear from Amber or her parents, and no police showed up to cart me off to jail. I told myself that maybe she'd backtracked. Maybe she'd realized that she'd contributed to what happened between us just as much as I had. But every time I had this thought, a loud voice clanged inside my head: *She told you to stop. You had sex with her anyway.* And then I felt ill, anxiety oozing through me, melting away any rationalizations in its path. It felt like a virus infecting my body's defense systems, a plague intent on taking me down.

I did what I could to fight it. As July progressed, I stuck to a strict schedule—I worked at night and slept at least eight hours during the day. I went for a five-mile run before each shift, trying to drain the constant tension that gripped me. I didn't speak with my father, and he made no effort to reach out to me. Even though it was clear that he hadn't talked to my captain about what happened the night of the tanker truck accident, I couldn't forgive him for threatening that he would. The things he'd said about me and Amber that afternoon in my apartment were still on repeat in my head. I kept my conversations with my mom as brief as possible, but she often called me, crying about the loss of her friendship with Helen.

"She won't even *look* at me if we both happen to be in our front yards," she told me. "She's acting like I don't exist."

I had to repress a sigh every time she complained, knowing that it was just her nature to elevate her suffering above everyone else's. She'd never admit it, but she was like my father that way. I'd often thought it was one of the deeper reasons their marriage didn't work.

"Have you seen Amber at all?" I asked my mother toward the end of the month. I wanted to know how she was doing, if she and Daniel were still engaged. I wanted to know if she would ever find it in her heart to talk to me again. I felt her absence in my life like a gaping wound. I hated not knowing if she was okay, hated thinking that I might have hurt her.

"A few times," my mom said. "She looks so different with her hair short." She paused. "It looks like she's lost weight."

When Amber was upset, she restricted her food. She had stopped eating entirely at the end of her freshman year in high school, which was what ultimately led to her heart attack and hospitalization seven months later. I remembered sitting with her at the Bryants' dinner table, wanting to grab a spoon, force bites of buttery mashed potatoes between her lips, and then cover her mouth with my hand until she swallowed. At the time, I didn't understand why she wouldn't eat. I didn't understand that anorexia wasn't so much a matter of food as it was a desperate need to feel in control.

Now, I thought about texting or calling Amber daily. I felt sure if we could just talk, we'd find a way to resolve things and we could go back to how we used to be. Despite Mason's suggestion, I didn't talk with a lawyer, worried that, if I did, I might hear something about my circumstances that would ramp up my anxiety levels higher than they already were. There were times when my heart would race and I'd check my blood pressure in the back of the rig, shocked at the elevated numbers I saw. If it were anyone else, any one of the victims I helped treat in the field, I would tell them they needed immediate medical help—that sustaining a systolic pressure over 130 and a diastolic of 100 would eventually do irreparable damage to their heart.

This was the thought inside my head one a sunny afternoon in August when Mason and I pulled up to the curb of a building where a teenage girl apparently had swallowed an unknown amount of her mother's narcotics. I'd gone for my daily before-shift run, but still, I couldn't ignore the ache in my chest or the way my pulse stuttered every time I took a breath. I'd promised Mason I'd get a handle on it, but the more I tried to do just that, the deeper it seemed to dig its sharp talons into my brain, more determined than ever to stay.

"Hey," I said, as we bounded up the stairs to the third floor. "Want to grab a beer tomorrow? Or lunch?" In the past, it wouldn't be uncommon for Mason and me to hang out together on our day off. But since the incident with Amber, my relationship with my partner had shifted. We still got our jobs done, but that was all. He no longer invited me over for dinner with Gia and the baby, we didn't shoot the shit about other coworkers or our boss—all we talked about was work. I missed the easy camaraderie we'd always shared, and part of me regretted telling him anything about what hadhappened at the party. Outside of Amber, I didn't have many close friends, so I was anxious to find a way to reconnect with Mason. I couldn't lose them both.

"Can't," he said, not looking back at me as we approached the apartment door. "Sorry." He didn't give an explanation—he didn't have to. A hot rush of shame washed over me. I knew that Mason, a man I looked up to and respected, believed that what Amber accused me of might be true.

"Any bets on whether the mother has a prescription for the meds?" Mason asked, changing the subject.

"I'd rather not think about it," I said. Too many times we'd encountered parents who left medications—legitimately prescribed or not—in the easy reach of a child. And too many times this ended in a deadly overdose.

Ignoring the curious stares of the neighbors who peeked out of their doors and windows in response to the siren, Mason pounded on the door of the address we'd been given, and a woman opened it, standing before us clad only in a white T-shirt that barely reached the middle of her thighs. Her skinny body and pockmarked face fit the physical characteristics of someone who abused drugs, and in my experience, if people looked like addicts, that's what they were.

What do rapists look like? I suddenly found myself thinking, struck by the memory of being inside Amber, the way her naked skin felt against mine still vivid enough that it could have happened just hours ago. I heard my father's voice: *I think you'd do just about anything to get into your sweet little Amber's panties.* Had he been right? Had I been willing to do anything in order to have her— including forcing myself on her after she told me to stop? A horrified shiver shot across my skin, and I began to shake. *If someone looked at me, is a rapist what they'd see?*

"Please, hurry!" the woman said, snapping me back to the present. She urged us inside her apartment. "You have to help her!"

"Where is she?" I asked. My eyes darted around the small living room, looking for the woman's daughter, hoping we'd made it in time to save her. The air was stale with old cigarette smoke; I spotted an overflowing ashtray on the coffee table, along with two empty bottles of wine. The place was a mess with stacks of pizza boxes and Styrofoam take-out containers. Not a good sign.

"This way," the woman said.

Mason and I followed her down a short hallway and into what felt like a hatbox-size room, littered with laundry and empty cans of diet soda. The walls were covered in posters of bands I'd never heard of. The girl lay splayed diagonally across her twin bed, arms askew over her head and legs spread-eagled. She was thin like her mother with the same black, but clean, hair, and wore green-striped, drawstring pajama bottoms with a tight, white T-shirt. For a moment, she reminded me of Amber the day I found her passed out on her bedroom floor, and I had to force myself to remember to breathe. *Goddamn it, Hicks. Stay focused.* The girl's eyes were closed and her lips were tinged a very light blue, but I thought I saw a slight rise of her chest.

"What's her name?" I asked as I dropped down next to the girl on the bed, immediately checking for a pulse on her neck. "How old is she?"

"Dakota," the woman whimpered. "She's fifteen. Is she okay? Is she breathing?"

"What kind of meds did she take?" Mason asked the woman.

She looked at him with wide eyes, and I knew she was afraid to tell us. Afraid that she'd be in legal trouble for possessing a narcotic without a prescription. Mason put his hand on the mother's shoulder and gave it a gentle squeeze.

"We don't care where the meds came from," he said. He kept his voice low and calm, so she would believe him. "We just need to know so the doctors will know how to treat her. Okay?"

The woman waited another couple of breaths before slowly nodding. "Oxy," she whispered. "And maybe some Valium. It was a mixed bag."

Mason shot me a brief, knowing look. "She's breathing, but barely," I said. As I looked back to the girl and lifted her eyelids to check her pupillary response, Mason kept his attention on the mother.

"How many milligrams were the pills, do you know? How many did she take?"

"I don't know," the woman cried, clasping her hands to the sides of her head. "I don't know, I don't know!" A ragged sob shook her body. "Please, just help her!"

"Pulse is thready and BP is ninety over sixty-five," I reported. I quickly inserted an IV into a vein on the back of the girl's hand, hooking the tube up to a bag of saline, and then shot a dose of Narcan into the line. Even if we didn't know how much the girl had taken, flushing her system with saline and a standard dose of an opioid antagonist could help reverse the effects of the pills. Maybe even prevent her from having a seizure or stroke.

Mason tried again for more information. "How many do you normally get in a baggie?" he asked the mother. "Are they small, like a Tic Tac, or big, like a vitamin?"

"Wait!" she said, as though she'd just thought of something, and then ran out of the room. She returned quickly with another clear plastic bag, full of pills. "It was like this, but most of it was already gone."

"That's good," I said, taking the bag from her. "That helps." Mason set the yellow backboard he had carried up the stairs on the bed next to the girl, and both he and I did a three-count and lifted her limp body onto it.

"All right then," I said, looking at the mother as Mason and I finished strapping the girl to the backboard. "We'll need you to come with us to the ER."

"Am I going to get that back?" the woman said, staring at the bag in my hand.

"No," I said, firmly, and she moved out of the room so we could carry her unconscious daughter down the hallway, through the living room, and out the front door. She watched us, pressing a fist against her mouth. I suspected she wouldn't show up at the hospital. In all likelihood, when the police came to follow up with her at the apartment, she wouldn't be there. She wouldn't care what happened to her daughter. And if she did take off, and it turned out that Dakota couldn't be saved, the woman wouldn't have to deal with the fact that her child's death was no one's fault but her own. The lengths some people would go to in order to avoid having to take responsibility for their actions never ceased to amaze me.

HYPOCRITE! a voice shouted inside my head. *After what you did to Amber . . .*

"Tyler!" Mason said. He gave me an irritated look. It wasn't the first time since the tanker truck accident that I'd been distracted on the job. "Help me lift her in."

I did as he asked, and then climbed in next to the girl while Mason jogged around front and got into the driver's seat. I checked her vitals again, secured the oxygen mask over her mouth, and then radioed in to the ER, letting them know what was coming. I glanced down at the bag of pills, which I had set on the gurney next to her. The smaller ones were a light yellow, and had the letter "V" stamped on them—Valium, for sure. There had to be at least a hundred of them.

I thought about my blood pressure, that no matter how many miles I ran each day, the undercurrent of anxiety coursing through me still put my health—and my sanity—at risk. I thought about how it was perfectly normal for a doctor to write a prescription to address a temporary bout of severe anxiety, which I told myself I was experiencing. Situational anxiety, incited by a stressful event. But I didn't need a doctor to tell me that the medication would help; I administered it on a regular basis to the victims I helped treat, then watched as their angst magically melted away. If I knew when *they* needed it, surely I could decide the same thing for myself.

With a quick look at Mason, who was hunched over the wheel, focused on maneuvering through traffic, waiting for the cars surrounding us to get out of the way, I quietly opened the baggie and reached inside, rooted around, and then pulled out a small handful of the smaller, V-marked pills—maybe twenty of them—leaving enough that Mason wouldn't notice the difference when we handed the bag over at the hospital. I turned to face the back doors, so my partner couldn't see what I was doing, hesitating only a moment before popping a chalky, yellow-hued bit of relief into my mouth. *Just for when things get really bad,* I thought as I slipped the remainder of the pills I'd taken into my pocket. *When I really need relief. And not every day. Only until the memories of what happened that night fade away and I find a way to never think about them again.*

Amber

Heather was in town for two weeks, and despite my parents' pro-
tests, I went out with her almost every night after I got off work,
visiting different bars and trying out clubs I'd never been to. I did
it for the distraction, for a sense of normalcy. *See?* I'd think. *Everything's fine. I'm out with a girlfriend. I'm laughing and talking and dancing like any other almost-twenty-four-year-old girl.* Going out kept me
out of my head; it restricted the amount of time I spent replaying
what had happened with Tyler, who seemed to creep in around
the edges of my thoughts no matter how hard I tried to push him
out. I woke up every morning in a cold sweat, breathing hard,
remembering the weight of him on top of me, feeling the stabbing
pain as he pushed inside. *You asked for it,* I told myself. *If you hadn't
acted like such a slut, it never would have happened.* It didn't matter
that my parents kept telling me that I should report him to the
police, because I felt certain that anyone who listened to all the
details of what went down would assume that I had wanted to
have sex. They'd judge me. They'd tell me to be more careful next
time, and that would be that.

When Heather and I went out, I kept myself to a strict one-drink limit, never accepting the ones sent over to us by strange men, and rejecting the invitations to dance with anyone other than my friend.

"Come *on*," Heather said the night before she would head back to Berkeley. We were sitting at a table at the Wild Buffalo, where a live band was playing some kind of bluegrass-rock blend, and I'd just refused a stocky, cute guy with bright blue eyes and a well-trimmed, brown beard who had asked me to dance. "You're killing me, Amber! It's just a dance!"

I gave her a tight-lipped smile and shook my head, knowing full well that that wasn't always true.

"Are you still pining for Daniel? Is that it?" Heather asked, but she didn't wait for me to answer. "Because you know what the best way to get over a guy is, right? Get under a new one!"

I laughed, but my heart skipped a beat at the mention of Daniel's name. I hated knowing that I'd hurt him, hated thinking that he would spend the rest of his life thinking the worst of me. But I also knew that someone as kind and good as him deserved better than what I was, now. Breaking up with him, giving him his freedom, had been the right thing to do.

I glanced over at the guy with a beard, who, after asking me to dance, had rejoined his group of friends. And then, without warning, a tidal wave of rebellion rose up inside me. "You think I should go for it?" I asked Heather.

"Oh my god, *yes!*" she said. "You so need this. Go dance. Give him your number. Live a little, girl!"

So it was her encouragement, coupled with an undeniable, swelling sense of reckless abandon, that urged me to stand up and make my way over to this stranger. It felt good to know that he wanted me. I didn't want to know his name; I didn't want to make bullshit small talk about our lives. I just grabbed him by the hand and pulled him onto the dance floor, throwing my arms up in the air and swaying my hips to the music. I knew I looked good—I'd had a stylist clean up the hatchet job I'd done to my hair, and that, coupled with my new asymmetrical, sweeping-bangs bob, actually made me appear more sophisticated than I ever had before. I'd put on heavy makeup, as was becoming my habit, even when I went to the gym. I'd worn a light green, flowered sundress that had been a little tight on me a few months ago but now hung loosely on my frame. I closed my eyes, feeling the heat of his body so close to mine, smelling the sour scent of beer on his breath. I didn't care about anything. I didn't even care when he put his hand on my back and pulled me against him.

I thought I would instantly rebel at this kind of touch, that I would shove him off of me, but instead, I did nothing. I *felt* nothing. As we danced, I hovered above my body, watching as I leaned in and whispered in the guy's ear. "Wanna get out of here?" I asked, and he nodded.

I watched as I led him out to the dark alley on the side of the building. I watched as I pushed him up against the brick wall and kissed him, letting my hands roam down his sides, lifted his T-shirt, and unbuttoned the top of his jeans.

"Damn, you're hot," he muttered.

"Shut up," I heard myself respond, and it was someone else saying the words, someone else unzipping his zipper and rummaging around in his boxers, until she got down on her knees and took him into her mouth.

"Holy shit," he groaned, and I watched as this other girl—the girl who wasn't me—switched to stroking him with her hand. A few seconds later, it was over. After he caught his breath, he zipped up and stood there awkwardly for a moment, not really looking at me. "Sooo," he said, smoothing his hand over his beard. "Can I buy you a drink?"

I didn't speak. Instead, I simply spun around and headed back into the bar on my own, not caring whether he followed. I saw Heather on the dance floor, where she was gyrating against a broad-shouldered, hipster-looking black guy with round glasses and skinny-legged jeans. I went to join them.

"Hey!" she said. "Where'd you go?"

"I was living a little!" I said, still overcome by a buzzing, detached sense of power, similar to how I felt when I went to a party and ate nothing while everyone around me gorged. It was a heady rush, and I knew that, once it was gone, I'd want it again.

"Ha!" Heather shouted. "I told you! You feel better, right?"

I nodded, and we continued to dance. Again, I closed my eyes, moving my body to the music, letting the bass and drums and guitar pulse through me until my head throbbed and my mind went blank. This was who I was now, a girl who danced with strangers and unzipped their pants in a filthy alley outside a bar. A girl in charge of every minute of her own life—a girl who would own a situation before it owned her.

I held on to this new mind-set every night for the rest of July, after Heather had left and I started going out to the bars on my own. I visited a few of the ones downtown, but more often I frequented the busy casinos in Ferndale and Lynden, since the influx of out-of-towners there gave me a better chance at the anonymity I craved. I stopped drinking anything except water, because being drunk reminded me too much of that night. I honed in on a different guy each time I went out, never asking for his name or telling him mine, never making more than a few minutes of conversation before dancing with him, and then leading him to a stall in the bathroom or outside in the alley. I never let any of them take the lead—I would pin their hands above their heads, or behind their backs and whisper, "Don't say a word," in their ears. That was usually enough to get them to comply, but if they tried to touch me anyway, to slip up my skirt, pull down my panties, or turn me around and bend me over, I shoved them away and took off. I ran to my car and went somewhere else to look for someone new. There was no lack of males willing to let me do this. I doubted they went home and cried about how some girl had taken advantage of them. It was so different for men—the more women they slept with, the more accolades they were given. A man who has sex with a different girl each night is considered a stud, a woman who does the same thing, a whore. I was just living up to what I'd turned myself into the moment Tyler had rubbed his erection against me on the dance floor and I'd done nothing to push him away.

"Honey, please don't go out tonight," my mom said one morning in late September, the day after my twenty-fourth birthday, which I'd insisted to my parents that I didn't want to do anything to celebrate or acknowledge. We were sitting on the couch in the family room, where I had my laptop open, studying, and she was reading a book. "You can't keep living like this."

"Like what?" I asked, popping the sugar-free mint gum I had in my mouth between my molars. My breath was terrible lately, and I knew it had to do with how little I was eating. My thigh gap was back, my rib cage showed through my pale skin, and I fit into the jeans I'd worn when I was fifteen. Part of me felt angry with myself for so easily slipping back into the behavior patterns that had almost killed me, but another, darker corner in my mind experienced shimmers of self-satisfaction when my stomach growled or I was dizzied by hunger. Suffering felt familiar—it felt like something I deserved.

"Like Tyler didn't rape you," she said, dropping her book on the coffee table in front of us.

"Can we *please* stop having the same *fucking* conversation?" I snapped my laptop shut, ready to head upstairs to the solitary comfort of my bedroom, but she grabbed my arm before I could.

"Don't swear at me."

"I didn't. I swore *near* you."

We held each other's gaze, waiting to see who would look away first. When she blinked and released her hold on me, I felt like I'd won, but then, she started to cry.

"I don't even know who you *are* anymore," she said. She wrung her hands together in her lap, and I noticed that her usually lovely, manicured nails were bitten to the quick. "You're not eating. You barely speak to us. You're gone all the time. We know you're hurting, Amber, and if you'd just slow down a minute, you'd see we'd do anything to help."

Something about seeing her like this poked a tiny hole in the brick wall I'd built around me. I sighed, and then sat down next to her again. "I'm just trying to get past it, Mom. I can't change it. I can't let it take over my life. It's better to keep busy."

She wiped her cheeks with her fingertips and shook her head. "Keeping busy doesn't fix anything. It only makes you *think* you're not hurting. You're numbing yourself, just like you did back in high school. Can't you see that? Can't you see that you're doing it again?"

"I guess," I said with a small shrug. "But it's my life. What happened, happened to *me*. I should get to decide how to get through it."

"Not when how you're dealing with it is just going to make things worse," she said. "Your dad and I have been doing some research—"

"On what?" I asked, instantly wary. I knew they had to be talking about me; I saw the way their conversations suddenly ceased whenever I walked in on them. At night, I could hear them whispering fervently to each other through a heat vent between our rooms, after they'd said they were going to sleep.

"The behavior of sexual assault victims," she said, "and what we might be able to do to help. What you've been doing isn't unique. Lots of girls try to go on like nothing's happened. But it doesn't work. Eventually, the trauma works its way to the surface, and it will keep doing that over and over again, making you feel worse and worse, unless you *talk* to someone."

"Talking won't do me any good," I said, fighting the wave of revulsion in my belly that rose up when I thought about telling anyone else what Tyler did to me. I was fine. I didn't need some person I didn't know to talk with about my feelings. What would I say, anyway? That I'd seduced my best friend and then changed my mind at the very last minute, and now I was out there almost every night, shoving my hands into strange men's jeans? That doing this felt how I imagined heroin addicts did when they stuck needles in their veins—it only seemed terrible if you didn't know the pure and merciful blast of relief that followed.

"But what if it did?" my mom asked. "Can you at least please try, if not for me, for your dad? He can barely make it through the workday, Amber. He's so upset. He keeps replaying what Tyler did, and it's having a terrible effect on him." She paused, and then lowered her voice, even though there wasn't anyone around besides me to hear her speak. "He didn't want me to tell you this, so you have to promise you won't say anything, but it's been so bad, he actually went to the doctor and got on antidepressants."

"Oh," I said, shocked to hear this. My dad was the sort who would avoid his yearly physical like he was being asked to enter a torture chamber; the fact that he had chosen to see his physician on his own accord said a lot about the state he was in. "When?"

"In August," she said. "About a month after he hit Tyler in the front yard. The meds are just starting to help." She gave me a hopeful look. "I found the name of a local counselor who specializes in situations like this. Would you consider talking with her? Please?"

"Fine," I said, letting loose a long sigh. I already knew what to expect; I'd spent enough hours with Greta at the hospital and in the support group after I was released to know that therapists were pretty much paid to listen to you and then repeat back your feelings in a way that might help you understand yourself better. I'd go see this woman my mother had found, but that didn't mean it would change anything—I understood myself perfectly well. I'd show up, go through the motions of a good client, and then I'd get back to doing what had been working for me so far. I'd stay busy, keeping my eyes on my future, so I didn't waste another moment wishing I could find a way to change the past.

I stayed home that night, as my mother had requested, figuring it was the least I could do to help show her I was fine. After our talk, she had immediately called the counselor she'd mentioned, and set up an appointment for the next day.

"She can't be any good if she doesn't have a waiting list," I remarked as my mom hung up.

"She happened to have a cancellation, so she's fitting you in," my mom said, defensively. "Don't be so quick to judge."

I'd gone up to my bedroom then, and locked the door, something I'd started doing since the morning after the party, when Tyler showed up at my house. I'd never had a reason to do it before.

"Fuck him," I muttered, as I dropped down on my bed and opened my laptop. I thought about studying, but for some reason, instead, I opened a search engine and typed in the words "unreported rape." My parents weren't the only ones who could do research.

A list of over two hundred thousand links popped up, and I found myself clicking on one after the other, reading estimates that only thirty-two out of a hundred rapes that occur are reported; out of those, only seven might lead to an arrest, and out of these, only two might lead to a conviction. I read that it's almost impossible to discern whether or not rape rates are increasing or declining due to the fact that rape is one of the most underreported crimes in the world. I read how the results of a forensic exam performed right after an assault are almost the only things presented at trial that can lead to a guilty verdict and result in the rapist spending time in prison. How a victim isn't supposed to be put on trial for her sexual past or proclivities, but most of the time, she is. *No wonder it's so underreported,* I thought. *My instincts told me the police wouldn't help, and it looks like I was right.*

Armed with this information, I drove to Fairhaven the next day after work, parking near Village Books and walking down Harris Avenue to find the counselor's office in a brick building near the bottom of the hill. VANESSA DOUGLAS, MSW, RM. 203, the sign on the directory informed me. I didn't want to be there, but I'd promised my parents. I needed to do something to assuage their concern, something to help my dad's tenuous emotional state, and if it took talking to a stranger for an hour, then so be it.

I made my way up a steep set of stairs, and then sat in the waiting room, alone. A few minutes later, I heard a door open down the hall, and the click-clack of heels coming toward me on the hardwood floor. I steeled myself as a tall, slender black woman appeared in the doorway and smiled. Her hair was short, maybe two inches sticking up all around her skull, and her eyes were almond-shaped, dark pools.

"Amber?" Vanessa asked, and I nodded, gripping the edges of my purse. I didn't know why I was nervous. I was only there to tell this woman that I was fine, that I'd already figured out a way to move past what Tyler had done. That even FBI statistics confirmed my belief that reporting him to the police would be a futile act.

"Follow me," she said. Once we were inside her small office, I let my eyes wander around the room, taking in the one red-brick wall, accented by three others painted a rich cream, and high, rounded-arched windows overlooking Bellingham Bay. It was a crisp and sunny autumn day, and the water and the sky were an equally eye-squinting blue.

"Nice view," I said, still standing by the door, which I'd shut behind me.

"Isn't it?" she said as she lowered herself into a bomber-jacket brown leather chair. "Please, have a seat."

I glanced over to the couch, which matched her chair, and was littered with several large, fluffy red and cream pillows. I sat in the corner furthest away from her and hugged one of the pillows to my chest.

"So," she said. "Can you tell me a little about why you're here?"

"My mother made the appointment. I'm sure she already told you."

"Yes," Vanessa said, "but I'd like to hear it in your own words. And rest assured, anything you say to me in this room is confidential."

"I don't really want to be here," I said, gazing out the window. It was too hard to look at her. It reminded me too much of my time with Greta in the hospital all those years ago. I couldn't believe I was back in this same place—I liked to think that I was tougher than I used to be. I thought I was smarter. But what happened with Tyler took that away from me. He took away everything.

"That's not uncommon," Vanessa said, setting her elbows on the arms of her chair and crossing her long legs under her sleeveless and fitted linen dress, the hem of which hit just below her knees. "Therapy is usually the last resort for people. Not exactly on anyone's bucket list." I looked back to her, and she smiled again, waiting for me to speak. When I didn't, she tried another approach. "Why don't you just tell me a little about yourself? Did you grow up in Bellingham?" I nodded. "Any brothers or sisters?"

"No," I said, and then launched into the "how I was a miracle who came into the world nine weeks early" story, taking my time, trying to burn through the hour I was supposed to spend in that room.

"Did you have a lot of friends growing up?" she asked, and the question sucked the air from my lungs. *Only one that really mattered,* I thought. *And he's the one who landed me on this couch.*

"Some," I said, when I felt like I could breathe again.

"Do they still live here?" Vanessa pressed, tilting her head to one side.

"One of them does." The truth was, from the moment Heather left my freshman year and my illness started to get worse, it had always just been Tyler and me. He was the only person who stayed by my side, who didn't seem to condemn me for what I'd gone through. Even Daniel hadn't understood me the way my best friend did. And now I'd lost them both.

Vanessa didn't say anything, making me realize that my mother must have already told her some of my history. About Tyler. I shook my head, feeling a scratching sensation in my throat. I coughed to clear it, and a few tears escaped. *Damn it. I might as well stop with the bullshit small talk.* I reached for the tissue box on the burled wood table between us and wiped the corners of my eyes.

"I didn't go to the police," I said, tucking my legs up under me as I tore off bits of the tissue I held and let them land on the pillow in my lap. I kept my head down. "I didn't go to the hospital and have an exam. There's no way I could prove what he did."

"What did he do, Amber?"

I shook my head again. My mom kept using the word "rape" to describe what Tyler did to me, but I still couldn't quite label it that way myself. The circumstances that led up to that moment in the bedroom at the party were too muddy—I was too complicit in what had occurred.

"Did you want to have sex with him?" Vanessa asked. Her voice was low, a therapist's well-practiced, soothing serenade.

"I thought I did. We'd been flirting a lot since I got home from school, but I was engaged to Daniel, and even though I was having second thoughts about getting married, I never should have gotten so drunk. I shouldn't have kissed Tyler or danced with him the way I did." I'd had these same thoughts so many times over the last couple of months, I didn't know how I could believe anything else could be true.

"Amber. Our society always seems to blame the victim, not the perpetrator, for a sexual crime. It says a woman shouldn't dress provocatively or drink alcohol or have any kind of flirtation or interaction with a man because that means she is asking for him to do whatever he wants to do to her, even after she tells him no. Just because you were kissing him doesn't mean you were asking for more."

"But I followed him upstairs. I let him put me on the bed and push his hips against me. I could *feel* what he wanted to do." I shuddered briefly, repulsed by the memory of that moment, repulsed by myself, for being stupid enough to let it happen.

"Nothing you did makes what Tyler did to you okay. If you told him to stop at any point that night, and he went ahead and had sex with you anyway, then what he did was rape. If you had oral sex, and after that, he forced his fingers inside you or had intercourse with you when you didn't want it to go that far, then it was rape. If you two had been sleeping together for years, and this one time, you told him no, and he went ahead despite that, it was rape. Tyler *raped* you, Amber."

I shook my head, still struggling with the guilt I felt that I'd led him on.

"You're not responsible for this," Vanessa continued, looking at me intently. "Yes, you were drunk. You might have kissed him. Everything about your behavior and your words might have said yes, but the moment you changed your mind, the moment you withdrew your consent either by physically struggling to get away or by telling him no, he was committing a crime. But the fact that you were drunk means that you were *incapable* of giving consent, so even if you *hadn't* struggled or said no and he had sex with you, it was still rape."

Her words struck a chord deep inside me. I'd never thought about the fact that being drunk had taken away my ability to give consent. Tyler should have *known* that. He should have realized that the state I was in made what he was doing to me wrong. Instead, he took advantage of how weak I was. He ignored my pleas for him to stop what he was doing—he let me struggle and cry and then he had sex with me anyway. Hearing Vanessa describe this as rape sounded different to me, somehow, than when my mom said it. Maybe both of them were right.

"Whether or not you decide to go to the police," Vanessa said, "you are entitled to be *furious* about what Tyler did to you. To be full of fear and pain and have moments where you wish he was dead. And I am here, if you want to work through all of those complicated feelings. You just have to give me a chance."

My eyes welled up again as she spoke, and this time, I couldn't hold back the tears. "It doesn't matter," I said, my voice crackling. "No one would believe me. He's, like, the nicest guy around. He's a paramedic. He *saves* people for a living. He's never hurt anyone."

"That you know of," Vanessa said. "And, Amber, he hurt *you.* The world is full of seemingly nice guys who assault women. Guys who don't have healthy attitudes about women and sex in general, who see sex as something they're entitled to, who hurt women and don't even know they're doing it because we don't educate our young men on how not to *become* rapists."

I thought about Tyler's parents then, about the parade of

women Jason had plowed his way through over the years—the crude and sexist comments he always made around his son, and the way he constantly made Tyler feel like he would never measure up. I thought about Liz, that however nice she might be, she was also way more concerned with getting her own needs met than with meeting Tyler's, or teaching him anything about what a healthy relationship should look like. I was certain that neither of them had ever had a conversation with Tyler about how not to rape a woman—if they had, he definitely would have told me about it. I doubted that there were many parents out there who had this kind of conversation with their sons, the same way girls are talked to about not walking alone to their cars at night, or how to not dress "suggestively" when they go out so men won't get the "wrong idea."

"A man doesn't have to be evil in order to sexually assault women," Vanessa said. "Most rapists *don't* look like what we're programmed to believe they should—they're not greasy-haired monsters who jump out from behind the bushes and tie up their victims in their basements. More often, they're someone's typical father, husband, brother, or son—but what they do to women *is* monstrous. Just because Tyler is 'nice'—here, she made air quotation marks with her fingers—"doesn't mean he's not capable of rape. Clearly, he is, or you wouldn't be talking to me."

"But what's the point of going to the police if he won't go to jail?" I asked. My thoughts were scrambled, pulled in a hundred different directions.

"I'm not saying you have to," she said. "I'm happy to just help you here, in this room. But I will tell you that I've worked with many women who've been through exactly what you're dealing with now, some of whom ultimately decided to file a report with the authorities, despite knowing the odds of getting a conviction were low."

"That doesn't make any sense," I said. "Don't most women just end up getting retraumatized by the judicial system, having to relive what happened to them over and over again? Their sexual histories questioned and their reputations torn apart? What's the point of going through all of that if the guy gets away with it anyway?" My body ached, the same way it had the moment Tyler rolled off of me. I felt the stabbing sensation between my legs the same way an amputee might feel ghostly pain in a missing limb. Every time I allowed myself to think about that night, it all came rushing back—I was in that strange house, stumbling down the stairs, desperate to find a way to get home. I didn't want to do this. I thought I was fine. But now, I found myself hoping that Vanessa would tell me there was another way, that she had a magic formula to piece my shattered insides back together. I wanted her to make me feel whole.

"The point is, that for some women, going through the process of telling their story to the authorities is cathartic. It gives them a chance to release some of the blame they point at themselves and pin it on the person who actually deserves it. And, most importantly, it creates a record, so that if their attacker ever does the same thing to another woman, there's a better chance she'll be taken seriously and he'll be indicted."

I'd never thought about the fact that Tyler might have already done this kind of thing to other girls. I hadn't considered that he might do it again, in the future, to someone else. The full weight of these possibilities crashed down upon me, and I knew I had to do something. I knew going to the police would hurt me more than it would hurt him. *There has to be something else. Some way to make him pay.* And if I was sure of anything, it was that sitting in a therapist's office, dwelling on what he did to me and whining about my feelings, wasn't going to be it.

Tyler

It was a warm afternoon in late September, almost three months since the party on the Fourth of July, and Mason and I were working a rare day shift, covering for another paramedic team who were both down with strep throat. We had just grabbed lunch from a food truck downtown when a call came over the radio, asking us to proceed to a local park, where a ten-year-old boy had shimmied his head through the bars on a wrought-iron fence and now couldn't get it back out.

"What the hell would possess a kid to do something like that?" I asked, as we tossed the remainder of our meal into the trash and headed back to the rig.

"He probably just wanted to see if it would fit," Mason said.

"That's what she said," I quipped, hoping to get a laugh out of my partner. Things had continued to be strained between us, even though I'd done everything in my power to be more focused when I was on the job. Some days, when my mind spun with fear that Amber still might send the police to my door, when my heart raced and I felt like a fat boulder was sitting on my chest, the only way I got through work was by taking half a Valium before I got to the station. I'd made good on my promise to myself to only take it when the pressure inside me was unbearable, when I knew I was at risk of cracking on the job, so I hadn't yet run out of the ones I took from the woman's stash. But I was getting close, and I didn't know what I'd do when they were gone.

Mason didn't laugh at my stupid joke. Instead, we climbed into the ambulance, not talking as he drove us to a park on the south end of the Guide Meridian. It didn't take long to treat the boy from the fence; the firefighters in attendance had already used bolt cutters to free him, so all we had to do was check him for serious injury, of which he had none, and then administer a couple of ice packs and ibuprofen for the slight irritation and swelling around his neck. His parents were there, too, and signed a waiver stating they didn't want him to be taken to the ER, so after they drove off toward home, Mason and I climbed back into the ambulance, where it felt like it would take a wrecking ball to knock down the wall between us.

"Hey," I said, hoping I could find a way to get through to him. To make things go back to the way they used to be between us. "Can we talk?"

"About what?" he asked as he stuck the keys in the ignition. He didn't look at me.

"I don't know, man. We used to hang out. We were friends, we joked around. Now you barely say anything to me unless it's about the job."

"We're partners," he said. "That's what we're supposed to talk about."

"Come on, Mason. You know what I mean." I wanted him to tell me that everything would be fine, that something else was bothering him and that's why he'd been keeping me at arm's length. I wanted him to tell me that he didn't think what Amber said was true.

"I'm not sure what you want me to say."

"Tell me what's going on with Gia and the baby. Go have a beer with me like we used to. Let's talk about what an asshole my dad is. Anything but this stick-to-the-facts bullshit."

He waited a moment before responding, and when he did, it was with a look full of strangled disgust. "I can't do that, man. Too much has changed. I can work with you, I'll do my job, but that's it."

This time, I was the one who needed to wait before speaking. I kept my eyes glued on his, trying not to look away. "Because of what happened at the party."

He bobbed his head. "I can't pretend that I didn't see how shaken Amber was. How she'd been crying. How she didn't want me to touch her. I should have realized she wasn't just drunk. She was in shock."

I slumped back in my seat and dropped my gaze to my lap, feeling sick to my stomach, when a thought crossed my mind. "I take it you've told Gia about all of this."

"She's my wife. I tell her everything."

I looked at him again. "So is this coming from her? Some kind of female solidarity thing? Did she tell you we can't be friends anymore?" The words came out nastier than I meant them—like something my father might say—and witnessing the stormy look in my partner's already dark eyes, I realized that I'd crossed a line.

"Screw you." He spat the words. "It has nothing to do with Gia. It's coming from me. I've been doing this job way longer than you. I've seen women right after they've been attacked. They look just like Amber did that night."

I waited, trying to absorb what he meant. "You think I raped her." My voice was quiet, full of fear.

This time, my partner didn't hesitate. "Yeah, man. I do."

Fuck. Even though I'd worried all along that he felt this way, I hadn't let myself believe it until now. Until he said the words. "So I guess that's it," I said, fighting the rising tide of nerves tingling beneath my skin.

Mason didn't answer; instead, he started the engine and pulled out of the parking lot, back onto the street. We didn't speak, even as he parked the rig in its spot at the station house, where we would wait until another call came in. As we walked up the stairs to the lounge, I thought about what I should say. I wanted him to tell me that he'd made a horrible mistake. But the only thing that came out of my mouth was one question, to which I wasn't sure I really wanted the reply. "What do you think I should do?" I asked, and he stopped at the top of the stairs, turned around, and stared at me, long and hard.

"Admit what you did," Mason said. "Deal with the consequences. And then get some fucking help, so you never do it again."

We didn't have any more calls that afternoon, so at the end of my shift, around nine o'clock, I drove toward my apartment, the buzzing undercurrent of energy beneath my skin convincing me that being home alone was the last thing I should do. I kept hearing Mason's voice, a record stuck on repeat: *Admit what you did. Deal with the consequences. Get help.* I thought about driving to the police station and asking to speak to a detective. I imagined describing the events of that night, taking the blame for what went wrong, even if the details were still disjointed inside my head.

I can't do it, I thought, as I directed my truck downtown, eventually parking near the Royal, a popular bar. *I can't say I did something I didn't do.*

I strolled inside, and saw that the establishment was already full of students and a few twenty- and thirtysomethings playing pool, shooting darts, and dancing to what sounded like eighties cover hits. Winding my way through the tables, I found an empty stool at the bar and sat down.

"What can I get you?" the young male bartender asked. He couldn't have been much over twenty-one himself.

"Pyramid Hefeweizen," I said, taking out a ten-dollar bill from my wallet and setting it on the counter. "With lemon."

"Coming up," the bartender said, throwing a white towel over his shoulder and grabbing a clean glass pint for my drink.

"You know only girls take lemon in their beer."

I turned to see where the voice was coming from, and smiled when my eyes landed on an attractive woman with wavy black hair who had dropped down onto the stool next to me. She wore a blue dress with a short, fringed skirt, and high heels. Her long legs were tan and bare. She looked too polished and professional to be a student, possibly a few years older than me.

"Is that so?" I asked. I told myself I'd come here for simple distraction, that I wasn't looking to meet anyone, but I knew that was a lie. I'd already taken a long run that morning, and half a Valium before my shift. Clearly, I needed something else, and since Whitney hadn't moved back into my building when school started again, I needed *someone* else.

"It is," she said with a mocking, solemn nod. "You might want to change your order."

"No, I'm good," I said, leaning my head a little closer to her.

"Comfortable with your masculinity, are you?"

"I am." I grinned at her, letting the rush of pheromones I felt sand away my sharp, nerve-racked edges. The bartender delivered my beer, and I made a show of taking the quartered lemon off the edge of the glass, squeezing it, then dropping it into my drink.

The woman laughed and held out her hand. "I'm Kylie."

"Tyler." I took a swig of my drink, and then glanced around the bar. "You here alone?"

"No," Kylie said, and she nodded her head in the general direction of the pool table. "I'm supposed to be having a drink with my boyfriend."

I ran my eyes over the four men she was looking at. Two were younger college students in baggy jeans—obviously not her style—and the other two were the clean-cut, banker types, wearing black slacks and dress shirts with their long-sleeves rolled up. The one with blond hair looked back at her and waved.

"He's not doing a very good job of it," Kylie said, lifting her glass in response to his gesture. He didn't even give me a glance before turning his attention back to his pool game.

"So you're trying to make him jealous?"

She smiled, a coy, flirtatious thing. "And what if I am?"

"Then I say we should give him a show." I gulped down almost the entire contents of my glass, grabbed Kylie by the hand, and pulled her to the dance floor. The DJ had just started playing a slow song, Foreigner's "Waiting for a Girl Like You," so I held her close, slipping one of my legs in between her thighs, and pressing my cheek against the side of her head. I moved her with ease, running my hand up and down her delicate back, dangerously close to splaying my fingers on top of her ass. I wondered what Mason would have said if he'd been there, if he'd accuse me of behaving the same way I had with Amber at the party. But I told myself that that didn't matter. Besides, Kylie had been the one to approach me; in fact, I was doing her a favor. I just wanted to dance, to lose myself in a feeling other than the constant state of panic I'd been in. Like Whitney, this woman was an opiate in human form—immediately soothing, a perfect, temporary reprieve.

"Is he watching?" I murmured in Kylie's ear. She smelled like something sweet; coconut, maybe. And some kind of rum.

"I don't know," she said, sounding a little out of breath. "Just keep dancing."

I felt her push her hips against mine, and I couldn't help but think about Amber then, how she and I had danced, how it felt to hold her. How she'd screamed when I walked into her room the next day. My heart banged around inside my chest, and my blood roared in my ears. "Come on," I said to Kylie now, as the song ended. I guided her toward the back of the bar, near the bathrooms.

"Where are we going?" she asked, still laughing. Her cheeks were flushed, her dark eyes were glossy and pupils dilated, a clear sign, I knew, that she was drunk.

"Just come on," I said, pushing her up against the wall next to the men's bathroom. It was a dark hallway, but by no means private. I put my hands on the sides of her head and leaned down to kiss her. She answered by slipping her tongue in my mouth, and I instantly realized that she was a smoker, something I normally couldn't stomach. But even that didn't stop me.

When I finally pulled back and opened my eyes, I caught a glimpse of another couple further down the hall, maybe about fifteen feet away. They were in shadow, but I could tell that instead of the guy pushing the girl up against the wall, it was the other way around. With my head turned, Kylie began kissing my neck, which somehow felt more like an annoyance than a turn-on, and I squinted at the other couple, thinking that the silhouette of the girl's body seemed familiar. And then it struck me.

"Amber?" I said, not meaning to speak as loudly as I did, but the girl down the hall stopped what she was doing as I spoke, and then looked at me. The light from the one fixture between us caught in her eyes, and I knew I was right. She looked different, thinner than the last time I'd seen her, with a harshly angled haircut and heavy makeup.

"Who's that?" Kylie asked, her gaze following mine.

I didn't answer; instead, I dropped my hands from her body and took a few steps toward Amber and the stranger she was with.

"Screw you then," Kylie said with disdain, and she spun around and headed back to the main part of the bar. I didn't care that I'd offended her. All I cared about was talking to Amber.

"Tyler . . . don't," Amber said. She stumbled backward, away from the guy, who, now that I could see him more clearly, I realized had to be in his late forties. He had a receding hairline, bags of flesh under his eyes, and noticeable paunch hanging over his belt. What the hell was she doing in a dark hallway, making out with a guy like that?

"Please," I said. "I just want to talk." I couldn't believe I had to beg just to speak with my best friend. I couldn't believe it had been three months since I'd last seen her.

She stared at me, eyes wide, and shook her head. The guy she was with swung his gaze back and forth between us. "Doesn't look like the lady wants to talk to you," he said, puffing out his chest.

Ignoring him, I kept my eyes on Amber. "I've been worried about you," I said, stopping when I was about three feet away from her.

"Hey," the guy said, stepping in between Amber and me. He swayed a bit on his feet, and I knew he was drunk. "I *said,* the lady doesn't want to talk."

"Back off," I said, using one arm to push him out of my way. "This isn't your business."

Amber took another step back, her eyes darting around, looking behind where she stood, and then over my shoulder, as though searching for escape.

"I'm *making* it my business," the guy said, and then he lunged at me, his right arm swinging. The punch missed, but the impact of his body hitting mine was enough for me to lose my balance. We tumbled to the floor, our limbs entangled. At this point, Amber leapt over us, and as I struggled to push the other guy off of me and get back on my feet, I saw her dart back into the main part of the bar and disappear.

"Shit," I muttered, wondering if I should run after her, but then decided I'd better not.

"Thanks for fucking that up for me, asshole," the guy said as he, too, managed to get back on his feet.

"You should stick to hitting on women your own age," I said bitterly, taking in the man's puffy face and the broken red capillaries around his nose, sure signs of a heavy drinker.

"That's where you're wrong, buddy," the guy said. "*She* picked up *me*. Pulled me onto the dance floor and then dragged me back here, all hot and heavy. Probably could have gotten a blow job if you hadn't butted in."

"Shut up," I said, feeling my fingers curl into fists at my sides.

"Or what?" the guy challenged me, and I almost let my anger take over. I almost let myself hit him. But then I thought about Amber, what she had been doing in a hallway with a stranger, and I felt sick. I knew that the best and safest thing I could do was leave.

Without another word, I charged my way through the crowd, and less than a minute later, I was in my truck, chewing on a wad of spearmint gum to mask the beer. I revved the engine, pulled out of my parking spot, and tried not to speed as I took a left on Railroad Avenue.

I still didn't want to go home. I thought about going to my mom's place, but I knew she'd only want to talk about how hard things were for *her* now that Helen and Tom weren't speaking to us. I thought about following Amber back to her house and demanding that we talk and work out this entire, fucked-up situation, but that, most likely, wouldn't get me anywhere other than the back of a squad car. I needed to talk with someone who could help me find a solution to what I was going through. I needed to talk to someone who would understand.

Ten minutes later, I parked in front of a building I hadn't been to in over a year. *Desperate times call for desperate measures,* I thought as I jumped out of my truck and locked it, heading through the front door that led to the faux-marble-floored lobby. Once inside the elevator, I pressed the button that would take me to the fifth floor, remembered the dread that used to fill me back in high school every time I had done the same thing.

The doors opened and I stepped through them, realizing that the air in the hallway smelled exactly as it always had—a mix of slightly damp carpet and bleach. I realized that my father might not even be home. He could be working; he could have gone out with one of his flavor-of-the-month girls. But I approached his front door anyway, rapping on it three times, holding my breath as I waited for him to appear.

"Just a minute!" I heard my father say, and I exhaled. His voice was gruff and muffled, and I wondered if he had been asleep. He opened the door, keeping his hand on the knob, just as I had on mine the last time he showed up, unannounced, at my place.

"Well, look what the cat dragged in," he said, lifting his chin in a slight, defiant motion. There were glints of silver running through the blond stubble on his face and the hair on his head; the skin along his jawline was beginning to sag. He'd turn fifty-two in September and despite his muscular physique, it showed.

"Hi, Dad," I said, standing up as straight as I could, my shoulders back, not wanting to look as weak as I felt. "Can I come in?"

"What for?" he asked, and it took all my willpower not to whip around and walk away.

"Something happened. I need to talk."

"You lose your shit on the job again?"

"No, Dad. Please. I need your help."

The tone of my voice must have gotten to him, because his expression softened just a little around its hard edges, and he stepped backward, gesturing for me to enter. We proceeded to the living room, where he still had the same dark green, fake leather couches he bought off Craigslist the year he moved out of our house. The TV was on, set to ESPN, and there were two empty beer bottles on the glass coffee table. The air smelled of fried food, and I saw a crumpled McDonald's bag on his kitchen counter.

"Have a seat," he said, gesturing to the smaller couch. "Want a drink?"

"Sure," I said, and I waited to sit down until he returned with a beer for me and a two-finger pour of whiskey for him. "Thanks," I said as I dropped onto the worn cushions where I used to sleep. The condo only had one bedroom; I didn't have any other choice. When he didn't answer, we both stared at the flat screen on the wall for a few minutes, not saying a word, until finally, I asked him to turn it off. He muted it instead.

"So, you going to tell me what happened or not?" he asked, keeping his eyes on the college football game he'd been watching.

"Yeah," I said, trying to ignore what felt like a golf ball lodged in my throat. "But can you turn that off, though? Please? This is important."

With a loud sigh, he clicked the off button on the remote and then looked at me, expectantly. "Happy now?"

"Yes," I said. I tried to sort out where to start, finally deciding on his visit to my apartment on the Fourth of July, before the party. "We were pretty shitty to each other the last time I saw you. I feel bad about the things I said."

"Get to the point, Son."

I gritted my teeth, wondering if I'd made a mistake in coming to see him. But then I began to describe what had happened with Amber. I told him everything I remembered, how she looked, how she acted, how drunk we both were, and how I went to her house the next day and she freaked out. When I told him that Tom had punched me, my dad's face flushed red.

"That fucker's always thought he was better than me. He was probably happy to take it out on you."

"Amber told them I raped her," I said, forcing myself not to scream that this situation wasn't about him. "I'm pretty sure Tom hit me because of that." I went on to say that my mom had told me about the sexual harassment suit, and that I had come to see him, hoping he had some advice on what to do.

"She told you about that, but didn't tell me that Amber's accusing you of rape? I swear to god, that woman is dumb as a box of rocks."

"Dad, please," I said again, not wanting to listen to yet another diatribe from either of my parents about how the other was an idiot.

"Have the police talked with you?" he asked as his glass clinked on the coffee table when he set it down.

"No. I don't think she called them."

"Well then, sounds like you don't have anything to worry about. She didn't report it."

"But she still could," I said. "What do I say if the police show up?" I shifted in my seat, still edgy from my conversation with Mason and the altercation in the bar. I thought about the few pills left in my bathroom at home, and wished I had one with me now.

"You say nothing," my dad said, firmly. "Not a word, you understand? You call me, and I'll call a lawyer."

It felt odd to have him tell me that he'd be there for me if I was in trouble; too many times he'd done the opposite, insisting that I needed to learn how to handle my own problems. "Mason thinks I should turn myself in."

"Mason's a moron. If Amber or her parents had any actual proof, they would have gone to the police already. The fact that they haven't tells me that it'd be your word against hers, and in cases like that, it's almost impossible to get a conviction."

I allowed myself to be buoyed by his words, grateful that he seemed—at least for the moment—supportive. "How do you know?"

"Because that's what my lawyer told me when that bitch I worked with accused me of promising to help get her on day shifts if she fucked me. She backed off once he showed her all the texts she'd sent me, begging for it on a regular basis." He paused, looking pleased with himself. "You said Amber kissed you in front of everyone there? That you two were grinding on the dance floor?" I nodded, pressing my lips together, instantly taken back to that moment in time, when I thought all of my dreams were about to be realized. And then, the next morning, when the nightmare began as she screeched at me to leave her room. "Well, there you go. If she didn't go to the hospital or the police, there's not going to be any kind of physical evidence."

"I honestly thought she wanted it as much as I did. I wouldn't have gone ahead if—"

He waved a hand at me, dismissively. "It doesn't matter. Even if you did get a little rough with her, a little forceful, any lawyer worth his salt can argue that she likes it that way. That she asked for it. Not to mention she was drunk as hell. Nobody watched you have sex, right?"

"Of course not," I said. "But Mason and Gia did see her right after. They drove her home." I repeated what Mason had said to me earlier that day about how Amber's behavior reminded him of other assault victims, about needing to tell the truth and deal with the consequences of my actions.

"And this guy's supposed to be your partner?" my dad said, with disdain. "What an asshole. Ignore him."

The pressure was building inside my chest. "That's easier said than done. I respect him, you know? He's taught me a lot."

"So you're going to let him convince you to get arrested?" my dad said. "Listen to me, Son. I know I said you didn't have it in you to go after that girl, and I'm sorry for that. You've got more balls than I thought." He scooted forward in order to perch on the edge of the couch, took a sip of his drink, and then looked at me, intently. "But if there's anything I know, it's women. I know what they want and how they want it. Only sometimes, once they get it, they start overthinking every goddamn thing. Like those college girls who accuse football players of rape. They want to screw the hot athlete, and then, after they do, they worry about what people will say about them . . . that they'll look like a slut, so they make up some bullshit lie to make themselves feel better. It's a load of feminist crap. Women say no because they want us to convince them to say yes. That's the way it works. Cavemen grabbed their women by the hair and dragged them into the cave for a reason. It's not violence. It's fucking biology. The natural order of things."

I gave him a hesitant nod, though I wasn't sure I agreed with everything he'd said. Sure, I believed that there were probably women out there who made false rape accusations because they regretted having sex, or because their reputations were at stake. But did I really think that was the case with Amber? Maybe she was worried about Daniel finding out. Maybe she knew he'd break up with her and she was afraid of having that happen, so she decided to act like she hadn't wanted to have sex. That I'd forced her. Or maybe she already *had* told Daniel what happened, and he'd ended things—why else would she have been with that guy at the bar tonight? Maybe I didn't know her as well as I thought I did. Maybe my dad was right—maybe Amber had told me to wait as a reflex, as what a "good" girl is supposed to say, knowing full well that I would keep going. Wanting me to. She hadn't *really* fought me. She didn't claw at my eyes or scream for help. She never actually used the word "no."

Seeing that I was confused, my father spoke again. "Tell me this. Did you force her up the stairs? Did you hold a gun or knife to her and threaten to kill her if she didn't have sex with you?"

"Of course not."

"Did you hit her? Did you tie her up and gag her so no one could hear her scream? Did you torture her or beat her into submission?" I shook my head, and he continued. "All right, then. It wasn't rape. You were two drunk, consenting adults, and now she regrets what she did. End of story."

His words reassured me, even though I had never liked how he treated women. Coming here had been a last resort, but it had surprisingly calmed me. For the first time in as long as I could remember, I felt connected to my dad, and I knew, no matter what might happen next, at least I had someone on my side.

Amber

A few weeks after my appointment with Vanessa, I sat, shrunk down behind the steering wheel in my car, parked about a block from the station house where Tyler worked. It was almost five a.m. on a mid-October morning, an hour before I would need to get to the gym to meet my first client, but I didn't want to leave until I saw exactly what time Tyler's truck would leave the station's parking lot. I'd been watching him for the last two weeks, trying to pin down his normal schedule, but the timing of his shifts varied—some nights he was off just after midnight, others, not until dawn—and I had discovered this was a more difficult task than I'd thought it would be. I figured if I stuck it out long enough, I could figure out a pattern and pinpoint the best time to approach him.

I wasn't exactly sure what I was doing, or how I would do it. I just knew that, after seeing Tyler with that woman at the bar, likely about to do to her what he'd done to me, I'd gone online and researched women who had taken revenge on their rapists. I was stunned by the level of violence the victims were capable of when carrying out their plans. I'd already heard of Lorena Bobbitt, of course—the woman who famously cut off the tip of her husband's penis after he'd come home drunk and raped her. But I also read about a woman whose little girl was raped by a man, and then, seven years later, when he saw her on the street and called out, "How's your daughter?" the mother followed him into a crowded bar, doused him with gasoline, and lit him on fire. There were stories of women in India cutting off their attackers' heads, of a Turkish woman who stabbed and shot her assailant in his groin, and then cut off his head, too. There was an American woman who lured her rapist into her house, tied him up, beat him with a baseball bat, and then tattooed the word "rapist" on his penis.

As I read these women's stories, as violent as they were, part of me couldn't help but cheer for them. I understood the desperation they felt, the reasons why they did what they did, even if I didn't think that mutilation or murder would be on my particular agenda when it came to holding Tyler accountable. What I wanted was much more subtle than that. Less final. I wanted him to suffer, yes, but in a way that would haunt him, the same way that I was haunted. I wanted him to ache with despair; I wanted him to wake up, breathing hard, worried that his heart might explode inside his chest. I wanted him to look in the mirror and be struck with self-loathing; I wanted his life to change forever, to have everything and everyone he loved be tainted—forever altered—by the ugliness of what he'd done. I wanted him to question everything about who he was, to hate himself as much as I did, me. I wanted him to pay a steep and painful price for what he did.

Still, as I sat in my car alone each morning, I didn't know how to make that happen. My parents continued to push me to go to the police, convinced—naïvely so—that the justice system would do its job and put Tyler away. They assumed I was reluctant to report what Tyler did because I was afraid I might end up getting put on trial myself, which of course was part of my hesitance, but mostly, I felt like the only way I could move on was to find a way to stop blaming myself, and the only thing that would let me do that was for Tyler to take the blame himself. If he admitted his guilt, I might find a way to alleviate my own.

I'd refused to go back and see Vanessa again, reasoning that there was no amount of talking that would fix what was broken inside of me. There was only action, only the idea of seeing a grainy picture of Tyler in the paper, the headline LOCAL PARAMEDIC PLEADS GUILTY TO RAPE written in bold, black letters above his face.

I watched as Tyler's red truck pulled out of the driveway and onto the street. I checked the clock on my cell phone—five thirty-six—and then slid down even further in my seat to make sure he didn't see me. I worried that he might recognize my car, but so far, he hadn't. At least, not that I knew of. It wasn't like he would call me now and ask if it had been me parked on the street.

And even though I tried to fight it, I felt a small pang of long-ing then, mourning the relationship he and I had shared for so many years. Just like that, it had vanished, all the days and hours we'd spent together, the laughter we'd shared, the sense of stabil-ity that no other relationship in my life seemed to match. There was a vacuum where our friendship had once been. He'd robbed me of the one constant in my world, besides my parents. He'd annihilated more than just my body that night—he'd crushed my entire life.

As he drove past, I squeezed my eyes shut, trying to fight back tears. How was I going to get him to admit what he'd done if I could barely stand the thought of him? How could I be in his physical presence without wanting to turn around and flee? He was so much stronger, he could easily overtake me. He could lure me in with sweet words of amends, promises of atonement, and then, without warning, he could rape me again. My entire body convulsed at the thought. I'd need something to even the playing field, something that would let me be in control. He could apologize, beg forgiveness, and the all the years I'd loved him might soften my heart and not make him confess. I needed something to remind me to be strong—to show him I couldn't be persuaded or sweet-talked. And then, my mind flashed to the image my father's black pistol, which was in his home office, locked away in the safe behind his desk. I knew where he kept the key—he'd shown me, years ago, in case I was ever alone in the house and needed to protect myself from anyone trying to break in. *That's it,* I realized. *The one thing that could make me more powerful than Tyler.* If I had a weapon, it would remind me that I was the one in control. There was no question it would give me the upper hand.

After I was sure he was gone, after I'd given him enough time to be blocks and blocks away, I finally sat upright in the driver's seat and started my car. Once at the gym, I went through the motions of my job, instructing Doris and my other clients through their workouts, cheering for them, correcting their positions as needed. But I was mostly thinking about that gun. How I could sneak it from the safe without my father knowing, how I would have to figure out a place to take Tyler where no one would interrupt us. How once I was holding that gun, I would be invincible.

"You're distracted today," Doris said as we finished up the last session of my shift and I walked with her into the locker room.

"Oh," I said. "Sorry. Just thinking about my test."

"Mmm-hmm," she said, skeptically. "You'll have to forgive me for saying this, dear, but I'm concerned about how much weight you've lost. You're wasting away."

"I'm just one of those people with a fast metabolism." I gave her a big, fake smile to make the lie more palatable. "I eat like crazy, but when I'm busy and a little stressed, the pounds just slide right off." I glanced down at my body, which, despite the valley between my hip bones and the ribs that showed through my skin, I knew could still stand to lose another ten pounds, at least. I felt disgusting. I pinched the skin of my stomach, sure there were fat cells multiplying beneath it, taunting me when I looked in the mirror.

Doris stared at me, lips pursed and her kind, cornflower blue eyes still filled with doubt. "If that's the case, you should talk with your doctor," she said, and I nodded, knowing that she meant well. But she didn't understand that every meal was a battlefield, that every bite was a bullet I put in my own mouth. Every pound I lost made me a purer version of myself.

As I drove home, I thought about how I could get Tyler to confess. I could hear a quiet, rational voice whispering in my ear, telling me I was out of my mind, saying that I should just go back and see Vanessa, let her help me navigate my life and stitch together the ragged remnants of my soul. But the louder voice inside me was that of anger—my absolute fury at the idea of Tyler getting away with this. If I let that happen, I was tacitly giving him permission to do the same thing to someone else.

I needed to get my hands on my father's gun.

When I pulled into my parents' driveway, I noticed an unfamiliar blue sedan parked in the spot next to mine. I wondered if it was one of my father's clients, who he sometimes invited over to sign paperwork if he was working from home. Feeling wary as I entered the house through the side door, I heard voices in the family room, just off the kitchen—my parents, and someone else.

"Hi, honey," my dad said, rising from where he had been sitting, next to my mother, on the couch. "Come meet Larry."

Larry was a tall, skinny reed of a man dressed in a blue suit that looked too short on his long limbs. He was completely bald, wore round glasses without frames, and his earlobes were huge, sticking out at a weird angle from his head.

"Hi," I said, dropping my purse on the counter and then crossing my arms over my chest, thinking that no good could come of a strange man in our house. Was he another counselor? A detective, maybe? Did my parents really have the nerve to bring the police to me when I'd refused go to them?

"Nice to meet you, Amber," Larry said, walking around the couch. He came toward me, holding out his hand, and so I shook it, quickly, and then crossed my arms again.

"Why don't you come join us?" my mom said. She was still on the couch, turned to look at me. Her eyes were rimmed in red, and I knew that she'd been crying.

My gaze bounced from her, to my dad, and then to Larry, and I shook my head. "I need to shower," I said. "And study."

"Amber, please," my dad said. "That can wait. We invited Larry over to speak with you."

"Without telling *me* about it first?" I said, unable to keep the anger from my words. "I told you, I don't want to talk to the police!"

"I'm not with the police," Larry said. His voice was low and calm. "I'm a lawyer, and I've represented several other women like you in civil cases against their attackers. It's my specialty."

"You *told* him?" I said, shooting an embittered look at both of my parents. I hated the idea that they'd discussed what Tyler had done to me behind my back, with a stranger, no less. I hated that Larry was looking at me now, picturing me with my dress pulled up around my hips, Tyler on top of me, holding me down.

"Just hear him out," my dad said, pleading. "You don't have to say anything. Just listen."

"Fine," I said, perching on one of the barstools under the counter.

"Don't be rude, Amber," my mother said. "Come sit down with us."

"That's okay," Larry said. He stayed standing, but leaned against the back of the couch, slipped his hands into the pockets of his slacks, and crossed one ankle over the other. I could see his pale skin above the blue and yellow striped socks he wore. I found myself thinking that his professional abilities had better be more polished than his fashion acumen. He looked at me for a moment, and then began to speak. "Your parents told me what happened to you in July. And that you decided not to report it to the police. Considering the circumstances, I can't say I blame you."

I raised a single eyebrow, my attention momentarily piqued by his affirmation of what I believed to be true.

"Unfortunately, our justice system, as it currently stands, regularly fails rape victims. There's rarely enough valid evidentiary proof in these types of situations to warrant an arrest, let alone a conviction."

"And that's my fault, right, because I didn't go straight to the hospital and have a rape kit done?" I said, feeling my defenses shoot back up.

"Amber . . ." my mom began, but Larry held up a hand to stop her.

"That's not what I meant," Larry said. "I was simply stating that in the majority of cases—and the majority *are* acquaintance rape—it's almost impossible to get an attacker to serve time for his crime. It's an ugly truth, but it's the way things are." He pushed up his glasses on the bridge of his nose. "But that doesn't mean there aren't other ways to bring attention to the kind of man he is."

"What other ways?" I ask, warily.

"You could file a civil suit, which only requires that we bring forth a preponderance of evidence that he raped you, instead of having to *prove* that he did beyond a reasonable doubt, which we'd have to at a criminal trial. You'd still have to testify as to what happened, but whether we win a legal judgment for damages against him or not, a suit of this sort would at least get his name out there, linked to being a rapist. People will know what he's done, and other women will be informed that he has the potential to hurt them. He might not go to jail, but some sort of justice could still be served."

Hearing this last sentence, I couldn't help it—I let out a sharp laugh. "So you want me to put myself out there and be dragged through the court of public opinion?" I shook my head. "No way. I've read about other women who've done just that. And what ends up happening is every boyfriend they've ever had, their entire sexual past, is put on trial instead of their attacker's. He's the 'good guy' who made a stupid mistake, and she's the whore who spread her legs and then regretted it."

I watched my parents both flinch as I spoke, and felt a little bad for being so blunt, but if they were bothered by my words now, I could only imagine how they'd feel when Tyler's lawyer searched out and cross-examined the string of men that I'd led into dark alleys over the last few months. I pictured these men sitting on the witness stand, describing how I'd pushed them up against the wall and reached into their pants. How I'd never even asked their names. I imagined describing for a jury the way I stood in front of the mirror in my bathroom when I came home after a night at the bars, staring at my reflection, hissing to it the same words I had when I was younger: *You're disgusting, you're filthy, you're fat.* Except now I added: *And you're a slut.*

"Are you worried about what Daniel will think?" my mom asked, and my lungs seized, realizing that if I followed through with my plan, if I managed to find a way to get Tyler to confess, Daniel would it read in the papers and know what had happened to me. He'd know the real reason I ended our engagement. I pictured him thinking back to our first date, when I'd brazenly pulled him inside my apartment and onto my bed, and I had no doubt he'd conclude that he should have known back then what kind of girl I really was; that a good woman, the kind of woman a man wants to marry, doesn't spread her legs on the first date. I imagined he'd be grateful that he got away from me when he did.

"Daniel doesn't have anything to do with this," I lied. "I haven't heard from him in months." I didn't say that I still checked my phone several times a day, hoping that he would reach out. I didn't say that every time I lured a man into an alley, I felt like Daniel was there watching me, repulsed and sick with regret for ever having touched me.

"And Daniel is . . . ?" Larry asked, looking back and forth between me and my mom.

"Amber's fiancé," my dad said.

"*Ex*-fiancé," I corrected.

"You were engaged at the time of the attack?" Larry inquired. I nodded.

"Would he be willing to testify on your behalf?" Larry asked.

"No," I said, at the same time both of my parents said, "Yes." I stood up from the barstool. "Look, I'm sorry, but there's nothing more to discuss. Nobody's going to be testifying about anything. I don't want to do this."

"Honey, please," my mom said. "You have to do something."

"No," I said, "I don't." I looked at Larry. "Sorry to waste your time." Not waiting for him to reply, I strode out of the kitchen, down the hall, and up to my room. My parents had no idea what I'd been up to; they had no clue that I planned to get Tyler to admit what he'd done and save me the pain—not to mention the expense—of bringing a suit against him. There was no way I could tell them; they'd just try to stop me. They wanted to believe that there was some other avenue I could take to expose him, but I knew that his confession was the only way to avoid the pitfalls of a system hell-bent on blaming women for the sins of men—the only way I wouldn't be victimized all over again. I'd been making myself suffer, caught in a cycle of pain I couldn't escape. I had to believe that getting Tyler to confess would finally put all the guilt and shame I carried where it actually belonged—onto him. *He* needed to suffer, now, and if the justice system couldn't make that happen, I would.

Tyler

For several weeks after I saw Amber at the bar, I spent a lot of time contemplating everything my father had said to me later that night. I went back and forth between agreeing with my dad that Amber was as much to blame as I was, and thinking his explanation of the biological imperative behind male-female sexual interaction was totally insane, a weak rationalization that had allowed him to treat women like shit over the years. But I couldn't deny it was good to feel like I had someone in my corner, especially one cold evening the first week of November as I climbed out of my truck and headed inside the station to begin my shift. I'd long run out of Valium, and while I knew that I hadn't taken enough of the medication since swiping the pills from the junkie mother's stash to be physically addicted, I still craved the chemical peace of mind the drug gave me. I often thought about where I could get more—the doctor, a psychiatrist, or our rig—but no option was ideal. If I talked to a medical professional, a diagnosis of an anxiety disorder would go on my insurance record and I might lose my job. If I slipped a few pills every now and then from the stock we kept for the victims Mason and I treated in the field, my partner would surely notice the discrepancy when he did inventory. The parameters were too tight, so I was basically out of luck. I'd have to find another way to cope.

Now, shivering from the bite of winter in the air, I greeted a few firemen as I entered the garage, where I knew my partner would already be, making sure the ambulance was properly stocked. Sure enough, as I approached the vehicle, I saw the back doors were open, and Mason sat with a clipboard in his lap, making note of what we had.

"Hey," I said. "Can I help?"

"Thanks, but I'm good," he said in the same clipped tone he'd been using with me for months.

"You sure?"

"Yeah." He hung the clipboard in its designated spot behind the driver's seat, and then looked at me. "You got a minute to go talk with the captain?"

"Uh, sure," I said, instantly feeling the muscles in my chest tense. "What's up?"

"I'd rather discuss it with him," Mason said as he climbed out of the rig and closed the doors. "He's expecting us."

"Oh." *This can't be good,* I thought, as I followed him up the stairs to the captain's office, which was adjacent to the kitchen, where most of the other men and women on shift were hanging out. *Did Mason report what had happened at the party? Am I going to get a black mark on my record for conduct unbecoming? Am I going to lose my job?*

Mason opened the office door, and Captain Duncan, who was sitting at his large oak desk, welcomed us in. "Have a seat," he said, fiddling with one thin end of his black handlebar mustache. Other than his eyebrows, it was the only hair on his entire head; the pink skin of his scalp reflected the fluorescent lighting above us. His uniform was perfectly pressed; he'd told us that his wife took pride in making sure his creases were straight as plumb lines.

Mason and I both sat down, and I noticed that my partner inched his chair slightly away from me. In a space so small, the motion seemed significant.

"So, Hicks," Captain Duncan said. "I need to inform you that Mason has requested a transfer to another station."

"What?" I said, swinging my gaze to my partner. I knew things were strained between us, but I had assumed that, with time, we'd go back to the way we were.

Mason didn't look at me; instead, he sat ramrod straight and kept his eyes on the captain.

"I know it's a hard thing, when a partnership doesn't work out," Captain Duncan said, "but it happens, and we all just have to learn how to deal with it." He looked at Mason. "I hate to lose you, but I've made your request official. As soon as an opening comes up, you can make the move."

"Thank you, sir," Mason said.

"Wait," I said. "Do I not get a say in this?"

"No," Captain Duncan said. "You don't. Just as Mason wouldn't have a say if you requested it." He paused, glancing back and forth between us. "I'm not going to have to deal with any bullshit between you two, am I? You can work together peacefully, for now?"

"Of course, sir," Mason said.

The captain turned toward me. "Hicks?"

I nodded, feeling the muscles along my jaws working as I clenched my teeth.

"Good," Captain Duncan said. He opened his mouth, about to speak again, but the radio behind him crackled, requesting units be dispatched to the corner of Eldridge and Meridian, where a traffic accident had occurred. "You heard them," the captain said, pointing to the doorway. "Get to it."

Mason and I made our way back down to the garage and

climbed into our rig, where he flipped on the lights and siren while I let dispatch know we were on our way to the accident. The air between us was thick and heavy as a rock; I had the futile urge to pick it up and toss it out the window.

"Am I really that bad?" I asked, keeping my eyes straightforward.

"I don't think we should talk about this right now," he said.

"I saw Amber at the Royal a few weeks ago," I told him. "She was making out with some disgusting old guy in a dark hallway." Mason didn't say anything, so I went on. "What I can't figure out is, if she's the kind of girl who grinds her body against her best friend, who kisses him and goes upstairs to a bedroom at a party with him, and *then* searches out a stranger at a bar, all while she's engaged to someone else, how can what happened with us be rape?"

"Dude," Mason said, shooting an angry glance my way, his dark eyes flashing. "You do *not* want to have this conversation with me."

"Yeah, actually," I said, "I do. Because seriously. How is a guy supposed to let a girl get him all turned on, make him believe that she really wants to have sex with him, and then just be okay with her suddenly changing her mind at the last second? If she's out at bars now, cheating on Daniel and making out with strangers, she can't be the girl I thought she was. She can't be the girl *you* thought she was." I felt desperate. If I could just get Mason to agree with me, to concede that Amber was guilty of at least part of what happened that night, I might be able to live with myself.

Mason jerked the steering wheel to get around a long string of cars that weren't pulling out of our way. "Is that you talking, or your dad?" he asked. "Because you sound like a stupid frat boy, trying to rationalize his way out of taking advantage of a wasted girl. You going to make a video, like those assholes at Yale, chanting, 'No means yes, yes means anal'?"

"What the fuck are you talking about?"

"Google it," Mason said harshly, as he continued to bob and weave down West Holly. "Stop thinking about yourself for a fucking second and get some education about what rape actually is. And for the record, most of the time it looks *exactly* like what happened between you and Amber. I don't give a shit who she's making out with in a bar or whether she's engaged to Daniel or not. The fact is that she told you to *stop* and you had sex with her anyway. *That's* the definition of rape. *That's* what you're guilty of, and the fact that you won't own up to it is why I have to get the fuck away from you. I have a daughter, man. And if some fucker did to her what you did to Amber, I'd do a lot more than punch him in the face. I'd *kill* him." He paused, breathing hard, and then spoke again. "You make me *sick*."

Tears pricked the backs of my eyes as Mason said these last words, and I looked away, out the passenger side window, blinking quickly to get them to disappear. Outside of Amber, Mason had become my closest friend, and hearing him tear me apart like this now, knowing that I triggered such feelings of disgust in him, made me feel like I was cracking open. Loud thoughts ricocheted inside my head, my dad's and Mason's voices, each vying to be heard, each telling me conflicting things. I didn't know who to believe.

As we approached the scene of the accident, my pulse was already racing, my heart pounding like a jackhammer. We both jumped out of the rig and raced around to the back to grab our gear. I went through the motions of my job, running a line, assessing airway, breathing, and circulation. Luckily, it was only a fender bender and no one was seriously injured; I was too distracted to have handled something like that.

Mason and I got through the rest of our shift, speaking only when we had to, doing our jobs, the fat elephant of what he'd said—*you make me sick*—still stuck between us. Maybe he was right. Maybe my father was just a womanizing asshole, and I'd been grasping at empty, meaningless straws by asking his advice. Maybe the desire to shift blame onto Amber was the only way I could keep it from clinging to me. Maybe the only way to get my life back was to admit what I did.

But then, a shock of terror pulsed through me as I imagined what would happen next. I imagined talking to the police, being handcuffed, put into an orange jumpsuit, and locked behind bars. I thought about losing my job, losing my reputation—losing everything I had managed to build for myself over the past several years. And I knew that no matter what I'd already lost, no matter that Mason would soon disappear from my life as Amber had, I wasn't willing to sacrifice myself. I might have doubts, I might share in some of the guilt for what happened that night, but I wasn't the only one.

Now, as I grabbed my bag from the rig after Mason had already gone home, I headed out the door into the parking lot. It was late, after midnight, and the air was chillier than it had been when I started my shift. I tucked my hands into my coat pockets, and began to make my way across the lot. I looked toward my truck, and suddenly, I stopped short, because Amber was waiting for me. She was standing next to my truck, her hands shoved in her coat pockets, too.

"We need to talk," she said, and like a hopeful idiot, I nodded, wanting to believe that she had changed her mind and was there to make peace. I wanted to believe this as I walked around to the driver's side door and climbed inside. I wanted to believe this as she joined me, slamming the passenger door. *We're going to work this out,* I thought, still believing that in the end, after everything, our friendship could win out. I believed she still might love me, right up until the moment when she pulled out the gun.

Amber

It's almost dawn when Tyler and I finally arrive at the cabin. The sky is a dusky mix of lavender and gray; a few stars still twinkle above us as we walk down a path surrounded by a dense forest of snow-dusted evergreens. The roar of the river fills my head—the water is only thirty feet away. When I was young, falling asleep to that sound was something I looked forward to every year. My mother called it nature's lullaby. It does nothing to soothe me now.

After we get inside and light a single lantern, I point the gun at Tyler and tell him to sit on the lumpy, plaid-patterned couch. The air is musty and cold; mouse traps, some of which have already done their job, litter the floor around us. I try not to look at the motionless rodents; I try to pretend that I don't smell death.

"So, we're here," Tyler says, as he complies with my request. "Now what?"

I take pleasure in hearing the tremble in his voice, but the truth is that I don't know what I should do. Getting him to the cabin was as far ahead as I had planned. I want him to confess. I need to hear the words "I raped you" coming from his mouth. But I don't know how to make that happen. I consider holding the gun to his head and forcing him to speak the truth, asking him to recite, in detail, the way he attacked me.

"Remember the first time you came here?" I ask instead, thinking back to the summer just before my freshman year. Even though Tyler and I spent the first nine months of our friendship at different schools, we had grown close during the many fall and winter evenings he spent at our dinner table, the weekends we watched horror movies together at his house because my mom wouldn't allow me to view them at mine. His parents' divorce was finalized in the spring, and my mom and dad decided to invite Liz and Tyler to the cabin with us for a weeklong vacation in June. We packed up several ice chests and plastic bins full of food, stuffing both family vehicles with sleeping bags, inner tubes for floating down the river, and board games we could play. Tyler and I rode with my parents, while Liz followed behind us. They'd both been camping, but neither of them had stayed this far into the woods before.

"Of course I remember," he says now. "You took me hiking and made me learn how to fish."

"And I taught you how to ride the river on an inner tube."

"You almost drowned," Tyler says, softly, and I know we are both thinking about the day my black rubber tube had unexpectedly flipped—how I got sucked into a circling undertow next to a giant, craggy rock. I remember kicking and flailing all of my limbs as hard as I could, trying to free myself from the strong funnel pulling me down, trapping me beneath the surface. But I couldn't, and it was Tyler who grabbed on to a fallen tree with one arm and managed to grab on to my hand and lift me to safety with the other.

"You saved me," I say, tears welling in my eyes. Remembering moments like this in our friendship only added to the nightmare of what he'd done to me in July. It magnified his betrayal, amplified my pain, and made me feel like I'd never be able to trust another man again. The friend Tyler had been to me for so many years was the polar opposite of the attacker he had become. Most of the time my mind didn't know what to do with this disparity. It made me feel crazy, one moment remembering how close we'd been, how often he was there for me, listening, refusing to abandon me when everyone else seemed to. Then I'd be hit with the memory of the weight of him on me, the stench of alcohol on his breath, and the sharp pain of him jabbing at me with his hips. I couldn't reconcile these two versions of the same person. My mind kept telling me it couldn't be real.

"Sometimes I think it was you who saved me," he says. His green eyes reflect the flickering light from the lantern on the table in front of the couch.

"What're you talking about?" I say, momentarily distracted from the fury I feel by the memory of that day. "You pulled me out of the water."

"I'm not talking about the river," he says. "I'm talking about how you came over and sat next to me at your parents' party after my dad threw me in the pool. Having you as a friend saved me in so many ways."

I let out a short, barking laugh and sit down in the pleather recliner, opposite him, and drop the gun into my lap. "You have a fucked-up way of showing your gratitude."

"I know," he says. "Trust me, please. I know how badly I screwed up. But you have to believe I never meant to hurt you."

"So you keep saying. And I keep saying that what you *meant* to do doesn't matter. What matters is what you *did*. You *raped* me, Tyler. Just say it. Just fucking admit it so I don't have to shoot you." I try to sound strong, worried he might call me out on my bluff. I don't know if I actually have it in me to pull the trigger. I don't know if I can follow through on my threats.

"You're not going to shoot me," he says, but there is a hint of uncertainty in his voice. He is testing me, seeing if he can come out the winner in this battle of wills.

"How can you be sure?" I ask, holding his gaze while I run my free hand over the cool steel of the gun. With one quick bend of my thumb, I turn off the safety and give him a challenging look. *Go ahead,* the look says. *Try me.*

"Because that's not who you are," Tyler says. "The only person you've ever been able to hurt is yourself."

"Fuck you," I whisper, knowing he's referring to the years I spent starving myself, the same way I've been starving myself since the night he led me up to that room and pinned me down on the bed. Restricting what I eat is my go-to act of self-defense; the best way I know how to feel strong in the midst of turmoil. I've lost twenty-six pounds since July, my weight sliding back into double digits. My old behaviors have snuck back in, embracing me like a familiar blanket.

"Is your heart okay?" he asks. "With all the weight you've lost?"

"Stop pretending like you give a shit!" I say. My tone is an octave higher than usual, on the verge of shrieking. "Nothing you say right now can make a difference, except admitting what you did!"

"What *we* did, Amber," Tyler says. "Don't forget how drunk you were, too. Don't forget that it was you who kissed me, first." His voice is still soft, but it's also laced with a hint of defiance, a fact that only serves to feed my rage. When we first climbed inside his truck, he'd said he was sorry—he'd said he hated himself for hurting me. And now he was going to blame *me?* Fuck that. Fuck *him.*

"Kissing didn't give you permission to have sex with me! I told you to wait! I asked you to stop! And you *ignored* me!" I lift the gun again and point it at him, my arm shaking so much that I have to cup the butt of the weapon with two hands in order to hold it still. "You made me bleed! You left bruises all over my body. I couldn't *move* without remembering what you did. Goddamn it, Tyler, just admit it! Admit it and promise that you'll tell the police. That you'll turn yourself in! That's all I'm asking you to do!"

"I'm sorry," he says, "but I can't. I'll lose my job. I'll lose everything."

"What about what *I've* lost?" I say. I stand up, arms held straight in front of me, gripping the gun. "You don't give a shit about that, do you? All you're thinking about is you. What might happen to you." I breathe in and out, rapidly, feeling my heart flutter, and I am suddenly terrified that I might have another heart attack. But then it hits me that I've come too far, fought through too much, to give up now. A renewed sense of determination flows through me. I'm going to right this wrong. "You know what, Tyler? You sound exactly like your father. Like an egomaniacal, self-absorbed, *rapist bastard.*"

He closes his eyes momentarily, and I know that I've hit him where it hurts most. *Good,* I think. *I want you to hurt. I want you in so much pain you feel like you're going to die.* He's just said that I couldn't shoot him. But there is a fiery ache in the pit of my stomach and I think I'm capable of doing anything it takes to get him to speak the truth.

"There has to be some other way," he says, sounding as though he is struggling to remain calm.

"There isn't," I say, cocking the hammer with my thumb. "Admit what you did. Say it. Promise you'll go to the police." If he refuses, there's only one thing I can do. One way to make him pay.

"Amber, I can't. You have to understand. If you'd just stop—"

"The same way *you* stopped that night?" I take a step toward him, and he freezes, realizing his mistake.

"We can find another way," he says, again. He stands up then, too, looking like he might come at me, like he's trying to figure out a way to grab the gun.

"No," I say, gripping the weapon as tightly as I can. With the safety off, all it will take is a single twitch of my finger. "Sit down. Now!"

He holds completely still, except for his eyes, which bounce between my face and my hands. I can see a thick blue vein pulsing in his neck, and beads of sweat sprout across his forehead, but he doesn't comply with my order. I am white hot with rage.

"You won't shoot me," he repeats. "Give me the gun, Amber. This has gone on long enough. You can't prove I forced you to do anything. If you could, I would have been arrested by now. Bringing me here was a mistake. If you stop this, if we just get in the truck and drive back home, I won't tell the police."

"Tell them what?" I goad him, preparing my stance the way my father taught me at the shooting range back in high school. "Steady legs and tight, strong torso gives you the most control," he said, and even though I never thought I'd have to use his advice, I'd never forgotten it.

"That you kidnapped me," Tyler says, taking one more step toward me. We're less than six feet away from each other now. "At gunpoint, no less." He waits, trying to stare me down. "I think that might be even more jail time than rape."

When I hear him suggest that it would be me who would be incarcerated instead of him, the fury inside me explodes, blotting out any restraint I might have left. This is not the Tyler who sat by my hospital bed, helping me find my way back from my own personal hell. This is not the Tyler who saved me from drowning. That Tyler is gone—he disappeared the night he yanked down my panties and speared me until I bled. This Tyler, the one who stands in front of me now, is pure evil, a spiteful, monstrous doppelgänger of the boy who was once my best friend.

With this realization, I meet his intense gaze with one of my own, and in that moment, everything changes. My breathing slows, and my body relaxes. I'm no longer afraid. No longer unsure. I feel calm. Full of resolve. I know exactly what has to happen next.

"Go to hell," I say. And then, just as he lunges toward me, his arms outstretched, I put my finger on the trigger, take aim, and shoot.

Tyler

The bullet from Amber's gun tears through my right shoulder, causing me to cry out and topple onto the dusty floor. The acrid stench of gunpowder fills the air. The pain is unbearable—a searing sensation my mind can barely process. I can't move.

"Mother *fucker*," I say, spitting the word through tight lips. *She shot me.* My best friend had done the one thing I didn't believe she would do. I lie on my left side, in agony, but manage to lift my free hand up against my shoulder, knowing I need to apply pressure to the wound.

"Say it," Amber says, standing above me, still holding the gun. "Admit what you did. Say you'll go to the police." She sounds like a maniacal windup doll, a haunting creature created for a horror movie, repeating the same words over and over again.

I squeeze my eyes shut. My deltoid muscle is on fire; I can feel blood oozing down my back, and I hope this means the bullet isn't lodged somewhere inside my shoulder, wreaking havoc on my joint. I might be okay if it went straight through, though it still could have bounced off the bone on the way out. It's possible I'll suffer nerve damage and maybe even lose partial function in my arm.

"Answer me!" Amber shrieks. "Tell me you'll do what I want and I'll drive you to a hospital right now!"

"First . . . get the aid kit . . . from my truck," I say, trying to ignore the seething heat radiating from my shoulder as it travels throughout the rest of my body. The metallic smell of my own blood is sickening; I can taste it in the back of my throat.

"No!"

"Please, Amber!" My words come out in short bursts, as I try to handle the pain by controlling my breath. "At least . . . give me something . . . a towel or a blanket . . . anything to stop . . . the bleeding."

"Why should I?" she asks. "You might not be able to see my wounds, Tyler, but you tried to kill me first."

She's not in her right mind, I think. The Amber I know would never have pulled that trigger. I'd tried to remain calm since we first climbed into my truck at the station. I didn't want to aggravate the situation by challenging her. I didn't want my own anxiety to make the situation worse. But when we got inside the cabin, I decided to change tactics. I thought I could intimidate her. I could force her down from the precarious ledge she'd been standing upon—I thought I might be able to convince her to capitulate and let me go.

"I'm sorry," I say, grinding my teeth. "I never—"

"If you say you never meant to hurt me one more time, Tyler, I swear to god I'll shoot you in the head." Her voice is calm again. *Too calm,* I think. *I've never seen her act this way. I have no idea what she might do next.* I think about my training, how I'd been taught to deal with mentally unstable people in the field. *Make them believe they're winning,* my instructors always said. *Keep them calm, let them think that you're on their side.*

"Okay," I say, looking up at her, my left hand still pressing where the bullet entered my shoulder. "I get it. But please . . . something to stop . . . the bleeding."

"Not until you promise to turn yourself in."

Had this been her plan, all long? Bring me to a secluded place, and then shoot me to make me confess? "Fine," I say. I'll tell her whatever she needs to hear just so we can end this. "I promise."

"You'll go to the police with me? You'll tell them you raped me?"

I nod, biting my bottom lip, willing to concede anything to get her to help me.

She hesitates, and then walks a circle around me, out of my reach, toward the kitchen, where she rummages around in a few of the drawers until she comes up with a sealed plastic box filled with dish towels. She returns to where I am lying with a stack of them, and throws them at me. "You have to do it." Her voice is dull now. Defeated. "You have to admit what you did."

I pull back my hand from my shoulder and try to gauge how much blood I've lost by looking at it, but there's no way to be sure. It's possible the bullet nicked the brachial artery, and if it did, I need to get to an ER sooner rather than later. I take a couple of the towels and press them hard against my shoulder, managing to sit up and lean against the side of the couch.

"I know," I say. I worry I might pass out from the pain. But there's no way Amber can carry me to the truck; I need to stay alert long enough for her to get us back on the road. I look at her, and try to keep the rage I feel from showing on my face. "I still need the first aid kit . . . from my truck. There's a special kind of gauze . . . that will make a gel and . . . seal off the wound. I'll need your help . . . wrapping it up."

"I should have aimed for your heart," she says, but there is no energy behind her words.

"Amber," I say. My breathing is still erratic. "Please. The kit."

She bobs her head, and then disappears out the front door, returning a few minutes later with the large red bag from under the driver's seat. It isn't your standard, pick-it-up-at-Target kind of kit.

I'd packed it myself with the same supplies that Mason and I use on our rig and in the field. She drops it at my feet, and I notice that she's no longer holding the gun. *Should I hit her?* I wonder. *Should I knock her down and make a run for the truck? Should I just leave her behind?*

I think these things, but I know I can't do them, not in my current state. I'd bleed out before I got over the hill and back on the highway. "I can't do it . . . on my own," I tell her. "Can you find the hemostatic gauze? I need you . . . to wrap the shit . . . out of my shoulder."

She nods her head again, picks up the kit, carrying it with her to come kneel next to me. We don't speak, though I can't help crying out a few times as she tears my shirtsleeve away and shifts me around in order to tend to the wound. When she's finished, she leans back to sit on her heels, puts her face in her hands, and begins to cry.

"Why did you do it, Tyler?" she asks, and there is so much raw, naked sorrow in her voice, it reaches inside me and claws at my heart. She drops her hands and stares at me. "You were my best friend. You're the one person I always thought I could count on, someone who would always believe in me, no matter what. And you just tore me up. I didn't know what to do. What to say. I needed my best friend and I couldn't talk to him because he was the one who hurt me." She pauses to wipe her eyes with a stray corner of gauze. "You destroyed me, Tyler. Everything I believed about myself, about my life, disappeared that night. I don't know who I am anymore. I don't know who I am without you there to help me figure it out."

I open my mouth, about to speak, but she shakes her head. "No, don't," she says. "There's nothing you can say to me that will change what you did. Nothing to fix us. But you can admit what you did. You can never do this to anyone else again. Please, Tyler. Tell the truth."

I stare at her, pressing my lips together as she says the same words Mason had said to me just a couple of months before. And I can't help but think that if Amber had been pushed this far—desperate enough to shoot me—what I did to her in that bed was worse. I know all too well that it's the wounds no one can see that cause the bloodiest, messiest pain—secret injuries that, no matter the years that pass, never quite heal. I think about the pills I'd taken to try to help manage my guilt, and then, the way I allowed myself to be comforted by the same logic I'd watched my father use to justify his poor treatment of women over the years—the treatment I'd always abhorred. I suddenly feel sick, not just because I've been shot, but because I realize that I'd let his criticism of me the afternoon of the party drive my behavior that night. I'd behaved like him long before that even, if I am really being honest with myself. I used Whitney for sex for months, maybe even coerced her that first time on my couch, not giving a second thought to her youth or vulnerability. I'd wanted Amber so much that I didn't listen when she told me to stop. All I heard in that moment was my father's voice in my head, telling me a girl like her would never want someone like me, and wanting to prove him wrong. I could rationalize it however I wanted, but if, in fact, Mason was right and the definition of rape is performing a sexual act without the other person's consent, then I was a rapist. Amber had given consent for everything up until that moment when I lay on top of her on the bed; she'd even instigated it. But she'd also told me to wait . . . to stop. I held her down and had sex with her anyway. And all I'd done since then was try to escape my guilt. All I'd wanted was to blame her so I didn't have to take it upon myself.

So instead of speaking, I simply close my eyes and shake my head, and begin to cry, too. I cry in a way I haven't for years. I cry because I know I am guilty, and the only thing I can do to right this wrong is turn myself in. I cry because I know that, even if I do this, I've still lost Amber forever. I'll lose my job, too. I might even go to jail. I'll be branded a rapist for the rest of my life, and though I still might not be able to reconcile that word with the man I thought I was, as Mason said to me the morning after he drove Amber home, we'd seen it on the job a hundred times—normal, everyday people are capable of doing horrendous things. Drunk drivers who kill another person are still murderers, even if that hadn't been their intent when they got behind the wheel. In that case, and now, in mine, intent doesn't matter. What matters is the result.

"I'm sorry," I say, my entire body shaking from my tears and the pain that throbs in my shoulder. "I'm so, so sorry. I'll tell the truth, I promise. I'll tell them what I did. I wish I could take it back. All I've ever wanted is for you to be happy and I fucked it all up."

"Yeah," she says, darkly. "You did." She wipes her eyes as she stands up, and then helps me do the same. She looks up at me with confusion and hurt and fear littered across her face. "Say it to me now," she says, and I know exactly what she means. She wants me to prove to her that I'll follow through on my promise, that I'll actually go to the authorities and admit what I did.

And even though every cell in my brain is screaming at me to clamp my mouth shut, even though I still long to hide behind all my manufactured justifications—I can't live another minute carrying this soul-choking suffering around. The pain in my shoulder is nothing compared to the one in my heart as I look at Amber and finally speak the truth.

"I raped you," I whisper, feeling my insides begin to crumble, and I know that everything in my life is about to collapse, that the world I've known is as good as gone.

Amber

I couldn't believe that I'd actually pulled the trigger. That moment, the entire night, had taken on a dreamlike quality, viewed through blurry eyes and filled with strange and shadowy, amorphous scenes. When I'd left Vanessa's office that day back in September, trying to think of a way to make Tyler pay other than reporting him to the police and hoping for the best, I never believed that this was where I'd end up. I'd thought that the threat of the weapon would be enough to get him to confess; I never imagined that I'd have to shoot him.

But even now, after watching him bleed and cry, after hearing the words I'd hoped would help ease my pain, nothing had changed. My body still felt his assault and my mind was still an exhausted mess of confusion, anger, and grief. I looked at him and saw not only my attacker, but the boy who'd held my hand while I lay in a hospital bed, fighting for my life. I saw the awkward teenager who'd grown into a strong and capable man; I saw someone for whom I felt as much love as I did hate. That, I realized, was the crux of my despair; this connection between rapist and friend, two labels that described Tyler—two words that would forever ring discordant in my ears.

"Come on," I finally said, blowing out the one kerosene lantern I'd lit when we arrived. "We need to get you to a hospital."

He nodded, grimacing as he got to his feet. We stepped outside into the cold midmorning air, and I breathed in the sweet, fresh scent of damp earth and pine, looking up to the tall evergreens in the forest around us. Long, curved branches swayed in a gentle wind, moving like a conductor's arms leading his musicians through a slow and beautiful symphony. I carried the first aid kit up the hill to the truck, opening the passenger side door for Tyler, who staggered slowly behind me, his left hand still pressing on his now-wrapped wound. I knew he had to be in agony, but I took less pleasure from this than I'd thought I would. *Don't go soft now,* I thought. *After all of this, don't let him think that he doesn't have to follow through.*

It took well over an hour to drive up over the logging road and get back on the highway that would lead us into the town of Monroe, where I knew the closest emergency room would be. My parents had taken me there one summer, years before we had even met Tyler and his family, when we'd gone to the cabin and I'd slipped on the rocks in the river and broken my arm. I was half-tempted to make him wait until we got back to Bellingham, where I could take him to St. Joseph's and the police could come and hear him confess from his hospital bed. I was afraid if I waited, if I let him think too long, he might go back on his word and the entire night would have been for nothing. But as I glanced at the sloppy bandage I'd wrapped around his wound, I could see that, despite the special gauze, it was already soaked through with a large spot of bright red blood. He needed a doctor, and I was too afraid of what would happen if I didn't get him to one. However much I hated Tyler, however much I wanted him to pay, I didn't actually want him dead. I wanted him alive and able to suffer the consequences of his crime. I wanted him to feel every minute of humiliation and loss that his confession would bring.

Tyler didn't speak during the drive; he only rested his head against the window, eyes closed, continuing to clutch his injured shoulder with his one good hand. He was pale, his breathing was rapid, and his skin was clammy. When I finally pulled up in front of the emergency room entrance and turned off the engine, it was me who broke the silence. "Are you going to tell them I shot you?" My heart raced inside my chest. I kept my eyes forward, unable to look at him as I waited for his reply.

"It was an accident," he said, and I could tell from the staggered pace of the words that he was in a great deal of pain. "You didn't know it was loaded." He must have sensed my hesitance, because he spoke again. "Don't worry. I know what to say."

I bobbed my head, still unsure whether I could trust him, and jumped out of the truck, quickly making my way into the ER. "My friend's been shot," I said. My voice trembled, and the woman at the front desk gave me a suspicious look, as though she was trying to decide whether to call for a doctor or security. I held my breath until she nodded and picked up the phone. A moment later, a man and a woman dressed in mint green scrubs appeared with a gurney. "This way," I said, leading them out to the truck, where Tyler was slumped against the passenger door.

"What happened?" the man asked, as the two of them carefully extracted Tyler from the front seat.

I kept my eyes on Tyler, my muscles tensed, wondering how he might respond. *He could easily turn the tables,* I thought. *He could tell them I kidnapped and shot him, and then every bit of this night, every moment I'd suffered, would be pointless. I could end up going to jail instead of him.*

"We were looking at her dad's gun up at their cabin," Tyler said through clenched teeth, groaning a bit as they moved him. "We didn't know it was loaded," he said. "It was an accident."

I let loose a quiet sigh of relief.

"Is that true?" the woman asked, skeptically.

I swallowed hard, wondering if she could tell that he was lying. Did she wonder if he'd tried to attack me and I'd shot him in self-defense? Did she think that maybe I'd shot him outright? "Yes," I said, and despite my exhaustion and frayed nerves, I manage to keep my tone calm and my expression neutral.

"We'll have to report it," the man said, as they pushed the gurney back inside, me trailing a few feet behind them. "Reception likely already called the police. It's protocol."

"Okay," I said, not knowing if I should stay with Tyler or wait for him by the front desk. I didn't want to be around him any more than I had to, but I also was worried what he might tell his doctors or the police if I wasn't standing right there. My stomach churned, as I was unable to think of anything but getting him back to Bellingham, to the police station, and making sure that he confessed.

Once Tyler was in a small room of the ER, the woman informed us that they were both nurses, and the doctor was on his way. They began running IVs, taking Tyler's blood pressure, and removing the gauze I'd slapped on his shoulder in order to examine the bloody damage. The female nurse took down our names, writing them on a chart that hung on the end of Tyler's bed.

I stood as far back as I could, not wanting to be in the way. A short, heavy man in light blue scrubs arrived and introduced himself as Dr. Morris, then listened to the nurses' assessment of Tyler's condition.

"The bullet went through and through," the male nurse said. "A reported accidental discharge. The police are on their way."

Dr. Morris glanced at me, where I cowered in the corner, arms crossed over my chest. "And you are?"

"A friend," Tyler answered for me. "We live in Bellingham, but Amber's family has a cabin out past Index, on the Skykomish. We were up there winterizing it, and unfortunately, when she picked up the gun, it went off."

"I didn't know it was loaded," I said, repeating what Tyler had already told the nurses, hoping I sounded more convincing than I felt.

"I see." The doctor began to examine Tyler's wound, ordering X-rays and an MRI to assess the damage. "Looks like you managed to stop the bleeding fairly quickly," he said.

"I'm a paramedic," Tyler said. "I had hemostatic gauze in my kit."

"Good thing," Dr. Morris said. "Depending on what your tests show, we might be able to avoid surgery." He rattled off instructions to the nurses, who made note of them as he spoke, and then the doctor and the female nurse disappeared from the room.

I watched as the remaining nurse hung a bag of clear fluid from the silver pole next to Tyler's bed and then injected something into his IV. "What are you giving him?" I asked, worried that if Tyler got too loopy from pain meds, he might start babbling about what really happened.

"Oxycodone," the nurse said. "Just enough to take the edge off."

"Oh," I said, feeling the word catch in my already dry throat. It had been hours since I'd had anything to drink, and well over a day since I'd slept. My eyelids felt leaden and scratchy as I blinked, fixing my gaze on Tyler's face, silently willing him to keep his mouth shut.

"Don't worry," the nurse said. "He'll be fine. If he doesn't need surgery, you should be able to take him home this afternoon."

"Thanks," I said, and then he, too, exited the room, leaving me alone with Tyler, whose skin was as white as the sheets he lay upon. He had to be as exhausted as I was—probably more so, considering the trauma his body had endured. Again, I struggled between having compassion for the boy I used to love and wanting the man who raped me to suffer. Confronting these two opposing versions of him in my head at the same time was excruciating—maybe as much as the rape itself.

"I can feel you worrying from here," he said, rolling his head to one side so he could look directly at me. His voice had taken on a softer edge, so I assumed the pain meds were doing their job.

"I'm not worried," I lied, trying to sound more confident than I felt. He could still hear my thoughts before I spoke them—would anyone else ever know me so well? Could I feel as safe with another person, the way I used to feel safe with him?

"Yeah, you are," Tyler said. "Trust me, you don't have to."

I took a few steps over to the sink on the opposite side of the room, grabbed a small paper cup, and filled it with water, gulping it down. I refilled the cup, drinking until my parched throat was finally quenched. I turned around, about to answer him—about to remind him that he'd stolen my ability to trust him when he held me down on that bed—but just as I opened my mouth, two uniformed police officers entered the room. I froze where I stood, the empty paper cup still in my hand.

"Amber Bryant?" one of the officers asked, looking at me. He was young, maybe even younger than me, reed-thin and tall, with closely cropped black hair and blue eyes.

"Yes," I said, but my voice cracked on the word, so I cleared my throat and spoke again. "That's me," I said, then crumpled the cup and threw it in the garbage beneath the sink.

"And you're Tyler Hicks?" asked the other officer—an older, thickly built man with salt and pepper hair and a full mustache.

"Yes, sir," Tyler said.

"I'm Officer Porter," the older cop said, and then he gestured toward the younger man, who was standing closer to me. "This is my partner, Officer Olsen." Tyler and I both nodded, and Officer Porter continued. "Can you tell me what happened to you, Mr. Hicks?"

"Yeah, of course," Tyler said, and again, as it had when I first entered the ER, my body tensed and I began taking shallow breaths. Everything hinged on this moment, what would come out of Tyler's mouth next. "Amber and I went up to her parents' cabin to winterize it," he said, maintaining strong eye contact with the older officer. "She picked up her dad's gun, and for whatever reason, it went off. The next thing I knew, I was on the floor and I was bleeding."

Officer Porter glanced my direction, and I nodded, still anxious, every nerve I had still shot through with fear, because no matter what Tyler said, it was possible the cops wouldn't believe him. It was possible that they'd poke and prod at our story until it fell apart.

"I don't know how it happened," I said. "I feel terrible." This was true. I *did* feel terrible, but not because of the shooting. It was so much more complicated than that. Tears sprang to my eyes, and I hoped that the officers would view this response as a show of remorse instead of what it really was—the dizzying confusion I felt about the fact that Tyler had chosen to protect me now, despite also being the one who tore my life apart. If, when we got home, he actually confessed to the rape, we would need to withhold the truth of how he had been shot from everyone—from the authorities and our parents. I would have to trust that he would forever be the keeper of this secret.

"How far apart were you when the gun discharged?" Officer Porter asked.

"About six feet, I think?" Tyler said, looking at me. "Does that sound right?"

I nodded again, not trusting my voice, worried it might break and give us away.

"She helped me put pressure on the wound and got me here as fast as she could," Tyler said. "We had to take the logging road, since the main road is still washed out."

The tension inside my chest began to lessen as Tyler spoke, and it looked as though Officer Porter believed what we had said. I watched as Officer Olsen made notes on the pad he carried, and then looked at his partner, expectantly. *He must be new,* I thought. *He's waiting for a cue because he doesn't know what to do next.* I felt a little better knowing that we were only dealing with one experienced cop, hoping this meant that they'd be less likely to doubt our story.

"Where's the weapon?" Officer Porter asked.

"In my truck," Tyler said, and I was glad I'd put it inside the console when I'd gone to get the first aid kit. If I hadn't, if I'd left it at the cabin, the cops might have thought we had something to hide.

"Did you check to see if the safety was on when you picked it up?" Officer Porter asked, turning toward me.

"No," I said, suddenly tearful again. "I should have. I'm so sorry."

"It's okay," Tyler said, locking his green eyes on mine. "It was an accident. A mistake. I know you didn't mean to do it. You'd take it back if you could."

His words landed like a boulder flung against my chest, since I knew that he wasn't only talking about what had happened with the gun. I started to cry then, in earnest. My shoulders shook and I put my face in my hands. "I'm sorry," I said. "I'm so, so sorry." But as I sobbed, I realized my apology wasn't about shooting him—it was more about the loss of our friendship. In that moment, listening to him lie to the police in order to protect me, I felt connected to him the same way I used to before the rape. I remembered what it was like to be in on something with him, to know something that only the two of us knew—to trust someone implicitly—and it hit me hard, then, that we'd never have that same kind of closeness again. Everything I believed about him, about *me,* had changed.

"It's okay," Officer Olsen said, awkwardly patting my back.

"We'll need to examine the gun," Officer Porter said as he handed me a tissue from the box on the counter next to the sink. "And file a report."

"Thank you," I said, sniffling as I took the tissue from him. I felt Tyler's eyes on me, too, but I couldn't look at him, for fear that I might totally fall apart.

"Do you need anything else?" Tyler asked. "Do we need to sign something?"

"No," Officer Porter said. "Seems clear this was an accident." He looked at me. "Don't beat yourself up too badly, miss. These things happen." He paused, and frowned. "But in the future, you might want to look into some gun safety training, if you're going to be handling a weapon."

I bobbed my head and blew my nose, just as the male nurse reentered the room. "All right, Tyler," he said. "Time to wheel you off for some tests." He looked back and forth between the officers. "Did you get everything you need?"

"Yep," Officer Olsen said. "Just need to take a look at the gun."

"I'll take you to the truck," I said, feeling like now that Tyler had made an official statement to the police that the shooting was accidental, I could leave him alone and not worry about him telling the hospital staff something else. I couldn't follow him around forever. On this one issue, I'd have to trust him—I had no choice.

Twenty minutes later, after the officers had inspected the gun and confirmed for their report that there had been only one bullet discharged, I sat in the waiting room of the ER. Except for me and one older man napping on a small couch, it was empty, which wasn't surprising. Monroe wasn't exactly a raging metropolis; anyone with more serious, life-endangering medical issues would likely be taken to Everett, to a bigger hospital.

As I waited, I wondered what my parents would believe had

happened, and how Liz and Jason would react to Tyler's injury. I decided that I'd better at least text my parents and let them know I was okay. I'd left a note for them before I'd gone to confront Tyler, saying that I probably wouldn't be home that night, but there was no way I'd be able to hide the fact that Tyler had been shot, and that I'd been with him when it happened.

I quickly typed out a text to both my mom and my dad, telling them that Tyler and I had gone up to the cabin to try to work things through. I said that I'd taken the gun from my father's office just in case, as a way to feel safe and secure around Tyler, and that it had accidentally gone off. I felt terrible for lying to them, and guessed they might suspect that I had purposely pulled the trigger, but as long as Tyler and I told the same story, no one would be able to prove otherwise. Again, I was struck by the oddity of this new and unlikely alliance with the man who raped me. This lie would forever link us.

My phone immediately began to chime with anxious return texts from both of my parents—"Where are you? How could this happen? Are you okay?"—so I told them where we were, that the doctors were taking care of Tyler, and that I was fine. "He admitted what he did to me," I told them. "He said he'll tell the police."

Knowing this would set off another litany of responses, I turned the sound off on my phone and shoved it back in my pocket. My stomach growled, but I ignored it, instead thinking about what the police in Bellingham would do when Tyler confessed. What kind of consequences he would endure. I had read enough about rape shield laws online to know that my name would be kept out of the paper unless I consented to having it made public, but Bellingham was a small town. People who knew our families were aware of how close Tyler and I were, not to mention there were other people who had attended the party and might put two and two together, remembering us making out on the dance floor, and then my abrupt departure with Mason and Gia. *I need to move,* I thought suddenly. *I need to find a place where nobody knows me.*

"Excuse me, miss?" a voice said, jerking my attention back to the waiting room.

"Yes?" I said, startling in my chair, realizing that I'd begun to doze off. I looked up to see the same male nurse who had taken Tyler for his tests standing in front of me.

"Everything looked good. He'll need some physical therapy, but the bullet missed the joint, so there's no need for surgery. We're going to clean the wound and pack it, put him in a sling, and give him some antibiotics and pain meds, and then you two can be on your way."

"Thank you," I said, strangely relieved that Tyler's injury hadn't been worse. Maybe the long shadow of our friendship would always be the first filter through which I saw him. Maybe, no matter the damage he'd done or how hard I tried to fight it, there would always be part of me that cared.

We left the ER in Monroe around two p.m., and spent an hour and a half in silence as I drove us north—home, to Bellingham. Tyler slept most of the way, but then, just as I turned on my blinker and took the Lakeway exit off of I-5, he spoke.

"Do you want me to do it today?" he asked. His voice was dull. Defeated. "Should we go downtown right now?"

"Yeah," I said. "We should."

"They'll want you to make a statement, too, I'm sure," Tyler said. "But probably not until after I've made mine."

"Okay." I wanted to say more, but I was so tired, my brain seemed to be running out of words. "I told my parents we went up to the cabin to try and talk things out, and that I brought the gun just to help me feel safe around you. I told them it went off on its own. That it was an accident."

"Then that's what I'll say, too," he said.

Out of the corner of my eye, I saw him turn and look at me, but I forced myself to keep my gaze forward as I turned onto Lakeway Drive and followed it until it became West Holly, a one-way street that led downtown. "You promise you'll tell them everything," I said, my voice an octave higher than usual. "You'll tell them what you did?"

"I promise," Tyler said, without hesitation.

I drove toward Grand Street, thinking that I'd need to have one or both of my parents come pick me up at the station and take me to get my car, where I'd parked it last night when I was waiting for Tyler's shift to end. I couldn't believe that barely thirteen hours had passed since the moment I approached him in the parking lot. It seemed like another lifetime; I felt like I'd aged a hundred years.

As I pulled into a parking spot and turned off the truck's engine, Tyler looked at me again. "I know this doesn't change anything," he said. "And I know it doesn't help, but I really am sorry. I'd do anything to fix it."

"Do *this,*" I said, keeping my voice hard, even though a small spot inside my heart ached hearing the angst threaded through his words. "Do what you promised to do."

"And that will make things right?" he asked, with a sliver of hope.

"Nothing can do that," I said. I wasn't sure I'd ever feel "right" again, whatever that meant. All I knew was that the idea of his confession and the punishment that would likely follow were the only things helping me to believe I might be able to get on with my life. Those steps had to be taken before I could find a way to move on.

We sat in silence for another moment, before Tyler used his free hand to open the truck door. Carefully, he landed on his feet on the cement below, and then looked back at me. I pulled the keys out of the ignition and handed them to him, even though I knew with his shoulder in a sling he wouldn't be able to drive. But that wasn't my problem to solve.

"I'm sorry," he said, again, and then I watched as he shut the door behind him and made his way up the steps to the police station's front doors. Part of me wanted to run after him, to make sure that he recounted every moment of what he'd done, but another part of me knew that I couldn't stand to hear it. What happened that night already played on a constant cycle inside my head; I didn't need any help remembering the details. I didn't need to hear them from Tyler's point of view. All I needed was the knowledge that he was headed inside that building in order to set the record straight. He was going to tell the truth.

Tyler

Three weeks after I walked into the police station and turned myself in for raping Amber, I made my way inside Bellingham Towers, where I had an appointment with my attorney, Peter Thompson, who my mom had hired as soon as I called her and said that I'd signed a document waiving my right to have a lawyer present during my confession. Hours later, after an officer had led me into a small room and recorded every word I said about what I'd done to Amber on the Fourth of July, second-degree rape charges were filed against me, and after one night in jail, my mom bailed me out and introduced me to Peter.

Today, I was headed to his office in order to discuss the plea bargain he'd been offered by the district attorney, and though I was determined not to let my anxiety get the better of me, I could still feel it surging in uncomfortable sparks beneath my skin. As I opened the single, smoked-glass door that led to the reception area of his office, my heart banged inside my chest, and I wished hard for a Valium to steady my nerves.

"Hi, Tyler," Peter's receptionist, Jane, said when she looked up from her desk and saw me. She was a short, skinny woman, likely in her late fifties, who wore red-framed glasses, and whose silver hair stuck straight up in messy spikes on top of her head. "How's the shoulder?"

"Better, thanks," I said, trying to smile, even though my lips trembled. The sling I'd worn since the morning at the hospital in Monroe came off a week ago, and though the wound still ached and itched as it healed, the pain was manageable with Tylenol. Every time I looked at it, though, every time I took in the red, puckered skin around the dark scab that had formed, I was reminded of Amber's face just moments before she shot me—the pure, rancorous anger in her hollowed-out eyes. I remembered the terrible pain that I had caused her. And even though I was terrified of what might happen to me next, I tried to hold on to the fact that at least I'd done what she asked—I'd given her the one thing that she needed most.

"Peter's ready for you," Jane said, nodding in the direction of his office. "Would you like anything to drink? Coffee or water?"

I shook my head. "No, thanks. I'm good." I wondered if it was difficult for her, as a woman, when her boss represented a client like me, who had confessed to committing a rape. The few times I'd been to Peter's office, she had never been anything but polite, but I couldn't help but think that she was probably just a good actress. I bet she went home and had a drink to blur out the uglier portions of her job.

I turned right and headed down the narrow hallway that led to Peter's office. "Hey," I said, as I entered the room and shut the door behind me.

"Good morning," Peter said. He stood up from his sleek glass-and-chrome desk, and walked around it in order to shake my hand. He was a little shorter than me, not quite six feet, with the body of a college football player who had lately spent more time on the couch than in the gym. He was fighting a receding hairline, and wore a blue suit and shiny black loafers. "How are you?"

"I'm okay," I said, as I dropped into one of the two high-backed, black leather chairs that sat closest to the door. I should have said I *wasn't* okay. I should have said that I was about to crawl out of my skin, wondering whether or not I was going to end up in prison. "As good as can be expected, I suppose."

"I take it you heard from your captain?" Peter asked as he returned to his own seat, across from me.

"Yeah," I said, unable to keep the bitterness from my voice. "He fired me." I'd gotten the call a few days before, after Captain Duncan had been contacted by the D.A., who informed him of the charges filed against me. The conversation had been short, less than two minutes, at the end of which my captain told me that I wasn't welcome back at the station—he would have someone clean out my locker and send me my things.

"Well, we expected that, right? The law doesn't allow for you to be a sex offender and a paramedic, too."

"I guess," I said, flinching at the use of the term "sex offender." No matter how hard I tried, I still couldn't believe that's what I'd become. "But that doesn't make it any easier. That job was my life. It's all I had."

Peter shrugged, and I shifted in my seat, feeling my face flush, suddenly furious that he could just brush off my entire career with a roll of his shoulders. What if someone came along and took *his* job away? How would he feel, then? *Knock it off,* I thought. *This isn't Peter's fault. You did this to yourself. You walked into a police station and told them what you did.* I tried to focus on remaining calm as he spoke again.

"So, we have a plea bargain on the table," he said, glancing down at the open file in front of him on his desk. "They'll reduce the charge to rape in the third degree instead of second—"

"What's the difference again?" I said, interrupting him. He'd explained it to me at our first appointment, but I couldn't recall the distinction now.

"Second degree is a Class A felony, punishable by up to life in prison and a fifty-thousand-dollar fine," Peter said, looking back up at me. "Third degree is a Class C felony, and gives us the option of a lower fine and negotiating for little or no jail time, depending on the circumstances of the rape."

"Oh," I said. "So you negotiated?"

"Yes," Peter said. "And since you stipulated to what you did, and that everything Amber told them in her follow-up statement was true, they're willing to waive jail time in lieu of you attending a two-year outpatient sexual offender treatment program and paying a ten-thousand-dollar fine."

"Jesus," I said, as I tried to let the weight of his words sink in. I wouldn't have to go to jail, but I'd have to spend two years in a room talking to a therapist, and possibly a bunch of sexual predators. I'd have to somehow find an extra ten thousand dollars to pay the state, despite the fact that I'd just lost my job and emptied my entire savings paying Peter's retainer. I knew my mom would help as much as she could, but after having bailed me out, she didn't have any extra money lying around. In fact, over the past couple of weeks, tired of trying to avoid running into Tom and Helen in the neighborhood, she had decided to list her house with a real estate agent, and while it had sold after only two days on the market, she ended up barely breaking even. She had just enough equity to buy a two-bedroom condo near Barkley Village, where I was planning to move in with her now that I wouldn't be able to pay rent. My father, since learning that I'd gone to the police and confessed, had refused to speak with me or offer any financial help. I wished I could say that his reaction surprised me.

"It's a great offer," Peter said, sitting back against his chair. He folded his hands together over the swell of his belly and looked at me with cool blue eyes. "You're lucky they're not trying to make an example of you."

"I get that," I said. "But still. A *treatment* program? Seriously?" My mind flashed with images of having to sit in a circle with a group of nasty old men with pockmarked faces and porn-style mustaches, listening to the horrifying things they'd done to women or, even worse, children. I couldn't fathom being among them; I couldn't believe they were anything like me. I gave Peter an imploring look. "This was a one-time fuckup. I made a mistake, but I'm fully aware of what I did and I owned up to it. Doesn't that count for something?"

"Sure," he said, carefully. "It's what earned you this offer."

"Can't you counter it? Bargain for a lesser sentence?" I racked my brain for the words that would make him realize all I really deserved was a slap on the wrist. If he just argued more, if he just emphasized that I was first-time offender, that my record was otherwise totally clean.

"No, I can't. That's not how plea bargains work." He paused and gave me a pointed look. "Unless you're willing to change your story about what happened at the cabin. You'd have to say that Amber meant to shoot you. Then we could argue that your confession was made under duress, and a judge might rule to throw it out."

"But that would mean Amber would be charged with assault, right?" I thought back to the small room where I'd told the detective on duty how I'd raped Amber, how he'd questioned me over and over again about if the shooting had been truly accidental. At the time, I knew he suspected there was more to the story—that it was too much of a coincidence that the same girl I'd raped had "accidentally" shot me, too. I'd protected her, though, because I'd promised I would. It was the one way I could show her that the friend I'd been to her over the years hadn't been a figment of her imagination. It was part of the price I'd promised to pay.

"Assault with a deadly weapon, yes. Which, considering the

circumstances, is more believable than it being an accident, and she'd probably be convicted. Then we could go back to the prosecutor and your case would take on an entirely different light. The confession wouldn't be admissible, you could plead not guilty, and without any physical evidence, the rape would be almost impossible to prove. You might even be able to get your job back."

I considered this, sorely tempted to do what Peter suggested. After all, Amber *had* purposely shot me. If reporting her for it would mean I could avoid having to register as a sex offender, if it meant that I could skip treatment and be able to do my job again, shouldn't I *want* to tell the police the truth about what happened? Hell, the prosecutor might even tack on kidnapping charges, and, as I'd told Amber that night at the cabin, *she* would be the one who went to jail.

But even as I thought these things, an undercurrent of self-loathing seized the muscles in my throat at the memory of Amber's strangled voice when she told me to stop as I pushed her thighs apart. I remembered her tears and the way she screamed the next morning when I entered her room. I thought about the conversation we had in the truck, the night she took me to the cabin, the anguish in her voice, the way she could have killed me if she had wanted to. But she didn't. She chose to let me live, despite the fact that I had raped her, only because I promised to admit what I did and endure the consequences. If I changed my story about the details of the shooting now, I'd be going back on my word. I'd caused Amber enough pain; I couldn't hurt her again.

"It was an accident," I told Peter, locking my gaze with his. "She didn't mean to do it."

"Well, then," he said with a sigh, "I don't have anything to go back to the prosecutor with. You admitted to *rape,* Tyler. This is the best deal you're going to get."

"Okay," I said, blowing out a puff of air along with the word, trying to settle the squirrely feeling in my chest. "What happens, now?"

"I'll tell the D.A. you accept the plea, and we'll get a sentencing hearing on the calendar. In the meantime, Jane will get you all the information you need to set up your first appointment with Dr. Philips, who runs the treatment program. He'll do an intake, and then you'll see him once a week, in addition to attending a group session with other offenders. After the hearing, you'll be assigned a probation officer, who will perform your drug tests and hopefully help you find a job."

"Who is going to hire me now?" I said, bitterly. I hated that I would no longer be a paramedic. I hated that I'd lost the one thing I'd worked so hard for—the part of me, outside of having been Amber's best friend, that I was proud of.

"There are businesses that participate in state incentive programs for hiring convicted felons," Peter said, leaning forward and shutting the file in front of him. "But your probation officer can tell you more about that."

"Okay," I said, standing up. He held out his hand, and I shook it, trying not to let the terror I felt show on my face. "Thanks for your help."

"Just doing my job," he said.

I nodded and turned around, toward the door, knowing that this was true. Peter probably didn't care what happened to me, one way or the other. He was happy because he'd been paid several thousand dollars to have a few meetings with the district attorney, and now, he'd simply move on with his day to another client, another case.

"Tyler?" he said, just as I put my hand on the doorknob.

"Yeah?" I replied, looking back over my shoulder.

"For what it's worth, I think you did the right thing, confessing. It took some serious balls. Believe me, most men in your situation wouldn't have gone through with it. I see far too many cases of sexual assault where the victim is the one who ends up paying the price in court. The trial traumatizes them more than the rape itself already did."

A lump formed in my chest as he spoke, and I only managed to bob my head in response.

"I know this is going to be rough for you," he continued, "and I don't say this very often, but in the end, with treatment, I'm hopeful you'll learn enough about yourself so you won't do anything like this, ever again. Eventually, you might be able to have a normal life."

A normal life. Standing there in his office, having just learned my immediate fate, I couldn't begin to picture what that would look like. I couldn't imagine finding a decent job, falling in love, getting married, or having children, as I'd always hoped I would. What woman would want a man who had admitted to rape? What community would accept me when they found out about my past? My blood pressure began to rise as I found myself suddenly picturing angry fathers screaming at me to stay away from their daughters, and I had to close my eyes. How had I ended up here? What was it inside me that had allowed me to do this terrible thing to my best friend? Why hadn't I *listened* to her—why wasn't I able to *stop* myself when she tried to push me off of her? What was *wrong* with me? My pulse sped up even more, almost as though it was attempting to answer these questions, and the possibility struck me that my issues with anxiety weren't as "situational" as I'd previously believed. Perhaps when I was lying on top of Amber, my brain had been chemically hijacked by swirling hormones and sputtering synapses, and, just like a hundred times before, I'd been desperate enough to do anything—even the unthinkable—to find relief. *That doesn't excuse what you did,* I scolded myself. *Even if anxiety played a part in enabling my behavior that night, there has to be something else, something* more *in the way I think—in my subconscious—that permitted me to cross that line.*

"Thank you," I said to Peter, even though I wasn't sure I believed that my life would ever be normal again. I was too confused, too screwed up, to even think it possible. And yet, after I made my way back down to the street, I knew the only thing I could do in order to get through this moment—and maybe the rest of my life—was to focus on what I'd finally been able to give to Amber, instead of everything I'd taken away.

On a Tuesday morning in mid-December, a week after my meeting with Peter, he and I walked into the courthouse and headed to the room where my guilty plea would be officially accepted and my sentence would be handed down.

I was terrified—anxiety raged through me like an angry river, practically drowning out the voice in my head that told me I was doing the right thing. I wondered if I could still change my mind. If I could tell Peter right now that Amber *had* kidnapped and shot me as a way to get me to confess to a crime I didn't commit. It was so tempting to travel down that road—one where my life wouldn't end up demolished.

But then I thought about what would happen to her, how I would be ruining her life more than I already had. I'd made my decision; I was going to be held accountable for what I did.

I took a deep breath and followed my lawyer into the courtroom, where my mom sat on one of the wooden benches. I thought she'd be alone—my dad had told her that he wouldn't be there: "I'm not going to sit there and watch my son throw his life away over a stupid girl," he'd said—and was surprised to see Mason sitting next to her. He and I hadn't spoken since the night we fought, the same night Amber had taken me to the cabin, and

I certainly hadn't expected to see him today. When I walked past them, he locked his eyes on mine and gave me a brief, tight-lipped nod. I imagined he'd only come to see that I actually went through with taking responsibility for what I'd done, but part of me hoped his presence meant more than that. Part of me hoped that, after all of this was over, we might find a way to be friends.

"I love you, honey," my mom said, wringing her hands in her lap. Her blond hair showed at least an inch of dark roots, and the skin under her eyes was smudged blue. She'd been working as much as she could, and had called in a favor from a friend who owned a diner in Ferndale, to get me a job as a dishwasher, at least until I could find something better. It was humiliating to think that, after being a paramedic, I'd be doing such a menial job, but I tried to swallow my pride and see it as only temporary, like everything else in my life right now. I needed a paycheck, and for the time being, scrubbing pots and pans would be how I earned one. I didn't have much of a choice.

Peter led me to a rectangular table and had me sit down with him, facing where the judge would be. To our right was the prosecuting attorney, and as I glanced over my shoulder, I saw Amber and her parents sitting behind him. Tom's gaze flickered to mine, and there was so much disgust in his eyes, I had to look away. It struck me that I wasn't just losing a friend—I was losing Tom and Helen, too. They'd been parents to me as much as my own parents were. I was losing three people I'd long considered part of my family.

The bailiff announced the judge as she entered, and we all stood up until she took her seat and banged her gavel. She was a heavyset, stern-looking woman with a black bun worn at the base of her neck. Blood rushed around inside my head, past my ears, making a roaring sound that made me worry I might pass out.

"Take a breath," Peter whispered, apparently having noticed me sway on my feet.

I nodded, just as the judge looked down at the file in front of her, and then looked back at Peter. "I understand that there has been a plea bargain reached in this case?" she said, glancing over to the prosecuting attorney as well.

"Yes, Your Honor," the attorney said. "Mr. Hicks has agreed to plead guilty to rape in the third degree, and lieu of jail time, he will register as a sexual offender and spend two years in an outpatient treatment program, as well as pay a ten-thousand-dollar fine."

"Is that correct, Mr. Thompson?" the judge asked Peter.

"It is," Peter said, standing back up.

The judge looked down at her file again and then over to where Amber sat. "Ms. Bryant," she said, more gently than she had spoken to the lawyers. "The D.A. has informed me that you would like to make a statement today, before Mr. Hicks's sentence is read into the official record?"

"Yes, Your Honor," Amber said. Her voice shook as she stood up and made her way to the table where the prosecutor sat. I was happy to see that she'd put on some weight in the month since I'd seen her last, the day she dropped me off at the police station. Her eyes looked brighter, and her cheeks were pink. She held a piece of paper in her hand, but she didn't glance at it as she began to speak. Instead, she kept her eyes on the judge, seeming to purposely not look at me. I couldn't blame her.

"Tyler Hicks was my best friend," she began, and I could see that her entire body was trembling. I blinked back tears and forced myself to focus on her words. My knee began to bounce under the table, and unobtrusively, Peter reached over and put his hand on my thigh to get me to stop moving.

"He was my best friend," Amber repeated. "Like a big brother to me, really, from the time I was thirteen years old. We did everything together. We talked for hours about our families and what we were going to do with our lives. He was the person I knew

I could always count on. The friend that I went to whenever I was upset or stressed or scared. He was there for me, no matter what, and I think I was there for him." She paused, and cleared her throat. "But everything changed almost six months ago, on the Fourth of July, when we went to a party. We both drank too much and started kissing, then headed upstairs to a bedroom." Amber's voice cracked here, and I watched her swallow a few times before going on. "At first, I kissed him back. But then something changed. It felt wrong to be with him. It felt horrible. And I told him to stop, but he didn't listen. I tried to struggle to get away from him, but he was so much bigger and stronger than me, there was nothing I could do. And even though I was crying and I told him I didn't want to do it, he forced my legs open, pushed up my skirt, and pulled down my underwear." She took in and released a quiet but shuddering breath, wiped away a stray tear that had escaped down her cheek, then looked back up at the judge. "He raped me. He forced himself inside me and jabbed at me until I bled. I had bruises on my body for weeks from where he held me down. I didn't think I'd ever feel safe again."

I felt sick to my stomach as I listened to what I'd put my best friend through. *No wonder she took me to the cabin,* I thought. *No wonder she shot me.*

"I couldn't understand how he could do it," Amber said, not trying to hold back her tears now. "Which was partly why I didn't go to the police. I blamed myself for leading him on, for giving him the wrong idea, because he'd always been such a good person. It didn't make sense that someone like him could do something as awful as this. He was there for me when I went through some incredibly tough times. He held my hand and listened and never asked me to be anything other than what I was. He was the person I trusted more than anyone else, but now, after what he did to me, I just don't think he *is* that person anymore. Something has to be seriously broken inside him for him to be able to rape me, a girl he supposedly loved."

She finally looked at me then, eyes glittering with conflicted emotions of revulsion and concern. "And honestly, Tyler, I'm glad that you finally confessed. I hope you find out what is wrong with you. I hope you get help and fix the fucked-up thinking that allowed you to attack me like that. To make me *bleed*. I hope there's a way for you to someday become the kind of man I always thought you were, instead of the one that's sitting in front of me right now."

She kept her eyes on mine the entire time she spoke those last words, and I made myself nod, once, as I held her gaze, hoping she would understand that I'd taken in everything she said. I made a promise to myself then, the same way I'd made one to her the day she shot me. I promised myself that I would start treatment with Dr. Philips as soon as I could. I needed to figure out why I hadn't been able to hear her pleas over my own desire and my conviction that we were meant to be together—that having sex was something we both wanted, even as she had begged me to stop. I would do as Amber had asked—I'd dig in deep and take it seriously. I'd try to figure out how I could have spent my entire life not wanting to be like my father, and still end up doing something so similar to what he might do. I'd try to figure out where my thinking went wrong, I'd be truthful about the depth of the anxiety I felt; I'd be willing to go on medication if that's what the doctor wanted me to do. I needed to do whatever it took so that I never hurt anyone else like this again

"Thank you, Ms. Bryant," the judge said, and then ordered that Amber's statement be made a part of the permanent record in regard to my case. A few minutes later, after I'd stood up and officially entered my guilty plea, Peter shook my hand and told he'd check in with me in a few days so we could get the final paperwork signed. I turned around to face my mom and Mason, both of whom had stood up, too. My mother hugged me, and I patted her back.

"It'll be okay," I said, and she nodded against my chest, before sniffling and pulling away.

"I need to get to work," she said. "I'll talk to you tonight." And then she left, avoiding making eye contact with any of the Bryant family, who were huddled together with Tom's and Helen's arms around Amber's shoulders. A moment later, they left, too, without so much as a glance in my direction.

"So," Mason said in a low voice, standing in front of me.

"So," I said. "Thanks for coming. It means a lot." He nodded, but didn't say anything more, so I spoke again. "You know I'm sorry about all of this. About everything." I stared at him, wanting him to know just how much our friendship meant, holding out hope that he would understand I wasn't just referring to what I'd done to Amber. Hoping that he might find a way to forgive me.

"Don't be sorry," he said, firmly. "Be better."

"That's the plan," I said. I held out my hand, and after a brief hesitation, he shook it.

"Good luck," he said. I knew it wasn't luck I needed—it was rigorous honesty. With others, of course, but mostly with myself. It was taking ownership of the mistakes I'd made and dealing with the consequences. And then maybe, after all of that, I'd earn a chance to start again.

Amber

The first week of January, at the beginning of a brand-new year and a little over a month since I'd made my victim impact statement at Tyler's sentencing hearing, I stood in the middle of my now-empty bedroom in my parents' house, my gaze traveling around the space to make sure I hadn't missed anything when I'd packed. My bed, dresser, and nightstand were already inside the U-Haul I'd rented in order to move, along with all my clothes and a few boxes of household items that I'd need for my new place—dishes, towels, and the like. I'd taken a personal training job at a gym in Edmonds, a tight-knit community just north of Seattle, and found a tiny studio apartment only a few blocks from where I would work. I'd registered to take my exam with the American College of Sports Medicine at the end of the month, and for the next few years, I planned on building up my experience and professional reputation before applying to work at the Seahawks training facility. Reaching my ultimate goal of being a trainer for the team was at least five to eight years out, but I had to start somewhere, and moving to Seattle was the next indicated step.

In the two months that had passed since the day I dropped

Tyler off at the police station, I'd spent a few hours a week in therapy with Vanessa, dealing with all my messy, convoluted feelings about everything that had happened since July, as well as another hour with Greta, the counselor in the hospital who'd helped me with my eating disorder all those years ago. She was in private practice now, and was helping me again, trying to get me to develop different and better coping mechanisms for stress, other than restricting what I ate.

"Remember that you're going to deal with this for the rest of your life," she'd told me yesterday, at our last appointment before my move. I'd gained back the twenty or so pounds I'd lost since the rape, but I still struggled with taking solace in food restriction whenever my emotions felt too big and unwieldy for me to handle. "Much like dealing with addiction to drugs or alcohol," Greta went on to say, "recovery from an eating disorder is a process, something you may have to deal with every day. There's no point at which you are totally 'cured.' But if you stay aware of your thought processes and behaviors, and ask for help when you need it, you can manage it. It doesn't have to rule your life."

Vanessa had said much the same thing to me about having been raped. "It will always be a part of you," she said. "You'll never forget what Tyler did or how you reacted. But it is your choice what you do with that. You can let it control you, or you can integrate it into your past as a traumatic experience, and not allow it to define who you are. It won't be easy, but you will find a way to survive it."

I'd nodded then, thinking about what she'd taught me about the concept of "trauma repetition," and how when I started sexually acting out with strangers after the rape, it was my way of trying to re-create the trauma of what Tyler had done by being in control of the men instead of them controlling me. "More women do this after being assaulted than you'd think," Vanessa said. "It's a self-destructive behavior, yes, but while they're doing it, they get a few moments of feeling safe again. Unfortunately, they're almost immediately flooded with feelings of guilt and self-disgust, because all they've really succeeded in doing is reinforcing the idea that they're sluts who deserved what happened to them."

I had already made appointments with two new therapists in Seattle, recommended to me by Vanessa and Greta. I'd also been toying with the idea of attending a sexual assault victim support group, but I hadn't quite decided if sharing what happened to me with a roomful of strangers would actually help. Still, Vanessa had given me the name of the organization that held the meetings, and a location near my new apartment, in case I chose to go.

Now, with one last glance around my childhood bedroom, I closed the door behind me and headed outside, where my parents were waiting. We were going to caravan together down to Edmonds—my dad and mom driving the U-Haul, and me in my own car—so they could help me move into my new place. It was a cold but clear winter day, and the sun felt warm upon my face.

"Hey, sweet girl," my dad said, as he loaded the last box onto the truck.

"Hey, Pops," I said, walking over in order to give him a hug. He wrapped his thick arms around me, and I felt grateful for the solidness of his body against mine. He smelled like coffee and sweat.

"You're sure you want to do this?" my mom asked, for what had to be the hundredth time since I'd told them my plan to move. "You'll be okay on your own?"

"I lived on my own at school," I reminded her, pulling out of my dad's embrace so I could look at her. She was wearing jeans and a gray PROUD WSU MOM sweatshirt, and her hair was in a ponytail at the base of her neck.

"I know, but that was before—" she said, stopping short before finishing the sentence.

"I'll be okay, Mom. I need to do this." I needed to get a fresh start, to build the life I'd always wanted. I needed to prove to myself that I was still a capable and worthy human being, and the only way I could imagine doing that was away from the environment where I had spent so much time feeling like I wasn't. But despite the fact that I'd already told my parents all of this, I knew they were worried about me. They were worried I'd slip back into starving myself, that I'd hide from life instead of learning to live it. And while there was no guarantee I wouldn't do these things, I had to give it a shot. I had to at least try.

A few minutes later, we climbed into our respective vehicles and made our way to the freeway. I had my hands-free headset on, in case my parents had to let me know they needed to make a pit stop, but as soon as we were driving past Lake Samish, the electronic voice in my ear began to speak. "Call from . . . Daniel Garcia," it said, and I instantly felt a lump form in my throat as I instructed my phone to ignore the call.

Since Tyler's confession and conviction had hit the papers back in early December, Daniel had left me a handful of voice mails and text messages. "Why didn't you tell me what happened?" he asked more than once. "I would have supported you. I would have been there for you through the whole thing." And while I appreciated that he had reached out, I couldn't bring myself to call or text him back. I was trying to focus on one thing at a time: to find the right words to speak at the sentencing hearing, and then to do the mental and emotional "homework" that Vanessa and Greta assigned me each week—practicing new coping mechanisms, telling the truth about my feelings to my parents, no matter how painful they were for me to talk about or for my parents to hear. I didn't feel like I could add an emotionally laden conversation with Daniel on top of all that. I knew I owed him an explanation; he deserved at least that much. *Now is as good a time as any,* I thought.

Still, I waited another twenty minutes, until we were just south of Mt. Vernon, before returning his call. I held my breath as the phone rang in my ear, once, twice, until he picked up.

"Amber?" he said, and hearing his voice nearly made me cry. I blinked rapidly and tried to steady my breathing so I wouldn't swerve out of my lane and cause an accident.

"Hi," I said, feeling more than a little awkward. "Sorry it's taken me so long to get back to you."

"That's okay," he said hurriedly. "I get it. You've had a lot to deal with."

"Yeah, I have." I didn't know what to say next—where I should start.

"Are you okay?" he asked, and there was so much tenderness in those words, the muscles in my throat ached, fighting back more tears.

"I'm getting there," I said, thinking that this was probably the most truthful answer I could give him. Everything was a process; *life* was a process. "It's been hard."

"I can only imagine," Daniel said. "I feel like such an asshole, for yelling at you the way I did that morning in your room. Accusing you of being a cheater. I'm so sorry, Amber."

"You didn't know," I said. "I get why you reacted the way you did. It's okay."

"You were right about something you said, though."

"Really? What?"

"That I asked you to marry me so quickly because it was about sticking to my own plan. How I always pictured my life playing out, having a wife before I finished my residency and went into private practice." He waited a beat. "Don't get me wrong. I loved you, and I *wanted* to marry you, but I didn't stop to think whether the timing was the right thing for you, too. I didn't show you the respect of really talking about it with you first. I'm sorry for that."

"Don't be," I said. "It meant a lot that you asked . . . I just . . . I wasn't ready."

"Why didn't you just tell me what Tyler did?" he finally asked, as he had in all of his messages.

I had to wait a moment before I could answer him, keeping my eyes on my parents driving the U-Haul in front of me, trying to sort out the best way to explain how I'd felt that morning. "I think I couldn't, because I hadn't even processed what happened in my own head. I didn't know *how* to tell you. I was so worried what you'd think of me."

"The only person I would have thought negatively about would have been him," Daniel said, vehemently. "That fucker. But I would have understood. I would have known it wasn't anything you did. It wasn't your fault."

"I get that, now," I said, slowly. "But at the time, in that moment, I felt like it was my fault. I blamed myself for letting it happen. I'm still working through all of that, and it's going to take some time. But I want you to know that I've appreciated your messages. They meant a lot."

"Can I see you?" he asked hopefully. "Can I come up and take you out for dinner or something? No pressure . . . just to catch up?"

Before I answered, I tried to imagine what it would be like to see Daniel now. To have him look at me with his dark eyes and kind smile, to perhaps let him hold me the way he used to. *Could I do it?* I wondered. *Could I sit down with him, open myself up, and try to reconnect?* But then I imagined telling him about how, after the rape, I'd gone out almost every night and picked up a strange man, and my stomach convulsed. It was too soon, I realized. I still had too much to work through.

"I'm actually driving down to Seattle right now," I finally said, and then quickly told him about my apartment, my upcoming test, and new job. "I need to get settled, and be on my own for a while. I'm not sure I'm ready to see you, yet. But that's not about you . . . it's about me, okay? You understand that, right?"

He was silent for a moment, and the only sounds were his breath in my ear and the low, vibrating hum of my car's tires on the road. "Yeah," he finally said. "I understand."

"Good," I said. "Because I want you to be happy. You deserve it."

"So do you, Amber. I miss you."

"Thank you," I said. "I've missed you, too." While this was true, I wasn't sure if I'd ever be able to be with him again. I wasn't sure if I would be able to be with anyone. Even though I understood why I'd sought out those strangers—why I'd kissed them and touched them and never learned their names—I felt sick every time I thought about the possibility of having sex. At this point, the idea of undressing in front of another man, being intimate with him, emotionally or otherwise, was unthinkable. With time, I hoped that might change, but until then, I needed to focus on myself.

"You can call me anytime, okay?" Daniel said. "Just to talk, or whatever. Just as friends. I'm here for you."

"Okay," I said. "Thanks." My heart swelled with so much regret, it felt like it might burst. Was I making a huge mistake, ruining my chances with the perfect man for me? Daniel was sweet and kind and smart. He made me laugh. Would I ever find someone like him again? I felt panicky, thinking that maybe Tyler had robbed me of the ability to let someone like Daniel close to me. Maybe I shouldn't let him go. Maybe I should see him as soon as I could, and let him touch me, kiss me, take care of me. If I didn't, I could end up alone for the rest of my life. I could lose out on the best thing that had ever happened to me.

But then, I thought about how the attack had forced me to dig in deep and find more self-reliance than I ever had before. For years, I'd allowed myself to be buoyed by Tyler and his friendship while I struggled with my eating disorder. Then, I relied on Daniel and his support as I planned out what I was going to do with my life. I'd never thought much about myself unless it was in relation to how a man felt about me, too. I defined my own worth based on Tyler's love for me and then Daniel's. It was time for me to learn to love myself, and let *that* love be enough.

"Take care, okay?" Daniel said, and I could hear the swell of emotion in his voice, too.

"You, too," I said, and then, after another quiet moment filled with unspoken words, we ended the call.

For the rest of the drive, my mind raced with what might have been if Tyler had never attacked me. I might have been shopping for wedding dresses with my mom today instead of moving. I might have been living with Daniel in Seattle instead of finding my own apartment. I might have already passed my certification test. My whole world, everything about it, would be different. *I* would be different.

But then I thought about what Vanessa had said, that I could choose how to let what happened affect me. Either it could control my life or I could rise above it and move on. The latter, I decided, was why I had opted to start over. I was going to do everything in my power to not let my past rule the present.

As my parents helped me carry boxes and furniture into my new apartment, I felt happy that I'd found this small space to call my own. It was painted a light gray with bright white trim around the windows and doors, and the hardwood floors were a pale bamboo. There was a closet, a tiny kitchen along the back wall, next to the door that led to the bathroom, and just enough square footage to contain my queen-size bed, a dresser, and a desk and chair. It wasn't spacious, it wasn't perfect, but I was grateful that it was mine.

"Let me take you grocery shopping," my mom said, after we'd

finished putting together the bed and setting up the rest of the furnishings in the room.

"I can do that after you guys head home," I said. "The market is just around the corner."

"Are you sure?" my dad asked as he adjusted the small flat-screen television that he'd just mounted on the wall opposite my bed. It was their gift to me, along with a substantial deposit in my bank account to help me get started.

"I'm sure," I said. "I appreciate everything you and Mom have done. I know I haven't made it easy—"

"Shh," my mom said, cutting me off. "You are the best daughter we could ask for. We love you so much, and we're so proud of how far you've come."

"Thank you," I said, once again feeling tears at the backs of my eyes. "I love you, too." I stepped over to where they stood, and they both put their arms around me. My dad kissed the top of my head, and my mom put her cheek against mine.

"We're here for you, however you need us," she said. "Anytime, day or night. You're only a little over an hour away."

"And you can always come home," my dad said, but I didn't say anything, because we all knew that my visits to Bellingham would be limited now, for fear of accidentally running into any of the Hicks family.

"We might even move down this way," my mom said, as the three of us finally pulled apart. She had tears in her eyes, too.

"Is that so?" my dad asked, but he said it with a smile. He knew my mother so well, and usually did whatever it took to make her happy. I imagined that it was hard for them to think about running into Liz, Jason, or Tyler, too. It might make sense for them to move.

"Maybe," my mom said, returning his smile with one of her own. "You never know."

"Let me walk you out," I said, and we made our way to the parking lot of my new building. It was late afternoon, and the sun had dropped low in the sky, so the air had taken on a much colder bite than earlier in the day.

"Thanks for everything," I said again as I hugged them both, individually. "I'll call you tomorrow, okay?"

"You'd better," my mom said. "Let us know how your first day at work goes."

"I will," I said, nodding. And finally, they climbed into the U-Haul and drove away.

I spent the next couple of hours tweaking the arrangement of my apartment, as well as hitting the grocery store, where I loaded up on frozen vegetables and chicken, along with a lot of fruit, some nuts, and a loaf of eight-grain bread. On my way to the register, on impulse, I grabbed a package of Oreos, too, my favorite cookie from my childhood. Greta had encouraged me to practice buying food that I might not necessarily be ready to eat, as a way to help me stop labeling food as either "good" or "bad."

"It's all just food," she said. "You eat what you like, what feels good to you in the moment, whatever that is, until you feel full. And then you stop. It's that simple. And it's that hard."

Once I was back in my apartment, I put away what I'd bought, then turned on the television, just for the background noise. The cable was paid for and ready for my dad to hook up when we got here, a perk the landlord provided, along with paying for water, sewer, and garbage. I dropped down onto my bed and picked up my phone, scrolling through my messages to find the text from Vanessa that held the address of the sexual assault victim support group. It was Thursday, the same day her therapist colleague held the seven o'clock meetings. I stared at the address, and then quickly looked it up on Google Maps, a little shocked to see that it was only four blocks from my apartment. It was six thirty, and if I wanted, I could walk over and attend.

I thought about Tyler then, how he would be spending the next couple of years in therapy, instead of in jail. I wondered if he would take it seriously; I wondered if what I'd said to him in my victim impact statement had sunk in the way I'd hoped that it would. My stomach didn't twist quite as much when he came to my mind now, but that could change from day to day. There were times I ended up heaving over the toilet, overwhelmed by the memories of what he did to me. There were moments I looked in the mirror and wanted to scream at the unfairness of how I would carry around this trauma with me for the rest of my days.

"It's less of a burden when you share it with other women who understand," Vanessa said, when I told her how I felt. "You'd be amazed at how much it helps."

Now, I drummed my fingers on the top of my thigh, exhausted from the long day of packing and moving, but before I knew what I was doing, I had jumped up, grabbed my purse and keys, and headed out the door.

It only took a little over five minutes to get to the office building, and another few to find the room where the meeting was being held. I stood outside the doorway for a moment, hesitant to go inside, and then a woman's voice startled me.

"The first time's always the hardest," she said, and I turned to look behind me. She was a thin blond woman about my age, but taller than me, with long legs and an athlete's broad shoulders. She was dressed in black leggings, a matching thick, black sweater, and knee-high, black leather boots. There was a bright red infinity scarf looped around her neck, and a multitude of silver bangle bracelets around her wrists. She looked impossibly hip, and I suddenly felt self-conscious about the ratty jeans and dirty sweatshirt I hadn't changed out of after the move.

"Is it that obvious?" I asked nervously. I shoved my hands deep into my coat's pockets.

"Maybe a little," the woman said, smiling. "I'm Charlotte."

"I'm Amber," I said. "I just moved here from Bellingham."

"Really?" Charlotte said, moving off to one side as a couple other women pushed past us and walked into the room. "My brother graduated from Western last year. I love it up there."

I nodded, but felt a dark look fall over my face, thinking how I used to love my hometown, too, and now couldn't imagine ever living there again.

Charlotte must have sensed the conflict I felt, because she quickly changed the subject. "But now you're here," she said. "Did someone give you the group's name?"

"My therapist," I said.

"Mine, too," she said, and then lowered her voice. "I was raped by an online date last year. What about you?"

"My best friend," I said, swallowing hard. "Just last summer."

"I'm sorry," she said, frowning. She jerked her head toward the room, where I could hear a low buzz of conversation among the other women. "Come on in. It'll be okay, I promise."

"Okay," I said, as I released a deep breath, hoping that what Charlotte said was true. Hoping that after everything I'd been through, after deciding to move and start my life over again, I'd found place where I would continue to heal—a place I'd find other women who understood me. A place where, no matter what else might happen, I could finally start to feel whole.

Acknowledgments

[[TK]]